From the rugged Scottish Highlands to elegant Regency drawing rooms, *New York Times* bestselling author

CANDACE CAMP

delivers pure romantic delight!

Praise for her Legend of St. Dwynwen trilogy

The Marrying Season   A Summer Seduction
A Winter Scandal

"Filled with sensuality, intrigue, and Camp's trademark romantic sparring.... Delightful."
—*Publishers Weekly*

"A charming courtship.... Readers will be captivated."
—*Booklist* (starred review)

"Sexy and sweet! Candace Camp delivers another beautifully written story with just the right touch of mystery and a generous helping of a scandalous romance."
—*Coffee Time Romance*

"A charming, sometimes suspenseful tale."
—*Romance Reviews Today*

Turn the page for more rave reviews!

Be sure to read Candace Camp's dazzling Willowmere novels. . . . Critics adore this breathtaking Regency trilogy about the unforgettable Bascombe sisters!

An Affair Without End

"[A] delightful romantic mystery. . . . Cunning intrigue. With clever and witty banter, sharp attention to detail, and utterly likable characters, Camp is at the top of her game."
—*Publishers Weekly* (starred review)

"Sprightly dialogue . . . [and] a simmering sensuality that adds just enough spice to this fast-paced, well-rendered love story."
—*RT Book Reviews* (4½ stars)

A Gentleman Always Remembers

"An intensely passionate and sexually charged romance. . . . A well-crafted, delightful read."
—*Romantic Times* (4 stars)

"A delightful romp. . . . Camp has a way with truly likable characters who become like friends. The action pops . . . and the relationships are strong."
—*Romance Junkies*

"Witty, heartwarming, and fast-paced. . . . Where the Bascombe sisters go, things are never dull."
—*A Romance Review*

A Lady Never Tells

"This steamy romp . . . will entertain readers."

—Publishers Weekly

"With a bit of mayhem, humor, misunderstandings, and enough sensuality to please any reader, this consummate storyteller writes a well-crafted and enchanting tale."

—Romantic Times (4½ stars)

"Superbly written and well paced, *A Lady Never Tells* thoroughly entertains as it follows the escapades of the Bascombe 'bouquet' of Marigold, Rose, Camellia, and Lily in the endeavor to make their way in upper-crust London society."

—Romance Reviews Today

"One of those rare finds you don't want to put down. . . . *A Lady Never Tells* carries an allure that captures the reader's attention. Candace Camp brings a refreshing voice to the romance genre. The touch of elegance mingled with the downright honesty of the main characters takes your breath away."

—Winter Haven News Chief

"Filled with humor and charm. . . . Fine writing."

—A Romance Review (4 roses)

Also from Candace Camp and Pocket Books

CANDACE CAMP

A SUMMER SEDUCTION

POCKET BOOKS

New York   London   Toronto   Sydney   New Delhi

Pocket Books
A Division of Simon & Schuster, Inc.
1230 Avenue of the Americas
New York, NY 10020

This book is a work of fiction. Names, characters, places, and incidents either are products of the author's imagination or are used fictitiously. Any resemblance to actual events or locales or persons, living or dead, is entirely coincidental.

This Pocket Books paperback edition June 2014

POCKET and colophon are registered trademarks of Simon & Schuster, Inc.

For information about special discounts for bulk purchases, please contact Simon & Schuster Special Sales at 1-866-506-1949 or business@simonandschuster.com.

The Simon & Schuster Speakers Bureau can bring authors to your live event. For more information or to book an event, contact the Simon & Schuster Speakers Bureau at 1-866-248-3049 or visit our website at www.simonspeakers.com.

Cover design by Lisa Litwack
Cover photograph by Michael Frost; hand lettering by Ron Zinn

Manufactured in the United States of America

10 9 8 7 6 5 4 3 2 1

ISBN 978-1-4767-8344-4
ISBN 978-1-4516-3954-4 (ebook)

Acknowledgments

My thanks go out to all the usual suspects: Abby and the great team at Pocket, Maria and the great team at Maria Carvainis Agency, and most of all to my own team here at home—my husband, Pete, and my daughter, Anastasia Hopcus. I couldn't do it without all of you. You deserve a fuller recounting of all the ways you've helped me, but that, I'm afraid, would make another book.

Special thanks to Mikey for gracing our lives. You helped me through fifteen years of writing books, and even worked your way into two of them. This is the first one in a long time without you, and you are sorely missed.

A SUMMER SEDUCTION

One

Her body was warm and yielding in his arms, her mouth sweet beneath his. The very air around them was electric with promise. A breeze touched his skin, sending a shiver through him, and in the distance, there was a low rumble of thunder.

"Jocelyn," he murmured, his arms tightening around her, and at that instant, she turned and slipped away from him, laughter trailing over her shoulder.

Alec started after her, his body thrumming with need, the thrill of the chase rising in him. She was white and silver in the moonlight, her gown fluttering behind her, dark gold hair streaming like a flag. Airy as a dream, she darted between the stones, always just out of his reach. He turned a corner, and she had vanished. He realized with a chill that the stones around them were grave markers.

Then her arms wrapped around him from behind, and her scent teased at his nostrils. Alec turned to her and claimed her lips, his hands sinking into the thick mass of her hair. Heat flared through him, his body hard and eager. She pressed up into him, her soft breasts flattening against his chest. He wanted her. Ached for her.

He lifted his head and gazed down into the huge amethyst pools of her eyes. Her alabaster skin gleamed in the moonlight, her thick black hair twining around his fingers. And in that moment he realized that she was not Jocelyn at all.

"Damaris!"

Thunder rumbled, and Alec jolted awake.

He lay for a moment, disoriented, the room unfamiliar, before his groggy thoughts gathered and he recalled that he was in an inn on his way to visit Lord Morecombe. Soft summer air wafted through the open window, stirring the sheer curtains, and thunder sounded again, low and distant. Alec's body still surged with lust. Was it for Jocelyn, he wondered, or for Damaris?

Letting out an impatient sigh, he sat up and swung his legs out of bed. It didn't matter. Either way, it was folly. Jocelyn's place now was in the graveyard. She had never been his, not really. As for Damaris . . . His thoughts turned to the attractive young widow who was Lady Morecombe's good friend. Hair thick and black as midnight . . . wide, expressive eyes of a deep blue, almost purplish hue, a distant look of cool amusement in them . . . an enticingly curved body that seemed to beckon a man's hand.

Alec shook his head, as if to dislodge his thoughts. However alluring the lady might be, Damaris Howard was not for him. He had not, he reflected, made the best of first impressions upon her, storming into Gabriel's house six months ago and launching into a fistfight with him. He had compounded his sins by being rude to the lady, flatly refusing her offer to show him the way to the village. Pride was a failing of his—an overweening pride, some might say—that disdained help as equally as it did pity or contempt.

After that inauspicious beginning, Mrs. Howard had regarded him with a prickly politeness that bordered on disfavor. That fact would not have stopped him from pursuing her, of course, for Alec Stafford was not a man to avoid a challenge. But she was a lady and, what was more important, a friend to Thea, one of the few people Alec respected, which meant that Damaris was not a woman with whom he could casually tumble into bed. And Alec was not foolish enough to be interested in a woman in any other way. Whatever mawkish feelings of love and marriage had once glimmered in him had died with Jocelyn.

He shoved away from the bed and strode to the window. The sheer curtain billowed out, brushing over his naked flesh, and he shivered once again, just as he had in his dream. There was no moon in the sky; it was growing close to dawn and the sky had begun to lighten.

Sleep, he knew, had been thoroughly chased off, so he turned away and began to pull on his clothes. It was less than a day's ride to Chesley, where Gabriel Morecombe now lived with his new wife and the baby boy they had adopted. If he set out now, he could reach the village by midafternoon.

By the time the sun came up, Alec was well down the road. He stopped for breakfast and to rest his mount, but as the miles passed and the village of Chesley grew closer, his pace quickened and his stops were more and more infrequent. He was not sure where the restlessness that had plagued him the last few months had come from, but it was becoming more and more familiar. It seemed as if no place contented him for long now. After visiting Chesley for young Matthew's baptism, he had returned home to dutifully escort his sister to London for the Season. A month later, boredom had sent him ricocheting back to Northumberland. But, unlike in the past, he had not been content at Castle Cleyre either. The days had seemed long and empty, the nights dull, until finally he had decided to return to the city early, making a side trip to visit his friends the Morecombes along the way, as if he had not just visited them in February.

It was odd behavior, he knew, but perhaps a man just grew bored when he reached a certain age. Or perhaps once Jocelyn had been found and he had been freed from his long, uncertain period of waiting, he simply no longer knew what to do with himself.

He came over a rise and saw Chesley before him, the Cotswold stone buildings gleaming a pale honey in the midday sun. In the distance, on the far side of the village, the square tower of St. Margaret's rose bluntly into the sky. It surprised him to feel his spirits rise. It was here that he had learned the grim truth about Jocelyn, not only her death, but the full measure of her deceit. She had been lost to him more than a year at the time, but he had still stubbornly clung to some small measure of hope until the events at Chesley. The village should hold naught for him but sorrow and loss, but instead he had a certain fondness for it.

He nudged his horse into a trot and was soon at the outskirts of the village. He passed the Blue Boar, where he had stayed last Christmas. When he had come for the baptism in February, Gabriel and Thea had welcomed him into their home—but Jocelyn's leaving had set the two men's friendship on a perilous path, and it had been only tentatively restored last winter. So he hesitated now as he rode past the inn, thinking he should perhaps stop and claim a room there. Instead he pushed forward. The road that led out to the Priory went past Damaris's home, and it would be only polite to call upon her . . . but better sense prevailed, and he continued to Gabriel's home.

The footman who answered the door at the Priory was quick to bow and usher him inside. Just as the servant turned to lead Alec to the drawing room, there was a high-pitched squeal, followed by a peal of laughter, and a small child ran out of the great hall. His chubby legs were spread wide for balance, as were his arms, and the skirts of his gown were tucked up into his swaddling band to keep him from tripping. A gleeful expression lit his face. Alec's heart clenched almost painfully in his chest. Behind him came a tall, slender woman dressed in a fashionable gown of sprig muslin. She, too, was laughing, her large expressive gray eyes alight behind her spectacles. Her cheeks were flushed, and several strands had escaped from her upswept reddish-brown hair to curl in an unruly fashion around her face.

The baby came to an abrupt halt when he saw Alec standing in the entry, and for a moment Alec thought that the child's laughter might turn to tears of fright. Alec was a tall, even imposing figure, and there was a certain fierceness, he knew, in his ice-blue gaze and angular, strong-boned face that did nothing to soften his appearance. More than once, children had turned and run to hide against their mothers' skirts when they met him. Matthew Morecombe, however, was apparently made of sturdier stuff, for after that brief pause, he grinned, let out a piercing shriek, and ran forward, holding up his hands to Alec. Alec gazed down at him in bemusement, not quite certain what he should do.

"Rawdon!" The woman hurried forward as well, now beaming at Alec. She let out a laugh. "You must pick him up, you know, or he will not give you an instant's peace."

Alec bent down and somewhat gingerly placed his hands on either side of the child's waist, lifting him. Somehow Matthew settled naturally into the crook of his arm, curling his dimpled fist into the lapel of Alec's coat. The boy was heavy and soft in his arm, smelling faintly of milk and lavender and child, and something in Alec's chest went loose and warm. The baby looked down at the woman as she stopped before them, and he let out another happy crow.

"Yes, you like being up there so high, don't you?" She beamed at the baby, then focused on Alec. "I am so happy to see you. Gabriel did not tell me you were coming; I shall have to scold him."

"No, pray do not; I am the one at fault. I beg your pardon,

Lady Morecombe, I did not write to warn you. I was on my way back to London from home, and I decided on the whim of a moment to pay a visit to my godson."

There was a flash of surprise, quickly hidden, in Thea Morecombe's eyes, and Alec flushed, deeply aware—though his hostess was too polite to comment on the fact—that the village of Chesley lay a good deal off the road from Northumberland to London.

"Well, we are excessively glad that you did," Thea said with a warm smile. "But I thought we had agreed that you must call me Thea. We are, after all, almost kin, surely, since you are Matthew's godfather."

Alec smiled back at her, the harsh lines of his face softening almost imperceptibly. "I am honored. Thea." Despite holding the child in his arm, he executed a precise bow. Matthew gurgled with delight at the movement and dug his fists more tightly into Alec's coat. "But only if you will call me Alec in return."

"Alec!" A tall, dark-haired man came striding toward them, grinning broadly. "Whatever are you doing here? It's devilish good to see you."

"Gabriel. Thank you. I fear I have dropped in quite uninvited." Alec moved toward his friend, reaching out to shake the hand Gabriel Morecombe offered.

"Nonsense. You always have an invitation extended to you, whenever you should wish to take it."

It felt quite natural to stand here with Gabriel—they had, after all, been friends since they were fifteen years old—but there was still a touch of awkwardness as well, for it was hard to forget the estrangement which had kept them apart for over a year. For a moment, Alec found himself at a loss for something to say. Then Matthew leaned forward, babbling and holding out his hands in a grasping manner to Gabriel.

"Are you leaving me, then?" Alec asked, amused. "Traitor."

Gabriel chuckled and plucked the child from Alec's grasp. "He is hopeful that my appearance means teatime is at hand." He bent and nuzzled the baby's neck, sending him into a paroxysm of giggles.

"I think, rather, that he is hopeful it means a bout of rolling about the floor with you," Thea corrected drily, coming forward and reaching out to take the baby. "Come here, you, it's time for your nap." She smiled toward the men. "I shall take Matthew to his nurse and give you two an opportunity to visit."

The two men stood for a moment watching her sweep up the stairs with the baby. "You must be very happy," Alec said quietly.

"I am indeed." The familiar white grin flashed in Gabriel's face. "I hope that someday you will know such happiness."

Alec smiled wryly, an expression he had perfected for countering such statements. "Alas, I fear I am destined by nature to be a bachelor." He did not glance at his friend; Gabriel was one of the few who knew how much he had once hoped to deny that fact.

"I would have said the same myself a year ago," Gabriel

responded cheerfully. "Before Thea opened my eyes." He gestured toward the rear of the house. "Come. Let's wash away the dust of the road, and you must tell me how you are."

They strolled down the hall to Gabriel's study, chatting as they went. Alec was surprised at how easy it was to fall back into their old pattern of conversation. But then, Gabe had always had a gift for putting one at ease, a talent Alec had never had or even understood how to acquire. It was fortunate, he thought, that he had little need for it.

"I feared I might find you had removed to London or Morecombe Hall," Alec commented as he settled down in a comfortable wingback chair. The darkly paneled study had a faint, pleasant scent of leather and tobacco.

Gabriel shrugged one shoulder negligently as he handed his friend a glass of Port, then sat in the chair across from him. "We spent a month at the Hall so Matthew could see his grandmother. And a while in London. Thea loved the plays, and I have never spent so much time inside bookstores and museums in my life." Gabriel looked faintly amazed at his own actions, and Alec had to chuckle. "But, quite truthfully, we missed the Priory. And Chesley. I have become utterly domesticated."

"It seems to suit you."

Morecombe nodded. "Thea says Matthew has me wrapped around his little finger. 'Tis absolutely true, I fear. She does not mention the fact that she does as well."

Alec was aware again of that feeling in his chest, a peculiar piercing mixture of pain and delight. "I could see Jocelyn in

Matthew's face." He did not add that he had seen Ian there, too. Best not to think about that.

Gabriel's eyes turned sober at his words, and he nodded. An awkward silence fell over them. Matthew's mother, Jocelyn, was Gabriel's sister, and when she had broken her engagement to Alec, running away from all of them, Gabriel had blamed Alec. It wasn't until Matthew had shown up in Chesley, abandoned in the village church and discovered by Thea Bainbridge, the vicar's sister, that the truth had come out. Pregnant by her married lover, Jocelyn had accepted Alec's proposal but, in the end, had been unable to go through with the charade. She had fled to the Continent to have her child and had lived there until finally, dying of consumption, she had returned to England to entrust her baby to her brother's care. She had not lived to bring Matthew all the way home, but everything had worked out finally and, as it turned out, the baby had brought Thea into Gabriel's life as well. Married not long after Christmas, they were raising the endearing child as their own.

Alec shifted in his chair. "How does the rest of Chesley fare? The Reverend Bainbridge? The squire and Mrs. Cliffe? Mrs. Howard?" He tossed out the last name casually and turned his eyes down to the drink in his hand.

Gabriel glanced at him, and a flicker of amusement touched his eyes. "Thea's brother is as ever. He will doubtless want to fill your ear with an article he read about Hadrian's Wall. I fear he finds me sadly lacking in the qualities he would wish in a brother-in-law; I told him I had visited you at Castle Cleyre several times yet not once had gone to look at the wall."

Alec chuckled. "That would, indeed, be anathema to him. I shall have to call on him. A scholar wrote me, asking if he could dig on my property for bits of some Roman encampment. I suppose I shall let him; I thought Bainbridge might wish to visit when he is there."

"Good Gad. You will have a friend for life in Daniel if you do so." He paused, watching Alec's face as he went on. "We must have a dinner party while you are here. 'Tis too bad that Mrs. Howard is not in Chesley."

Alec was aware of a distinct sense of disappointment, but he was too well schooled in concealing his thoughts to reveal it. "Indeed? I am sorry to hear it. I am sure that Lady Morecombe must miss her."

"No doubt. But she will not be gone long—merely a trip to London. Shopping, I understand, was the driving factor."

"Ah. Well, pray give her my regards."

"Of course." A mischievous light glinted in Gabriel's eyes. "A beautiful woman, Mrs. Howard."

Alec shot a sharp glance at his friend, but he had never been immune to Gabriel's humorous bent, and after a moment, he chuckled. "Oh, the devil take you! I am not interested in Mrs. Howard."

Gabriel made no answer, but the skepticism was clear on his face.

"I'm not," Alec reiterated. "I can appreciate beauty without planning to acquire it."

"Mm. And yet, how often are you taken with a work of art and do not purchase it?"

"If money were all that was involved, trust me, it would be a different matter," Alec retorted. "But I fear that the price of a lady like Mrs. Howard would be far too high for me."

The lighthearted humor dropped from his friend's face, and Alec knew that Gabriel realized all too well what lay behind Alec's disinterest in pursuing a lady of quality. Alec glanced away; he had no desire for any man's regret or apology, still less for his pity.

"Well, we shall do our best to keep you entertained," Gabriel said easily. "Even without the charms of the lovely Mrs. Howard. Come." He set aside his drink and stood up. "Let me show you up to your room, else Thea will scold me for not giving you a chance to rest after your journey."

"Of course," Alec agreed, rising to his feet and following him. It made no difference that Mrs. Howard was not in town. He had come here to see his friends and his godson. Dreams did not matter in the light of day.

Gabriel was true to his word and kept his friend well entertained. In the country, it seemed, one could whip up a dinner party on a day's notice, and though the squire's family, the vicar, and a retired colonel were not exactly sophisticated, they were a convivial lot who, at least, were not too urbane to be amused. As Gabriel had predicted, Daniel Bainbridge was rendered almost speechless with delight at the prospect of getting to dig about in a Roman ruin, and he insisted that

Alec come for tea the next afternoon to chat about the pro-
posed visit.

But in truth, Alec derived the most amusement simply
from being with baby Matthew. The sight of Matthew's
sunny face never failed to warm him and he found that if he
held the lad high over his head, Matthew burst into a cascade
of giggles. Sometimes it was as if a spectral hand clutched at
his heart when he looked at the son of the woman he'd once
loved.

Best of all was when, as now, Matthew came running at
Alec as fast as his chubby little legs could carry him. Alec
squatted down, his arms out to meet Matthew, who, much to
Alec's surprise, planted a wet, sticky kiss on his cheek.

"You look quite natural holding him," Thea told him with
a smile.

"Do I?" Alec raised his eyebrows. "I cannot imagine why. I
can't remember ever holding a child before."

"No? I suspect it does not require a great deal of practice,
only willingness. I knew scarcely a thing about them before
Matthew."

"He changed a number of lives, didn't he?" Alec murmured, looking down into the baby's wide blue eyes.

The nurse came to take Matthew up for his nap. Alec
found himself oddly reluctant to hand the child over, but
it was time to take tea with the vicar. He excused himself
to Thea, and since it was a pleasant summer afternoon, he
decided to walk through the ruins of the old abbey rather
than ride his horse the long way around to the vicarage.

The Priory, where the Morecombes lived, and St. Margaret's Church, on the opposite side of the ruins, were the only buildings remaining intact from the large convent that had once lain there. The cloisters and various outbuildings were now nothing more than a few partial walls and jumbled heaps of stones. Beyond the ruins lay the graveyard of the church, and seeing the stone markers, Alec was reminded of his dream the other night, in which he had run after Jocelyn through the gravestones. He thought of how he had caught and kissed her, only for her to turn into Damaris in his arms.

He pulled himself from his reverie and realized that he had come to a complete stop, lost in thought. He was utterly alone, with only the sturdy old stone church looming before him. On impulse, Alec turned toward the church instead of continuing across the little bridge to the vicarage.

The ancient wooden door closed firmly behind him as he passed through the vestibule into the sanctuary beyond. It was silent inside, light filtering in through the stained-glass windows lining the outer walls, casting soft colors across the high-backed wooden pews and ancient stone floors. The church, like many other old churches, was laid out in the shape of a cross, a shorter pair of arms thrusting out to either side just before the altar.

Alec drifted into the small chapel on the left side. It was partially separated from the rest of the church by iron fretwork and contained only a few short pews. Against the far wall, beneath the windows, lay two stone sepulchers of a long-ago lord and his lady, both topped with recumbent effigies. They were washed in the faint blue and yellow light streaming through the stained glass. On the wide wall near Alec stood a statue of St. Dwynwen, the Welsh patron saint of love, which that same medieval lord had taken from its place in Wales, along with a Welsh wife.

Damaris had recounted the legend to Alec when they were in the church for Matthew's baptism—how the lord had credited the saint with winning his lady love for him and so had brought the statue home and built the chapel in her honor. Since that time, according to the local lore, prayers to the saint were granted if one prayed with a true and loving heart. Alec was not certain exactly what that entailed, but he noted that two candles burned in the votive stand beside the statue. Clearly someone believed.

He moved closer to the statue and stood for a moment gazing down at it. It was rough and obviously quite old, with a chunk missing here and there and a decided crack running through it. Yet there was something soothing about the crudely chiseled face, a look of peace, even love. Alec turned and sat down in the pew, gazing out across the church at the baptistry, which lay in the opposite short arm of the sanctuary. He thought about the day in February when he had stood there at the ornately carved baptismal font.

Gabriel and Thea had stood next to him, the baby in Thea's arms, arms and legs waving about, as Daniel Bainbridge had read out the solemn words. And across from Alec, on the other side of the font, had stood Damaris Howard. She had worn a velvet cloak in the wintry chill of the church, and its dark purple had deepened the intense color of her eyes. He remembered gazing at her, his eyes caught by the thick gloss of her black hair, the creamy softness of her cheeks, the lush curve of her lips. He had, he recalled, indulged in decidedly unholy thoughts about her in this holiest of places.

He wondered what Damaris was doing in London. Shopping, Gabriel had said; that was no surprise. Every time Alec saw her, she was dressed in the height of fashion. No doubt she was visiting the theater and the opera as well. Dancing at parties. Perhaps if he'd remained in London, he would have run into her.

Not, of course, that that mattered.

He moved restlessly on the hard wooden seat, leaning forward to brace his arms on the pew in front of him and lean his chin on his crossed hands. He thought of the baptism again, of Thea's and Gabriel's faces, alight with love. The love still burned in them. Of course, it had been only months, but Alec had no doubt that the emotion would continue. They would raise Matthew with happiness and care; likely there would be siblings to join the boy. They would grow old together.

He could not help but feel a twinge of envy. He did not begrudge them their joy. Indeed, he felt himself warmed by it, rather like standing beside a roaring fire. The fact that his own life seemed dry and empty by comparison was not their fault. Once, for a brief while, he had hoped that his own future would be as bright, as sweet, as theirs, but of course such hope had died almost as soon as it was born. Now, for just a moment, before he could cut it off and lock it away, Alec felt the sharp ache of his solitary life, a brief, desperate something that yearned for that joy in his own life.

Letting out a small noise of disgust at his maunderings, he pushed himself up from the seat. It was folly to think this way. There was nothing wrong with his life; indeed, many would envy it. He was the Earl of Rawdon, and it was time to stop drifting about like a cork on the ocean. Time to get back to London. To his life.

He walked out of the church without looking back.

Two

Damaris twisted in front of the mirror above the dresser, craning her neck to see the back of her dress, and gave a wistful thought for the full-length cheval glass in her bedroom at home. Madame Gaudet's assistant had brought the first set of new dresses Damaris had ordered, and Damaris was eager to wear one of them to the theater tonight. She had chosen a silk frock in a pale blue hue, its froth of an overskirt held back with knots of seed pearls. Around the base of her throat, Damaris wore a circlet of creamy pearls to match. She only wished that she could get a complete view of the delicate demi-train that fell from just below her shoulder blades to the ground.

However, though the snug little house her man of business had found for her was fashionably located in a small crescent just off Half Moon Street, its furniture left something to be desired, at least when it came to mirrors. It was clear, Damaris thought with some irritation, that the place had been furnished and leased by men, for the few mirrors scattered about the place reflected only the upper portion of one's form. With a sigh, she turned toward her maid, raising her eyebrows in question.

"You look beautiful, ma'am," Edith assured her, reaching out to twitch a fold of the skirt into the perfect place. "Just another pearl pin for your hair, I think." She reached for a pearl-topped hairpin and slid it into position in a cluster of Damaris's ink-black curls.

"Is Mr. Portland here?" Damaris asked, picking up her gloves and fan.

"Yes'm, these ten minutes or more. Hawley set him up with a glass of Sherry, and he seems quite content."

"Good." Damaris slid on her gloves as she started out the door. She did not like to be overly late—though Mr. Portland would never complain, of course—but sometimes one's hair simply would not curl as one wished, no matter how expertly Edith twisted and pinned it.

Portland rose to his feet as she entered the small drawing room, setting aside the delicate glass of Sherry and offering a heartfelt smile and a punctiliously correct bow. "Damaris, my dear."

"Gregory." She smiled back at the graying gentleman and offered him her hand. It still felt strange to call her father's friend and banker by his given name, for she had known him since childhood. However, Portland had been her banker—and friend as well—for years now, ever since her father's death, and he had insisted that she drop the more formal appellation. "It is a pleasure to see you again."

She had, of course, called upon him at the bank when she

first arrived in London two weeks ago. Going over various monetary matters, after all, was one of her reasons for visiting London. She had also discussed investments with her man of business and some small legal concerns with her solicitor. While she was in general able to oversee her financial affairs by mail from her home in Chesley, she thought it wise to visit her advisors in person at least once a year. The shopping and evenings at the theater were her reward for executing the more boring duties.

"I am looking forward to this evening," she told the older man as she settled her gossamer evening wrap about her shoulders. "I have heard that Mrs. Cummings's return to the theater is quite the event."

"Indeed." The banker offered her his arm, and they walked out. "She has been absent now for almost two years, and the company has not been the same without her. There were those who feared she might never return, but I never believed she would stay away. Love is all very well, but . . ." He shrugged eloquently.

"Yes. It rarely lasts, does it?"

There was, perhaps, something in her tone that made the older man glance at her, a faint frown forming on his brow. "My dear, I did not mean to—"

"Nonsense." She smiled brightly. "I know you did not. It is very true, of course. Love is not enough." Her thoughts went to her friend Thea back home in Chesley, now so happily married to Lord Morecombe and an instant mother to his sister's child. "Well, except for a select few. I told you, did I not, that my friend Miss Bainbridge has made a love match?"

"Yes, indeed. I have met Lord Morecombe, an excellent man."

He handed her up into his carriage, a glossy black equipage, and they settled back into the plush maroon leather seats, chatting pleasantly as the vehicle rolled through the streets. Damaris had always enjoyed the older man's company. Having known her all her life, he was aware of her circumstances, which made it easy to talk to him, and he treated her with both affection and respect.

He realized, for instance, that despite her pleasure in the sophisticated delights the city had to offer, Damaris was rather constrained in her opportunities to enjoy them. Her visits to the milliner's or modiste's and other stores could, of course, be respectably carried out with the accompaniment of her maid or even alone. However, she could hardly attend such entertainments as the theater or the opera without an escort, and the only people in London she knew were the men who handled her business affairs. Her social life since she had been in the city had, frankly, been less full than it was in the country.

She was grateful, therefore, that Mr. Portland was perceptive and kind enough to offer her his escort to an evening at the theater. If a man who was the closest thing she had to a fond uncle was not the male companion she would have most wished for, Damaris refused to let herself think about the escort she might prefer.

Damaris glanced around as they walked inside the grand theater. She was *not*, she told herself sternly, looking for anyone in particular. Least of all the Earl of Rawdon. If it had, once or twice, occurred to her that she might run into him in London, she was not naïve enough to believe it was likely. They did not move in the same circles … or even in ones with any possibility of overlapping. Indeed, she had just received a letter from Thea, written only a week ago, which said that Rawdon was at the Priory.

It was unlikely he had even left Chesley yet. And if by chance he had arrived in London, he did not seem the sort to attend the theater tonight simply because everyone was talking about the return of a popular actress to the stage. Rather, she suspected, he was more likely to refuse to come to it simply because it was the popular thing to do.

So when she had been seated and her gaze fell upon a familiar blond head, she nearly gasped, her heart suddenly racing. It was Rawdon; she was certain of it. There was no mistaking that pale shock of hair, a trifle longer and shaggier than most gentlemen wore theirs, or the high, wide cheekbones that gave his lean face such a fierce and distinctive aspect. It was impossible, of course, to see the compelling pale blue of his eyes from this distance, but Damaris remembered it well. Indeed, his icy gaze made him almost impossible to forget.

He was seated at the nearest end of one of the loges, and beside him was a young woman whose light blond, almost silvery hair and patrician face suggested to Damaris that she was related to Lord Rawdon. To her other side was a much older woman of regal bearing—a mother, or even grandmother, perhaps.

Damaris realized that she was staring and hastily turned her gaze away. How awful if Rawdon were to catch her gaping at him like a moonstruck girl! She folded her hands demurely in her lap and turned to talk to Mr. Portland, determinedly refusing to even glance around the theater again. It was a relief when the curtain went up and she was able to focus her gaze on the stage.

All through the first act, she found it difficult to concentrate on the actors, for her mind kept returning to Lord Rawdon, and she had to fight the urge to turn and peer through the darkness at him. She wondered if he had happened to see her, too. If he had, would he approach her during the intermission? Damaris knew that her face and form attracted many men, but she was not sure that Lord Rawdon was one of them. He was a cold, proud man, and it was also clear that his heart—if he had one to give—had been claimed by Gabriel's sister, Jocelyn.

Still … there had been a flash of something in his eyes once or twice that set her stomach to fluttering. Of course, there was always the possibility that the flutter had been only on her part. In any case, she was not about to seek him out or angle to place herself in his path. She considered not even prom-enading through the theater lobby during the intermission, but when the act ended and her companion offered her his arm, she took it. It would, after all, appear odd if she insisted on remaining glued to her seat. But Damaris was careful not to look around as she and the banker strolled along. If Lord Rawdon saw her, he would have to seek her out.

Mr. Portland had just started to inquire whether she

wished a glass of Champagne when Damaris heard a deep voice say, "Mrs. Howard?"

A frisson of excitement darted through her, and Damaris was glad she was not facing in Rawdon's direction because she suspected her face revealed that fact. Pulling her features back into their usual composure, she turned around, but she could not hold back a smile when she saw him.

"Lord Rawdon. What a pleasant surprise."

She had been sure that her memory had exaggerated how tall he was and how squarely his shoulders filled out his jacket, but she could see now, with a little fillip of appreciation, that she had not. He was a large, lean man, and his looks were well suited to his severe black suit and contrasting snowy-white shirt. A signet ring decorated his right hand, accentuating his long fingers and the bony outcroppings of his knuckles. He was not exactly handsome; there was something too gaunt and predatory about the angular structure of his face and the slightly coiled tension in the way he stood. Yet Damaris could not deny that every time she saw the man, a ripple of something raw and tantalizing ran through her.

"The pleasure is mine, I assure you." The slight movement of his mouth could hardly be called a smile, yet it shifted the planes of his face and lit his pale eyes in a way that was distinctly warmer. His gaze held hers a moment longer than was strictly polite before he shifted and went on. "Pray, allow me to introduce you to my sister, Lady Genevieve Stafford. Genevieve, this is Mrs. Howard. She is a friend of Lady Morecombe. We met in Chesley."

"Mrs. Howard." The fair-haired woman on Rawdon's arm nodded toward Damaris. Her attractive, strong-boned face was as smooth and difficult to read as her brother's, but Damaris was certain that it was curiosity she read in the other woman's blue eyes. "I am afraid I have not yet had the pleasure of meeting Lady Morecombe. My brother speaks highly of her."

Damaris smiled at the thought of Thea. "He is quite right to do so. Lady Morecombe is delightful. I hope you will become acquainted with her soon. Please, allow me to introduce you to Mr. Portland."

There was another exchange of pleasantries. Damaris was very aware of Rawdon's gaze on her throughout. She wondered what he was thinking; it was impossible to tell from his face. Finally the polite greetings and comments regarding the weather and the play dwindled down, and a lull fell upon the conversation. Genevieve glanced at her brother, then faintly cleared her throat. Damaris wondered if Rawdon was not paying attention or was simply refusing to take the girl's hints. Damaris started to say something in order to keep them there a moment longer, but Rawdon spoke first.

"I was recently at the Priory," he told Damaris. "Lord and Lady Morecombe send their regards."

"How nice. Thank you. And did you find Master Matthew well?"

His smile was more definite now, the corners of his eyes crinkling. "Indeed. Hale and hearty. He is walking."

"Oh, yes." Damaris chuckled. "He leads everyone in a merry chase. I find I quite miss him."

"Have you been in London long?" Rawdon asked.

"No. Only a fortnight. I have taken a house for a month."

"Indeed? So short a time?" Did he looked disappointed, or was that merely her imagination? "That will be London's loss."

"Very prettily said, my lord." Damaris's eyes twinkled. She had almost forgotten how invigorated she felt when crossing verbal swords with this man. The challenge of making his controlled face spark with humor or surprise or even irritation was almost irresistible. "Still, one cannot help but think that such finely honed compliments must come from frequent repetition."

She was rewarded by the faint widening of his eyes in surprise, and his voice lifted with a hint of laughter.

"You imply that I am a flirt, madam?" Beside him, Rawdon's sister looked startled, but he did not seem to notice her slight involuntary movement as he went on. "I fear you would find yourself alone in that opinion."

"I would never call you a flirt," Damaris demurred. "'Twould be most uncivil of me."

"And are you always civilized?" he retorted. The light in his eyes was unmistakable now.

"Indeed, one must always try to be." A small, slightly wicked smile curved her lips. "But I fear that I do not always succeed."

Lady Genevieve was openly staring at Rawdon now. She cleared her throat, then turned to Damaris, offering her a quick, polite smile. "Pray excuse us, Mrs. Howard. Mr. Portland. It was a pleasure to meet you. But I fear we must speak to Mrs. Haverbourne."

Damaris nodded. "The pleasure was mine."

Lord Rawdon remained rooted to the spot despite his sister's discreet tug at his elbow. "I am sorry my grandmother did not get a chance to meet you. She remained in our box."

"Pray convey my regards to her."

"I will. Thank you. But perhaps you will come to Genevieve's party tomorrow evening. I know the countess would enjoy meeting you."

"I—" Damaris's gaze went to Genevieve's frozen expression. She should refuse, she knew. There were a hundred reasons why she should not attend a *ton* party, not the least of which was Lady Genevieve's hastily concealed astonishment.

Rawdon turned toward his sister, and Genevieve forced a smile. "Yes, do say you will be there," she told Damaris, her tone devoid of enthusiasm.

Normally Damaris would not have accepted so tepid an invitation. If Genevieve had any idea of the truth about Damaris's past, she knew the girl would not have proffered even that. She opened her mouth to refuse, but then she made the mistake of looking at Lord Rawdon.

"Thank you," Damaris said instead, smiling. "I would love to join you."

"But who is this girl?" The Countess of Rawdon leaned forward to fix her grandson with the full blast of her faded blue eyes. Her eyes lacked the icy hue that was a hallmark of the

Stafford family, though they carried enough authority and hauteur to quell almost anyone. But tonight her grandson seemed immune to their power.

He simply said, "Her name is Mrs. Howard, Grandmother. I believe I mentioned it."

"Yes, of course, but that does not tell me who she *is*."

Genevieve, beside her, was scanning the audience with her opera glasses. She had had to wait until her grandmother's guest had left their plush box before spilling out the news that Alec had invited a woman to their party the following evening, and now there was little time left before the lights went down for the next act.

"There!" Genevieve exclaimed softly. "She is that stunning black-haired woman in the pale blue gown." She handed the glasses to her grandmother, gesturing toward the audience below them.

"Genevieve! Really! Don't point." Lady Rawdon snatched the glasses from her granddaughter, shooting her a look of cool reproach. "It's vulgar."

"Of course, Grandmother. I'm sorry. She is in the second seat from the aisle almost directly below us."

"Ah, yes. I see." The countess studied Damaris for a moment, then handed the glasses back to Genevieve. She cast an assessing glance at her grandson, but before she could speak, the house lights went down and the curtain was raised. Lady Rawdon pressed her lips together and turned back to watch the play unfold.

Alec relaxed in his chair and, with his grandmother's

attention focused on the stage, stared down into the audience. It was impossible to see Damaris well now, but Alec could remember quite clearly how Damaris had looked. His memory had not played him false; she was as beautiful as he had recalled. Perhaps even more so. He thought of the creamy white pearls scattered throughout her lustrous black hair, echoing the strand around her neck, drawing the gaze downward to the inviting expanse of alabaster chest . . . the swell of her breasts above the fashionably low neckline . . . He shifted in his seat and turned back to the action on the stage.

But his thoughts remained on the woman below, so that he could not have said later what had transpired in the second act. He had no interest in the farce, anyway. He had come only because Genevieve had wanted to do so. It was, apparently, the most important night to see and be seen at the theater. And if he was being honest, he had to admit that the thought had occurred to him that it might be the likeliest time for Mrs. Howard to attend the play as well.

Still, even knowing that there was some possibility that she might be there, a little jolt had shot through him when he scanned the audience and saw her sitting there. He was glad that he had glimpsed her first and had some time to adjust before he engineered running into her in the lobby. Even so, he had felt foolishly stiff and awkward. There was always a look in Damaris Howard's eyes that made him certain he amused her in some way, an expression which both intrigued and challenged him. It was not an expression he was accustomed to, as it seemed that women were more given to viewing him either nervously or greedily or, often, a combination of the two.

Genevieve's presence in the conversation had not helped, of course, for he had been well aware that his sister was observing him keenly. It was useless to think he could get anything past Genevieve, who knew him better than anyone. Not, of course, that there was anything he really wished to hide from her . . . yet he could not help but think, every time he thought about Mrs. Howard, that he really did not want the rest of the world to know how he felt. Indeed, he had the suspicion that he would prefer that even he didn't know how he felt.

And *that* was a perfectly idiotic notion. Of course, it was no more idiotic than the vague, eager, twitchy sensations that rose up in him whenever he was around Damaris—as if he were a schoolboy again! He had never been the most socially adept man—and he counted it his good fortune that his reticence was invariably put down to arrogance rather than awkwardness—but it had been years since he had felt as uncomfortable as he did when talking to Mrs. Howard. Yet as soon as he saw her, he had been plotting to run into her between acts.

There was no question of speaking with her again after the second act, something that would be sure to cause talk. But he was not inclined to let his grandmother quiz him more about Damaris, either, so as soon as the curtain dropped again, he was on his feet, offering to bring the ladies back refreshments. By the time he returned, their box was obligingly full of visitors, two of whom were thrilled when he invited them to stay for the third act as well. By no twitch of her expression did his grandmother indicate the slightest surprise at his saddling them with her dead sister's friend and that woman's empty-headed daughter, but Alec saw the sharp glance Genevieve threw him, and he knew that he had only put off the inevitable.

He was prepared, then, for the countess's fixing him with her ruthless gaze the moment they left the theater and were safely settled in their carriage, away from prying eyes and ears.

"You did not answer my question, Alec. Who is this Mrs. Howard? Why have I never heard of her?"

"I could not say, Grandmother. She is a widow, and I believe she lives a rather retired life."

Lady Rawdon made a noncommittal noise. "Rather young and attractive, I would say, to have retired from life."

"Perhaps grief overcame her."

"She does not appear to be in mourning."

"Grandmother." He looked at her evenly. "I do not know the woman well enough to answer your questions."

"Yet you know her well enough to invite her to our party." She smiled faintly. "She is quite lovely, of course. But then, no one can accuse you of bad taste."

"I fail to see what my taste has to do with it." Rawdon's cool gaze would have intimidated a lesser creature than the countess. "I merely invited Lady Morecombe's friend to your ball. She is here for a short visit; I doubt she knows many people in London."

Lady Rawdon narrowed her gaze. "You expect me to believe that you extended an invitation—the first time you have asked anyone to one of our parties, by the way—simply to be nice to one of Lord Morecombe's wife's rustic friends?"

Amusement lit Alec's eyes. "'Rustic friends'? I assure you, Mrs. Howard does not have bits of hay clinging to her hair, Grandmother. Most of the people I met in Chesley were quite civilized."

"Chesley." The countess dismissed the village with a scornful flick of her hand. "Do not attempt to throw sand in my eyes, Alec. The point is: What do you know about this woman? Where does she come from—and do not say the Cotswolds; I am well aware of where Chesley is. What I want to know is, who are her people?"

"I am sorry, but I did not think to interrogate Lady Morecombe about her friend's background. All I really know is that she is a widow. I think you will find her speech and manners unexceptionable. You needn't fear that her presence will be an embarrassment."

The countess's gaze flicked across him, sharp as a knife. "Pray do not take that tone with me, Rawdon. I have been fending off the overtures of jumped-up mushrooms for a good many more years than you have been alive."

"I have no reason to think that Mrs. Howard, or her late husband, were 'mushrooms,' Grandmother. She is a friend to the Morecombes, and I believe you will allow that they are of adequate lineage to associate with Staffords. Lady Morecombe was a Bainbridge, a cousin to Lord Fenstone."

"Fenstone!" The countess lifted her head, sending a long look down her nose at her grandson, clearly registering her disregard for the earl. "Your father's ancestors were guarding the border long before Richard gave Fenstone to that lot."

"Yes, yes, I know, and we were throwing our lot in with the Percys against the Nevilles. But I really do not think that the War of the Roses is pertinent to asking Mrs. Howard to Genevieve's party."

"Being a friend of a Bainbridge is little recommendation," Genevieve inserted hotly. "Lord Fenstone is always run off his legs, and we all know what sort of man Ian is."

Alec started to retort sharply, but a glance at his sister's pink cheeks and flashing eyes made him soften his response. "I know how you feel about Ian, and I appreciate your loyalty to me. But believe me, Mrs. Howard is in no way connected to him. She had never even met the man before we cast her Twelfth Night party into shambles."

It had been at Damaris's masque ball six months earlier that they had all learned the full story of how Ian, once Alec's friend, had betrayed him, seducing Alec's fiancée and leading her to break their engagement and flee the country.

"I will not allow anyone to hurt you." Genevieve's eyes were as fierce as a she-wolf's.

He smiled faintly. "Pray do not worry. Whoever Mrs. Howard's antecedents are, it makes no difference. I am not about to lose my head over her. Certainly not my heart."

Three

Damaris took a deep breath as she smoothed the long, elegant white kid gloves up her arms. It was not too late. She could still change her mind and decide not to go to Lady Genevieve's party.

She had spent the entire day telling herself that she should not go. It was a selfish, foolish thing to do. If her presence there was noticed . . . if anyone knew who she was or discovered her identity, it would not reflect well on the Staffords, who would never have extended an invitation to her if they had known the truth about her parents. Indeed, it had been clear from Genevieve's expression that she had had little desire to extend Damaris an invitation even without knowing Damaris's history.

Why Rawdon had forced the issue was a question that sent a tickle of excitement through her. No matter how much she told herself it was silly to be flattered that he wanted her to come to the party, she could not convince herself to feel otherwise. Yes, other men had been interested in her, sought her company. She had flirted with any number of suitors—

and, truth be known, men far more adept at flirting than Lord Rawdon. But that did not matter; those men had not made her stomach quiver and her pulse speed up. They had not made her blood sing through her veins.

Alec Stafford did.

So, each time she decided that she would not go, every time she decided that her presence at the *ton* ball would be inappropriate and she sat down to write a polite note of apology to Lady Genevieve, she had wound up going to look through her dresses or to contemplate what jewels she would wear or whether to tie her hair up in rags so that it would have just the right amount of curl. After all, she rationalized, attending the party would not do anyone any harm. It was extremely unlikely that anyone there would have the slightest idea who she was.

Damaris had gone to school on the Continent when she was fourteen, and she had not returned to England until last year. No one would connect her last name to that of her father, and certainly her father's family would never have mentioned her. And it was unlikely that the scandal concerning her marriage would be common knowledge, since it had occurred in Italy. Besides, even if someone did learn her secrets, surely it would not stain Rawdon or his family in any serious way. She was only a casual guest at a large party, after all.

Besides, it would be too bad, really, not to seize the chance to wear the new confection of a ball gown that Madame Gaudet had made for her. The deep-purple silk was overlaid with silver tissue, so that the result looked like a sugared plum, and her amethyst and diamond earrings would echo the rich color. A silver ribbon running through her curls and an amethyst pendant nestled in the hollow of her throat finished off the picture perfectly.

So she had chosen her clothes and bathed and primped and now here she was—ready to go and yet still unprepared. As she stood there, lost in indecision, one of the parlor maids appeared at her door and bobbed a curtsey, saying in an awed voice, "Lord Rawdon is below, mum, waiting to see you."

Damaris stared at her, for a moment unable to speak or move. "Lord Rawdon? Here?" Her voice came out almost a squeak, and she cleared her throat before inclining her head in a dignified manner and saying, "Tell him I shall be right there."

She turned away, clasping her hands together and drawing a deep breath to calm the nerves that were suddenly dancing inside her. What was Rawdon doing here? She started down the stairs, her stomach curiously hot and her hands cold, her emotions bouncing wildly between excitement and fear.

Alec stood at the foot of the stairs, facing away from her. He was dressed all in black and white as he had been the night before, but the crisp severity of his clothing could not completely hide the touch of wildness that clung to him. Damaris thought of the first time she had seen him, when he had stormed into Gabriel's house, his angular face raw with rage, silvery blond hair windblown, pale eyes burning. He had been all elemental power then, intense and furious, his body coiled to strike. And yet over it all had lain an aura of control. Even in his fury, he was cold and in command. Damaris was not sure why, but she could not deny that the sight of him, as it always did, called up a swift, primitive response in her.

Rawdon turned at the sound of her footsteps on the stairs. Though he did not smile, his face brightened subtly, his eyes suddenly alert. "Mrs. Howard." He swept her a bow, and as she reached the bottom stair, he took the hand she offered him, guiding her needlessly but politely onto the floor beside him. "You are a vision."

He bent to brush his lips over the back of her hand in a gesture that should have been nothing but courtesy but instead made her tingle all over. "And you, sir, are a dreadful flatterer . . . but I appreciate your words, all the same."

"'Tis scarcely flattery when one speaks the truth." His eyes slid down her in a quick, comprehensive way that verified his words. "You take a man's breath away."

To Damaris's annoyance, she felt a blush creep into her cheeks. She was more knowing, surely, than to be so easily affected by a man's admiration. More bluntly than she would normally have spoken, she went on, "I am surprised to find you here. Surely you should be at your party."

"'Tis Genevieve's party, and my grandmother's. My presence is considered more a bother than a necessity. And I could hardly be so ungentlemanly as to invite you, then leave you without an escort."

"Ah." Damaris could not keep from slanting a challenging glance up at him. What was it about this man that always made her want to push at him, like a child poking a tiger with a stick?

"Then you are here out of duty, not desire?"

"My dear Mrs. Howard . . ." The faint lines that bracketed the corners of his mouth deepened, drawing her gaze to his lips. "Where you are concerned, 'tis always desire."

Warmth curled in her abdomen even as she chuckled at his deft parry of her verbal thrust. "I must remember that I should not try to cross swords with you."

"No, pray, do not cease. It is one of the things that I enjoy most about you." His hand tightened a fraction on her fingers, and Damaris realized that he was still holding her hand long after courtesy would have had him release it. More startling was the fact that she would like him to continue holding it.

"I can only thank you for being so thoughtful as to escort me," she told him rather formally, slipping her hand from his. "'Tis much more than I expected."

"I hope you will accept this as well." He reached over to the narrow entry table and picked up a small box, handing it to her.

She opened it, the heady scent of gardenias floating out before she saw the flowers. A delicate wrist corsage lay inside. Damaris drew in a little breath. "Rawdon! How lovely!" She took the corsage from the box and smiled up at him.

"Seeing you smile, I can only wish I had brought you two of them." Alec took the corsage from her hand and settled it on her wrist, tying the delicate ribbons.

"You are a man of many surprises," Damaris murmured, lifting her wrist to drink in the aroma of the flowers.

Her maid hovered at the edge of the entry, holding

Damaris's wrap of sheer silver voile and eyeing the earl with interest. When Damaris looked at her, she came forward, holding out the shimmering material, and Alec took it, draping it around Damaris's shoulders. She felt the brush of his fingers against her skin, and it was all she could do not to shiver.

He gave her his arm and led her out to the town carriage that awaited outside. A family crest in dull gold adorned the door of the polished black vehicle, and a liveried footman stood ready to open its door and let down the step. As Rawdon handed her up into the carriage, Damaris could not help but reflect how very different their circumstances were. Though she had never lived in anything less than comfort, the life she had always known was clearly a step below the elegance and formality that permeated the world of an earl.

However, she was not one who would allow herself to be intimidated, so she faced Rawdon with equanimity as he sat down across from her and the carriage started forward. "I am surprised that you knew where I lived."

"I have my ways, Mrs. Howard." His face relaxed in the manner that she was beginning to understand was a smile in another man.

"I am sure you do." She kept her voice light and wry.

"I wondered whether you would cry off tonight," Rawdon said after a moment. "I am glad you did not."

"I am not so fainthearted as that."

"No," he agreed, his eyes steadily on hers. "I don't believe you are at all faint of heart."

Damaris could not tear her gaze from his. She could feel the hard pulse in her throat, and she wondered if he could see it. He looked at her so intently that she thought he must see everything about her, clear through to the excitement swelling inside her. Her breath grew short, and she tensed imperceptibly, suddenly envisioning Rawdon moving across the carriage and taking her in his arms.

Then he looked away, breaking the moment, and Damaris let out her breath. She hoped, heat rising in her face, that he had not heard it. More than that, she hoped he had not suspected what she was thinking. Fortunately, the trip to his house did not take much time, and soon they pulled to a stop in front of a white stone mansion that stretched to either end of the block. Across the street was a small crescent-shaped park, a pleasant touch of green in the midst of the city. Streetlights illuminated the area, revealing the line of carriages unloading their passengers.

Rawdon whisked Damaris up the steps to the imposing front door, where another footman in full livery stood, admitting guests. He bowed to Rawdon and took his hat, and Rawdon, with a nod here and there, slipped around the guests to a knot of people at the door of the ballroom.

Damaris recognized his sister, talking to a man whose back was turned to Damaris and Rawdon. Genevieve's dress was white, and the pale pink satin ribbons that trimmed it gave her a bit of color without contributing any appreciable warmth. The strand of graduated pearls around her throat was as cold as snowdrops, accentuating her milk-white skin.

Lady Genevieve's eyes fell upon Damaris and Lord Rawdon, and her face tightened.

The man in front of her turned, following her gaze. He was a handsome man, slightly shorter than Rawdon, with thick cropped hair of a golden-brown color almost the same shade as his eyes. His dark green coat was tailored to his well-muscled chest and arms, and his snowy-white neckcloth was tied in an intricate arrangement, centered by a single large emerald. His eyes lit up appreciatively when he saw Damaris, and he cast a quick, speculative glance toward Rawdon as the two of them approached.

"Mrs. Howard," the man said when they reached him, and he swept her an elegant bow. "What an unexpected pleasure. I did not know you were in London."

Damaris smiled back at him. "Sir Myles. I am happy to see you again. I have been here for nigh on a fortnight now."

"And I have just now learned this?" Sir Myles assumed a wounded expression, which sat so ill on his strong-jawed face that Damaris had to laugh. "I shall have to have a word with you, Rawdon." He turned to his friend, eyes dancing. "Clearly you have been keeping Mrs. Howard hidden from the rest of us."

Rawdon merely shrugged, and Damaris lifted her eyebrows. "Lord Rawdon has little to say about my whereabouts, I assure you. I chanced to meet him and his sister at the theater last night, and they were kind enough to invite me."

Sir Myles had started a lighthearted flirtation with Damaris six months earlier, when he accompanied Lord Morecombe to Chesley for Christmas. Damaris suspected that wherever and with whomever he went, Sir Myles was certain to have a lighthearted flirtation going with someone, and she placed little weight on his words. But she did enjoy talking to him, and he was a better dancer than any other man who had ever asked her out on the floor. She also knew that there was a bedrock of loyalty and true friendship beneath his easygoing banter. He had been the only one of Morecombe's friends who had maintained his friendship with Rawdon after Alec and Gabriel came to blows.

"How do you do, Mrs. Howard?" Genevieve stepped up to greet Damaris. "I am so glad you could come. I see you have already met Sir Myles."

"Yes, I was fortunate enough to make his acquaintance last Yuletide."

"It must have been a large gathering at Lord Morecombe's," Genevieve commented. "We quite missed Rawdon from our celebrations."

"But fortunately Miss Bainbridge and her brother included Lord Rawdon in their Christmas party," Damaris inserted smoothly. "I know you are grateful to them that your brother was not alone on such a festive occasion."

"Yes, of course." Genevieve turned a considering look upon her. She was not, Damaris thought, as practiced as her brother in concealing her emotions, but while Genevieve could not match Rawdon's air of indifference, she seemed equally proud.

It was not hard to see where both had learned such qualities. The white-haired woman standing beyond Genevieve was ramrod straight and regarded the world with a regal expression. Diamonds glittered in matching hair combs and were echoed among the sapphires that encircled her throat. Though time had worked its way in the wrinkles lining her face, it clearly had not softened her. The blue gaze she turned on Damaris was incisive, and Damaris felt sure the countess did not miss a single detail of her appearance.

Genevieve introduced her grandmother, who nodded in response to Damaris's polite curtsey.

"Mrs. Howard. I am surprised I have not met you before," the countess said to Damaris.

"I have been back in the country for only a year or so."

"Indeed? You were living on the Continent?"

"For much of my life, yes." Damaris smiled but did not elaborate.

"Fascinating. We must talk more later in the evening. I have a number of acquaintances in Vienna."

"It is a lovely city, though I confess I have not spent much time there. I look forward to chatting with you." Privately Damaris determined to stay as far away from the woman as she could. She could well imagine the exhausting effort it would entail to evade the countess's subtle interrogation regarding her history.

"No doubt you will enjoy that, Grandmother." Rawdon inserted himself into the conversation, firmly taking her arm. "But first I must claim Mrs. Howard for the waltz. I believe it should be starting soon. Mrs. Howard?" He nodded toward the others. "If you will excuse us, I should introduce Mrs. Howard around."

Rawdon neatly separated Damaris from the other three and steered her away. She sneaked an upward glance at him.

"To whom are you planning to introduce me?"

"Why, no one if I can help it," Rawdon replied imperturbably. A grin lit his face and was gone in an instant. Damaris realized that she would very much like to bring that smile to his lips again. "I can see that Sir Myles would like to steal you for the evening, and I have no intention of giving him or some other fellow the opportunity."

"Lord Rawdon! That sounded almost as if you were flirting with me."

"Almost? Clearly I have fallen short of the mark."

Damaris let out a little chuckle and whipped her fan open, wafting it gently. "If you do not plan to introduce me, what are we to do? Do you mean to promenade about the room, then abandon me to fend for myself?"

"I am sure you will not spend any time alone," he replied drily. "However, my intention was to find some old dragon of a female sitting along the wall and settle you down beside her. Two old dragons, preferably, so you will have guardians on either side." He glanced down at her. "Although I have little doubt that will suffice. I shall be lucky if you are not surrounded by admirers while I am still standing beside you."

"Since you have had ample opportunity to be alone with me several times before this, I believe I shall take your words with a grain of salt."

"Ah, but that was in Chesley. We are in London now; a man must be more careful."

"The city renders my company more desirable?" Damaris tossed back.

"My dear Mrs. Howard, I am sure you realize that your company is always desirable." His sideways glance held a flash of heat. "But in the city, there is so much more competition. I feared if I did not lay my claim early, I would lose all hope of a waltz with you."

"I would not have thought you the type to shy away from competition, my lord."

He let out a soft chuckle. "I confess, I do not . . . in most situations. But you see, with you, I must seize every advantage. You have not heretofore seen me at my best."

Damaris glanced up at him. "Indeed. Perhaps not. Have I seen you at your worst?"

He lifted his brows a trifle. "I sincerely hope you will not witness me doing anything worse than knocking a man down in his own house."

Damaris's mouth curved up provocatively. "Still, I have not yet been frightened away."

She saw the little leap of light in his eyes, and she glanced away, startled by the sizzle that ran through her in response. Lord Rawdon was not the sort of man it was wise to tease. It was even stranger that she should have the desire to do so. Since the disaster of her impulsive marriage and the further pain of its aftermath, she had been the most cautious of women, unflappable and steady, even a trifle boring. When she had flirted, it had always been with someone like Sir Myles, uncomplicated and lighthearted, the sort of man who enjoyed the art of flirtation itself and would press for nothing more.

Yet here she was, with a man who was anything but uncomplicated, beneath whose still surface lay a wealth of dangers—and she found herself wanting to push at that controlled calm just to see what would rise to the surface. She had for years avoided danger, and now she was enjoying the thrill of standing on the edge. It was beyond foolish, she knew, but somehow she could not seem to turn away.

They stopped at the periphery of the dance floor and watched as the cotillion wound to a halt. Then Alec led Damaris onto the floor for the first waltz. She realized suddenly that nearly every eye in the place was on her and Rawdon. She had not taken into account the ripple of interest that would follow when Lord Rawdon took the dance floor with a stranger to the *ton.* Clearly she would not be unnoticed, as she had foolishly hoped.

But still, she reminded herself, no one would know who she was; they would not know her connections. Even if Rawdon or his sister were willing to answer any questions about her—and she could not imagine either one of them deigning to respond to impertinent inquiries—they knew nothing about her, really. The curiosity would die down as soon as she returned to Chesley; the *ton* was nothing if not fickle. There was no need to worry.

She refused to waste this dance fretting about such matters. It was a heady feeling to be standing so close to Rawdon, almost in his embrace. Whatever careful inches separated them, it was impossible not to feel surrounded by him. The heat emanating from his body warmed her; the faint scent of cologne, cigar, and brandy teased at her nostrils. Damaris looked up into his face. She was so close she could see the clear striations that ran through his light blue eyes like shards of glass, giving his gaze its glittering quality. His strong-boned face was compelling. She realized that she would like to run her fingers across the flaring bones of his cheeks. She wanted to see that firm mouth curve once again into a smile. She wanted, in fact, to feel that mouth against her own.

Damaris realized that she had been staring into his face for far too long, and she pulled her gaze away, glancing across the dance floor. She saw Genevieve dancing with Sir Myles, and the pair of them made a pretty picture, with Genevieve all white and silver beside Myles's dark green jacket and golden-brown eyes and hair.

Rawdon did not try to make conversation as they danced, and Damaris was grateful. She was too full of unaccustomed sensations. It was so much nicer simply to float in the music and the pleasure of dancing, to gaze up into Alec's face and think about kissing him, to feel the pressure of his fingers at her waist, subtly guiding her through the turns. It was with regret that she heard the music build to its crescendo and stop. They remained standing together for a moment after the music ended, then his hands dropped away from her. There was a hint of regret in his eyes, and Damaris wondered if he could see the same emotion in hers.

As they walked off the dance floor, first one man and then another made his way toward them to greet the earl. Casting a dry glance at Damaris, Rawdon introduced her to each of them, and in a few moments, she found herself in the midst of an admiring group. Rawdon, with a bow, excused himself, and Damaris spent the next few minutes bantering with the men as she filled up her dance card.

The rest of the evening was filled with dances and conversation. Damaris could not help but feel a touch of pride to think that even though she was all of twenty-eight years old now and a widow from the country, she could still fill up her dance card and have a covey of admirers clustered around her. Yet she could not suppress a niggling sense of disappointment that Rawdon did not return to join her as the evening wore on. She saw him dancing at one point with his sister and another time with his grandmother, and now and then she caught sight of him around the room, engaged in conversation. It was impossible to tell from his face whether he was enjoying himself or filled with boredom.

It was circumspect of him, of course, not to stand up with her more than once on this, her introduction to London society. Nor would it do for him to dance attendance on her. Such things would only serve to make her noticeable in the wrong way. Still, she could not help but wish that he were a little less able to stay away from her, no matter how correct it was.

And no matter how foolish she was to wish it.

Damaris realized that a small headache was beginning to form at the base of her skull and she wanted very much to slide out of her slippers for a few minutes. She had left one dance empty on her card before the midnight supper, out of an unacknowledged hope that the earl might return and claim it. Now she seized the opportunity to slip away and enjoy a few minutes of solitude. Making an excuse to her last partner, she made her way toward the other side of the ballroom, where a set of double doors lay open to a side corridor.

A knot of people stood not far from the doors she sought, and for a moment, Damaris thought that there was something vaguely familiar about one of the men whose back was turned toward her. Quickly she looked away, for fear he might turn and see her and she would have to stop politely to chat. As she walked past, a woman said, "Excuse me, Mr. Stanley." Ah, so not someone she knew, after all—the name Stanley was unfamiliar to her. But a moment later the woman strode past her, then whirled to stand directly in Damaris's path.

The lady who faced her rather belligerently was younger than Rawdon's grandmother, perhaps, but not by many years. Her hair was still brown in the back, but the front and sides were heavily streaked with pewter gray, and her eyes, hooded by age, were an oddly similar hue. Those metallic eyes now flashed at Damaris.

"You!" Her low voice shook with barely suppressed rage. "How dare you come here? In front of all the *ton*!"

Four

Damaris stared at the older woman. "I beg your pardon?"

"You heard me." The other woman came two steps closer, and it was all Damaris could do not to back away from her fierce gaze. "Do you think you can appear here and humiliate us like this? Do you intend to try to wring some gold from us in order to save ourselves the embarrassment?"

Damaris blinked. She had never seen the woman before, but it was not hard to guess who she was. "I presume you are Lady Sedbury."

"I suppose I should be grateful you did not try to call me Grandmother."

"Trust me, I will never do that." Damaris carefully kept her voice dry and detached. She could see the resemblance to her father in the woman's gray eyes. His had been a lighter shade, with a hint of blueness, but the shape was the same, large and wide-set, though age had made the woman's lids heavier.

"Why are you here?" Lady Sedbury went on. "You must leave immediately."

"I am here because I was invited, and I hardly think it is your place to order a guest out of Lord Rawdon's home."

"Just how do you think the Staffords would like it if they knew that their 'guest' was the bastard daughter of a common actress?"

"I think they would be most surprised to learn that my father was your son," Damaris replied, relieved that her voice did not shake. "Do you care to tell them?"

"Of course not! Is that what you are threatening?"

"I threaten nothing. I believe it was you who mentioned explaining my birth to the earl and his family."

"It has been so long—I thought you at least must have the decency not to show yourself in polite society. Lord knows, your father left you well enough provided for that you should have no need to importune us."

"I have no interest in you," Damaris said flatly. "Whatever you think, you are wrong. I would have lived the rest of my life quite happily never seeing your face. Nor do I have any interest in 'disgracing' your name or whatever you imagine I am about. I have said and done nothing to suggest to anyone that I am in any way connected to the Sedbury family." Lady Sedbury's face flamed with dangerously high color, but before she could say anything, Damaris plowed ahead. "However, just because you were able to make your son desert his child and the woman he loved, just because you could bend him to your will and make him marry a 'suitable' girl, do not for an instant think that you are able to make *me* do anything. As you said, I am amply provided for, and you have made it clear that there is no familial feeling between us. You have no power over me, and I shall live where I see fit and visit whom I wish."

"You impudent little cat!"

"Now, unless you want to arouse precisely the sort of interest among the Staffords' guests that you profess to hope to avoid, I suggest that you get out of my way." Damaris started forward, moving around Lady Sedbury.

To her surprise, Lady Sedbury reached out a hand and clamped it around Damaris's forearm, stopping her. "I will protect my family, just as I have always done. Get out of London. Immediately. Or I shall make sure that you will wish you had."

With that parting shot, she turned and walked away, leaving Damaris gaping after her.

A little shudder ran through Damaris; she was suddenly cold despite the warmth of the crowded ballroom. She blinked away the tears—of fury, she told herself—that had formed in her eyes, and strode through the open doors into the hallway beyond. Pausing only long enough to get her light silver tissue wrap for her shoulders, Damaris left Rawdon's home.

It was wrong of her, she knew, not to at least take her leave of her hostesses, and she felt sure that Lady Genevieve and her grandmother would take note of her rudeness. But she could not face hunting them down in the throng of guests and making the excuse of a headache. And, really, what did it matter? She would not see either of the women again. She should have listened to her inner voice and not come to this party; from now on, she would follow her own advice.

Damaris stopped on the stoop, remembering only now that

Rawdon had escorted her tonight, so she did not have her carriage. After a moment's hesitation, she started down the street, thinking she would hail a passing hack. She heard something rustle off to the side of her, deep in the shadows between the houses, and she turned her head toward the sound, startled. But at that moment, she heard a voice calling from the stoop behind her.

"Mrs. Howard!"

She whirled and looked back, her heart sinking. It was Lord Rawdon. She could not ignore him, but talking to him was the last thing she wanted right now. She tried to summon up a smile.

"Lord Rawdon."

"Are you leaving? Is aught amiss?" He frowned as he came toward her. He wore no hat, having obviously left in a hurry. "I saw you go out the door, and I . . . was concerned. I hope no one upset you."

She wondered if he had witnessed the scene between her and Lady Sedbury. Damaris brightened her smile. "No, indeed. It is a lovely party, and I appreciate so much your inviting me. It was most rude of me not to bid you good-bye. But I have a headache, you see, and I—"

He shook his head. "There is no need to explain. I am sorry that you are not feeling well. I shall give your good-byes to Genevieve and Lady Rawdon. You must not worry about that." He came another step closer and looked down into her face. "I can see that you are . . . not feeling yourself." He reached up to trace the line that had formed between her eyes.

Damaris felt the muscles in her forehead relax. She had not even realized that she was frowning. His gentle gesture made her feel foolishly like bursting into tears. She looked down, swallowing the impulse. "Thank you. You are very kind."

"Let me see you home." He took her arm, turning her back around and moving down the walkway alongside her.

"It really isn't necessary . . ."

"Nonsense. I brought you here; I will escort you back."

Damaris gave in and tucked her hand into his arm. The truth was, it was easier not to think of the scene with Lady Sedbury now that Rawdon was with her. He tended to crowd out all thoughts of anything besides himself.

"I spoke the truth, did I not?" he asked, and when she looked at him quizzically, he added, "About the men lining up to sign your dance card."

"Oh." She smiled. "Yes. I would almost think that you urged them to it."

"Hardly. I am not known for my generosity."

"Come, now. I believe you are the same man who went out into a snowstorm last Christmas to hunt for Matthew."

He made a half shrug. "It was a matter of a child. Somewhat different from giving up my advantage where you are concerned."

"Your advantage?" Damaris could not resist a saucy smile up at him.

"I already know you. That is an advantage, is it not?"

"And now so do they."

He grinned. "Ah, but I know in which village you live."

She laughed. "True. Yet somehow I doubt that you—or any of them—will trek out to Chesley to call on me."

"'Tis most unfair of you to say so. I was just there."

"To see your godson," she reminded him. "On your way to London."

"One trip can have multiple delights."

Damaris chuckled. "Very well, sir, you have bested me."

Rawdon raised his hand as they reached the cross street, and a hackney pulled over beside them. Rawdon helped Damaris step up into it, but when she turned to take her leave of him, she saw that he was climbing into the vehicle after her.

"But what are you—"

"I told you I could not let you leave unescorted. I shall see you to your house."

"No, that is too much trouble," Damaris protested, but the driver had already set the carriage in motion.

"Nonsense. 'Twill be only a short walk home, I'm sure."

"Yes, but you are neglecting your other guests." When he shrugged, she said, "Your sister and grandmother surely will not be happy about that."

"I have already stayed at the thing longer than I normally do," he told her lightly. "I am sure they will be well pleased with that."

He seemed to realize that his words had revealed perhaps more than he would have liked, for he glanced away, looking out the window. Damaris was content to sit in silence and study Rawdon's profile. She remembered that her friend Thea had expressed surprise when Damaris had once described Lord Rawdon as a handsome man. He was not, of course, the very pattern card of male attractiveness that Gabriel More-combe was. Lord Rawdon was unusual, with his soaring cheekbones and pale, shaggy hair and those striking blue eyes. Damaris was sure that there were women who found Rawdon more fierce than good-looking, cold rather than ardent.

But Damaris was all too familiar with smooth, handsome men who spoke easily of passion and devotion. Weak men like her father. Scoundrels like Barrett Howard. Those who promised love one day and slipped away the next, leaving one with only sorrow to hold. Damaris was drawn to the strength in Alec's face, the steady resolve beneath his cool exterior. He was the sort of man you could not forget once you'd met him.

Apparently feeling her gaze, Rawdon turned to look at her, and he smiled. And when that rare event happened, Damaris thought, his face was more compelling than that of any man she had ever known.

He escorted her to her front door, as he had promised, and surprised her by following her inside.

"There is no footman here to open the door?"

Damaris turned an amused gaze up at him. "Not all of us are earls, my lord. I took the servants with the house when I let it. There are not many, and I saw no sense in anyone staying up to answer the door. My maid is doubtless waiting for me in my chamber." She stopped, a blush creeping into her cheeks. Somehow, with Rawdon's gaze upon her, it was embarrassing even to allude to the nightly ritual of changing into her bedclothes.

His eyes darkened, his mouth subtly softening, and Damaris knew he was thinking of the same thing. His reaction stirred a new sensation inside her, something entirely different from embarrassment. She could not help but think now of what it would be like to have his hands, not her maid's, on the fastenings down her back, of his fingers slipping beneath the opened sides of the gown and pushing them apart, gliding over her bare skin, brushing the lace of her chemise. Just imagining the touch of his fingers, her skin was suddenly alive with anticipation. Heat curled deep in her abdomen. She could not help but wonder what the reality of his touch would be like.

Would he be tender or forceful? His hands rough and impatient or slowly stoking the heat in her? It would be easier, perhaps, to still be a maiden, she thought, to have no idea of what lay between a man and a woman. If she had never known a man's kiss, she would not wonder now how Alec's mouth might taste or how soft his lips would be against hers. She would have no hint of the way fingertips brushed over her bare flesh could make her shiver. But she did know, and she could well imagine ...

Alec reached out, brushing his thumb along the line of her cheek. Damaris looked up into his face. She knew she should protest, should move away, but she could not.

"Your eyes are so beautiful," he murmured. "Their color ..." The corner of his mouth quirked up. "No doubt hundreds of men have written poetry to your eyes."

"Hardly hundreds."

"I have no way with words. But when I look into your eyes, I feel as if ... I am drowning and I have no wish to be saved."

"I think," Damaris breathed, "that you are doing quite well with your words."

His eyes widened just a fraction, his lips pulling back in a flash of a smile, and he bent and kissed her.

Damaris stiffened, her hands coming up to his chest, but instead of pushing him away, her fingers curled into his jacket, holding on as he pulled her into him. His mouth lingered on hers, answering all questions of how he would kiss her. He tasted her as one might a fine wine, his lips and tongue teasing and exploring, slowly savoring her.

A long shiver ran down Damaris. She felt as if her whole body was opening up to him as surely and completely as her mouth. Her hands relaxed and moved up his chest to loop around his neck. She stretched upward, her body sliding up his, until she stood on her tiptoes, her lips locked with his. She was washed with heat, intensified by the furnace of his body.

Rawdon was flush against her all the way up and down, his arms wrapped around her, enveloping her. His kiss deepened, his mouth consuming her, and his hands glided down to her hips, pressing her up into him so that she felt the length of his desire digging into her. She was dizzy with the taste and scent and feel of him, and she thought that she might fall into a limp, trembling mass on the floor were it not for the hard strength of his arms clasping her to him.

His hand came up to curve around her breast, and her gasp was swallowed by his kiss. He caressed her, his fingertips burning through the material and arousing her nipples to hard points of yearning. A liquid warmth pooled between her legs, spurred by the delicious ache forming there.

With a groan, he pulled his lips from hers and buried his face in her hair. She could feel the stir of his breath upon her hair, hear the thunder of his heart. She felt strangely will-less, loath to move away or to pull herself back under control.

He released a long breath, a faint shudder of a laugh at the end, and pressed his lips once, softly, to her hair. "Sweet God." His voice trembled slightly. Then he released her and stepped back, tugging his jacket into place. "I should apologize." He hesitated, then added, "But I fear that I cannot. I enjoyed kissing you far too much, and I am not at all sorry for it."

Damaris glanced up at him, a laugh gurgling up in her throat. "My lord!"

"Do not 'my lord!' me." He grinned at her, grabbing her by the arms and pulling her up for a hard, quick kiss upon her lips. "My name is Alec, and I should like to hear it on your lips."

"Alec," she whispered, and he kissed her again, this time neither as hard nor as fast.

His hands dropped away from her arms and he stepped back reluctantly. "Good night, Damaris."

"Good night." She watched him walk out of the house. Her legs folded beneath her and she sank down onto the bench in the entry, landing with a small thud.

What had she just done?

The next morning Damaris still was not sure of an answer to her question. Lord Rawdon—Alec—was a mystery to her, and right now she felt somewhat the same way about herself. She was rarely so careless, so impetuous. The lessons she had learned had been hard, but well remembered.

Yes, she was a woman who enjoyed life, who lived more or

less as she pleased, but she made certain to always stay on a clear, easy path, one where she could not be harmed, where she would not stumble or fall. One, in short, where she was above suspicion and free from danger. From the kind of heartbreak that could never be forgotten.

But last night she had apparently taken leave of her senses and jumped right into—well, she was not sure what it was, but clearly it was anything but safe.

How could she have been so foolhardy? She had ignored all the warning signals her brain had sent her. The Season was still at its peak; Rawdon was an *earl*, for pity's sake. Of course some member of her father's family would be there. That was where they belonged; she was the one who was out of her element.

And of course they had seen her, no matter how large the ball was. She was a stranger; it would be of some note when the Earl of Rawdon singled her out for the first waltz. Moreover, she was not so foolish as to deny that an attractive mystery woman was bound to receive a certain amount of attention from all the male guests, especially since the earl had shown her such obvious favor. The cluster of men about her all evening would have drawn anyone's eye.

Damaris could see now that she had been willfully naïve in believing there would be no harm in accepting Rawdon's invitation. And more so still not to foresee what had happened last night when Rawdon brought her home. It had been simmering beneath the surface since they first met. She had seen the glances he sent her way during her Twelfth Night ball six months ago. Even during Matthew's baptism four months ago, her eyes had kept returning to Alec—no, Rawdon; she must keep the formality—only to find each time that he was watching her.

She knew that the only reason she had accepted his invitation, the thing that had swept her into impetuously appearing at a *ton* party, was the prospect of seeing him again—of flirting with him, dancing with him, even, yes, kissing him.

Damaris could not help but smile at the remembrance of that kiss. It had been laughable, really, for her to imagine that she had any idea what Alec's kiss would be like, just because she had been wooed and wed. She had been kissed by only one man—well, two, if she counted that silly brief struggle in the garden with an inebriated Italian count—and that had in no way prepared her for the incendiary touch of Lord Rawdon's lips. She could not term his kiss sweet or forceful or tantalizing or, indeed, any other description easy to define and dismiss.

Alec's kiss had taken her over, had consumed and changed and shaken her.

And that was precisely why it could not happen again. She would not allow her senses to control her. She must not be swept away on a tide of emotion and desire. Already she had gone too far. The only sensible course open to her was to leave London as quickly as she could and return to Chesley. If she remained here, it was all too likely that she would let herself be persuaded to see Alec again, and it would be very wrong of her to let him or his family become any more involved with her. As it was, if her past came out, the Staffords could easily shrug it off, as surprised as anyone else. But if she was seen with Alec, if he called on her or pushed his sister into inviting Damaris to dinner, if the Staffords were seen to be "taking her up," then they would be embarrassed by the eventual revelation of her birth.

She would tell her maid to begin to pack for the return home. She would finish up her errands here in London, and she would write a pleasant note to Lady Genevieve, thanking her for the invitation to her party and mentioning that she must unexpectedly return to Chesley. There was little joy in the prospect of not seeing Rawdon again, but it was the only sensible thing to do. There could be no relationship between them other than that of a nobleman and his mistress, and that was something she had vowed never to allow. It would be better to cut it off quickly, before any deeper feelings could take root.

Her decision made, she rang for Edith and set her to the task of packing. Damaris kept her appointment at the modiste's for her final fitting for the clothes that were not yet finished and left her with instructions to ship them to Chesley when they were done. After that, she made stops at the glover's and the milliner's shops and finally ended her day at Bedford House, picking up a few notions such as ribbons and handkerchiefs and such. She had contemplated going by Gunter's for an ice, but in the end, she hadn't the heart for it, and it was long past teatime so she simply went home.

The carriage let her down in front of her house, then drove on toward the mews. Damaris started toward the short walkway up to her house, but a man's voice stopped her. "Mrs. Howard!"

She turned and lifted her hand to shade her eyes. The setting sun was shining directly behind the man, so that it difficult to make out his features. As he drew closer, she saw that he was no one she knew, and she began to frown in puzzlement. He wore the rough jacket and trousers of a workingman, with a cap pulled low on his head. Footsteps sounded behind her, and Damaris started to turn, but at that moment two arms went around her from behind, wrapping a garment around her.

Before she could move, he whipped the two sides of the garment, which she recognized now as a cloak, around her and behind her back, effectively pinning her arms to her sides. She opened her mouth to scream, but the other man, who had leapt forward, clamped his hand across her mouth, effectively cutting off any noise. Damaris struggled, panicked, but the first man wrapped his arm around her tightly, clamping her to his side, while the other man shoved a wad of cloth into her mouth, then yanked the hood of the cloak up over her head.

Damaris squirmed and fought, trying to spit out the cloth, but the two men held her firmly between them as they whisked her up the sidewalk toward a waiting carriage. There was no one on the street in front of them, and she knew that even if there was a witness to the scene at a distance, it would look merely as if two men were helping a woman who had fainted or fallen ill. No one would assume that she was being abducted.

It did not take long to reach the carriage. One of the men yanked the door open, and the other one picked her up and shoved her inside. Damaris landed on her knees and, unable to raise her hands to shield herself, she pitched forward head-first against the opposite door. Her head cracked painfully on the handle of the door, and she crumpled to the floor.

Five

The man jumped into the carriage after her, and the vehicle rolled off. Damaris lay on the floor, dazed. When the man casually shoved her legs aside with his foot, she realized that he must think he had knocked her head so hard she had lost consciousness. Instinctively she rolled limply with the movement. It was better that he believe her immobilized, and now she was facing away from him. At a bump in the road, she turned even further, so her shoulder was now against the opposite seat, completely hiding her face and front from her abductor. The recent movements had loosened the cloak around her enough that Damaris was able to raise her hands up and pull the rag from her mouth.

Her reticule was still looped about one wrist, and she carefully edged it open and slipped her fingers inside. There was not much in the way of weapons there, but she did have a small leather coin purse, filled with coins. She tugged off her gloves and made sure the jewel of the ring on her right hand was facing out. Then she wrapped that hand tightly around the coin purse, to add a bit of weight to her fist. With her other hand, she located the small sewing kit, no more than three inches long, opened it, and pulled out the little scissors. The blades were no more than an inch in length, but they were sharply pointed. She held them in her other hand like a hilt on a knife.

Then she waited. The carriage was moving at a steady clip; it would be foolish to try to jump out, even if she could make it to the door. But she worried that the vehicle would take her so far from home that she would be unable to find her way back. What if they removed her to the countryside? Or perhaps into the dark, twisting alleys of the East End? She thought of the tales of white slavers that she had heard whispered, and she wondered if she had been too swift to dismiss them. The idea seemed absurd, but she could think of no other possibility. Why would anyone abduct her? Who would want to, and what could they hope to achieve? She was, she mused, an ordinary sort of person living an uneventful life.

The carriage slowed to a stop, and Damaris tensed. The man opened the door and stepped out of the carriage, reaching back inside to pull her out. As he did so, Damaris rolled to her back, jackknifed her legs and kicked straight out. Her feet, fortunately clad in heeled boots instead of soft slippers, hit him squarely in the chest and, caught by surprise, he staggered back, letting go of her.

Damaris scrambled out of the carriage. He reached for her, but she jammed the tiny scissors into her abductor's forearm, following up with a punch of her be-ringed fist into his cheek. The man howled, reeling backward, and luckily for

Damaris, he stumbled over the uneven cobblestones of the street and went down on his backside. His cohort, still in the act of climbing down from the driver's seat, stared at the scene in astonishment.

Damaris did not wait to see what they would do. She whirled and pelted back up the street in the direction from which the carriage had come. She heard a man shout, but she had no idea what he said or whether it came from a passerby or one of her pursuers. A wagon rolled down the street toward her, and at the last moment, she darted across in front of it. The driver yelled at her, but she managed to avoid the horse, and she hoped that the wagon would slow the men following her. A man stood on the street corner, staring at her, and she ran up to him.

"Please! Sir, please help me! Those men are—"

"Here! Grab her!" yelled a voice from behind her. "She's mad!"

The stranger looked at her uncertainly, his hand coming out to take her arm. "Here. What's going on, now?"

Damaris was suddenly aware that she probably did indeed look like a madwoman, clutching her embroidery scissors, points out, her eyes huge with fright and her hair escaping every which way from the cloak having been thrown over her head. Who would believe her wild tale of abduction? Her pursuers were almost upon them, confident man-to-man smiles on their faces.

Damaris whirled and ran, yanking her arm away from the stranger and leaving him holding only the cloak. She ran up the side street as the men let out shouts and started after her again. She knew she could not avoid them for long. However, it was reaching dusk, and deep shadows had begun to collect about the houses, so she would soon have at least the cover of darkness.

Something crashed behind her, and she risked turning her head back to look. It startled her to see how close her pursuers were, but fortunately, the one in the lead had run into a man who was stepping out from a door. The second abductor was too close behind to stop, and stumbled over them, sending all three to the ground. Damaris seized the chance and turned right at the next lane. Unlike the street she had just left, several of these houses had small front gardens. She darted across the street and threw herself over a low iron fence into a garden. Bushes grew across the foundation of the house, and she crawled in among them, squirming her way to the very deepest, darkest corner of the house, where she crouched, curling in on herself and tucking her head in so that her face was completely hidden.

She waited, doing her best to calm her gasping breaths. It was nerve-wracking not to be able to see, but she dared not look up and perhaps reveal a flash of pale face at precisely the wrong moment. She heard the sound of footsteps in the distance, running at first, then slowing and coming to a halt. There was a scrape or two of shoes upon the street, then a low curse. A shout came from a distance, and the footsteps retreated quickly.

Damaris counted to ten, then risked looking up. She could

see nothing beyond her shelter of branches, so, every nerve screaming, she forced herself to crawl from her hiding space. There was no one in the yard or on the street. She thought of going to the door and asking for assistance, but the house was dark and she was afraid of exposing herself for too long to the full view of the street, knocking and waiting, without anyone answering. Besides, her recent experience had left her fearful that anyone who answered the door would assume the worst about her, given her unkempt appearance. No doubt she now had leaves and twigs clinging to her as well, after her foray in the bushes.

If her abductors appeared again, claiming she was the escaped lunatic they guarded, she might very well be handed over to them, and she could not count on being able to escape them again. No, the best thing was to find her way home, staying in the shadows and ready to leap into hiding along the way. She scurried over to the fence and knelt, staring up and down the street. There was no sign of her assailants. Cautiously, she slipped from the yard, using the gate this time, and started off, hoping that she had been correct about the direction the footsteps had taken and that she was headed the opposite way.

She had no idea where she was or where to go, but she kept walking, keeping as much in the shadows as she could, always glancing around for any sign of her followers. When she had been thrown into the carriage, it had taken off toward the west, and it had not taken a good many turns, so she continued moving in a generally eastward direction. The houses around her were not poor, but as she walked, they seemed to increase in size and grandeur, which heartened her. Surely she was going the right way.

When she saw a man approaching, she thought about stopping and asking him for directions, but she was too shaken. She was not sure she would recognize her abductors; the man could be one of them. She slipped quickly across the street, glancing back to see if he followed her.

Her legs ached, and she was beginning to rub a blister on her right heel. She was chiding herself for having been so distrusting of the recent passerby, when she stopped at a corner and looked around, suddenly realizing that she was not far from her house. With renewed energy, she crossed the street and hurried to the next one and turned right. Her steps quickened; she was on her own street now, less than half a mile away. She glanced across the road and saw two men walking purposefully down the street ahead of her. Her stomach lurched, and she froze, her heart slamming in her chest.

It was her kidnappers; seeing them now, she was certain. And they were walking to her house! She whirled around and started in the opposite direction, forcing herself not to run. She must not do anything to attract their attention. When she turned the corner, she glanced back. The men had stopped and were talking to each other; one of them glanced her way. Damaris slipped around the corner and took off at a run. She ran without any idea of where she was going, turning up first one street and then another, desperate only to stay away from the kidnappers.

A crescent-shaped park down a side street brought her to a sliding halt. She knew that park! It was right across from Rawdon's house. Rawdon! Hope surged in her, and she raced down the street. Just as she darted up the steps to his front door, she saw her two pursuers turn onto the road from the opposite direction. They caught sight of her and started forward at a run.

Damaris pounded on the door, her stomach clenching frantically, watching the two men running toward her. The door was opened by a liveried footman. His carefully trained face did not change at the sight of Damaris's disheveled state, though there was a cautious note in his voice as he said, "Yes? May I help you?"

"Rawdon!" Damaris cried. "I must see Lord Rawdon." She cast a glance back. The men were only yards away. Heedless of propriety, she jumped through the doorway, shoving the footman aside, and slammed the door shut behind her.

"Ma'am!" The footman stared at her in shock and consternation.

"Rawdon!" Damaris called, then turned to the footman. "Do not let those men in! They must not—" She gestured toward the door. "You must lock it! Where is the key?"

"What? What men?" The footman planted himself in front of her again. "Madam, I am afraid that I must—"

Damaris went around him, calling Rawdon's name again, and at that moment Lady Genevieve popped out of the drawing room. "What is—Mrs. Howard!"

Her grandmother appeared beside her in the next

moment, and the two women stared at Damaris in astonishment. Damaris swallowed against the hysteria bubbling up in her throat, about to break out into uncontrollable laughter or tears, she was not sure which.

"I—I beg your pardon for—for bursting in on you this way. But I'm—I must see Lord Rawdon. Is he here?"

"My dear Mrs. Howard," the countess began icily, "a lady does not come calling on a gentleman. I don't know what you hope to accomplish by—"

"Damaris!" Rawdon appeared at the top of the stairs. "What is it? What is the matter?"

"Oh, Alec!" Tears sprang into her eyes now; she could not keep them out. She started toward him. "Thank heavens you are here."

He ran down the stairs and pulled her to him. "What has happened?"

Damaris went limp with relief against his hard chest, closing her eyes.

"Alec!" If Lady Rawdon's tone had been icy before, it was positively glacial now. "This is most irregular. What is this woman doing here? Let go of her at once. I will not allow—"

Rawdon sent the countess a single swift look, and she stopped speaking, astonishment clear on her face. "Pray have a cup of tea brought for Mrs. Howard, Grandmother. We will be in my study." He turned, keeping one arm curled around Damaris's shoulders, and began to walk with her toward the back of the house. "Come, sit down and tell me about it."

Behind them, the countess made a choked noise of protest

at this social solecism, but she did not try to stop them. She and Genevieve watched in shocked silence as Rawdon led Damaris along the hall and into his study.

It was a dark, masculine room, obviously in frequent use. A comfortable chair and hassock sat beside the fire, a book open on the low table beside it. Alec steered Damaris to the chair and sat down across from her on the hassock, taking her hands in his. "Now, what happened?"

"I—I'm not sure. These men—I was coming home." Damaris stopped and drew a breath, looking into his eyes. The cool blue gaze somehow steadied her, and she began again. "I had been shopping, and I got out of my carriage in front of my house and started toward the door. Two men came toward me and—and they seized me and threw me into a carriage."

"The devil!" Alec's eyes blazed, and his hands tightened on hers. "Were you hurt?"

"No. I mean, well, of course, a little, but they did not hit me, just pushed me into the carriage, and we took off. One of them drove, and the other man got in the carriage with me."

"What did he do to you?" Alec looked thunderous. "Did he dare to touch you?"

"No, nothing, really; he just sat there. But when the carriage stopped, he pulled me out. So I hit him and ran away."

Rawdon's brows went up. "Did you, now?"

Damaris reached into her reticule and pulled out the embroidery scissors and coin purse, holding them up for him to see. "I used these."

Alec smiled faintly. "Ah, I see."

"They were all I could find in my reticule. He wasn't watching me in the coach; I was on the floor—"

"The floor!"

She nodded. "Yes. When he threw me in, I fell." Alec let out a low curse, but Damaris shook her head. "No, it was good that I did. I cracked my head a bit on the door, and he thought I had been knocked unconscious, I think. I was able to hide from him that I was searching in my reticule. He'd thrown a cloak around me, you see, to immobilize me."

She shuddered at the memory of the enveloping cloak around her, and the rest of her story came tumbling out of her. "I couldn't move at all, and he threw the hood up over my head so no one could see me. I couldn't scream because he stuffed a rag in my mouth. But I pulled it out in the carriage, and I got these out of my bag. When he reached in to take me out of the carriage, I kicked him, and—"

Rawdon, whose expression had grown ever more fierce as she talked, let out a sharp bark of laughter. "You kicked him? Good girl!"

Damaris grinned at him. "It felt quite nice, I don't mind telling you. I stabbed him in the arm with these scissors, and I hit him with my other hand." She looked at the slightly mangled coin purse in her hand. "It added a bit of weight to it."

Rawdon laughed again. "Good for you."

"Then I ran. He and the driver pursued me, but they collided with someone or I wouldn't have managed to get away. I hid; it was dark, and they couldn't see me in the bushes. I didn't know where I was, but I just kept running and running. Finally I managed to find my way home, but they were already there ahead of me! So I turned and ran again, and they came after me. Then I saw the park, and I knew you were here." Damaris wavered to a halt. She felt suddenly, unutterably weary, and she realized how disheveled she must look. Her hair was straggling down around her face, and she suspected that her cheek was probably smudged with dirt. Leaves and twigs littered her clothes. She reached a tentative hand to her hair. "I—I am sorry for barging in on you like this. Your grandmother must think I am some sort of madwoman."

"Nonsense. Don't worry about the countess." Rawdon dismissed the problem of his grandmother with a wave of his hand that Damaris knew would have incensed that aristocratic woman had she witnessed it. "Coming here was exactly what you should have done. You are safe now. I promise."

He leaned forward and brushed a kiss across her forehead. His lips were warm and soft against her skin, and their touch made Damaris shiver. She was tempted to throw herself into his embrace once again.

"You're cold. Here." Rawdon took off his jacket and draped it around her shoulders.

The jacket was much too large for her, but it was warm and smelled reassuringly of Alec. Damaris pulled it more tightly around her. "Thank you. You are very kind."

A grin lit Rawdon's face for an instant and was gone. "I doubt you will find many to support that theory."

At a discreet noise in the hallway, Rawdon raised his head.

The butler stood in the open doorway, holding a tray. "Ah. Dunworth. Good. Set it down over here." He nodded toward the small table beside the armchair.

Turning back to Damaris, he reached for the scissors and purse still clutched in her hands. "Now, if you will allow me to take your weapons . . . I don't think you shall need them here."

Damaris released the objects, and he tucked them into a pocket. Going to a cabinet on the other side of the room, he picked up a decanter and brought it back to pour a healthy splash of brandy into her tea. "No doubt you could use a bit of a restorative."

She wrapped her hands around the cup, soaking in the warmth, and took a sip. Even forewarned, the strength of the doctored tea made her eyes water, but it also sent a trail of heat down her throat to warm her from the inside out. She continued to drink, grimacing a little at the taste. Glancing over at Rawdon, she saw the spark of amusement in his eyes, and she almost chuckled. He was right, she thought: the brandy-laced tea was quickly restoring her spirits.

The butler had brought in a plate of dainty breads and cakes along with the tea, and when Damaris's gaze fell upon it, she realized how very empty her stomach was. Not only had she been running across the city, but she had missed tea-time as well. She dug into the delicious-looking comestibles, reflecting that it no doubt reflected her plebeian blood that she was able to eat heartily after such a misadventure. A true noblewoman should have been laid prostrate from the experience, unable to eat a bite.

Rawdon, however, gave her an approving nod. "Good. Now, I am going to leave you in Genevieve's care. I am—"

"Rawdon! No!" The last thing she wanted was to be stuck in a room with his disapproving sister and grandmother. "I mean, truly, there is no need. I will return to my house."

He gave her a long look. "Do you really think I would send you back alone to your home after what just happened?"

"Well, no," Damaris admitted. "Frankly, I hope you will escort me."

"And so I would … if you were going there. But I am going to look for your abductors right now, and I want you to be here and safe while I am gone. The servants will have instructions to open the door to no one. You need not worry." He turned away from her and went to his desk, where he pulled a box from the lowest drawer and opened it. Inside lay a set of dueling pistols.

"Alec! What do you mean to do?" Damaris's voice rose in alarm. "Do you plan to shoot those men?"

"I don't *plan* to. I intend to deal with them at closer than ten paces." A chilly smile whispered across his lips. "These are just a bit of insurance, since you said there were two of the chaps." He began to load the guns with a cold efficiency.

Damaris sprang to her feet. "No, you mustn't go after them alone. There were only two who seized me, but there is nothing to say there were not more where they were taking me. You could get hurt."

His face softened fractionally as he looked at her, and he reached out to take her hand. Bringing it to his lips, he kissed her knuckles gently. "It is good of you to worry. But I shall be fine. I promise. I shall take Myles, if that will make you feel easier. He and I were planning to go to our club, anyway, so he should be here at any moment."

He released her hand and went back to the desk. Damaris watched him, unconsciously caressing with her thumb the spot his lips had touched. Alec opened a drawer of the desk and removed a sheathed knife, which he slipped inside the calf of his boot. Damaris's eyes widened a little.

"My. You seem to be quite, um, lethal."

"I learned to take care of myself." He turned back to face her. "Now . . . tell me about these men again. Did you recognize them? Do you have any idea who they were?"

"No." Damaris shrugged, frustration edging her voice. "I had never seen them before. At least, not that I remember. I have no idea why they would try to kidnap me."

"I can think of one or two," he responded drily. "Though it does seem most peculiar that they would simply snatch you off the street in broad daylight. And in Mayfair."

"Yes. It seemed so . . . so planned. Organized. It wasn't just two men walking along and deciding to grab the first woman who came along. They came at me from either side. I think they had been waiting for me. Oh!" She straightened. "I just remembered! He called me by name."

"What? Really?"

"Yes. I'd just gotten out of the carriage, and I was about to go up the walk to the house, and he called out, 'Mrs. Howard!' That is why I turned toward him. Then he walked toward me, and the other fellow came up from behind and wrapped the cloak around me." The memory of that terrifying moment curled through her, and she squared her shoulders against the shiver of fear. "Rawdon . . . I am going with you."

"What?" His eyebrows vaulted upward. "No. That's out of the question."

"I thought there was not going to be any danger."

"I didn't say that. I just said I didn't think it would come to shooting. I'm handy enough with my fists, and Myles spars regularly at Jackson's. But I cannot take a lady into a mill."

"But there won't be a mill, or even a possibility of one, unless you take me," Damaris countered. "How do you intend to identify the culprits? I can tell you that they were two average-size fellows wearing brown coats and caps. And the man who threw me into the carriage had light-colored eyes and a large nose and was a bit unshaven. I did not see the other man as closely, so I do not know his eye color. I would recognize them if I saw them, at least the one who was facing me, but I cannot describe them to you any better than that. Nor can I tell you where they took me. They did not say the address, and I don't know London well enough to know what area I was in. I think I might be able to find my way back there—though I would not swear to it—but I am *certain* that I could not tell you how to get there."

He stared at her for a long moment. "Bloody hell." There was the sound of voices down the hall. "That will be Myles, no doubt." Rawdon let out a sigh of frustration. "Very well, then. It seems you are coming with us," he told her rather ungraciously, and took her arm. "Let's go find your kidnappers."

Six

They found Sir Myles in the drawing room with the ladies of the house. He was standing by the fireplace, elbow propped on the mantel, clearly in the midst of telling a story. Lady Genevieve was smiling, and for an instant her lovely face warmed with humor, blue eyes dancing. Even the countess looked amused. But almost immediately Alec's sister pulled her face back under control, returning to her usual icy beauty.

"Really, Sir Myles, what a Banbury tale," Genevieve drawled. "I am sure you are having us on."

"Lady Genevieve!" He pulled a face of mock indignation. "Do you mean to say you don't believe me?"

"I make it a policy to believe only half of what you tell me, and I suspect that is rather too much," she replied. She turned toward the door and saw Damaris enter with Rawdon, and her expression tightened. "Mrs. Howard. I hope you are feeling more the thing."

"Yes, thank you. I apologize for imposing on you this way."

"Mrs. Howard." Sir Myles swept her an elegant bow. "What a delightful surprise to find you here."

In the luxurious surroundings of their drawing room, faced with the fashionable perfection of the Stafford women's clothes and hair, Damaris was once again acutely aware of the miserable state of her own appearance.

"It is very kind of you to say so, Sir Myles. I fear I must look a fright."

"Has something happened?" Myles asked solicitously. "May I be of some assistance to you?"

"We have it in hand," Rawdon told him crisply. "It seems there is a change of plans for us, Myles. Mrs. Howard has been accosted by ruffians, and we are going to find them."

Myles looked startled, but quickly agreed. "Of course. What happened?"

"I shall tell you as we go," Rawdon promised. "Time is of the essence."

"Rawdon, this is most irregular," the countess protested.

"I know, Grandmother, but I fear we really must make haste. I shall tell you all about it when we return, I promise."

"But surely Mrs. Howard is not accompanying you."

"I would have her stay safely here as well," Rawdon assured his grandmother, though Damaris suspected that the woman was far less concerned with Damaris's safety than with propriety. "However, I need her help to identify the men."

Lady Rawdon looked as if she would offer further argument, but Genevieve said, "I am sure there is no reason to worry. Rawdon knows what he is about; they won't be in any danger. Sir Myles will be along to help him, and I am told he is an able pugilist."

"For all my other sins," Sir Myles murmured, shooting Genevieve a sardonic glance. Genevieve ignored him, saying, "Pray take my shawl, Mrs. Howard." She stepped forward, taking off the wrap of warm blue cashmere and handing it to Damaris. "At least you will not have to go about with Rawdon's jacket hanging off you."

"Thank you," Damaris replied, shrugging out of the coat, even though truthfully it cost her a pang to part with the garment.

Sir Myles joined Damaris and Rawdon as they left the drawing room. When Rawdon handed him one of the pistols and pocketed the other one himself, Myles made no comment, merely took the gun and stuck it in an inside pocket of his coat.

"Ruins the lines of one's jacket, doesn't it?" he commented drily, straightening his lapels.

"Perhaps you should carry a knife in your boot instead, as Rawdon does," Damaris tossed back, and Myles chuckled.

"The man's a barbarian," Myles told her confidentially. "Border lord, you know."

"Are you on about that again?" Rawdon said. "One would think we were still raiding cattle from the Scots, to hear you and Morecombe talk."

"Mm. Or landing your longships on the northern shore," Myles riposted.

Rawdon tossed him a wicked grin that, in Damaris's opinion, did little to deny the notion that he was descended from ancient Viking raiders. He stepped aside to give instructions to one of the footmen, then joined them at the front door.

Outside, Rawdon waved for a hack, saying, "Better to be anonymous, don't you think, if we are going to be driving up and down some rum streets?"

"No doubt I would agree, if I had the slightest notion what we were about," Myles retorted.

So Damaris recited the story of her abduction again, and she was pleased to note that she was able to review it in a more calm and collected manner. Even so, Myles's brows lifted with each detail until she thought they might soar into his hairline.

"Good Lord," he said finally as a hackney stopped and they climbed in. "I rather thought Rawdon was jesting, at least in part. What a dreadful ordeal for you. Do you have any idea who the men were?"

"No, none at all," Damaris confessed.

"But it was not random," Alec put in grimly. "One of the louts called her by name."

"He knew who she was?"

"Or he wanted to make sure he had the right woman."

"Ah, yes, of course. In that case . . . you think he was hired by someone else to capture Mrs. Howard?"

"That would be my guess. We'll get it out of them soon enough—provided we can find them." They drove past Damaris's house first to see if her attackers might again be lurking around. However, they saw no one loitering about nor any carriages near her home.

"I should go in and let the servants know I am all right,"

Damaris said, struck by guilt that she had not thought of it earlier.

"I sent a footman to inform them," Rawdon assured her, and told the coachman to drive on.

Damaris backtracked along the route she had taken in her escape as best she could in the dark streets. More than once she mistook a turn, but eventually in their meanderings they came upon the yard in which she had sought shelter, and from there, it was an easy enough task to return to the place the abductors' carriage had stopped.

"This is it."

"You're certain?" Alec peered out of the window at the rather ordinary street.

"Yes. We stopped just beyond that red door. I know that."

Rawdon exited the carriage, calling up to the driver to wait. Damaris and Myles got out after him, and for a moment, they stood glancing around them.

"Somehow I was imagining someplace far . . . seedier," Myles commented. "By the wharves, perhaps."

"Yes, it seems fairly respectable," Rawdon agreed. "But I doubt the abductors live here. Which door shall we try first?"

"I don't know which house they were planning to enter," Damaris said. "There was a cart of some sort in front of us, so it could have been that house they were going to rather than the one right in front of us."

"We'll start with this one," Rawdon decided, and glanced at Damaris. "Perhaps you should—"

"I am not going to wait in the carriage," Damaris replied bluntly, forestalling him. "It will hardly help if I cannot see to whom you are speaking."

Rawdon had to admit the sense in her reasoning, though he looked as if he would have liked to argue the point. "Very well, but stay behind us."

There was no answer to their knock at the narrow house in front of them, so they went to the red door, which led into a small entry with an inner door and a stairway, indicating that each floor contained a separate flat. Rawdon pounded on the inner door, again receiving no answer, but after a moment there were heavy steps above them, and a man appeared at the landing above them.

"'Ere! Wot d'you think you're doin'? A man can't sleep around him for all that noise you're makin."

Rawdon turned, his eyes narrowing. "I have a few questions."

"Do you, now?" The other man crossed his arms over his chest. "And wot makes you think I'll answer 'em?"

Rawdon was across the entryway and up the stairs before the other man could even take a startled step backward. He grabbed the man's shirtfront in his left hand and twisted it, tightening his grip to hold the man firmly in place. "Because I can see from your face that you are an honest fellow. Aren't you?"

"Happen I am," the man retorted, setting his jaw. "Don't mean I'll be flapping my gums to some swell like you just 'cause you ask."

"Ah, but I intend to do more than ask." Rawdon bared his teeth in what could only loosely be termed a smile. He glanced down at Damaris. "Is he one of them?"

"No. He's not," Damaris said hastily. "There is no need to threaten him."

"Then you don't know Rawdon," Myles told her drily, and went up the stairs to join the other two men, who were glaring at each other pugnaciously. "Please, allow me to help. It may surprise you, Rawdon, to find that a friendly face opens more doors than a doubled fist." He turned to the man in Rawdon's grasp. "Perhaps you could help us. We are making inquiries about a certain incident that took place in front of this house earlier this evening. Mayhap you chanced to witness it—two men pulled a young lady from a carriage, and she took off running, with them giving chase."

"Wot? 'Er?" The man looked down the stairs at Damaris. "The swell mort?"

"Did you see her?" Rawdon asked curtly.

"Never seen 'er in me life," he replied in a surly voice. "Now be on your way, why don't you?"

"What about the people who live on the ground floor here?" Myles went on.

"Wot about 'em?"

"Who are they? The sort to go about abducting young ladies?"

"'Ow should I know?" His gaze turned crafty. "And if I did, why should I tell you?"

Rawdon released the man and reached into his pocket,

pulling out a coin and holding it up. "I believe this, Myles, is what opens doors most efficiently," he said in an aside to his friend, then turned back to the other man. "Does this give you sufficient reason?"

"Best in the world," the man replied, looking a good bit more cheerful, and nipped the coin out of Rawdon's fingers. "Wot you want to know?"

"The people downstairs."

"Family—man and wife and a passel of little ones. Usually runnin' about shriekin' all hours."

"Doesn't seem likely. What about the house next door?" He pointed in the direction of the first house they had tried.

"It's to let. Been empty awhile. Some swell like you owns it."

"Have you seen this 'swell'?"

"Nah. Just 'is agent, wot comes round to get the rent ever week."

"Did you see anyone there recently? This afternoon or evening?"

He shrugged. "No. Like I said—" He paused, looking thoughtful. "No, wait, I lied, I did see a bloke there earlier, 'bout the time I came home. Only one, though. And she weren't there." He nodded toward Damaris.

"What did he look like?"

"Oh, regular, like."

"Could you be a bit more specific? This information is hardly worth a shilling, let alone a crown."

The man sighed and twisted his face up in thought. "Well,

'e 'ad medium sort of 'air. Blue eyes—not like yours," he added, looking at Rawdon. "More …"

"Regular?" Myles suggested.

"That's right." The man nodded. "Sort of this tall." He gestured. "Brown jacket. Oh!" He brightened. "The bloke 'ad a big nose. I remember that."

"Did he?" Rawdon reached into his pocket and pulled out his card case. "Here is my card. Should you see this fellow at that house again, there's a Yellow Boy in it for you if you come tell me. I'd very much like to have a chat with him."

The card disappeared into the man's pocket with the coin, and he nodded. "I'll remember that."

"Sounds like your fellow," Rawdon commented to Damaris as they left the house.

"Yes, his description fits—though I suppose it could fit a number of other men as well. Do you think there's any chance of his returning?"

"I don't know. But if he does, I think our friend will come running to tell me. Let's see if there might be anyone else here who saw the men."

They spent some time canvassing the houses across the street and on the other side of the house in question, but they could not discover anyone who had noticed either the men or Damaris at the house earlier. Finally, they got back into the hackney and returned to Rawdon's house.

When Alec got out and turned to offer Damaris his hand to exit the carriage, she looked at him in some surprise. "But I am returning to my house."

"Nonsense. You are staying right here."

Damaris's eyebrows shot up at this autocratic statement. "I beg your pardon?"

Alec grimaced. "Don't balk, Damaris. I am sorry to be blunt; Genevieve always tells me I am lacking in diplomacy. But surely you must see that it is impossible for you to return there until we locate your abductors and put them in jail. What is to stop them from trying again?"

"I cannot stay here!"

"Why not? There is plenty of room. I told Genevieve to have a chamber made up for you. And if you are worrying about the proprieties, there is no need. My grandmother's presence makes it perfectly respectable. Not to mention my sister."

"No hint of impropriety would dare attach itself to Lady Genevieve," Myles agreed with a grin.

It was not the propriety that made her hesitate, Damaris thought, so much as the fact that she was sure his grandmother and sister both disliked her. However, she could hardly say that to Rawdon. The truth was, she would prefer not to go home; she knew that if she did, she would probably lie awake all night, listening for odd noises. With Rawdon nearby, she felt safe. And *that* was something she had even less desire to admit to him.

"But my clothes—my maid—" she began, castigating herself for her weak attempt at refusal.

"Are already here," he finished for her. "The servant I sent to your house earlier was charged with telling your maid to pack some of your things and bring them here for your stay."

"Edith is here?" Damaris smiled, warmed by the idea of his thoughtfulness. She gave Rawdon her hand and stepped down from the hackney. "That is very good of you."

Inside, Genevieve and Lady Rawdon waited for them, looking so much the same that one could almost have believed no time had passed. Lady Rawdon's hands were busy with a piece of needlepoint, but Damaris noted that Genevieve's embroidery hoop lay idly in her lap. She shoved it aside when they entered and rose lithely to her feet.

"Are you all right?" Her eyes skated over Rawdon, then Myles, and she relaxed fractionally. "I assume from your lack of bruises and cuts that you did not get into a mill."

"Lady Genevieve, I am touched to hear your concern," Myles told her, grinning.

"I am always concerned for my brother's well-being," Genevieve retorted, shooting Myles a quelling look. "Especially when he is in the company of a scapegrace." She turned to Rawdon. "Did you find the men you were seeking?"

"I fear not," Alec replied. "They had disappeared. Hopefully, something will turn up. In the meantime, Mrs. Howard will be staying with us."

Damaris could not see that this news excited Genevieve, who merely said, "Of course. Please, allow me to take you up to your room, Mrs. Howard. I am sure you must be exhausted."

"Thank you, yes." Damaris took her leave of the others and followed Lady Genevieve out of the room.

Rawdon's sister said little as she walked up the stairs and along the paneled corridor to Damaris's room, though Damaris could see from the corner of her eye that Genevieve was watching her with shrewd, assessing eyes. She could hardly blame the girl, of course. Genevieve must wonder who Damaris was and why her brother was taking such an interest in her. No doubt she found it forward of Damaris to run to Rawdon for help. In Genevieve's place, Damaris suspected that she, too, would be wary of her. Still, it did not make Damaris any more comfortable in Genevieve's aloof company.

"Here is your chamber," Genevieve said, stopping in front of one of the doors and opening it. "I hope you will find everything acceptable. Just ring for a servant if you need anything."

"I am sure it is perfect," Damaris told her honestly. She doubted that much was ever out of place or lacking in a household run by the countess or her granddaughter. "Thank you. It is good of you to take in a stranger like this. I am sorry to impose so on you."

Genevieve gave her a smile that did not reach her eyes and said, "Pray do not consider it. Rawdon is a generous man."

On that ambiguous note, she nodded to Damaris and left. Damaris went into the spacious room, which was decorated with the same formal elegance as the rest of the house, with velvet draperies of a deep russet and a tester and bed hangings of the same material. Coals glowed in the small fireplace, warming the evening coolness, and Damaris's maid was at the dresser, laying out her silver-backed brushes.

"Oh, ma'am!" she cried, turning and seeing Damaris. "I'm

ever so glad to see you. I was worried when you didn't come home!" She took Damaris's hand and pulled her toward the vanity table. "Here, let's take off those clothes and get you a bath. Then you'll feel more the thing."

Damaris sank down onto the stool in front of the mirror, and Edith went to work taking the pins from Damaris's hair. With a sigh of relief, Damaris closed her eyes and gave herself up to her maid's competent ministrations.

"Ah! Excellent!" Myles took another sip of his brandy and leaned his head back against the chair.

Alec sank into the chair across from his friend and stretched out his long legs in front of him, crossing them at the ankles. He swirled the liquid idly in his glass. "I thought we were never going to get away from the countess. Lord, what a night."

Myles grinned. "Yes. I have to tell you, your grandmother frightens me silly."

Alec chuckled. "You are not the only one. She's terrorized Castle Cleyre ever since I can remember. However, she likes you, so you needn't worry."

"Good. I should hate to be in her bad graces."

"Well, I know that state well, and I can tell you that it is not pleasant. I suspect she will freeze me for the next fortnight to demonstrate her displeasure."

"Does the countess dislike Mrs. Howard?" Myles asked, surprised. "She seems a most agreeable and refined woman to me."

"She does not *know* Mrs. Howard," Alec told him. "And that is even worse, in Grandmother's eyes. Worse, rather than allowing the countess an opportunity to grill the lady on her ancestors and life history, I whisked Mrs. Howard off. I am sure she suspects there's something deeply smoky about the woman. No lady, to the countess's way of thinking, would get herself carried off by ruffians."

"It is a demmed peculiar thing," Myles commented. "Who do you suppose those men are? Why were they after Mrs. Howard?"

"Beyond the obvious?" Rawdon shook his head. "I have no idea. She said she'd never seen either one of them and had no idea why they attacked her. Clearly, she would stir any man's lustful nature, but still …"

"Not the sort of thing one would think would happen in Mayfair, particularly in daylight. Didn't she say she'd just stepped out of her carriage?"

"Yes, and she had only to walk a few feet to her door. I think it is clear that they were lying in wait for her. It was no happenstance."

"What do you plan to do?" Myles asked.

"I'll set my Bow Street Runner on it. See what he can find out."

"You are the only gentleman I know who has his own Bow Street Runner," Myles pointed out.

"There are those who would dispute terming me a gentleman." Rawdon smiled faintly. "The problem is that, other than seeing she doesn't go out without an escort, I am not sure what to do."

"It might be best if Mrs. Howard returned to Chesley," Myles suggested.

"Mm." Rawdon went back to studying his drink.

Myles was silent for a moment, watching his friend, then said casually, "Mrs. Howard is certainly a beautiful woman."

"Yes."

"I was surprised to learn she was in London. Did you, ah, know she was coming here?"

"Ran into her at the theater the other night."

"I see. And when you introduced her to Lady Genevieve, she decided to invite Mrs. Howard to her ball?"

"Yes."

"Hmm. Odd, Lady Genevieve taking to someone quickly like that."

Rawdon glanced up and met Myles's twinkling eyes. "Yes, isn't it?"

He stood up and strolled over to the liquor cabinet to retrieve the decanter, then returned to replenish both their drinks.

"Rawdon …" Myles began when his friend sat down again. "I'm beginning to think that you are developing a *tendre* for our Mrs. Howard."

"I? I believe it was you who kept dangling after the woman last Christmas."

Myles grinned. "I will admit I enjoyed flirting with her."

"You enjoy flirting with everyone."

Myles laughed. "I will not deny that I like the company of women."

"But what about this particular woman?" Rawdon asked, his gaze sharpening. "Are you enamored of her? Do you mean to woo her?"

Myles's brows went up at his friend's suddenly serious tone, but he shrugged and said lightly, "No. Much as I admire the lovely Mrs. Howard, I get along with her far too well to fall in love with her."

Rawdon cast him a sardonic glance. "Then …"

"Would I object to your pursuing the eminently pursuable Mrs. Howard?" Myles grinned. "Not at all. Indeed, I think it might provide me a good deal of entertainment, watching the chase."

"That was not what I was about to say."

"It should have been. Come, Alec, an earl cannot remain unmarried forever. And you would have difficulty finding a better prospect than Mrs. Howard. She is entrancing, and your relatives disapprove. What could be more appealing?"

Rawdon snorted. "I can assure you, my grandmother's approval—or disapproval—has no role in my pursuit of a woman. But I have no intention of wedding Mrs. Howard or anyone else, for that matter. I am done with such nonsense."

"But surely you will marry one day."

"I suppose I must, if only to keep my cousin Hubert from inheriting the title." Rawdon shrugged. "But I will take a wife as a Stafford does, for her bloodlines, not because in some juvenile way I fancy myself in love."

Myles glanced at him, his brow furrowing. "Jocelyn was an aberration, you know. Not all women are like her."

Rawdon downed the rest of his drink. "No? Still, I fear I cannot escape myself."

Seven

$\mathcal{D}$amaris awoke to find a pair of bright blue eyes staring at her. They were set in a flat little pink-nosed face with a cloud of white fur bursting out around it. Damaris blinked, surprised. The cat gazed steadily back at her from its perch on the wooden footboard, unblinking and unmoving except for an occasional twitch of its fluffy tail.

"Well," Damaris said. "And who might you be? I wonder."

The animal continued to regard her with its unnerving stare. Damaris felt vaguely at a disadvantage lying on the bed, looking up at the cat, so she sat up. At that moment, the door opened and Edith slipped quietly inside. She glanced over and saw the cat, and her mouth twitched in irritation.

"So you managed to get in, did you?" Edith hissed, coming into the room and laying down the dress she was carrying. "I'm sorry, ma'am. He's been trying to sneak in here this past hour. The chambermaid must have let him in."

The maid made shooing motions at the cat, and Damaris watched in some amusement as the feline ignored Edith, lifting its paw and beginning to wash it. Finally, just as Edith started for the small fireplace broom, the cat stood up and jumped lithely to the ground. With a regal air of unconcern, it stalked to the door, its long, full tail held high, and paused at the door, waiting for Edith to open it.

"Sorry," Edith said again, heaving a gusty sigh as she closed the door behind the cat. "His name is Xerxes, and he belongs to the young miss."

"Lady Genevieve?" He was, Damaris thought, a perfect pet for Alec's sister, with the same aristocratic manner and piercing blue eyes. Even the white fur was not far different from Genevieve's pale blond tresses.

"Yes'm. When I came down the hall this morning, he was climbing the drapes in the hall. They say he likes to lie on top of them and jump down on the maids. He's a terror, but the young miss is terrible fond of him."

Damaris thought it better not to comment on the "young miss's" own personality. After all, she barely knew the girl, and having a visitor thrust upon one like this could not be easy. Besides, perhaps there was more to Genevieve than her frosty manner showed. Alec could scarcely be termed a warm man, either, yet it was clear he had undiscovered depths. Or was she merely indulging in romantic nonsense about him? True, he had come to her aid immediately, and she could not but think that she was right in assuming he was the man to turn to in danger. But it might be simply that he welcomed a fight, not that his concern was aroused. And even if it was, it did not signify. It was beyond foolish for her to think about the Earl of Rawdon.

Indeed, it had been foolish of her to come here. Last night, as she lay in bed, Damaris had done a good bit of thinking that she had not paused to do earlier, in her panic. When she considered what had happened, it seemed clear to her that it had not simply been a matter of two ruffians deciding to have their way with her. It had not been a spontaneous attack. They had obviously planned it out, had even brought a carriage to carry her away in. They had apparently leased, or at least found, an empty house to bring her to. Of course, there was the possibility of white slavers, but that seemed unlikely. The men had been after her specifically; they had called her name. Why would a ring of white slavers have targeted a woman in such a neighborhood, where they were much more likely to be noticed?

No, those men had had no interest in her other than as the subject for which they were being paid. She felt sure they were acting at someone else's directive. It seemed equally clear to her who must be behind their actions. There was only one person— or family—who would like to be rid of her. Unfortunately, it was most likely her own grandmother who had hired the ruffians.

It seemed absurd that anyone would go to such lengths to avoid the possibility of a scandal. However, Damaris had no other enemies. After all, the only people she knew in England were her friends in Chesley, and she thought it unlikely in the extreme that any of them would have hired someone to kidnap her. Her grandmother, on the other hand, had been furious with her at the party, and she had obviously feared Damaris would flout her parentage before the *ton* and bring down disgrace on her father's legitimate family. And while it had been satisfying to defy her grandmother, she could see that it had perhaps not been the most prudent thing to say. Her attitude had doubtless only increased Lady Sedbury's fear that Damaris meant to humiliate them, and the woman must have taken steps to make sure it could not happen.

She did not think that Lady Sedbury would have gone so far as to order the men to kill Damaris. At least, she hoped her own grandmother would not do that, no matter how much she held her in contempt. After all, the men had taken her to a house in a decent enough area; she imagined the house had not been uncomfortable inside. Probably they planned to threaten Damaris with dire consequences if she did not leave England, or perhaps they intended to transport her out of the country themselves, taking her across the Channel to Calais or some other port.

It was not a pleasant notion, realizing her father's family hated her to such an extent. However, it had taken away much of Damaris's fear. All she had to do to avoid the danger was to leave the city. Damaris tried to ignore the way her heart clenched at that thought. It was the only thing she could do. If she stayed, it would embroil Alec in her battle with the Sedburys, and it would be unfair of her to place him in conflict with another aristocratic family. No, she must leave.

But she could not keep her steps from dragging later as she made her way downstairs to the breakfast table. Glancing up, she spotted the white cat perched on the top of one of the draperies, peering down over his white paws. Damaris narrowed her eyes at him, remembering Edith's tale of his trick with the maids.

"Don't you dare," she warned, and the cat's tail lashed, but he stayed where he was.

As she neared the breakfast room, she heard the sound of Alec's voice, followed by the higher tone of his sister's. Damaris was relieved not to hear his grandmother's.

"... only Myles," Genevieve was saying scornfully as Damaris drew near enough to distinguish their words.

"I cannot understand what you hold against Myles," her brother responded mildly. "He is usually quite popular with young ladies."

"Exactly," Genevieve retorted. "The man is an inveterate flirt."

"Ah, then you are looking for a man with serious intentions," Alec mused, and Damaris realized with a little start of surprise that he was teasing his sister. Somehow, playful sibling teasing was not something in which she would have envisioned either of them participating.

"I am not looking for a man at all," Genevieve shot back, and suddenly laughter gurgled up out of the girl, light and melodic and so unexpected that Damaris came to a dead stop in her surprise. "Oh, stop mocking me. One would think I was still fifteen, the way you act."

"It has not been that long, Genny."

"Hah. Ten years. I am a veritable ape leader now, as you well know."

"I would never call you such a thing."

"Only because you know I would make you regret it."

Damaris paused at the open doorway, taking in the pleasant scene before her. Alec sat at the head of the table with his sister at his right hand, the summer sunshine streaming in warmly through the open window beyond them. The window looked onto a small side garden, shielded from the noises of the street by a high brick wall. Roses bloomed in profusion beneath the window, their heady scent drifting inside. Alec and Genevieve sat looking at each other, their fair hair and light blue eyes strikingly similar, laughter and affection giving their expressions a warmth normally missing.

Then Genevieve glanced over at the doorway and saw Damaris, and her face settled quickly into its usual remote lines. "Mrs. Howard. Good morning."

Unlike Genevieve, Alec's smile broadened, and he turned, coming to his feet. "Mrs. Howard."

His pale blue eyes were bright, and it seemed to Damaris as if they burned right into her. She felt suddenly breathless and blushing, and no matter how she told herself it was absurd for her to be this way, she could not hold back the smile that spread across her face. He came forward, then stopped a bit awkwardly. Damaris held out her hand to him, and he took it, a light flashing in his eyes, and he bowed over her hand.

"I trust that you are feeling improved after your experience last night." His fingers tightened fractionally on hers, and Damaris was very aware of his skin warm and bare against hers. She had not, she reflected, ever seen him early in the morning. He was even more handsome, the subtle colors of his skin and hair and eyes clear and distinctive in the golden wash of the light.

"Yes, indeed, thank you." She realized that her own fingers had tightened in response to his touch, and their hands were still together long after they should have broken their hold. A trifle embarrassed, she released his hand and turned toward the table, her eyes flickering over to Genevieve to see if she had noticed. From the carefully blank expression on the woman's face, Damaris felt sure she had.

"I hope you found everything to your liking," Genevieve said as Rawdon pulled out Damaris's chair for her. She reached out and politely poured their guest a cup of tea.

"Yes, thank you. It is a lovely room." That was no more than the truth. "So elegant." She smiled at Genevieve and added, "I believe I met your cat this morning."

"Xerxes?" Genevieve looked startled, then wary.

Alec let out a small snort. "'Satan' is more like it."

"I hope he was no trouble to you," Genevieve continued, ignoring her brother's comment.

"Not at all. He merely dropped in for a visit. Such a beautiful animal. I don't believe I've ever seen such blue eyes on a cat."

"He is an Angora. One of Grandmother's friends brought him to her from Paris."

"He likes no one but Genevieve," Alec put in. "So he soon became her pet rather than the countess's. He is the scourge of the rest of the household."

"You are just jealous because Xerxes sent your dog off with his tail tucked between his legs."

Alec chuckled. "Yes. Poor Shadow."

As they spoke, a footman had been dishing up food onto

Damaris's plate, and she set to eating it with some enthusiasm, her stomach reminding her that she had eaten little the day before. Genevieve and Alec kept up a casual, desultory conversation which necessitated little input from Damaris, and she was just as glad, for her own mind was occupied with making plans to leave London. After a moment, she was aware that the conversation had paused and both Alec and Genevieve were looking at her, and she realized, with a guilty start, that she must have been asked a question.

"I'm sorry. I am afraid my mind drifted," she began.

"Perfectly understandable," Genevieve said. "You have been through quite an ordeal. Rawdon had asked about my plans, and I was saying that I had a few calls to make this morning. But no doubt you are not feeling up to making calls."

"Thank you for asking," Damaris replied quickly, though, she reflected, Genevieve's statement had not actually included an invitation, only a plausible reason for Damaris not to accompany her. "But you are, of course, right. I don't think I shall make any calls today."

"Perhaps you should just stay in, too, Gen," Alec began.

"Oh, no," Damaris hastened to say. "Pray, do not change your plans for me, Lady Genevieve. I will manage quite well on my own. I have a number of things to attend to, in any case."

"You are most kind," Genevieve replied, rising to her feet. "There are a number of visits I really must make, so if you will excuse me . . ."

Alec rose politely as his sister left the room, but sat down again immediately and turned his gaze on Damaris. "If you have things to attend to in the city, I shall be happy to escort you. I have some business I must settle this morning, but I will be back this afternoon, and—"

"There is no need for you to rearrange your schedule," Damaris assured him. "I need only to visit my banker and, of course, I must return to my house."

"Damaris, we discussed this. Your maid brought your things over here."

"Yes, of course, but surely you must see that I cannot continue to live here indefinitely."

"I am not talking about indefinitely. Only until I find out what is going on. I plan to set a Runner to hunting for your abductors today. He is quite good, I've found, and I expect it will be no more than a matter of days before he tracks them down."

"Alec! No." Damaris's voice rose in some alarm. "Truly, it is not necessary. You must not put yourself to any bother about this."

"'Tis no bother."

"No, please. Really, there is no need. I have been thinking, and it is clear to me that what I should do is leave London."

"Leave!" His brows drew together. "But why—is there something you are not telling me? You said you didn't know those men."

"I don't! I have no idea who they are. But I—I believe I may have overreacted."

"To two men grabbing you in the street and tossing you in a carriage? How could you have overreacted?"

"What I mean is, they did not hurt me. I don't *know* that they would have hurt me."

"I cannot imagine what else you could think they meant to do."

"You don't understand."

"No, I don't. Because you have not said anything that makes sense."

She paused, drawing a breath, then said, on a sigh, "I am not sure, but after I thought about it, I decided . . . well, I believe it is a family matter."

She had succeeded in astonishing him into speechlessness. He stared at her for a long moment. "Your family is trying to kill you?" He lifted his brows. "Perhaps my family is not as bad as I thought."

"No, I don't think they are trying to kill me. I just told you, they didn't hurt me. That was what made me realize . . ."

"So, if it is your family, why are you running away from them?"

"I'm not running away!" Damaris retorted indignantly.

"What else would you call it?"

"Being prudent. That is what I would call it. There is no reason for me to be in London. I merely came to make some purchases, see a few plays, and so on. I have done that. Leaving is a simple solution to the problem. If I am not here, they will not be able to abduct me again."

"Unless they follow you," he pointed out. "If someone means to do you harm, why would they stop because you remove yourself from London? They can attack you in Chesley just as easily—probably more so. Or on the road as you travel."

"I am not going to Chesley. I have a mind to visit the Continent. I might summer in Switzerland."

"Switzerland! Devil take it, Damaris, you mean to flee the country? What is going on? Please don't expect me to believe that you are ready to run to the Continent over some trifling 'family' matter."

"It isn't trifling, at least not to them." Damaris glanced at him and away.

She knew she ought to tell him everything. It was the only way to make him understand why her family would resort to such lengths to get rid of her. But she could not bear to see his face when she told him who she was … what she was. She had already been aware of what a proud man Rawdon was, but being here in his house, meeting his grandmother and sister, she had realized that she had probably underestimated that pride.

"I cannot tell you the details about my family," she said in a low voice.

"You do not trust me?"

"It is not that. But it would be unfair of me to—to reveal their secrets."

"Blast it, Damaris." He stood up, shoving back his chair impatiently. "I am not asking you for gossip! How do you expect me to protect you when you will not tell me what is going on?"

"I *don't* expect you to protect me. That is what I have been trying to tell you."

"And what am I supposed to do?" Alec glared. "Stand idly by while you go out to be taken by ruffians again?"

"I don't plan to be taken by ruffians." Damaris stood up, too, to face him.

"I hardly think you planned it the first time."

"Of course not." Damaris slapped her napkin down on the table. "But I was not prepared for it then. Now I am. I am taking actions to keep from being harmed."

"Have I given you reason to think that I cannot take care of you? Keep you from harm?" Alec lifted his chin, looking down at her from his superior height, appearing so much the essence of cold aristocratic hauteur that it made Damaris fairly vibrate with antagonism.

"It is not your responsibility to take care of me!" she shot back.

"You came to me; that makes it my responsibility."

"No, it does not. And I am beginning to wish that I had gone somewhere else."

"Well, you did not." He gave her a long, baleful look, then swung away and walked to the door. He turned back. "I am going to find out who attacked you. And I am going to put a stop to it. When I return, we will thrash this all out. But in the meantime, you stay here. Inside. Do not go out and put yourself into danger." He paused, and when Damaris made no response, he said in a goading manner, "Am I clear?"

Damaris crossed her arms, her chin jutting mutinously. "Oh. Perfectly clear."

She had the satisfaction of seeing uncertainty flicker

across Rawdon's controlled face before he turned and left the room. Damaris refrained from picking up her cup and tossing it out into the hallway after him, though she had a strong and childish urge to do so. She stood for a moment, fulminating, then walked out, moving in long, purposeful strides down the hall and up the stairs to her room.

"Edith, pack my things," she said as soon as she entered her chamber.

The maid, who was busy sewing up a ripped flounce on one of Damaris's evening gowns, gaped at her. "But—" Edith glanced around and returned her gaze to Damaris. "But I just unpacked them."

"Yes, I know. It's a bother, but Lord Rawdon never should have ordered you to bring them here in the first place."

"Are we going back home?"

"Yes. Well, I mean, you are. I plan to leave for Dover this afternoon."

"Dover!"

"Yes. I am making a trip to Calais. In the meantime, you are going to pack up our things and take the carriage back to Chesley."

"By myself?" Edith stared. "Why? Why can't I go with you? I should be with you. Who will do your hair? Your clothes? Are you angry with me?"

"No. No, of course not. It's not that I don't want you with me. But I need to draw some people away. I don't want them to know about the house in Chesley."

"But who, miss? Who is trying to hurt you? Is it them? The ones your poor mother hated so?"

"Yes, I think so." Damaris nodded. "I saw Lady Sedbury the other night, and she was very clear that she wanted me to leave London. So I intend to oblige them. I want them to think I am going back to the Continent to live. But I'll stay only a week or two, long enough to make sure that they are not keeping tabs on me, and I will return to Chesley. That is why I need you to take charge of getting yourself and my things back home."

Edith looked somewhat reluctant, but she merely nodded. "Yes'm, I'll get to packing right away."

While her maid was thus engaged, Damaris went downstairs to take a polite leave of the ladies of the house. She found Genevieve and the countess in the sitting room. The countess was by the window, taking advantage of the light to pursue her needlework. Genevieve had apparently abandoned her plans to make calls, at least for the moment, for she sat in a nearby chair, reading aloud from a scandal sheet. The large white cat was curled up asleep in her lap, looking like nothing so much as a large ball of fur.

Genevieve looked up at Damaris's entrance and stopped reading, causing the cat to lift its head, too, and stare resentfully at Damaris. "Mrs. Howard. Good morning again."

The countess, who had been smiling faintly in response to whatever Genevieve had been reading, assumed her usual contained expression and let her hands fall idle in her lap. "Mrs. Howard."

"Lady Rawdon. Lady Genevieve. Pardon me; I do not wish to disturb you, but I wanted to thank you for your kindness in giving me shelter last night. I must take my leave of you now."

Genevieve straightened. "Leave? But Alec said you were to stay here."

"It is most courteous of him to take such an interest in my welfare, but I am certain that I will be fine now. It is broad daylight, after all, and I will have my maid with me. There are some errands I must attend to before I leave the city."

"You are leaving London?" the countess asked, and Damaris could see no sign of regret on her features. "So soon?"

"Yes, I believe I shall take a trip to Switzerland or perhaps Italy."

"Oh. How lovely." The countess went so far as to smile at this news.

Genevieve, however, was frowning slightly. "I don't think Rawdon will like this."

Damaris suppressed a spurt of irritation. "Indeed, I hope he will not be distressed. You may assure him that I will have my driver with me, as well as one of the footmen, while I go about my errands. Pray give your brother my regards, as well as my deepest thanks. I shall leave a note for him, if I may, expressing those sentiments."

Genevieve obviously remained doubtful about Alec's reaction to Damaris's leaving, but there was little else she could say. The countess, on the other hand, was quite cheerful and even went so far as to send a servant to have their town carriage brought round to return Damaris to her house. After a few more expressions of thanks and well wishes, Damaris bid them good-bye and returned upstairs.

Edith had finished packing the small case of clothes she had brought with her the night before, but Damaris took the time to sit down and pen a short note to Rawdon. She hated to leave in this hasty and secretive manner, but she knew that if she stayed to say good-bye to Alec, it would result in a long and doubtless acrimonious argument. Rawdon was not a man who liked to be gainsaid, and Damaris was too long accustomed to taking care of herself to submit to his making decisions for her.

Perhaps she was taking the coward's way out, she thought. If she stayed and discussed the matter with Alec, she would have to tell him the truth about herself, and she did not want to face that. It was better this way, really—quicker and cleaner. There could be no hope of anything between them, ever. It would be easier for both of them to make the break now.

It was difficult to choose what to say, and she started over more than once, but finally, she gave up and contented herself with a few lines expressing her gratitude for his help. Sealing it, she wrote his name on the front and left it on the hall table, then walked out of the house.

Eight

Alec trotted up the steps of his house, realizing with some astonishment that he was whistling beneath his breath. He stopped in the entryway and managed to hand his hat and gloves to the footman with his usual demeanor. A glance in the drawing room told him Damaris was not there, and he considered running upstairs to see if she was in the less formal sitting room. It occurred to him that he was probably a good deal too eager to see her, so instead he headed to his study.

He spent a few idle minutes there, poking about his desk and thinking of the many matters about which he needed to talk to Damaris. It had taken him longer than he expected to find the Bow Street Runner, and the whole thing had been rather fruitless. By the time he had explained Damaris's situation and answered the Runner's questions, he realized that what he did not know about Damaris was a great deal more than what he did. Having assured himself of the fact that there were a number of perfectly adequate and logical reasons for talking to Damaris, he got up and went upstairs.

He could hear his sister's voice coming from the sitting room, and he strode toward it, coming up to the doorway, when he saw that Genevieve and his grandmother were talking with his grandmother's bosom friend, Lady Hornbaugh. He would have liked to back out of the room, but of course they had spotted him.

"Rawdon!" Lady Hornbaugh trumpeted. The daughter of an admiral, the woman had a voice that could be heard across stormy decks, and governing over a large brood of children and an even larger collection of grandchildren had done nothing to decrease its volume. "It's been an age since I've seen you. Come here, young man, and give an old woman a kiss. Bets tells me you've been marooned in that castle of yours for months."

"Lady Hornbaugh." Alec forced himself to bow politely and step forward to give the old woman a kiss on the cheek. He had never understood the attraction between his formal and aloof grandmother and the bellowing, even bumptious Lady Hornbaugh. It was also hard to envision the countess being called "Bets."

There was nothing for it except to sit down and engage in a few minutes of polite chitchat with the woman. He could not leave without offending her, and he was not about to inquire into Damaris's whereabouts with Lady Hornbaugh here; he could only praise whatever good angel had prompted his relatives to keep Damaris away from her. After a seemingly unending twenty minutes, Lady Hornbaugh departed, and he was able to turn to Genevieve and ask after Damaris.

Genevieve shifted a little uneasily, which was not like her, and said, "She left."

He stared at her blankly. "Left? What do you mean?"

"It seems rather self-explanatory. I mean that she came and told us she was leaving, and then she did so. I believe she wrote you a note."

Alec stood up. "Genevieve!" He turned to his grandmother. "Is this your doing? Did you say something to send her away?"

The countess lifted her brows. "Really, Rawdon, are you accusing me? Of what?"

"I don't know. But I specifically told you Damaris should stay inside today." He swung back to Genevieve. "After what happened to her yesterday, how could you have let her go out?"

Genevieve jumped to her feet to face him, a dangerous light glinting in her eyes. "I could hardly hold her prisoner here! What did you expect us to do? She said she had things to attend to. She said she planned to leave the city. She is a grown woman, Alec, not a child. I cannot see how I have any right to stop her from doing what she wants."

"You could have persuaded her not to go! You could have made a push to get her to stay."

"Really, Alec, who is this woman and why are you acting in such an absurd manner over her?" Lady Rawdon chimed in.

"I have never heard of her, and suddenly you are thrusting her upon us and berating us because she left."

"Who is she? What the—" He stopped, aware that he was on the verge of saying something rude to his grandmother, and drew a breath, then continued in a more measured tone, "She is Lady Morecombe's friend. And mine as well, I hope. Forgive me for raising my voice. I am concerned about her." He turned to Genevieve, his voice as cool as it was calm. "When did Mrs. Howard leave, may I ask? Did she say where she was going?"

"She said she had errands. She took her maid, and we gave her the carriage. I am sure she is quite safe. It was almost two hours ago, I suppose. Not long after you left."

He nodded abruptly and stalked out of the room.

"Alec!" Genevieve called, and hurried out into the corridor after him.

He turned, waiting for her impatiently at the top of the stairs.

"She said she was leaving you a note."

"I'll look downstairs." He started to turn away.

"What do you mean to do?" Genevieve asked. "You cannot force her to come back, you know."

His face tightened. "I have no interest in forcing her to do anything. But she is in some sort of danger, and I must do what I can to protect her."

"Alec … do you … do you *care* for this woman? You scarcely know her."

"Of course I don't—" He stopped abruptly. "I have to leave. There isn't time to stand about talking nonsense."

He turned and trotted down the stairs, leaving his sister staring after him, frowning with concern.

Damaris held on to the strap as the post chaise bounced into and out of a rut in the road. Perhaps, she thought, she should have taken her own carriage instead of hiring the vehicle. The post chaise's suspension left much to be desired.

But no, it was the better way. She was certain that, as she emerged from the Staffords' carriage, she had spotted a man lurking down the street, pretending to be vastly interested in the railings of the house in front of him. With any luck, he had followed her as she went about getting cash and a letter of credit at her bank and hiring the chaise to take her to Dover. She hoped that he was even now on her trail. If she had taken her own carriage to Dover, there was the possibility that he might follow it back and discover her home in Chesley, which would make all her pretense of fleeing to the Continent for naught.

There was always the possibility, of course, that the men might follow her and attack her later, but, given that they had seemed more interested in spiriting her away than in harming her, she continued to believe that her grandmother's only wish was to see her gone, not to have her killed. Surely even Lady Sedbury, dislikable as she seemed, would not be likely to do away with her own flesh and blood. Just in case, though,

Damaris had pulled out the dainty pistol her father had given her long ago and loaded it, then put it in her reticule. She often took it with her when she traveled, though she did not usually carry it on her person, preferring to keep it in its box in the side panel of her carriage. This time, however, she wanted it close at hand.

They had left London without incident and had traveled for two hours without any sign of attackers. So far, the worst aspect of her trip had been the rough ride of the post chaise—that, and having far too long a time to think about the Earl of Rawdon. She could not help but dwell on his reaction when he found out she had left. Would he be furious? Would he feel resentful and betrayed after all he had done for her yesterday? She could not help but feel that leaving his home without telling him face-to-face had been the act of a coward, and she could not blame him if he was angry. Even worse was the thought that he might simply shrug and regard her departure as a problem taken care of without any effort.

She thought more than once of turning back and going to him, telling him everything. But that, she knew, was folly. She could not remember a man about whom she had felt this sort of chaotic longing and liking. When he had kissed her, every nerve in her body seemed to sizzle. But that, of course, was what made continuing to see him such a bad idea. Quite simply, she liked him too much. He was not someone with whom she could keep up a light flirtation, as she had done with Sir Myles. With Alec, something deep and serious lay beneath the surface; it would be far too easy to be pulled under.

There was no hope of a future with Alec Stafford, and because of that, she could not allow her feelings to grow. Her parentage might not matter to some other man, but it would to the Earl of Rawdon. He would never marry her, and she refused to be a man's mistress, so that way lay only heartache. Which did not mean, of course, that she should not give him a better explanation for her actions, but she did not think she could bear to see the look in his eyes change when she told him who she was and why her grandmother did not want her in London. It would be too painful if she saw the subtle alteration of expression that meant he now viewed her as a lesser being, someone beneath his notice except for her obvious attractions of the flesh.

Damaris enjoyed the spark she saw in Alec's eyes when he looked at her, the way heat flashed for an instant in the midst of all that cold calm. But she did not want to know that that heat was all he felt for her.

She was still plunged in her gloomy musings when she heard a shout. A moment later, it came again, this time closer to them. Puzzled, she moved the curtain aside and glanced around but saw no sign of anyone. Finally, turning and leaning out the window, she was able to see directly behind them. A man on a black horse was riding toward them. At the sight of her, he kicked his heels into his steed's sides and charged after them. His hat flew off, and white-blond hair flashed in the sun.

Alec!

Damaris's heart started beating like a hammer, and happiness leapt inside her. Alec had come after her.

"Stop!" he shouted again, and the authority in his voice obviously swayed the postilion, who pulled the horses to a halt. Twisted around in the seat as she was, the sudden cessation of movement sent Damaris sliding off onto the floor, where she landed with a thump. She had barely pulled herself back into her seat when the door was flung open and Alec looked inside.

"Bloody hell, Damaris! What the devil do you think you're doing?" His silvery blue eyes blazed with temper, the cool demeanor he normally showed the world shattered. "I turn my back for a few minutes, and you've sneaked out of the house and taken off!"

"I am not answerable to you!" Damaris jumped out of the vehicle to face him. She was not about to sit cowering in a carriage while he ranted at her. "The last I heard, I am an adult, free to go where I choose."

"Free to get captured again!" he retorted. "What an utterly nonsensical thing to do!"

Damaris's eyes narrowed dangerously at this insult. "I beg your pardon! There was nothing nonsensical about it. I gave it a good deal of thought."

"All of ten minutes, no doubt. Genevieve said you left the house right after I did. You told me that you would not leave."

"I did nothing of the sort!" Damaris shot back, planting her hands on her hips. "You asked me if you had made yourself clear, and I said you were quite clear about it. I did not say that I agreed to stay shut up in your house like some . . . some odalisque in a harem."

"An odalisque!" His eyes flared brighter, and to Damaris's astonishment, he reached out and grabbed her arm, pulling her up hard against him.

She let out a little "Oof" as her body met his, but then his lips were on hers and she was rendered incapable of speech. For a moment she was conscious of nothing—not the sun bathing them in soft light nor the breeze that stirred her hair nor even the amazed stare of the post boy on the lead horse— nothing but the heat that flooded her and the exquisite plea- sure of his mouth. His kiss was hard, almost punishing, and his arms wrapped around her in the same way, pressing her into him as if she could become part of him. His embrace was all strength and passion and fire, explosive in its intensity, as if the emotions inside him were bursting their way out of him and into her.

Damaris shuddered as dizzying sensations flooded her. She went up on her toes, wrapping her arms around his neck, meet- ing his desire with the force of her own. She felt him twitch, a small groan sounding deep in his throat, and his lips dug deeper into hers. The fire between them was consuming, as if it could burn them into nothingness, but Damaris embraced it will- ingly, rushing toward the hunger, reveling in the ache that filled her. She wanted him, her entire body trembling with an impet- uous eagerness, and the fact that he could bring her to such a state in one deep kiss would have been frightening—if her mind had been clear and cool enough to think.

At last he tore his mouth from hers, though he did not let her go. "An odalisque," he murmured again, and his lips, soft and darkened, almost bruised-looking from their fierce kiss, curved up in a trace of a smile. His eyes caught and held hers. "I can imagine you as an odalisque, skin like cream, a wisp of sheerest silk to cover you, lying on the sultan's couch." He let out a long sigh, leaning his forehead against hers. "Ah, Damaris, what you do to me . . . I have never known the like. I am usually a measured man."

Damaris could not help but giggle. "Oh, indeed, I have seen how measured you are—bursting into the Priory and smashing your fist into Gabriel's chin, riding out into the snowstorm to find little Matthew, charging out to track down my traveling chaise."

He had the grace to look chagrined. "Perhaps I can sometimes be impetuous. But I promise you I do not make a habit of stopping carriages and kissing young women by the side of the road."

"You are fierce, is what you are," Damaris retorted. She was not about to add that his fierceness thrilled her down to her toes. Instead, she forced herself to pull away from him. Reaching up to adjust her hat, which his rough embrace had knocked awry, she said with all the calm she could muster, "I am sorry I did not tell you. I knew you would argue and make it difficult to leave."

"Of course I would. Why will you not allow me to help you? Why are you exposing yourself to danger this way?"

"I'm not!" she insisted. "It was the rational thing to do. I removed myself from London so that those men could not seize me again."

"And what if they seized you on the road?"

"Really, Alec, it's broad daylight. They are not going to attack m—"

She was interrupted by the sound of a shot. Damaris jumped and whirled to see four men charging at them. Before she could move or even think, Alec picked her up and threw her into the carriage. Once again finding herself deposited rudely on the floor of the vehicle, Damaris scrambled up and looked out to see Alec, who had pulled a pistol from his pocket, coolly take aim at the rider bearing down upon him. He fired, and the other man jerked as the ball hit him in the shoulder, yanking on the reins as he slumped to the side. His horse reared, and he fell heavily. The animal, thus unencumbered, took off at a run.

Alec neatly sidestepped another horse, but one of the other men launched himself out of his saddle at Alec and the two men went tumbling to the ground. Damaris reached into her reticule and pulled out her little pistol. One of the remaining attackers slid down from his horse and ran toward her, and she lifted her pistol and fired. Her shot, unfortunately, went wide of the mark, smacking harmlessly into a tree. It was enough, however, to make the last rider's horse rear, whinnying in fear, and the ruffian was too occupied with trying to control his mount to come to the aid of either of his companions.

The assailant whom Damaris had shot at let out a curse and ran forward again. Her weapon, having been fired, was useless now, and as he reached the carriage, she swung it at him. It caught him flush on the forehead, splitting open his skin and bouncing off, but it did not fell him, only made him roar with rage as he reached up, grabbed her arm, and pulled her from the coach. Damaris resisted, kicking at him and clinging with her other hand to the door.

He jerked her free of the coach and dragged her toward his horse. Damaris dug in her heels, slowing him down as best she could, and reached up to her hat. Pulling out the long, decorative hatpin that secured it to her hair, she brought it down hard, stabbing her assailant in the arm. The man let out a high-pitched scream and released her instantly. Damaris, having been pulling away from him with all her strength, stumbled back and sat down hard on the ground.

"You bitch!" the man roared, clutching the arm she had stabbed and lunging toward her. Damaris scrambled backward, glancing around frantically for something to throw at him. She had managed to keep her grasp on the hatpin, but she knew it was a pitifully poor weapon against the man's strength now that she no longer had the element of surprise. There was nothing close at hand, so she clutched the long pin firmly and started to her feet to meet him.

At that moment Alec came barreling into the man, knocking him to the ground. The two of them rolled across the ground, punching and wrestling as the horses danced nervously around them, wild with the noise and excitement. The horses pulling the carriage were equally affected; it was all the postilion could do to keep them under control.

Damaris got to her feet and started toward the struggling

men. Alec was on top of the other fellow, slamming his fist into the man's face, so she glanced around her, looking for what danger might spring up next. Her eyes took in the chaotic scene of whinnying, stamping horses. The man who had first attacked Alec was on the ground, sitting up with a dazed look on his face, and the other man, whom Alec had shot, lay a few feet away from him, clutching his shoulder and moaning. The last of the men had finally settled his horse and dismounted. As she caught sight of him, he reached down and picked up a rock and ran toward Alec.

"Alec! Watch out!"

Alec half turned at Damaris's scream, and the rock the other man swung at him hit him a glancing blow on the side of his head instead of crushing his skull. It was enough, however, to send Alec crumpling to the ground. The man raised his hand as though to strike again, but Damaris got there first and sank her hatpin into the assailant's leg. He howled and dropped the rock as he flailed out, knocking Damaris to the ground. Alec's horse, which had been nervously stamping and turning near the fighting men, reared up, hooves lashing out. This was apparently the final blow to the man's courage. He scrambled away from the horse, as did the other man whom Alec had been beating, and they ran for their mounts.

"Alec!" Damaris dropped down on her knees beside him, scarcely noticing as the others struggled onto their horses and clattered away. She had eyes only for Alec. Blood streamed from the cut on the side of his head, staining his pale hair red.

He let out a low groan before his eyes popped open, and he started to push himself up.

"No! Lie still. You're hurt." Damaris laid her hand on his shoulder. "Oh, Alec! I'm so sorry!" She dug into her reticule, which was still, rather absurdly, dangling from her wrist, and she pulled out a handkerchief to press against Alec's cut.

"What in the bloody hell is going on?" Alec sat up despite her restraining hand. His blue eyes were stark in his dust- and blood-smeared face, and a light still burned in them so fiercely that it was enough to make anyone want to flee. "Who the—" He winced and raised his hand toward his head. "The devil!"

"Don't move. Don't worry. They have all left. We're safe. Let me get something to bind your head." Damaris turned toward the post chaise, starting to rise.

"No!" she cried in dismay, and jumped to her feet.

The sounds of horses running had not been only their attackers. Right behind them, galloping away at full speed, was her post chaise.

Nine

Damaris spit out a word she had learned from her French schoolmates and dropped back to her knees beside Alec. "The carriage is gone."

"So I gathered," Alec said drily. He reached up gingerly to touch his head, where Damaris's handkerchief was now stuck to it with blood.

"Oh, Alec, I'm so sorry. I didn't mean to involve you in all this."

"In what? What is 'all this'? No, wait." He held up a hand. "This is neither the time nor place to discuss it. We need to get away from here."

He got to his feet with Damaris's aid. He swayed for an instant but remained standing. His horse had calmed down considerably with the departure of the other animals, and now he came over to Alec and butted his head lightly against Alec's chest. Alec reached up and rubbed his head. "Aren't you the good chap?"

"He was indeed," Damaris told him. "It was your horse that sent that man fleeing. My poking him wouldn't have kept him away long." She lifted her hand, which, amazingly, still clutched the hatpin.

"Good Gad," Alec said with some awe, looking at the lethal ornament. "You stuck that thing into him?"

"Yes, after he hit you with the rock. It was the only thing I had. I'd already fired my gun."

The corner of his mouth twitched. "I heard. I feel quite extraneous."

"Don't be absurd. You are the only reason I'm still here." She paused, then added, "Thank you. I am sorry to—"

He shook his head. "It's not necessary, I assure you. And we really should be on our way."

"You're right. We need to see to your head." He was, she thought, even paler than usual, and the blood that had streamed over one side of his head and face was horrifying.

"What we need is not to be here if our friends decide to come back."

"Do you think they might?" A thrill of alarm ran through Damaris. "Surely not. They were wounded."

"Only one of them was seriously wounded. I'm not at all sure they won't get down the road a bit, assess their damages, and decide that they would be better off ridding the world of the witnesses to their crime."

"You're right. We'd best go." Damaris ran to pick up her little pistol and stuff it back in her reticule, then retrieved Alec's as well. "Oh, look, here is another gun. The man you wounded must have dropped it."

She went over to get the other gun, and, turning back,

she saw that Alec was leaning against his horse, one arm on the animal's neck, his head resting against that arm, his eyes closed. Her heart clenched inside her and she hurried back. Alec straightened at her approach and gave her a reassuring smile, but Damaris was not fooled. There was still a dazed look in his eyes that did not bode well.

"You'll have to ride in front of me. Erebos won't like it, but he'll manage." He bent and cupped his hands to vault Damaris into the saddle, but she shook her head.

"No, there's a stump over there. Let's use it. There is no need for you to lift me."

"Are you saying I haven't the strength?" He slanted a look down at her in his familiar arrogant way, which, she realized with a start, was beginning to seem rather endearing.

Damaris grimaced. "Clearly that knock on the head took away some of your sense." She started toward the stump without glancing back to see if he followed. She took it as a sign of his feeling weak that he did so without any more protest.

Even with the added height of the stump, Damaris had some difficulty getting on Alec's horse. Not only was Erebos tall, but he was also skittish at the idea of her climbing into his saddle. It did not help that she was not dressed for riding. Alec held the stallion's head, talking soothingly to him and stroking his nose, and finally, on the third try, Damaris was able to squirm her way onto the horse's back. Scooting up as far as she could, she decided to damn propriety and ride astride, even though her skirts did not completely cover her legs. Alec, too, used the stump to mount, confirming Damaris's suspicions regarding his weakness.

His arms went around her to hold the reins. Damaris's back was pressed against his front, and she found herself relaxing into him. It was impossible not to feel safer with his strength wrapped around her like this. She felt the movement of his arms and thighs as he turned Erebos and started across the road, and she could not deny that something stirred in her in response. It occurred to her that she must indeed be shallow to be so aware of the intimacy of their physical situation. Alec was injured. They were fleeing dangerous men. And she was thinking about the breadth of his chest and the heat of his body. Sternly she tried to pull her thoughts onto more appropriate matters.

"Are you not taking the road back?" she asked, surprised, as he struck out across the land.

"If they come looking and find us gone, that would be the obvious direction we would have taken. Strong as Erebos is, I have ridden him hard this afternoon, and he's carrying double now, so we cannot travel fast. They could catch us on the road. Better to stay off it. Beyond that meadow, the trees look fairly thick. With luck we should lose any pursuers."

Their pace through the meadow was quick. Alec kept glancing back at the road for any sign of their attackers, and when they reached the stand of trees, they both let out a sigh of relief. They picked their way through the woods at a much slower pace, heading generally east as the sun dropped lower in the sky behind them.

When they came to a shallow stream, Damaris insisted that they stop to clean Alec's wound. He protested for a moment, but gave in. As he dismounted, Damaris saw him waver, so she hastily slid off the horse before he could reach up to help her. Soaking her handkerchief in the clear stream, she began to carefully wash the blood and dirt from his face.

Alec sat on a rock, level with her, watching her as she worked on him. Damaris found it faintly unnerving to stand this close to him, looking into his eyes. She put her fingers on his chin to hold his head steady as she worked, and she was tinglingly aware of the sensation of his skin beneath her fingers, the faint scratch of the beginnings of his beard. It did curious things to her insides, and she felt jumpy and strangely unsure of herself, as if she might suddenly do something over which she had no control.

He drew in a quick, hissing breath as she drew closer to his wound.

"I'm sorry." Her hand stilled.

"No, go ahead. We have to find a place to spend the night, and the less I look like a vagabond, the better."

She resumed her cleansing, and after a few more minutes, she had cleared away the blood and dirt from his hair, revealing a small cut, thankfully no longer bleeding.

"It's not as bad as I thought," she said with relief.

"Scalp wounds always bleed a great deal," he said casually.

Damaris let out an indelicate snort. "You, obviously, are accustomed to being knocked on the head with rocks."

"It's more ordinarily fists, though once Gabe and I got into a mill with some chaps at school, and one of them threw a tankard at me."

"Good thing you have a hard head."

"Aye. 'Tis the border blood." He adopted the thick, faintly lilting Northumbrian accent.

She chuckled, the twinkle in his eyes warming her. She was aware of a strong—and very inadvisable—desire to lean in and plant a swift kiss on his lips. She also thought of kissing that sharp jut of cheekbone . . . or the strong line of his jaw . . . and how would the tender skin above his eye feel beneath her lips? Indeed, she wanted to hold Alec's face between her hands and kiss him all over. Heat and danger fizzed up in her, and her breath caught in her throat. She was, she realized, feeling a bit wobbly herself.

She told herself that it was just gratitude she felt, and a lingering excitement. The aftermath of fear and anger were fueling her outrageous, licentious urges. She could not allow herself to give in to them. She would be appalled and embarrassed later, when she was herself again.

With an effort, Damaris took a step backward. "I—um, I haven't a clean handkerchief to dry your wound and bandage it."

"Don't worry, it will dry. And at least I won't look the fool with a great strip of white wrapped around my head."

"No, wait, I have an idea. I don't suppose you are still carrying that knife of yours?"

He cast her a smug look and reached down to his boot

to pull the hidden knife from the sheath strapped to his calf. His gesture was somewhat spoiled by the fact that the sudden movement made him sway and he had to grip the edge of the rock upon which he sat.

"Alec!" Damaris reached out to steady him. "I *knew* you were hurt worse than you'd say."

"Just felt woozy for a bit. I am fine." He gave her a wicked grin. "Though feel free to hold me up if you'd like."

Damaris snatched her hand away and grabbed the knife. Ostentatiously turning her back to him, she bent over and raised the front of her skirt to cut through a ruffle of her petticoat. She felt Alec's hand curve over her buttocks, and she jumped and whirled, her insides a sudden, clanging mix of astonishment, indignation, and pure roaring lust.

"Alec!"

"I could not resist." The devil-may-care grin on his face had widened. "You were right there in front of me."

"Well, you had best curb your impulses," Damaris told him, trying her utmost to sound stern despite the yearning heat that had blazed up deep in her abdomen. She stepped away and ripped the rest of the ruffle from its moorings, then cut the strip into pieces, handing him one. "Here, you can dry your own face if you are going to act like that."

The truth was, she was not sure she trusted herself to do so without giving in to her own base impulses. It was pure effrontery for him to caress her in that way, and she should be furious. But what she felt was not anger but a rush of excitement. Foremost in her mind was a thrilling curiosity about exactly how that hand would feel on a number of other parts of her body.

She turned and walked a few feet away as she folded another piece of the strip into a pad, using the time and distance to pull herself under control. Adopting what she hoped was an adequately freezing look, she stalked back to him and pressed the pad to his wound. Alec's face was once again stamped with its usual undemonstrative expression, but there was an undeniable heat in his eyes, and Damaris could not keep her fingers from trembling slightly.

"Hold this," she ordered, pleased that at least she sounded crisp instead of the decidedly liquid way she felt inside, and she began to wrap the last strip of cloth around his head to hold the pad in place.

"You are determined to make me appear foolish, I can see."

"Don't whine. We can't have you bleeding on someone's doorstep if we hope to make a good impression."

He grasped her wrist and lifted her hand, turning it, to press his lips gently into her palm. Damaris stood, unable to move, scarcely daring to breathe, caught by surprise at the tender gesture. Impulsively she reached out to smooth her other hand over his shock of silver-gold hair. It was soft and fine, like silk beneath her fingers, and she wanted to sink her hand into it. She wanted to pull his head against her breast.

"Thank you," he murmured. "You are an angel."

"Far from it," she retorted shakily. She felt nothing like an angel at this moment. "Come. We should leave."

It took an effort to step away from him, and if he had resisted, if he had pulled her to him, Damaris was not sure what she would have done. But Alec let go of her hand and rose, his gaze lingering on her face for an instant before moving away.

Alec made no protest this time when Damaris climbed onto the horse by herself, merely guided Erebos to a rock so that she could do so more easily. When he settled in behind her, she could feel the tension in his body. Damaris was even more aware now of his body curving around hers as they rode, of the brush of his breath against her hair and the shift of his thigh muscles as he guided the horse, the tautness of his arms around her, his hands holding the reins, resting against her stomach.

He turned Erebos into the shallow stream, traveling downstream for some distance before crossing to the other side and continuing east. As the afternoon settled into dusk, they wound through the trees and emerged on a track, taking it along the edge of a low stone wall until they ran into a lane. Still there was no sign of a village with an inn where they could take refuge for the night.

Alec had no more familiarity with the area than Damaris, having in the past done no more than pass through it on the main toll road. They had seen a small cottage in the distance when they first set out, but they had stayed away from it, wanting to put more distance between them and the men who had attacked them. As darkness fell, Damaris began to worry that they might be caught outdoors for the night.

Clouds had begun drifting in late in the afternoon, heavy and dark, contributing to the encroaching gloom, and it seemed likely that it might soon start to rain.

It would be exceedingly uncomfortable to spend the night outdoors, Damaris thought, much less in the rain. Worse, she was worried about Alec. He was not at his normal strength, and more than once as they rode, she had felt his body relax against hers until he was leaning against her, his head on hers, and his hands had gone slack on the reins—obviously slipping into unconsciousness until she said his name sharply, snapping him back awake.

The last time he began to drift, she took the reins from his hands, fearful that he would drop them altogether. It was somewhat awkward to guide the horse this way, without her feet in the stirrups and sitting so far forward, and she was afraid that Erebos would recognize the unfamiliar hand on the reins and balk, but he kept moving forward, though once or twice he shook his head as if disturbed. As she felt Alec's body grow limp behind her once more, she began to fear that he might fall off the horse altogether. She tried not to think of stories she had heard of people striking their heads, then slipping into a slumber from which they never wakened.

Damaris reached down and took Alec's arm, wrapping her own arm around his and pressing it against her stomach in an effort to keep him steady. He shifted in his sleep, his head slipping to her shoulder, and he wrapped his other arm around her waist as well. Damaris tried to ignore the intimacy of their position. It was, after all, more secure this way. But the practicality of it was not what her body was responding to; it was the sheer physical pleasure of his close embrace, the touch of his breath upon the sensitive skin of her neck.

Damaris wished more than ever that they would come to a village. Or even a farmhouse. Anywhere they might be able to get off and rest. A hot meal would be wonderful, too. She still had her reticule, and she had enough money in it to pay for a room—though, annoyingly, she had stuck the bulk of the money she had gotten from Mr. Portland into the valise for safekeeping, so it was now resting uselessly in the long-gone post chaise.

Thunder rumbled in the heavy clouds, confirming Damaris's fears of a storm, and within minutes, drops began to fall. Erebos skittered to the side at the sudden noise, and Damaris struggled to control the animal. Alec awoke behind her.

"Good God, did I go to sleep?"

"A little." Damaris was relieved to have Alec take charge of Erebos, and he nudged the horse to a faster pace.

The rain increased as they rode, turning the road slick with mud and soaking them to the skin. The storm had brought a wind with it, chilling them further. With relief, Damaris spotted a glimpse of light through the trees, and shortly thereafter, they came upon another lane. At the end of it stood a sturdy farmhouse.

Alec dug in his heels and clicked to his horse, but Erebos needed no urging to run toward shelter. As they drew closer, they saw a man, swathed in a cloak and carrying a lantern, cross the farmyard to the house. He stopped on the porch and turned to watch them approach.

Alec pulled Erebos to a stop at the bottom of the steps. "Good day to you."

"And to you, sir. Best come inside and get warm," the man responded cheerfully. "Looks like the storm caught you out."

"Indeed." Alec swung down off the horse and started toward the stranger. Suddenly he faltered, then collapsed onto the ground.

Ten

"Alec!" *Damaris slid off the* horse and ran to him, but the man on the porch reached Rawdon first, leaning over him and setting the lantern on the ground so that it shone over Alec's face.

"Looks like a nasty wound there." The rain had soaked Alec's bandage, and the diluted blood had stained the entire pad, making it appear even worse than it was. Alec's pallor did nothing to contradict the man's assessment. "Best to get him in out of the wet," the man went on placidly. "Mayhap I can carry him."

Damaris doubted that, given Alec's size, but the man, though not nearly as tall as Alec, was strong, and between the two of them, they wrestled Alec to his feet. He regained a groggy consciousness as they pulled and tugged at him, and he was able to make it into the house with the stranger and Damaris on either side of him, supporting him.

"Emmet!" A woman hurried toward them. "What's happened? Here, put him by the fire."

She brought a sturdy wooden chair from the table and put

it down in front of the large fireplace. Emmet and Damaris steered Alec toward it and tried to ease him down into it, but he sat down with a thud.

"I'll put his horse away in the barn," the man offered, "whilst you get them warm and dry, Babs."

The woman went to work, nodding toward the cluster of children gazing at them in wide-eyed fascination. "Here, now, Maud, set the kettle to boil for tea. Henry, fetch the bottle of Madeira your pa keeps in the cabinet. Josie, get me a blanket off our bed."

The children all hurried to do their assigned tasks while the efficient Babs began to remove Alec's sodden jacket. Damaris hurried to help her. As they pulled Alec forward, his eyes fluttered closed again and he slumped against Damaris, shivering with cold. She held him steady while the other woman peeled off his coat.

"I'm Babs Putnam," their hostess told Damaris as they worked.

"Damaris Howard," Damaris responded. She started to introduce Alec, but hesitated. Not only did it sound very odd for an earl to be running about the countryside like this, but she had a suspicion that Alec would prefer not to have his name given out freely. She finished somewhat lamely, "And this is Alec. I'm sorry. It isn't the best way to meet, but we are very grateful to you for letting us in."

"'Tis a terrible storm out there," the woman said as she cast a quick encompassing glance over Damaris.

Damaris realized with dismay how disreputable she and

Alec must appear. They had both lost their hats in the struggle, and Damaris's dress was thoroughly bedraggled—wet, muddy, and sporting a large tear across the front. Her hair had come undone and hung dankly down over her shoulders, clinging to her face and neck. To make it worse, they were dripping all over the woman's spotless plank floor.

"I'm so sorry. We are making a terrible mess." A shiver ran through Damaris despite the warmth of the fire. Alec had not stopped shivering since they came in. "I know you must think us utter vagabonds."

The woman waved away her concern. "Now, never you mind. As if I couldn't tell quality the minute I see it. Alan, get them some towels, now, step to it. First thing, we need to get you two warm." She started on the buttons of Alec's waistcoat, saying, "Looks like you had a mite of trouble besides the storm."

"Yes, we were, um, attacked on the road." Damaris wondered exactly what she ought to tell the woman. Some explanation was necessary, obviously, but it seemed best to keep it as simple as possible. "We fought them off, but our post chaise ran off, and we had only Alec's horse."

"Thieves!" The woman tsk-tsked, shaking her head. "Are you hurt?"

"No. One of them hit Alec with a rock. It bled terribly. I think it's weakened him. And he kept nodding off as we rode."

"I've seen it before." The woman shook her head sagely. "Ethan's cousin fell out of his hayloft last summer and struck his head. Took him some time to come to, and then he passed out again and never woke up. Died two days later." Seeing

Damaris's panic-struck face, she waved away her comments, saying, "There, now, I've let my tongue run away with me again. Not likely to happen to your man. Anyone can see he's strong as an ox."

One of the boys, a freckle-faced adolescent, brought his mother a cup and a bottle, and she poured a healthy amount of wine into the cup. "Here, see if you can get him to drink this. That'll warm him up a mite."

While Babs struggled to tug off Alec's boots, Damaris shook him awake. "Alec. Wake up. You need to drink this."

He opened his eyes blearily. "Damaris."

"Yes, I'm here. I want you to drink this, now. It will make you feel better."

He murmured something she couldn't understand and put his hand on the cup, but he was still shivering with cold, so she helped him bring the vessel to his lips and drink. A great shudder ran through him, but he grasped the cup more firmly and continued to sip. By the time he was finished, Babs had managed to wrestle him out of his neckcloth and boots.

"We just need to finish getting your husband out of these wet things," Babs told Damaris.

Damaris started to correct Mrs. Putnam's assumption that she and Alec were married, but she caught herself just in time. Given the state of their appearance and the holes in her story if she tried to explain exactly who they were and why the men were after them, Damaris decided it would be better to take the path of respectability and let her believe she and Alec were lawfully married. This woman might have been able to tell from their clothes and speech that Damaris and Alec were gentry, but the assumption of a high station in life would not compensate for a lack of morals. As Babs turned away to take the towels and blanket from her children, Damaris surreptitiously slipped one of her rings from her right hand onto the third finger of her left.

"You just take your gentleman into our bedroom there," Babs told Damaris, gesturing at an open doorway down a short hallway. "You can get him out of the rest of his things and wrap this blanket around him."

Color rose in Damaris's cheeks as it sank in that the woman expected her to undress Alec. She was well and truly caught by the fact that she had not corrected Babs's misconception earlier. In her moment of indecision, Alec, despite his grogginess, spoke up, relieving her of making a decision. "Can do it myself."

He started to rise, and Damaris quickly moved to support him, slipping one arm around his waist. He curled his arm over her shoulders, leaning subtly against her. Damaris looked up into his face, and even though it was still quite pale and his eyes a trifle glassy, she thought she detected a wisp of a smile on his mouth.

"Dear wife," he murmured, bending to press his lips to the top of her hair.

Damaris tightened her arm sharply. "I can see you are feeling better," she told him with a touch of asperity.

Fortunately, Babs did not seem to notice her tone, for she was already bustling toward the open door with her pile of cloths. Damaris had little choice but to follow with Alec. Their benefactress laid the towels and blanket down on the bed as one of the boys popped in to light the fire.

"There, it'll be warm as toast soon," Babs told them cheerfully. "I'll just dish up a bit of stew for you, if you don't mind humble fare."

"That would be wonderful," Damaris responded honestly. Her stomach felt as if she had not eaten for a week. "If it's not too much trouble," she managed to add politely.

Babs beamed. "No trouble at all. Got a nice loaf of bread as well. You just get the gentleman out of those wet things and into the bed. He'll warm up real well like that."

"Oh, you must not give up your bed," Damaris protested.

"I'll sit by the fire," Alec added.

"Nonsense. After what you've been through? You hop into that bed now," Mrs. Putnam told Rawdon in the same tone she had used with her sons. "The mister and I'll do fine with the youngsters. Don't you worry about it."

She was gone in an instant, shutting the door behind her, and Damaris was alone with Alec. The bed loomed up only a few feet away, dominating the room. Damaris knew she was blushing again. She cleared her throat.

"Well." This was no time for delicacy, she told herself. She turned around to face him. Alec was leaning against the wall beside the fireplace, his eyes closed. His face was stamped with lines of pain and weariness, and Damaris's heart went out to him.

She crossed over to him and began to undo his shirt. She

noticed that her hands trembled a little on the buttons as she tugged them open. His eyes opened a slit, and she caught a gleam in them. "You make an excellent valet, wife of mine."

Damaris's eyes narrowed suspiciously. "If you are only pretending, Alec, I shall throttle you."

"How unkind." The corner of his mouth quirked up. "Not a proper wife's statement of affection." He paused, then added with a devilish delight, "Or obedience."

"Do be quiet. I didn't know what else to say to her. She assumed you were my husband, and I—well, it seemed a good idea at the time." Damaris shrugged. "Bend over a little so I can pull this off you."

She tugged the ends of his shirt from his breeches and yanked it up over his head. He bent obligingly so that she could draw it the rest of the way off, but he swayed as he did so and let out a low curse, grabbing at the fireplace wall to steady himself.

"I'm bloody muzzy-headed," he murmured.

"Not surprising. I wonder if that cup of Madeira was really the best idea." Damaris kept her words as calm and brisk as she could, given that she was facing the broad expanse of his bare chest. Her eyes roved over his flesh, taking in the hard lines of bone and muscle, and she was aware of a most inappropriate urge to run her hands over his wet skin.

Somewhat unnerved, she reached out to the top button of his breeches. Her heart was pounding, and her hands felt clumsy and slow. Her nails brushed against the bare skin of his stomach, and she jerked them back. She looked up into his eyes. There was definitely a gleam there now and tension crept into his posture, as if something was coiled and waiting inside him. Damaris imagined sliding her fingers down beneath his waistband.

Swallowing hard, she clasped her hands together behind her back, like a guilty child standing before a tin of sweets, and whirled away. "I think you can manage the rest."

Damaris picked up the folded blanket Babs had laid on the bed and shook it out. Holding it up as high as she could, so that her vision of Alec was blocked, she walked back to him.

"Such modesty," he drawled, amusement mingling with something darker and fiercer. "You are a widow, after all. Surely you have seen a man's body. Even touched it."

Damaris's throat went tight and dry, and her voice came out hoarsely as she snapped back, "Not yours."

At the smack of his wet clothes hitting the floor, Damaris wrapped the blanket around him, and Alec took it from her hands, pulling it closed. He gave a violent shudder, as though the warmth wrapping around him had released him from his control.

"Here, get in bed," Damaris ordered, going to the bed and turning down its covers. "You'll get warmer faster."

He did not argue, but sat on the bed and let her prop the pillows behind him, then pull up the covers to his waist. "You should get out of your wet things as well."

Damaris shot him a sharp glance as she picked up a towel and began to wrap it around her wet hair. "I haven't anything to put on."

His grin flashed. "I don't mind."

"I do."

He reached his hand out to tug back the covers beside him. "I'll share."

At that moment, there was a knock at the door, and Babs peeped in. She had brought a tray of food, which she carried inside once she saw that Alec was decently covered. "Well, you're looking better, sir. Mayhap this will pick you up more. There's a bowl for you as well, missus, and hot tea."

"Thank you." Damaris gratefully took one of the cups.

"You'll need something to wear as well," Babs went on, bustling over to the dresser and opening one of the drawers. She pulled out a flannel nightgown and handed it to Damaris. "Now, you slip out of those wet things and hand them out to me. I'll see what I can do about getting them dry for you whilst you sleep."

Damaris hoped she managed to conceal the alarm that had run through her at the woman's words. It had just struck her that not only would she have to undress right here in front of Alec, but she would also be expected to share his bed. It should have been obvious to her earlier, she knew, since she was pretending to be his wife; but somehow in her worry over Alec and her desire to seem proper in front of their hosts, she had managed to overlook this fact.

She cast a quick glance at Alec. He was sitting with the tray on his lap, digging into his bowl of stew with eagerness. But he cut his eyes toward her; they flashed almost silver in the dim light, and she knew that he was fully aware of her quandary.

As soon as their hostess left the room, he said casually, "Best hurry, now; you won't want to risk catching cold. I am sure you'll look quite fetching in your new nightrail."

"I think I preferred you when you were unconscious."

He hid his smile by taking a sip of tea. "Honestly, Damaris . . . you've nothing to fear from me. I'm weak as a kitten; I couldn't do anything to sully you even if I were cad enough to try it. Look: I'll even close my eyes while you undress."

Ostentatiously he closed his eyes and covered them with one hand. Damaris was too cold and wet not to accept his offer. She turned away and peeled off her clothes, toweling off as quickly as she could. She stacked the damp things just outside the door, after dropping the nightgown over her head. It was far too large for her, as Mrs. Putnam possessed a wider girth than she, but it was a trifle short despite that, for the woman was also several inches shorter. Well, she thought, catching a glimpse of herself in the mirror above the washstand, at least she would not have to worry about appearing seductive. The high-necked, long-sleeved, plain gray flannel gown did little to enhance her looks.

She turned back and found Alec watching her. She scowled. "You promised to close your eyes."

"I did. For quite some time. I cannot help it if you are slow." He grinned, setting his bowl aside and leaning his head back against the pillows. His eyes drifted closed and he opened them again with effort.

Damaris picked up a small crocheted blanket that lay folded across the foot of the bed and wrapped it around her shoulders. She came over to take the tray from Alec's lap. His eyes were half-closed again, but he murmured, "You have a lovely back, by the way."

"My back is hardly an appropriate topic for conversation," Damaris replied tartly, and whisked away the tray.

She set it down on the dresser, then picked up the other bowl of stew and sat down on the stool in front of the fire. She took a spoonful into her mouth and let out an unconscious sigh of pleasure. The soup was thick and meaty and deliciously hot. For the first time in an hour, she was beginning to feel warm again. Damaris glanced over at the bed. Alec had reclined, his eyes closed, and his chest was rising and falling softly in the slow rhythm of sleep.

Damaris wondered just how much of her he had seen, and heat rose in her cheeks. He was a complete scoundrel, of course, to take advantage of the situation like that, but it stirred something inside her to think of him watching. She could not help but wonder what ran through him as he looked at her—and what might have happened if he had not been "weak as a kitten."

She supposed that it must make her rather wanton that such thoughts set up a warm ache between her legs. It was always rumored that widows were likely to be promiscuous, that having known a man's touch, they were more inclined afterward to seek it. But that had not been the case with her. Barrett Howard had not been a harsh lover, but the few times he had lain with her, he had not lingered along the way, but had raced to the conclusion of the act, and Damaris had found all the fuss over the experience rather overblown. After their brief marriage was over, she had had little urge to take any man into her bed. She had had some twinges of feelings now and then, she would admit that, but all in all, it had not been difficult to remain chaste.

But now, thinking of Alec, she could not deny that she felt . . . well, unusually loose and warm. Her mind went back to the sight of his bare chest and arms, his skin slick from the rain, stretched taut over the thick pads of muscles. She wondered what it would feel like to tease the tip of her tongue across that skin, how it would taste. Truth be known, if she could have looked past the blanket without his knowing while he took off the rest of his clothes, she would have done so.

Damaris shook her head, faintly shocked by her own thoughts, and turned her attention back to finishing the stew. When she had done so, she set the bowl aside and unwound the towel from her head. Using her fingers, she worked through her wet hair in front of the fire, separating the strands and doing her best to dry it. Her hair was thick and long and rather tangled, and it was not an easy task. She found a wide-toothed comb on the dresser and used it to bring some order to her tresses, letting the heat of the fire dry it. She hoped Babs would let her borrow a few hairpins tomorrow to wind it into a simple coil, but for now, she simply braided it into a thick plait and tied it with a bit of ribbon she found in her reticule.

Once that was done, she found herself nodding off on the stool, too warm and full to stay awake. Blearily, she raised her eyes and looked over at the bed. Alec was curled up on his side, burrowed under the covers; she could see little of him except for the tumble of bright hair on the pillow. He would not notice if she crept under the covers, too. And where else was she supposed to sleep? There was not even a chair in this small room, only the stool upon which she sat. Her only option besides the bed was to wrap a blanket about herself and sleep on the floor, which seemed excessively hard and probably cold as well.

Standing up, she tiptoed to the side of the bed opposite Alec and stood indecisively. He was asleep, she reminded herself, and weakened from the loss of blood. He was bound to have a headache and a variety of other aches and pains from the fight. Even if he woke up and realized she was sleeping beside him, surely he would not feel well enough even to want to take advantage of the situation. Besides, he had promised, however jokingly, that she was safe from him, and Damaris was certain that whatever else Alec might be, he was a man of his word. Anyway, she was likely to awaken before him, given the state of his head, and she could slip out of bed again without him ever being the wiser.

Damaris hesitated for a moment more; then, taking a breath, she put aside her makeshift crocheted wrap and slid beneath the covers. She lay for a moment, breathing shallowly, but Alec did not stir. It was warm as an oven under the sheet and blankets, for Alec's large body gave off a tremendous amount of heat, and as she lay there, Damaris could not help but relax. Turning onto her side, she snuggled into her pillow and gave herself up to sleep.

Eleven

She was blazing hot, and there was a heavy ache between her legs. Pleasure tingled through her nerves and across her skin. Alec murmured to her, and she shivered at the low timbre of his voice. She moved her legs restlessly, wanting him, eager for him. Hunger was like a sword stabbing through her.

Damaris's eyes flew open. She was lying in bed, suffused with heat, her back up against a hard male body—Alec's. She was in bed with Alec. He engulfed her, his body curled around hers, his head resting on her hair. His breath teased at her ear, sending little ripples of excitement through her. And his hands . . . good Lord, his hands! His arms were wrapped around her, one large hand covering one of her breasts, and his other hand—Damaris drew in a shaky breath. His other hand was between her legs, pressed firmly against her, and though the cloth of the nightgown lay between them, it presented little barrier.

And she was utterly, scorchingly on fire, inside and out. She needed to get out, she thought, and tried to edge away, but in his sleep, Alec's arms tightened on her, holding her in place. He mumbled incoherently, snuggling into her hair.

She was trapped.

If she pulled too hard, he would come awake, and there she would be in this embarrassing position. Her nightrail had gotten hiked up in her sleep, exposing much of her legs, and one of his legs was curled around hers. She could feel the brush of the hair on his leg against her skin. She could feel, moreover, the thick ridge of flesh prodding into her backside. Worst of all, though, was the fact that his hands were on her so intimately, as if she were his.

No, worse than that was the desire flooding her, the hunger that sizzled through her veins and swelled, pulsing, between her legs. Her breasts were full and heavy, the nipple prickling against his palm. His hand moved fractionally on her breasts, sending the material of her gown sliding over the sensitive nub, and pleasure radiated out from it. His lower hand wriggled deeper, pressing into her, and to Damaris's abashed amazement, her legs reflexively moved farther apart, giving him access to her.

What was the matter with her? She knew she must move, must break the embrace and jump out of bed. If she moved quickly enough, even if the movement awakened him, he might not realize how intimately they had been twined together.

And yet she continued to lie in his arms. He made a soft noise in his sleep, nuzzling into her hair, and his fingers moved insistently between her legs, rubbing the gown against her. Damaris's breath turned ragged. His skin flamed against hers, and he pushed her hips deeper into his pelvis, his fingers sliding rhythmically up and down.

Damaris closed her eyes and concentrated on lying very still so that she would not awaken him. He mumbled something—was that her name? Or perhaps it was only a curse.

Desire knotted in her, each stroke of his fingers ratcheting up the tension. Moisture flooded between her legs, but she could not even find enough strength to be embarrassed. He was having his way with her—and he wasn't even awake! But she could not bring herself to care. All she cared about was that coiling ache within her, the flesh that swelled and hungered for his touch until she had to clench her teeth to keep from moaning aloud. She wanted to move against his hand, to hurry the pleasure that danced just beyond her, to sob with the need that burgeoned inside her. The hard, twisting something built and built . . .

It exploded within her, a burst of pleasure so intense she had to bite her lip to keep from crying out. Waves of it washed through her, inundating every part of her, and her whole body trembled under the force of the explosion.

She felt Alec jerk, and she knew he had awakened. She kept her eyes closed, unable to face him. If he believed her to be asleep, he would not know how she had stayed beneath his hand, unable to forgo the pleasure. She waited, forcing her breathing into a slow, calm rhythm.

He let out a little groan close to her ear, and she felt his lips press into her hair. Slowly, he pulled his hands from her, sliding over her in a final caress before he released her. He bent to kiss the point of her shoulder, his breath searing her skin, then sat up. It was hard to keep herself from reaching out and pulling his hands back onto her.

She heard him release a long breath and felt the bed give as he slid out. He roamed about the small room, pausing at the fireplace to poke at the embers and going to the window to pull aside the curtain and look out. It was incredibly difficult to keep up her pretense of sleep. She kept thinking of his long, leanly muscled body naked in the morning light, and she had to fight the urge to open her eyes and look at him.

At last he wrapped the blanket around him and cracked open the door. He let out a little grunt, then closed the door again. He had not left, and Damaris wondered what he was doing, but then she realized that the soft noises she heard were the sounds of him getting dressed. He must have found his dried clothes waiting outside the door. Finally, when Damaris thought she could not keep her eyes shut a moment longer, he left the room.

Damaris blew out her breath in a burst and rolled over onto her back, staring up at the ceiling. What had just happened? Her body tingled all over, her blood was thrumming in her veins, but at the same time she felt warm and languid and loose, as if her very bones had turned to jelly. Though her marriage had been brief, she had thought she knew what took place in the marital bed. Clearly, her knowledge was severely lacking. Everything that had happened between her and Alec, from that first heated kiss to this morning's caresses, had been a revelation. If this was what most women found in marriage, she could understand the reputation widows held for wantonness.

She closed her eyes, luxuriating for a moment longer in the sensations still resonating in her body before it occurred to her that she ought to get up and dress before Alec returned to their room. She slid out of bed before she recalled that she, no more than Alec, had any clothes to don. Last night after she had undressed, she had set her wet things outside the door just as Mrs. Putnam had told her. A quick glance around confirmed that her frock had not magically appeared.

Remembering what Alec had done earlier, she opened the door a crack, but there were no clothes lying conveniently there, either. There was, however, Alec, striding out of the large central room down the short hall toward her. He carried a mug in one hand, and in the other, a pile of cloth, which Damaris recognized with a blush as her underthings. He smiled when he saw her.

"Ah, wife of mine."

Damaris frowned at him, though she doubted her expression would make much impression on him. He seemed in remarkably good spirits for a man who had suffered a blow to the head and been chased through the rain by brigands. Handing her the garments, he stepped into the room, so that she had to fall back and let him enter.

"Where is my dress?" she asked, taking the chemise and

petticoats. Her delicate stockings lay in a dainty pile atop the folded frilly underpants. Just the sight of Alec's long fingers on the garments did strange things to her insides.

"Now, don't fuss, sweetling," he said in that same droll and insinuating way that told her he was thoroughly enjoying playing the role of husband.

Damaris found his act as annoying as he found it amusing, and it was made all the more so by the horrifying knowledge that deep inside she wanted to spring on him and kiss the smile from his face. It was even worse because his eyes roamed appreciatively over her form, and though the loose nightgown was too thick to see through, it was soft enough that he could certainly see her nipples tighten and thrust against the material just from the touch of his gaze.

"The good lady of the house is even now mending a rent in the skirt, but she fears you will find the gown sadly insufficient. The silk did not, she said, hold up well to a soak in the rain."

Damaris let out a groan, clutching her underclothes to her. She could easily believe that her French silk gown had not fared well. "What am I to do?"

"Take a sip of tea," he replied, holding out the cup. "I offered to bring it to you, which I must say earned me a great deal of admiration from our Mrs. Putnam and Maud, though I could tell that young Henry found me a poor figure of manhood for doing so."

Damaris took a drink of the warm liquid and found that, surprisingly, it did help to restore her spirits. "Thank you."

"You are most welcome." He sat down on the bed, lounging back and watching her. "Mrs. Putnam says she will lend you one of her frocks, which will fit in perfectly with my plans. I suggest that we go forward as an ordinary sort of couple—a farmer and his wife, say. I discovered, by the way, that I am now Mr. Howard."

"Oh. Yes, I told her my name, and then she assumed we were married, so . . ." She could feel the heat rising in her cheeks again, and she turned away, taking another drink. "I didn't know what to say. I feared she would not be so welcoming if she knew we were not, I mean . . ."

"Quite right. And I was able to cover my surprise at my new name well enough that I think they suspect only that I am being discreetly quiet about my title."

"I see." Damaris smiled a little. Looking at Alec, she could see why they would assume he bore a title. Even lounging there in breeches and a shirt that looked somewhat worse for wear, his pale hair a tousled mess, he still looked every inch a lord.

He came off the bed in one sudden, lithe move and, laying his hands on her hips, pulled her into him. He bent to take her mouth in a kiss that left her breathless. He lifted his head, his eyes gleaming down at her. "God, but you are beautiful!"

She gave a little laugh. "I fear for your eyesight, Lord Rawdon. I must look a slattern; my hair—"

"Your hair is magnificent." He emphasized his words by sinking his fingers into the heavy mass. "Black as night and so thick a man could get lost in it. Ever since I met you I have dreamt of seeing your hair spread across my pillow. Of burying my face in it."

His mouth was on hers again, urgent and hot. His hands cradled her head, holding her in place as his mouth ravished hers. All the hunger and heat that he had stoked into life in her earlier now burst into flame again. Damaris clutched his shoulders, her fingers curling into the cloth of his shirt. She ached with the need to touch him, hold him, feel him all around her, consuming her in his fire.

He tore his mouth from hers, his lips moving down the line of her throat, teeth nipping lightly at the tender skin, teasing her into shivers of delight. He groaned, soft and low in his throat, and the sound inflamed Damaris. She ran her fingers up into his hair, tangling in the silken strands. His mouth came back to kiss her deeply, and his hands roamed slowly down her body, caressing her through the soft cloth of the gown. Her breasts swelled as if to find his touch, and she moved her hips instinctively against him. He made a noise, part laugh, part moan, and he swept his hands down to grasp her buttocks, digging into the soft flesh and lifting her up and into him. His maleness pulsed against her.

Yearning blossomed between her legs, empty and aching to be filled by him. Only some last vestige of modesty kept her from lifting herself up and wrapping her legs around him. He kissed her face, her ears, her throat, as he bunched her nightgown up in his hands, lifting it higher until he was touching her bare flesh, caressing her buttocks, squeezing and lifting, pressing her into him. His breath rasped in and out. He stumbled backward, pulling her toward the bed.

A knock sounded on the door. "Sir? Ma'am? I've brought your dress."

Alec buried his face in her neck, muffling a curse.

"Just a moment!" Damaris managed to squeak out.

He squeezed her for an instant, then released her, turning away and going to stand before the fireplace and stare into its depths. Damaris brushed back her hair and straightened her gown and started to the door, her steps a little unsteady. There was nothing she could do to hide the evidence of her kiss-bruised lips, she knew, or the luminous glow in her eyes. She hated to imagine what Mrs. Putnam would think of her, standing in a stranger's house and letting a man kiss her into insensibility.

She wiped her hand over her face, drew in a breath, and opened the door. Mrs. Putnam stood outside, holding Damaris's dress before her. She took in Damaris's face in a quick glance and looked down to hide a smile.

"I fear it's the worse for wear," Babs said with a sigh for the state of the luxurious material.

Though the tumultuous state of Damaris's emotions left little room for thought of anything else, she could plainly see that the rain had ruined the delicate silk, leaving it streaked and warped. Mrs. Putnam had done her best with sewing up the tear, but nothing could make the dress anything but crumpled, shrunken, and stained.

"You are welcome to wear one of my gowns, if you'd like," the woman went on tentatively. "They're not what you're used to, I know, but your mister said you wouldn't mind."

"Of course I would not mind," Damaris assured her. "But I cannot take one of your dresses from you!"

"Oh, ma'am, I'd be honored!" Mrs. Putnam beamed at her so brightly that Damaris could not help but believe her.

"If you are certain," Damaris said, adding, "I shall send it back to you as soon as I get home, I promise."

Babs went to the dresser and opened a drawer, pulling out a simple gown of yellow cotton. It laced up the back and was decorated with a contrasting sash. "Would this suit?"

"It's lovely," Damaris told her, taking the dress. "You are very kind."

"That's that, then. Now, breakfast is almost ready, so you just put that on and come join us."

With a nod and a smile, she left the room, and Damaris turned slowly to face Alec. She had not dared even to glance at him the whole time their hostess was with them. He had apparently been keeping his attention just as steadfastly on the fireplace, for now he pivoted toward her. His face was still stamped with the unmistakable lines of desire, his lips fuller and softer, his eyes the color of the center of a flame. He offered her a faint smile.

"Much as I would like to, perhaps 'twould be best if I did not stay to watch you dress."

Damaris nodded and glanced away. "What are we—do you have any plans? Of what we should do, I mean."

"Putnam said he would take us in his wagon into town. A mail coach comes through there every day."

"A mail coach!" Damaris stared, laughter bubbling up in her at the thought of the aristocratic Rawdon riding shoulder to shoulder with farmers and merchants and grocers' wives in a mail coach.

"Not my preferred mode of travel, I admit. But unless you have more of the ready than I, we are not plump in the pocket."

"No, nor I. I have a little in my reticule, but most of it I put in my baggage for safekeeping, along with my letters of credit." Damaris sighed at the thought of her vanished trunks.

"And while no doubt I could sell my tie pin, I cannot but feel we would be less noticed if we traveled like ordinary folk. Putnam has offered to lend me clothes and a hat. We shall be entirely unremarkable."

Damaris refrained from pointing out that with his height and unusual coloring, Alec would stand out in any crowd no matter how ordinary his manner of dress. "Is it really necessary to disguise ourselves? Do you think those men will still be searching for us?"

Alec shrugged. "I shouldn't think so. But, frankly, I would not have thought they would pursue you out of town and attack you on the road, either. I think it is better to make preparations, just in case they are persistent."

"But what about your horse?"

"I shall leave Erebos here. I went out to look at him when I woke up, and 'tis clear Putnam took good care of him last night. Fast as Erebos is, we are safer, I think, without him. We are too easy to spot, and, riding double, we slow him down. Besides, I could not persuade Putnam to accept any gold for taking us in and giving us their bed, but he was willing to board Erebos for a fee, holding it a business transaction, not a favor. I shall send a groom to fetch Erebos once we are home."

"It was good of you to find a way to pay them."

He gave her a sardonic look. "I am aware you think I am arrogant beyond measure, but I do spare a thought now and then for others."

Damaris looked away from his bright gaze, abashed. "No, indeed, I know that you can be most kind. You have certainly been so to me. It is only . . . well, in my experience noblemen are not inclined to notice people of lesser station, much less take their problems into account."

"'Let them eat cake?'" he quoted, watching her quizzically. "My grandmother will tell you that I have an unfortunate affinity for those of lesser station, but it was usually they who hid me."

Damaris glanced up at him, startled by the peculiar remark. Had he said *hid* him?

Rawdon, too, looked faintly surprised at his words, and he went on quickly, "It is to be hoped that I have improved myself in your estimation." He sketched a playful bow toward her. "Now, I will leave you to put on your fetching frock."

Aside from the fact that it was obviously both too wide and too short for Damaris, Babs Putnam's dress was not much different from the simple styles in muslin and cambric that were the fashion these days. However, Damaris soon found out that it was nearly impossible to tie the fastenings up the back, at least the top ones, no matter how she stretched and twisted. Finally, she opened the door, intending to call to Mrs. Putnam to help her.

Alec was standing at the end of the short hall, looking into the room beyond, engaged in conversation with one of the younger Putnam children, a boy of about five. The boy was talking earnestly to Alec, who was gazing down at him with a bemused expression. The lad held out a colored wooden top as he jabbered away, his towhead tilted far back to gaze up at Alec. By the color of his hair, he could almost have been mistaken for Alec's child. Damaris's heart squeezed within her chest.

She thought of little Matthew, remembering his baptism, when Thea had handed Matthew to Alec and he had gazed down at the baby, his face a mingling of horror, awe, and a hint of yearning. Then, too, tears had clogged Damaris's throat, even as she smiled. She watched now, her eyes shimmering wetly, as Alec reached down and took the top.

"Do you mean me to spin it?" he asked gravely, squatting down as he wrapped the string around the toy. "Well, Master Jem, it has been years since I have done this, you understand." He gave a twist of his wrist, whipping the toy out onto the floor with the string, so that its tip struck the wooden floor and spun madly.

The boy let out a crow of delight, chasing the top, and Alec chuckled as he stood back up. Damaris could not help but laugh, and Alec turned and saw her. His gaze brightened as he ran his eyes down her, taking in the too-large dress as well as the sight of her bare ankles sticking out beneath it.

"Mrs. Howard, what a sight for sore eyes you are."

Damaris grimaced at him. "Do come here. I cannot fasten it by myself."

"Ah." Comprehension touched his features, and she thought his eyes turned even brighter. He turned back to the boy, saying, "Pray excuse me, Master Jem, I must answer my lady's call for help." He strode toward her, saying, "I am happy to serve as your maid, my dear."

Damaris stepped back and closed the door after him. "I could hardly call Mrs. Putnam with you standing right there."

"Of course not. 'Tis your husband's prerogative, anyway, to help you dress." His eyes danced, but there was a trace of heat in them as well.

Damaris could not keep her gaze from going to his mouth, remembering the taste and feel of his earlier kisses. She flushed and turned away, presenting him with her back. She pressed the sides of the dress to her back to conceal as much of her skin as possible, but it still sagged open in the middle, revealing a strip of skin down the column of her spine.

He reached out and, light as a feather, ran his forefinger down the bare skin.

"Alec . . ."

"Yes, dear?" He seemed lost in contemplation.

"You were going to tie the ties?"

"But of course. I am merely assessing the situation."

He scooped up her hair and lifted it away from her back, letting it fall over her shoulder. Damaris tried to control the tremor that ran through her as his fingertips grazed her skin.

"I must say, Mrs. Howard," he commented, taking the top ties in his hands, "you have a way of testing my control." There was a ragged edge to his voice.

"I do not mean to," Damaris replied.

"That makes it all the more enticing." He tied the last set of ribbons, then slid his hands around her waist to take the sides of the sash and pull them back. Damaris's stomach quivered in response. He tied the strands in a neat bow. "There." He pressed a kiss soft as a butterfly's touch on the nape of her neck.

Damaris hardly dared turn around. She did not want him to see what she was sure must be on her face. But neither could she resist looking at him. His face was as she had thought it would be—desire softening his lips and tinting the sharp line of his cheekbones with pink, his eyes fierce and compelling—and the sight of him made desire flicker teasingly deep within her.

He reached out, his hand cupping her cheek, and he brushed his thumb across her lips. "I will have you in my bed. I promise."

Damaris lifted her chin. "And do I have nothing to say about it?"

"Of course." His lips lifted slightly. "You shall say, 'Yes.'"

Twelve

$\mathcal{D}$amaris stared at him, unable to speak. It took all her concentration to keep her knees from collapsing and sending her to a puddle on the floor. She was not sure what she would have done if Alec had pulled her into his arms, as he had earlier this morning. But, fortunately for her composure, he stepped back, his hand falling from her face, then turned and left the room. Damaris released a long, shaky breath and leaned against the footboard of the bed until her heart returned to its usual rate. It was, she thought, a very good thing that she would be back in London this evening and not trapped in a bedchamber with Alec.

She heard the sound of voices and the clatter of dishes, and a moment later a timid scratching at the door proved to be Babs's oldest girl, Maud, informing her with a shy smile that breakfast was on the table. Donning a pretense of calm, Damaris followed her into the large room at the front of the house.

The Putnams were gathered around a sturdy wood table on one side of the room, with Alec seated in the place of honor at the head of the table. The spot to his left had been left vacant, obviously for Damaris. She scarcely glanced at Alec as she slid into her seat, for fear that what she felt would be clear on her face for everyone to see. She wasn't sure how she would get through the meal.

But, as it turned out, it was difficult to remain tense in the midst of the cheerful, chattering Putnam brood. Damaris soon relaxed and dug into her food with relish, finding that it provided her a good deal of amusement to watch Alec, accustomed to gold charger plates and servants at his elbow dishing out his food, as he adjusted to spooning out porridge from a large bowl passed all around or receiving a hunk of bread from a child's hand. He glanced over at Damaris after one particularly unnerving moment involving young Jem, a slab of butter, and a jar of jam, and surprised her by grinning like a boy.

She smiled back, her hand going out impulsively to his wrist, and he turned his hand, taking her palm in his. His hand swallowed hers, warm and strong, and happiness bubbled up in Damaris, as light and airy as summer, utterly at odds with their stranded circumstances.

After breakfast, Mr. Putnam went out to hitch his team to the wagon, and Alec went into the bedroom to change into the farmer's clothes. While Babs and the girls cleared the table, Damaris made herself useful by wiping it clean. She had just finished and was about to take the damp cloth back to Mrs. Putnam when she saw Alec emerging from the bedroom.

A snort escaped her at the sight of his long, elegant form clad in Putnam's loose cotton farming smock, though she immediately tried to cover her amusement by dropping her cloth and bending down to retrieve it. On second glance, however, he appeared equally absurd, and she could not keep from dissolving into laughter.

"I fail to see what you find so amusing," Alec said, drawing himself up in his haughtiest manner.

"Oh, Raw—I mean, Alec, you would not say that if you could see yourself."

"I did," he admitted, a smile tugging at the corner of his mouth. "That is why I am wearing my own breeches and boots. If you had seen me in the others, you would have howled."

He settled a shapeless straw hat on his head, and that set Damaris off into another gale of laughter. Alec rolled his eyes and came over to take her arm. "Come, my dear, before our benefactors decide that I helped you escape from Bedlam."

They bade good-bye to Mrs. Putnam and each of the children. Damaris noticed that Alec managed to slip a halfpenny into each child's hand as he shook it. He lifted the sack in which he and Damaris had put their other clothes and they walked out to the wagon.

It took them over an hour in the slow-moving wagon to reach the village of Little Fornton, the nearest spot where they could catch a mail coach heading back to London. At Rawdon's insistence, Putnam set them down near the church, and Alec and Damaris started toward the inn on foot to wait for the mail coach.

"Why did you want him to leave us here?" Damaris asked.

Alec, the sack slung over his shoulder, was carefully watching the street around them. "It is safer that way. I can get a better idea of the lay of the land as we approach the inn."

"Are you always like this?"

"Like what?"

"Living your life as if it were a . . . a campaign?"

He shrugged. "I prefer to know what's coming at me. It is especially handy when one is running from something."

"You sound as if you are accustomed to running from things."

Alec cocked an eyebrow at her. "Mrs. Howard! Are you calling me a coward?"

"Don't be absurd. You know I am not. In fact, I would almost think that you enjoy a fight."

"Perhaps I do, at that. But I much prefer a fight where I win, which is easier to do if one plans ahead." He cut his eyes to her, then went on, "There were some chaps at school who liked to lie in wait for me. That's how I met Gabriel, you know; he jumped in to help me once."

"Why did they attack you?"

"I was new. And they took exception to my manner. I may have told them that I had little concern for their opinion."

"Imagine that."

"Yes. No doubt you will have trouble believing it of me, but I could be a mite insolent when I was young."

They had reached the yard of the inn, and Alec paused at the edge, casting a long look around, before they continued to the door. Inside, they slid into a table at the edge of the public room. There were only a few people besides the tapster behind the bar, but every eye in the place turned to look at them. Damaris knew that her face was fairly well hidden by Mrs. Putnam's bonnet, but neither that nor the clothes Alec had donned could hide the fact that they were strangers here.

They were far too full from Babs's breakfast to eat, but Alec ordered a glass of porter, and after a few minutes, the other occupants of the room stopped staring at them. Damaris glanced around the room with some interest. She had never been in the public room of an inn before, for when she had traveled, she had, of course, always eaten in one of the small private rooms.

It was smaller than she had expected and rather dark, with only one old mullioned glass window and plaster walls smudged with years of soot from the large fireplace at the far end of the room. The bar along one wall was made of walnut, scarred and nicked and slightly uneven. Damaris looked over at Alec. Despite his clothes, it was clear that he did not belong here. He had turned his ring around so that the square chunk of gold etched with the design was hidden from view, leaving only the plain gold band, but his long fingers were too pale and uncallused, the hands of a man who had worn gloves most of his life. And no one, she thought, could look into that face and not see the generations of aristocrats who had formed it.

Alec stiffened beside her, and she followed his gaze. Two

men had walked into the room through the other door and were headed for the bar. Alarm shot through Damaris. Even from the back, she recognized them, and when one of them turned his head to glance toward the fireplace, she was certain. They were two of the men who had accosted them on the road yesterday.

Quick and quiet as a cat, Alec slid out from his chair, settling his hat low on his head. Damaris looked down so that the wide scoop brim of her bonnet would hide her features, and she slipped out after him. Just as Alec whisked her into the hallway, she saw out of the corner of her eye that the attacker was turning toward her. An instant later there was a shout behind them. Alec ran for the door, pulling Damaris after him.

Damaris was glad for the too-short dress Mrs. Putnam had given her, for there was no danger of its dragging on the ground as they tore across the courtyard. A rider had just dismounted from his horse and handed the reins over to a groom when Damaris and Alec darted toward them. The horse reared, and the groom stumbled back and fell to the ground.

Alec scooped up the reins, tossed Damaris onto the horse's back, and vaulted into the saddle after her. The groom let out a shout, as did the owner of the horse, but before either of them could reach them, Alec dug his heels into their new mount's sides and they charged off down the street. Behind them the courtyard erupted into a cacophony of shouts and curses.

Alec shoved the sack he had been carrying into Damaris's hands. She grasped it with one hand and wrapped her other arm around Alec's waist, holding on tightly. She was in a far more precarious position than she had been yesterday, for she was sitting sideways, and she could do little but hang on and hope for the best.

Two men standing in the street, chatting, looked up and jumped aside as they raced toward them. A woman leaving a shop shrieked and dropped a package. At the village green, Alec turned their horse up the intersecting road. It, fortunately, was deserted, and they flew unimpeded down the lane toward the church where Putnam had let them off only a few minutes before.

A few yards past the church, Alec pulled the horse up short and slid from his back, reaching up to lift Damaris down, too. He gave the animal a sharp slap on the rear, and it took off at a run. Alec took the sack from Damaris and grabbed her hand, and they raced along the side of the church. Damaris saw now what Alec had apparently noted earlier—a narrow track that led away from the lane and disappeared into a copse of trees no more than fifty yards before them.

Alec flung the sack over his shoulder, and they ran. Damaris did not waste time looking back. If they could reach the trees before their pursuers reached the church, Alec's ruse would work, at least for a while. Since the men would either have to run on foot or wait for the groom to get their horses, she and Alec just might have enough time to disappear.

She heard no hue and cry as they darted into the trees.

They were forced to slow down for fear of stumbling over a root or running into a low-hanging branch, but even so, it did not take long before they were deep in the trees, hidden from sight. Alec came to a stop and turned to Damaris. She leaned over, gasping for air. Alec, too, was breathing hard, but he looked around them, assessing their situation.

"How—" Damaris gasped out, "—did you know about this place?"

"I noticed it when Putnam was letting us off earlier. I have no idea where this track goes, but if we've any luck, they will follow the horse out of town until they find him riderless. Even then, they can't be sure of where we dismounted." He paused. "Are you all right? We should go on."

Damaris nodded. "It has been some time since I've run like that, but I shall manage."

She looked at him. His floppy straw hat had flown off when they charged away on the horse, and Alec's hair was wild and tangled about his head. His blue eyes snapped with excitement, and his cheeks were stained with color.

"You're enjoying this," she said accusingly.

He laughed. "Perhaps I am. Nothing like a chase to bring up one's blood."

"Well, I would just as soon not be the quarry," Damaris commented, and started off down the track, which was barely discernible beneath the trees.

Alec followed her, pulling off his farmer's smock, revealing his own shirt beneath, and stuffed the smock into his sack. They walked steadily and soon emerged from the stand of trees. Damaris felt dreadfully exposed without the concealing shelter of the woods, but there was nothing for it but to continue walking. The path ran along one side of a meadow, then over a stile and onto a lane. There was more risk of getting caught on the road, but the going was so much faster and easier that they could not pass up the opportunity. The lane eventually reached another, larger, road.

"I am utterly lost," Damaris confessed as Alec looked up and down the road. "Have you any idea where we are?"

"The sun hasn't reached the middle of the sky yet, so that way must be east. Unless I am mistaken, Little Fornton is that direction." He pointed vaguely to his right. "I think this road might run parallel to the one by the inn. I'd say, let's go this way."

After a few minutes of walking, they heard the distinct sound of someone whistling merrily. Hastily, they crossed to the other side of the road and took shelter behind a stand of flowering bushes. Soon a cart come trundling into sight, drawn by a pair of oxen, and a sturdy country lad walked beside them, directing the pair. Damaris relaxed and looked at Alec.

"What shall we do?"

"I suspect that, for a few shillings, that lad would be happy to let us ride on top of his turnips. The cart appears only half-filled."

"But if those men should happen down the road . . ."

"Yes, we would be quite exposed." He hesitated, looking down at her. "I'd take my chances in a fight with them . . ."

"I am sure you would," Damaris murmured.

He slanted a quelling glance at her and continued, "However, I cannot in good conscience expose you to further danger."

"The danger is because of me," Damaris reminded him. "I am the one who has exposed you to it. And if I remember correctly, I managed to hold my own in that fight."

The corners of his eyes crinkled. "So you did. You have your hatpin at the ready?"

Damaris reached up to touch the side of her bonnet, into which she had slid the long pin for safekeeping. Alec chuckled.

"Very well, then. I say we ask the young man for a ride. We'll not get very far on foot."

As Alec had predicted, the youngster, though startled to see two people emerging at the side of the road, was happy enough to earn a bit of money to let them ride on the cart. Alec handed her up with all the elegance of a gentleman assisting a lady into the finest carriage, and they settled down in one corner.

"It's a good deal too bad I lost my hat," Alec commented, sliding a sideways glance at Damaris, who let out an unladylike snort of laughter. "You may laugh," he told her sternly, "but my smock is simply not the same without it."

"No doubt. Still, I think it was a disguise well lost. You were not—how shall I say this?—entirely believable in the role."

"I thought I made an excellent farmer," Alec retorted loftily.

Damaris rolled her eyes. "Oh, indeed. I am sure that no one noticed the set of your chin or the way you look just so . . ." She tilted her head up and cast a supercilious look down her nose.

Alec's brows vaulted up and he lifted his chin in much the same gesture Damaris had just employed. "I beg your pardon."

Damaris burst into laughter, and Alec's eyes glinted with humor.

"It has been a refreshing journey, really," he went on in the same vein. "An invigorating tramp through the woods, a relaxing ride down a country lane . . ."

"Don't forget the jaunt through town on a stranger's horse this morning."

"True."

"And we have met so many interesting people."

"Indeed," Alec agreed, adding judiciously, "It makes me appreciate how dull my life was before I met you." Alec picked up her hand and laced his fingers through hers.

Damaris looked down at his long, aristocratic fingers tangled with hers and said in a suddenly sober voice, "I am very grateful to you, you know."

He made a quick gesture of denial. "No, really . . . I assure you . . ."

"No, do not think you can slip out of receiving my thanks." Damaris clasped his hand firmly and placed her other hand on his as well, holding it to her chest and looking at him earnestly.

"Dear lady, I would not dream of taking my hand from where it rests."

Damaris grimaced. "And I will not allow you to quip your way out of my gratitude, either. I hate to think what would have happened if you had not ridden after me. Even though I had refused your help, you came to my aid. I have not always . . . thought the best of noblemen, shall we say? But you have truly been a gentleman. I—" She faced him squarely, her blue eyes looking deep into his. "However much I may tease you, I admire you."

She felt his skin flare with heat beneath her fingers, and his eyes were almost silver in the sunlight. "Damaris." His voice was husky. "Your teasing is a source of infinite pleasure to me." He raised her hand to his lips and kissed it. His breath was warm on her skin, sending feathery ripples through her.

"Now, here," he went on, reaching out to untie the ribbons of her simple bonnet and remove it. He pulled her to him, settling her into the crook of his arm, her head on his shoulder. "'Twill be a long way to town, I am sure. You get some rest. I will keep watch for marauders."

Smiling, Damaris nestled against him, and, lulled by the steady beat of his heart beneath her ear, she dozed off. It was a long time later that she came awake, roused by the peal of church bells. She sat up and glanced around. They were rolling into another town.

"Welcome to Dartford, wife," Alec said cheerfully.

"Dartford?" Damaris repeated, anxiety rising in her. "We are back on the road to Dover?"

"We will cross it," Alec agreed. "So we must keep an eye out for our friends. But young Ned tells me that public stages stop here at the White Bull, where he will so kindly let us off, and I intend to find one going in an entirely different direction."

As they rattled through the streets of the town, Alec pulled his jacket from the sack and put it on, and wrapped his neckcloth around his neck, securing it with the ruby tie pin. "No doubt I look a thorough sloven in these clothes, but I fear the farmer's smock would only make me more recognizable to those men, now that they saw us in Little Fornton."

Damaris looked at him critically. Mrs. Putnam had done her best to clean his clothes, but it was clear that they had seen better days, being rather rumpled and stained, with a tear on one sleeve that Mrs. Putnam had carefully darned. "Perhaps you look a mite ... purse-pinched."

"Delightful. So I shall only appear in the basket—better, I suppose, than appearing to be foxed."

"Of course your ruby pin is at odds with the look."

"No doubt everyone will assume it's paste." He flashed a quick grin at her.

The cart boy let them out in front of the inn's courtyard, and they found that they were in luck, for a stagecoach sat in the courtyard, its team being changed out by the ostlers. A few questions to one of the ostlers won them the information that it would be departing as soon as the driver and guard had finished their meals.

"But it is going to Gravesend," Damaris whispered as they walked into the inn. "Not London."

Alec kept his watchful gaze on everything around them as he answered, "Yes. However, it is leaving immediately, which at the moment I find more appealing than any destination. Besides, I have something in mind."

A comprehensive look around the public room apparently convinced Alec that the place held no dangers for them, and he turned to Damaris. "Sit here and keep your eyes open. I shall purchase our seats on the stage." He paused, looking vaguely uncomfortable. "Ah, it seems that—I fear that I am about to run out of coins." He raised his hand to his tie pin, looking thoughtful. "There is scarcely time to find a place to sell this."

"Don't be silly. There is no need. I have money in my reticule." Damaris pulled out a few paper notes and thrust them into his hand.

Looking somewhat reluctant, he took the bills and walked away. Damaris slipped into the nearest chair. A large woman in a purple bonnet was sitting at the table next to her, watching her with interest. She nodded cheerfully at Damaris and said in a confidential tone, "My man was allus the same way—money ran through his fingers. I had to keep it for him."

"Oh. Yes, well. He has, um, experienced some losses."

"I knew it." The woman nodded again. "Are you taking the stage, then? I'm visiting my sister Meg. Expecting again, so I'm to take care of them. My Hal, he said she didn't need me, but he don't know Meg like I do. Fourth little one."

"Oh. My." Damaris was somewhat overcome by the woman's spate of words and unsure how she was supposed to respond.

Apparently no response was necessary, as the woman swept on, "I'm Ethel Sanders, by the by."

She looked expectantly at Damaris, and Damaris fumbled for an answer, "Oh, um, Mrs. Powell."

"Pleased to meet you." The woman moved on. "Was it gambling?"

"Excuse me?" Damaris stared at her blankly.

"That made him fall on hard times." Mrs. Sanders jerked her head in the general direction of Alec. "Was it gambling? It's allus what gets them, isn't it—the gentlemen, I mean. And he looks like a gentleman. You can allus tell a gentleman by his hands, I say."

She rattled on, and since Damaris realized that the woman needed little response to continue, she soon gave up trying to follow the jumps and starts of her new companion's conversation, making do with a smile or a nod or a "Really?" every now and then.

"My dear." Alec reappeared at her side, and Damaris realized, with a guilty start, that she had not been paying attention to the people around them.

"Oh. Yes." Damaris sprang to her feet. "Is it time to go?"

"You've time yet," Mrs. Sanders assured her. "They haven't even blown the horn. Not used to traveling the stage, are you?" She turned to Alec. "Good thing you came to your senses."

"I beg your pardon?" Alec's brows rose slightly, and his voice was tinged with frost.

"You've a fine wife; it's not worth throwing it all away in gambling dens."

"My good woman—" Alec began, ending with a small grunt of pain as Damaris brought her foot down on his. He turned to her, frowning. "What—"

"Mrs. Sanders was just saying that she could tell you were, you know, experiencing financial difficulties. That is why we have to take the stage."

His eyes widened slightly, but he said only, "Yes. I see. Well. Um."

"No need to be embarrassed," Mrs. Sanders said grandly. "Some are good with their coins and some aren't. Just let the missus take care of it, and you stay away from the cards, and you'll be back on your legs in no time, I'll warrant."

A horn sounded loudly in the courtyard, and Mrs. Sanders stood up. As they followed her out of the inn to the coach, Alec leaned down and murmured, "Did you have to tell her I had gambled away my money? Couldn't I have been a poor but honest clergyman?"

Damaris giggled. "I didn't tell her anything. I cannot help it if you have that dissipated look about you. Oh, and you are Mr. Powell."

"Mr. Pow—oh, very well. I shall simply keep my mouth shut."

"In that regard, I can assure you that you will have no choice."

The coach was nearly full, and Damaris had to swallow a smile at seeing the Earl of Rawdon squeezed into a seat between a sour-faced old man and their new friend Mrs. Sanders, who proceeded to regale Alec with her story of going to help her poor younger sister, though her delicacy of mind prompted her to leave out so many details of her sister's condition and to use so many euphemisms that it was difficult to understand precisely what she was talking about. But the confused expression in Alec's eyes was soon replaced by a glazed one that lasted the rest of the way to their destination.

The trip seemed unending, and though Damaris's nerves were stretched, fearing that at any moment their pursuers were going to stop the carriage and find them inside, the ride was also profoundly boring and uncomfortable. The seat was hard, she could not even talk to Alec, and the swaying of the big, clumsy coach made her slightly ill.

It had turned dark by the time they reached Gravesend. Damaris was glad to climb down; though they had stopped once to change horses and she had been able to get down and stretch her cramped muscles, she was once again quite stiff. She emerged rather cautiously from the carriage, glancing about as she took Alec's hand.

The courtyard was lit only by the ostler's lantern, leaving the corners darkly shadowed. She told herself that it was most unlikely that the men who had chased her would be here. How could they have known she would come here? Anyone would logically assume she was headed for Maidstone or Dover. Still, she could not help but feel a little tingle of dread up her spine.

She had been afraid that they would not be able to get away from their newfound friend Mrs. Sanders, but luckily the woman turned her attention to getting her bags, which had been stored in the rope "basket" on the back of the carriage, and Alec and Damaris were able to slip out of the inn yard unnoticed.

There was still money in Damaris's reticule, though it was dwindling, and Alec used it to get them a place at an inn that looked more respectable than some of the others they had passed. Weary as she was, Damaris followed Rawdon up the stairs, scarcely taking notice of their surroundings. It wasn't until he had closed the door behind them and Damaris had dropped down onto the settee by the fireplace that she took a comprehensive look around and realized, with a sudden sizzle of nerves, that once again they were sharing a bedroom.

Thirteen

Damaris's eyes flew to Alec's face, and what she was thinking must have showed in her expression, for he shifted uncomfortably and said, "I am sorry. They had only one private room left. I did not like to leave you alone, in any case. I'm not sure I could get to you in time if you needed me. This seemed . . . for the best. I hope you will not think that I have any intention of putting you in a situation that—well, I mean, of maneuvering or forcing you into—oh, devil take it! I am no good at prettying up my language. I know that what I said this morning might make you think otherwise, but I did not do this to compel you to sleep with me."

"I know." Damaris had experience with men who were happy to lie to a woman to get what they wanted, and she knew that Alec was not one of them.

But she also knew what had happened this morning, and the memory of it made her shiver. Not just the consuming kisses after Alec returned to the room. Not only his blunt words that still reverberated through her, the promise that he would have her in his bed. More than all that, it was the thought of the blissful pleasure his seeking hands had awakened in her early this morning that made her wary of spending a night in this room with him. Alec had been asleep and dreaming; no doubt he had no idea what had transpired, but Damaris had been fully aware, and she knew she would never forget the passion that had surged through her, shattering her into a thousand pieces.

There was a very real danger in staying in this room with him, a danger to her heart and to the comfortable, content life she lived. She knew the kind of life that awaited her if she gave herself to the Earl of Rawdon, and she was determined not to fall into that trap.

Damaris straightened, pulling her strength together, and said, "It is a, um, very inappropriate situation." She sounded horridly miss-ish, even to herself. "You would not wish to have your sister in a similar position, I am sure."

"Good Gad, I should think not!" The horrified look on his face was enough to make Damaris laugh, but she kept her lips firmly clamped together. He swung away, then turned back. "But I should not wish her to spend the night unprotected, either. Especially not if someone had been chasing her across the countryside. I—I shall put this chair in front of the door and sleep in it."

Damaris cast a doubtful glance at the rather rickety narrow chair.

"Unless you prefer that I sleep in the hall across your door." His voice assumed some of its old hauteur.

"No, of course not. I am not *unreasonable*, I hope."

"I assure you that I am capable of not acting upon my baser instincts," he told her, lifting a brow.

Damaris was not about to tell him that she was not entirely certain that she could say the same about herself. She turned away, saying stiffly, "I am sure that we can manage here together well enough, as long as we are mindful. Careful."

"Of course."

Damaris looked around her. She did not know what to do or say. The room was small, and the bed seemed to fill it. There was no place to sit other than the one chair or the bed, and it seemed much too suggestive to sit casually on the bed. Her face and hands felt gritty, and she was sure that beneath the bonnet, her hair was a mess. For some reason, the realization that she did not even have a brush was enough to make the tears start in her eyes. She blinked furiously and drew a steadying breath.

"If you will excuse me," Alec said, "I believe I shall go downstairs and see if I can procure us something to eat."

Damaris turned and smiled at him. She knew he was tactfully giving her a chance to be alone, and she was grateful. "Thank you."

"Mm. You may wish to hold those thanks until you see what I manage to find."

After he left, Damaris pulled off her bonnet and did what she could to freshen up. At least there was a washstand in the room and water in the pitcher so that she was able to wash. There was little help for her hair except to take out the few hairpins she had left in it and run her fingers through it to disperse some of the tangles. She was trying in vain to restore some order to her tresses when a soft knock sounded at the door and Alec entered, carrying a tray.

"Alec!" Damaris's voice lilted upward in delight as a delicious aroma filled the air. "Food?"

"I was able to wheedle some scraps from the cook. Meat pie, mostly, and a bit of bread." He set the tray down on the bed.

"Anything sounds wonderful to me. I am starving," Damaris admitted, going over to inspect the tray. "Oh! You even got a bit of cake."

"Bought by flattery and a sixpence." He had set the tray down more or less in the middle of the bed, and he whisked off his boots and perched on the other side. "Sit down. Enjoy it." He made a show of tucking a napkin into his neckcloth, then whipped another one off the tray and handed it to her. "Meat pies are messy business."

Damaris laughed and followed his example, sitting down on the bed and picking up a small meat pie. It was so hot it burned her mouth, but she was too hungry to care. It was a messy meal, the crust flaking everywhere, and she had cause to be thankful for the placement of the napkin. But she had rarely enjoyed a meal more. Her hunger added a zest to the food unequaled by any sauce, and the cup of milk tasted better than the finest wine. Best of all was sitting there, feet tucked up under her, with Alec cross-legged on the other side of the tray, as if they were picnicking on the bed. They talked and laughed, going over their day's adventures again and repeating choice bits of Mrs. Sanders's conversation.

"Is *that* what she was talking about?" Alec exclaimed when

Damaris explained to him that the woman's sister's affliction was pregnancy.

"Yes! And apparently the poor woman has to endure a months-long visit from her every time she has a child."

"That would be enough to put one off of having children forever. Hmm." He looked thoughtful. "Yes, I can see how if one left out every reference to giving birth or pregnancy or lying-in that it might come out that way. I thought the poor woman was wasting away of some unmentionable disease, though I could not imagine what."

"Mrs. Sanders would not want to bring up such lewd topics with a gentleman," Damaris told him.

"Oh, aye, especially an inveterate gambler such as myself," he retorted. "Feel free to slander my character any other time you choose, by the way."

"I did not!" Damaris protested, laughing. "It was Mrs. Sanders who was sure you had lost your money on cards and dice. She said it was always so with gentlemen."

"No doubt." He took a bite of the cake, then leaned closer and popped a bit of it into her mouth.

His fingers brushed her lip, and suddenly the food became flavorless on her tongue. She was overwhelmingly aware of the state of her hair falling loose around her shoulders and that they were sitting together on a bed. Entirely alone and distant from everyone they knew. She gazed at him, her eyes caught by his ice-blue gaze. She thought of his lips on her. His hands. The heat that had surged up in his skin when he touched her, as if someone had laid a spark to a torch.

No one need ever know what happened here tonight. The thought dangled tantalizingly in front of her.

Except, of course, that *she* would know. She would hope and dream, and gradually her comfortable life would slip right through her fingers, no longer in her control. Damaris turned away and slid off the bed. Reaching down, she ripped another bit of ruffle from her mistreated petticoat and used it to tie her hair back. She turned back to face him.

"Thank you for supper," she said, her voice and face formal.

"You are welcome." His face changed, too, and he followed her lead, leaving his relaxed position on the bed and standing up. He set the tray aside on the dresser and turned back to her. "It is time to talk, is it not?"

The grave expression on his face, the way he stood, arms crossed over his chest, sent little prickles of warning through her. "About what?" She suspected that she knew what was coming, and she had little desire to face it. However, she could not continue to keep Alec in ignorance. He had done too much for her, taken too many risks.

"About those men. Who are they? Why are they after you? I find it difficult to believe that this is simply a 'family matter.'"

"It seems excessive," Damaris agreed. "Truly, Alec, I do not know who they are. I have never seen them before the other day when they seized me. I assume that they were hired."

"Who hired them?"

"I don't know, but I think ... perhaps ... it was my father's mother."

"Your *grandmother*?" He stared at her in disbelief. "Are you seriously telling me that your grandmother hired a bunch of ruffians to abduct you? Why?"

"Because I am a scandal to her. I am a reminder of the way her son flouted her for years, how he brought shame to the family name. I am . . ." She took a breath and said quickly, "I was born on the wrong side of the blanket."

He continued to look at her. She could not read his expression.

"I am sorry," Damaris went on quickly. "I should have told you earlier. But it is not the sort of thing one blurts out when one first meets someone. Clearly, I should have told you when you invited me to your party. I shouldn't have gone to it. It was very wrong of me to put you and your family in that position."

"That doesn't matter. I am glad you didn't stay away from the ball. If you had, I would not have been able to waltz with you."

She gave him a fleeting smile. "That is very nice of you to say."

"My dear girl, I think you have me mistaken for someone else. You keep telling me I am kind or nice, and I promise you that I am not known for either quality. Nor is 'good' a word that is usually attached to my name."

"You have been all those things to me. And I have repaid your kindness poorly. I should not have accepted the invitation. I know that no one would fault a man such as yourself for . . . keeping company with a woman like me, but it is a different matter for your sister and your grandmother. They would not like the *ton* thinking that they are friends with a woman whose mother was an actress and who was not married to her father."

"I am not sure that my grandmother is friends with anyone," Alec told her lightly. "However, I am confident that she has known other people whose parents were not married—at least, not to each other."

"I will not tell you again that you are kind, since you seem to mislike it. But I am not naïve or foolish enough to believe that your grandmother would not be most upset if she knew who I was. She would think, rightfully so, that I had deceived all of you, and she would be embarrassed in front of society."

"I can promise you that my grandmother would not for a moment accede to the idea that anyone else had the right to disapprove of her or what she did. As a result, she is rarely embarrassed. You need not worry about that." He paused, frowning. "But I fear I still do not understand why you think your grandmother would hire thugs to abduct you. The scandal was years ago, after all."

"Yes, but I think she fears that it would all come up again if I were in London, going to *ton* parties. You see, I have never done so before. I went to school in Switzerland, and after my father's death, my mother and I remained on the Continent. I did not return to England until last year, and I have stayed in Chesley all that time. I don't believe any of them knew I was here. But she saw me at your party. I did not even realize who she was, but she knew me. She came up to me during the ball, and she was livid. She told me she wanted me to leave England, that I would bring shame and scandal on her family."

Damaris was not about to tell him the rest of her scandalous past. She was not even sure that her grandmother knew about her hasty marriage or that it played any part in Lady Sedbury's fear of scandal. In any case, it was not something Alec needed to hear. "That night, when I came to you, I had no idea who the men were or why they would have attacked me. It was only afterward that I realized they must have been hired by Lady Sedbury to remove me from England."

"Lady Sedbury is your grandmother?" At Damaris's nod, Alec went on, "Then your father was . . .". He looked thoughtful. "The present Lord Sedbury's father?"

"Clement, yes. Did you know him?"

"Vaguely. I saw him at the club a time or two when I was first on the town. We did not really move in the same circles."

"My father was a quiet man, the sort who liked his hearth and home, except that he did not really like the home he was born to."

"I don't remember any scandal surrounding him."

"You would have been too young. When my father was a young man, he fell in love with an actress. So much in love that he not only bought her a pretty little house, but he went to live with her there, as if they were man and wife."

"If your mother looked like you, it is little wonder that he was willing to face scandal to be with her."

"One could argue that he might have shown some restraint . . . or maybe enough courage to stand up to his family," Damaris retorted tartly. "But he was unable to do either. When his father died and he inherited the title, his family convinced him that he must do his duty and marry a suitable woman. Someone from his own class. And so, when I was eight, he left us." Her eyes flashed, and she lifted her chin. "He could not stay away entirely, of course. He visited my mother now and then. He would chuck me under the chin and tell me I was his girl. But I knew, of course, that it was no longer true. I was his bastard daughter, the one he would not openly acknowledge." Tears sparkled in her eyes, and she dashed them away angrily. "Oh, blast it all. I am not going to cry about him."

Alec went to her, but she turned her head aside, unwilling to let him see the hurt in her eyes. Gently he took her chin in his hand and tilted her face upward so that she had to meet his gaze.

"He loved you," he said firmly. "No matter what he did or how many other children he had, he loved you. I am sure of it."

"So he told me. But such assurances meant little to an eight-year-old girl who was used to her father tucking her in every night. He vanished, turning up every now and then with a present and a kiss. It was hard for me to understand that he had another family now, that they were somehow better than we were."

"Oh, Damaris." His arms went around her, and he pulled her to him.

For a moment, she remained stiff in his arms, resisting; but then, with a sigh, she gave in and rested her head against his chest. The ache in her chest somehow did not hurt so much when she was standing in the warmth and strength of his embrace and his heart was beating reassuringly against her ear.

"He provided for me always," she said, pushing back the tears that swelled in her throat, choking her. "He paid for me to go to a proper school for ladies, far from England, where they would not despise me for who my mother was. When he died, he left me well provided for. But it wasn't the same as having a father."

Alec curled down over her, resting his head on hers. "Sometimes, it is better not to have a father," he said, his voice grim.

His tender gesture pierced Damaris to the heart, and, surprising herself, she burst into tears, clinging to him and crying out her pain against his broad chest. Alec scooped her up and sat down in the old wooden rocker, cradling her to him. He rocked her gently, murmuring low words of comfort as his hand moved soothingly up and down her back.

When, at last, her sobs quieted and she rested, drained and still, against him, he said, "Your father was weak, I know, but do not doubt that he loved you. I know the demands that were put on him. No matter how well he loved you and your mother, no matter how much he preferred to live happily with you, there is a burden that weighs on one along with the title. Your life is not always your own. It is something you learn from the cradle; duty to your family is drummed into you at every turn."

He pressed his lips against her hair, silent for a moment, then went on in a voice tinged with remembered pain, "Everything you do has consequences for your family. When I— when Jocelyn ran away, the scandal did not scorch me only. It caused untold embarrassment and pain for my sister and grandmother. They had to endure the whispers about my fault in the matter, the speculation that I was a cruel monster who had sent a sweet young girl running in panic."

"No, Alec, that is so unfair!" Damaris stirred in his arms, lifting her head to look at him. Her lovely face was streaked with tears, eyelashes clumped together in starlike bursts around her eyes, so that she looked, if possible, even more beautiful. "You are not cruel at all."

He smiled and cupped her face, wiping the tears from her cheeks with his thumbs. "Don't cry for me. I am long past all that. Sweet as it is, I am not asking for your sympathy. What I want to say is that, hard as it was for me, it was worse, I think, for my family. There were even one or two old cats who snubbed Genevieve and my grandmother, and everywhere they went, they had to endure the rumors, the looks, the disdain of people not worth a tenth of them." His voice hardened, his gaze turning inward. "Grandmother feared it had even harmed Genevieve's chances of making a spectacular marriage—though Genevieve swore to me that she never cared about that. The truth is, my actions caused them harm. I knew Jocelyn did not feel for me as I felt for her; I was stubbornly, selfishly certain I could make her happy, could make her love me. But by chasing my foolish dreams of love, I hurt everyone around me."

"But you should not have to give up what you want," Damaris protested.

Alec shrugged. "'Tis harsh, perhaps. But the truth is, when you are given so much, you have to accept the responsibilities, too. And that is what your father did. He took on that burden for his family. He sacrificed his happiness—and it is dreadful that his act caused you such pain. But it did not mean he did not love you. All those times he came back to see you, it was because he loved you; that was where he was happy. His home and heart were with you."

"Thank you for telling me." Damaris's heart swelled with warmth and tenderness. She knew Alec was not a man who shared his secrets easily, and it touched her that he had revealed himself to such an extent in order to make her feel better.

He looked down at her in that way of his, in which only his eyes smiled, and laid a caressing hand against her cheek. "Why didn't you tell me about yourself?"

"It is not the sort of thing one tells a stranger."

"And I am a stranger?" There was a hint of hurt in his eyes.

"No. Of course you are not. But I—I wanted to hide it from you. I didn't want you to look at me differently. As if I was . . . less than you had thought."

"And you thought I would? That I would hold your birth against you?"

"I think that you are an earl. And a man." She pulled away from him and stood up. She could not lie in his arms and say the rest. "And I am the illegitimate daughter of an actress. I did not believe you would despise me. But I would no longer be a lady to you. I didn't want you to—to try to seduce me because I am not a lady. I did not want to be someone you could bed because my virtue need not concern you." Her voice shook, and she turned aside, annoyed with her own weakness.

"Damaris." He rose to his feet and faced her. "I feel nothing different for you than I did before I knew who your mother was or what your father did." He raised his hand and stroked his knuckles gently down her cheek. "And I can promise you, without any doubt or prevarication, that my desire to have you in my bed has nothing to do with your father or the circumstances of your birth. You are the reason I want you. Only you."

His eyes were bright, with that cold clarity that seared as much as any heat, and Damaris's heart warmed within her. Impulsively she went up on tiptoe and pressed her lips to his briefly. "Thank you."

She had pressed her hands against his chest as she went up to kiss him, and she felt the heat rush in him, even through his shirt. His hands went to her waist, his fingers sinking into her flesh. She knew he was about to kiss her. She could see the hunger in his face—in the softening of his mouth, the intensity of his gaze. He wanted her, and Rawdon was a man accustomed to having what he wanted. He moved closer to her, his face looming above her, and Damaris's head fell back.

She waited for his kiss; she wanted it. Her nerves were alive, sizzling with the memory of his hands on her this morning, the pleasure of his long, skillful fingers. She leaned into him, her body drawn toward its desire as surely as the tides to the moon. Her breasts were tender and aching for his touch. His hands slid restlessly down her side and curved over her hips, then back up. They stood, balanced on the razor's edge of passion, for a long, yearning moment.

Alec pulled himself back, his hands releasing her, and with a final heated flash of his eyes, he turned away.

"You should get some rest. I—I'll take a walk."

Damaris watched him walk out the door.

It was good that he had left, she knew. She would have been filled with bitter disappointment if he had taken advantage of the moment and tried to seduce her into his bed. Not only had he refrained, but he had given her privacy to undress and get into bed. The revelation of her parentage had not caused him to react as she had dreaded that he might.

But still . . . desire hummed in her veins, so that she was aware of even the sensation of her clothes against her skin. And she could not help but wish that he had not played the gentleman. That he had lowered his head that last little bit. And kissed her.

Fourteen

Alec stared out the narrow window at the street below, which slowly brightened with the sun edging over the horizon. He ran his hand back through his hair and released a breath. It had been a very long night with far too little sleep. The narrow chair had not been conducive to rest. He had managed to drift off a few times with his head tilted back against the wall, but had soon jerked awake. And knowing that Damaris lay only a few feet from him, curled up snug and warm beneath the covers, wearing only a shift ... when he did manage to drift off, he was plagued by fevered dreams of her naked and pliant beneath his hands.

He turned and looked over at Damaris. The dawn light revealed her lying on her side, her thick black hair spread out across the pillow and drifting over her creamy shoulder. The cover had worked its way down through the night, so that it now lay tangled around her legs. Her upper body was covered only in the simple white cotton shift. It was scooped low across her breasts, exposing most of her upper chest and shoulders. A ribbon pulled taut beneath her bosom made the material cup her breasts. The soft white tops of her breasts pressed against the upper edge of the undergarment, and he could see the dark circle of her nipples beneath the thin cotton.

It would be so easy to slide into bed beside her, to stroke and tease her lush body into wakefulness. He could almost feel the velvet softness of her lips under his, the smooth texture of her skin upon his fingertips. Lust gnawed at him. It had become a familiar sensation. He had spent most of the last two days in that state. He remembered coming awake yesterday morning to the feel of her in his hands, warm and soft, her breast heavy in one palm, and his other . . .

He swung away, swallowing hard, and considered how foolish it was to torture himself again with that memory. But it was damnably difficult to turn away from that sweet pain, to forget how Damaris had felt beneath his fingers, hot and wet and eager in her sleep, her legs opening unconsciously to his touch.

And there—his treacherous thoughts had done it again. He was hard as a rock, his skin burning like a fever, and with no relief in sight. He leaned his head against the windowpane, grateful for its coolness. He had done the right thing last night, he was sure of that. It had required every ounce of self-control he possessed not to take her soft, lithe body into his arms and make love to her. But after what she had told him, he would have been a cad to do so. It would have confirmed her worst fears. She would have thought he believed her less than a lady, someone whom he could bed with no compunction, no thought or regret. She would have assumed that she meant nothing to him except a momentary means of easing his hunger.

And what *did* she mean to him? His mind skittered away from that thought.

He had managed to do what he ought: accept her little kiss of gratitude for what it was, not an invitation to something more. He had shown her that he respected her, valued her, that he was not about to seduce her because he had found out that she was some gentleman's by-blow.

Of course, that did not change the fact that he wanted very much to seduce her. Indeed, it had been the thought foremost in his mind for the past few days, ever since he had looked across the theater and seen her sitting there. No, if he was honest, it had been lodged in his brain from the moment he met her. Even then, angry and distraught as he was over Jocelyn, he had looked across the room into those amazing eyes and found it hard to look away.

Damaris was the most beautiful woman he had ever seen. The kind of woman an artist's hands would itch to draw. To whom poets wrote sonnets. And over whom less sensitive men, men like himself, might start a war, or at least a blood feud. It was rumored that some long-ago ancestor of the Staffords had been a Viking raiding the British shore. He had no idea if it was really true, or simply part of the lore of blood and violence in which his family took pride. But when he looked at Damaris, he felt that Viking blood singing in his veins, the wolf not far beneath the surface.

He could understand sweeping up such a woman and carrying her off. Or grabbing your sword to hack to death whoever might try to take her from you. His fists doubled at his sides as he thought of the ruffian who had grabbed her beside the carriage the other day. A red rage had filled Rawdon then, and only a rock to the head had stopped him.

Gazing down at her now, he was determined to protect her. It galled him that his money and influence were useless here, where he was unknown. He had headed to Gravesend thinking to catch a boat back up the Thames. It had seemed the easiest way to get to London without running across her abductors again. But last night, during his long, restless watch, he had realized where he must go. Not to London, where she would be surrounded by strangers, still vulnerable to attack. No, like any marauding raider of the past, he knew where he must carry her to keep her safe. He would take her home.

Damaris made a soft noise and stirred in the bed, and Alec swung back to the window. He stared at the street below, not really seeing it, his whole being attuned to the faint noises behind him.

"Alec?" Damaris said, her voice thick with sleep. "What time is it?"

"Just after dawn." He turned toward her, keeping his face impassive.

She was sitting up, the blanket pulled up to her shoulders. Her hair tumbled down around her face in a tangle, and she looked deliciously warm and soft and still hazy with sleep, presenting, in short, a picture that was guaranteed to make a man want to crawl into the bed with her.

"I shall get us breakfast," he said quickly. "I was merely waiting for you to wake up."

"I can get dressed and go down with you."

"No, they have no private rooms to eat in, and it isn't the sort of place for you."

"Is this inn so bad?"

"No. No, of course not. I would not have brought you here if I thought it was a den of thieves. But still, it is not the sort of place for a lady." The truth was, he doubted that the public room had many, if any, patrons in it at this hour, and if there had been, he did not truly think they would offend Damaris's sensibilities. But he wanted to get out of this room for a few moments, away from Damaris and the constant onslaught that her nearness made on his senses. He trusted that she would be dressed by the time he returned and no longer sitting there in bed, all rosy and drowsy and scantily dressed. And that he would have regained a firm grip over his desires.

He pulled on his jacket and turned back to Damaris. She was so lush and delectable, sitting there with her cloud of sleep-tangled hair spilling over her shoulders, it was all he could do not to pull her up from the bed and kiss her. "Lock the door behind me," he said hoarsely, then turned and left the room.

Damaris took advantage of Alec's absence to get dressed. She tried valiantly to finger-comb her hair into some semblance of order, but that, it seemed, was well-nigh impossible, so she once again tied it back with the bit of ruffle she had pulled from her petticoat. She was, she supposed, simply going to have to ignore vanity. She could twist her hair up and secure it well enough to pull on her bonnet when they went outside. And Alec had already seen her looking like a slattern, so it really should not matter.

But it did, of course, she thought, wishing for a mirror. It was Alec's opinion, unfortunately, that mattered the most.

There was a light knock on the door, followed by his voice, and Damaris hurried to open it. Alec carried in a tray, once again filled with food. Damaris grabbed a piece of bacon from the tray as he went by.

"'Tis clear your charm works wonders on the kitchen staff," Damaris said, taking a bite. "Mmm. This is delicious."

They tucked into their breakfast with relish and soon put away most of it. Finally Damaris laid down her fork and leaned back against the headboard, sipping her tea. She cast him a teasing glance. "No doubt you will think I am an absolute pig, the way I have eaten since we got here."

"Not at all. I enjoy watching you eat." He smiled, then glanced away, saying in a more formal tone, "You have every right to be hungry, since we spent all yesterday dodging kidnappers."

"How are we going to go about dodging them today?"

"I had planned to take a boat to London from here."

Damaris nodded. "That's clever. They'll stick to the London–Dover road, don't you think? It would offer the best odds of their finding us, and they cannot have *that* many people to set searching."

"True. We might make it back to London without incident. But that would only be tossing you back into the fire, since it is where they first attacked you."

"Then, do you think I should go to Dover after all? Sail to the Continent as I had planned?" Perhaps it was the most sensible thing to do, but the thought sent a stab of disappointment through her.

"No." His answer was swift and adamant. "I think we should go home."

"To Chesley?" The idea of traveling cross-country to Chesley had some appeal.

"No. My home. Castle Cleyre."

Damaris stared at him blankly. "In—Northumberland?"

He nodded. "Yes. It is some distance, I know, but not that long a trip if we go by sea. If I hire a boat, we could be in Newcastle in a day or two, I'm sure."

"But . . . but why?"

"I can keep you safe there." His eyes burned with a fierce light. "In London, even in Chesley, I have no idea where your attackers might come from or when. You could not go out for a walk alone, and I know you do not like being trapped in my home like a prisoner, especially with my grandmother there. She and Genevieve would plague me with questions as well."

"I have no desire to stay at your house in London," Damaris agreed. "But surely it would be easier for me just to leave the country."

"You are assuming that if you flee to the Continent, it will settle the matter. The fact is, you have no idea if that is true.

We don't know what they want from you or even who they are, or who hired them. I realize that your grandmother was upset at your presence in London, but forcing you into hiding seems a rather extreme solution, don't you think?"

"Yes, but who else could it be?"

He shrugged. "I don't know. But the Runner I hired is searching for your abductors. I shall write my sister to tell her where we are going and charge her with recovering Erebos. I shall include a letter to my Bow Street Runner, describing the further information we have about our pursuers. I am certain he will be able to find something with this much to go on."

He leaned forward earnestly, taking her hand. "Until we know who they are, even if you leave the country or return to Chesley, you will have to be ever on the alert, unable to relax. But at the castle, you will be safe. It was built to withstand border raids. Any stranger would be noticed the instant he sets foot in the village or on my lands. Here, you and I are outnumbered. At Cleyre, the entire countryside will come if I call."

Damaris lifted a brow. "Everyone roundabout would jump to defend you?"

"The lands and the people are mine." The words would have sounded odd and outdated coming from someone else, but they rang true issuing from Alec's mouth. He was, in that moment, very much the Earl of Rawdon, the lord of Castle Cleyre. "Just as I am theirs. We are bound to each other and have been throughout history."

"My. How very feudal of you."

A faint smile lifted one corner of Alec's mouth. "In my grandfather's time, Rawdon still mustered his own personal army."

"I scarcely know whether to be in awe or simply frightened."

"Hadn't you heard? We are a bloodthirsty lot, us northerners, and clannish, as well."

"I see. But, Alec, think, I cannot go haring off to your northern fortress alone with you. Word would be bound to leak out. My reputation would be in tatters."

"But it won't." His expression lightened. "Aunt Willa is always at the castle; she will suffice for a chaperone."

"But what are we to do if your Runner cannot find those men?"

"Then we shall enjoy a peaceful sojourn in the country. And we'll make plans to resolve your situation some other way. I may have to have a chat with Lord Sedbury."

"Alec, no!" Damaris reached out to lay a hand on his arm. "You must not place yourself at odds with the Sedburys. I would not have you entangled in my affairs, opposing another family of the *ton*, people with whom you have to live."

"I don't recall that I have ever had to live with a Sedbury, even at school," Alec replied flippantly.

"You know what I mean. People of your own class, peers of the realm. People who come to your sister's parties and are members of your club."

"What have I ever done to make you think I care whether other members of the *ton* approved of me?" Alec asked.

"But your sister and grandmother ..."

"My sister and grandmother have little use for anyone who goes against me." His voice was flat and matter-of-fact. He looked into her eyes, his gaze unswerving. "I intend to see that you are safe, Damaris."

"I—I see." His words warmed her—more, she supposed, than they ought. "Then I can only say thank you."

He smiled and swung lithely off the bed. "Good. I am going to the docks to find us transport."

"But how will you pay?" Damaris went to the dresser and picked up her reticule. "I have a pound note left, but I fear that is all."

"It's bloody inconvenient that I know no one in Gravesend," Alec grumbled. "I shall just have to go to a moneylender. The publican downstairs gave me a name of one he says is fair and reasonable. I have my tie pin and cuff links to secure the debt."

"I have jewelry you can use. Here, take my ring." She pulled the ring from her finger.

"Your wedding band?" he exclaimed, widening his eyes in a pretense of shock. "My dear wife, I am desolate to think you would give it up."

Damaris made a face. "Don't play the fool. Take it. And my earrings. They are only pearls, but still, they will fetch something." She reached up and began to pull out the dangling drops.

"Damaris, I am not taking your jewelry."

"Don't be silly." She whisked the drops out of both ears

and took his hand, firmly putting the ring and earbobs in his palm. "I am the one for whom you are doing all this. I should be the one bearing the responsibility, not you. At least allow me to contribute."

He hesitated, then closed his hand around the jewels. "Very well. I will use them if need be. But I promise you, I shall send someone to redeem your baubles when we reach Cleyre." Alec started toward the door. "I will return as soon as I can."

"I'll go with you. Then we won't need to come back here."

"Take you to a moneylender?" This time Alec looked genuinely shocked. "Damaris, please. I may not be considered a perfect gentleman, but even I am not so lost to propriety as that."

"Honestly, Alec—"

"No. Absolutely not." He had that expression on his face again, the one Damaris thought of as his aristocratic face, a sort of blank hauteur that no amount of appeal or force could change. "Besides, the less you are seen about town, the better. For all we know, our 'friends' may be in Gravesend looking for you. Or they may appear later and go about asking for a woman fitting your description."

"You are far more noticeable than I," Damaris retorted.

He grinned. "If you honestly believe that, you are blind, my dear."

Damaris could make little argument against him, for she was well aware that their pursuers would be looking for a couple, not a man by himself. She grimaced at him and sat down with a sigh on the chair.

"Good. Lock the door behind me."

She followed him to the door and locked it, then sat down to wait. Since there was nothing to do, she had ample time to think; but no matter how much she thought about the matter, she could not understand why anyone would try to abduct her. Damaris was not so naïve that she failed to realize men existed who might grab a woman off the street and force themselves upon her. She supposed that could have been why the men had seized her in front of her house. But it strained belief to think that a man with that in mind would go to such lengths as hiring several thugs and tracking her down on the toll road, much less searching the nearby towns for her when she got away.

Such action showed a personal grudge against her. Her grandmother fit in that category, but, as Alec had pointed out, it seemed a bit extreme for the woman to go to such lengths just to get her out of the city. Most people would try to persuade or intimidate her before they resorted to hiring ruffians to kidnap her. And if she wanted her to leave London, why, then, had the men tried to seize her when she had already done exactly that?

But if these men had not been sent by her grandmother, who were they? And who had sent them? She was merely a widow of little importance, with no enemies that she knew of beyond a social rival or two, a rejected suitor here and there. Her late, unlamented husband had been the sort of man who had enemies, but he had been dead for ten years now. She could not imagine what any of his enemies might hope to gain by abducting her now.

Even if she had garnered some unknown enemies along the way, they would live on the Continent, where she had spent most of her adult life. Why would any of them have decided to travel to England to abduct her so long after the fact? Nor could she think of any enemy she had acquired during the year she had lived in England. It was ludicrous to think that someone in the village of Chesley might wish her harm, and if they did, they would have done so at home, surely, instead of waiting until she went to London.

It made more sense that the men were hired by someone who lived in London, but she knew almost no one in the city. Alec and his family. Sir Myles. Mr. Portland. It was nonsensical to think that Alec or Myles would have hired the men, much less Alec's starchy grandmother or sister. Mr. Portland had been her father's friend and banker and then Damaris's friend and banker for years.

She stopped and forced herself to look past her instinctive rejection and consider Mr. Portland. Could there be any reason that kind and dignified man would want her gone? Money was a powerful thing, and he did, of course, handle her money. He was one of the trustees who had been placed in charge of the trust fund her father had left her, and he was the one who actually handled the money. The other two were her father's solicitor and one of her father's friends.

Could Mr. Portland possibly have been embezzling money from the trust and now be trying to keep her from finding out? But that made no sense. She had never seen anything wrong in the figures he showed her; if he was stealing money from her, she obviously had no knowledge of it. It would be much more likely that the solicitor and his fellow trustee might discover it, so that would be the person to get rid of, not she. Unless, of course, Mr. Portland and the solicitor were working together to defraud her.

Damaris burst into giggles as she tried to imagine those two distinguished gentlemen engaged in such skulduggery. No, it was absolutely absurd. The only villains possible were her father's family. She was merely grasping at straws, reluctant to admit that her own blood kin despised her enough to do this to her.

She sighed and lay back on the bed, staring at the low ceiling above her. Whatever motivated her attackers, there was nothing she could do about it now. Of more immediate concern was Alec and his involvement in her affairs. She had to admit that there was something primitive and thrilling about the way he had come to her rescue. It warmed her that he wanted to protect her, and there was a part of her that wanted to bathe in that warmth, to relax in the strength of his embrace.

But it was wrong, surely, to encourage him in siding with her against her family. Whatever he said about not caring what his peers thought of him, she knew that he was not immune to the sting of gossip. And the fact that his name had already been embroiled in the scandal about Jocelyn would only make it worse if he was involved in an argument with the Sedburys over one of the late lord's by-blows.

Still, even though it might be wrong to involve him, Damaris could not refuse his help. She was in desperate need of it, frankly; she knew that she would not have managed to get this far without his aid, and she would face a world of difficulty if she tried to go back to London without Alec. His plan seemed more likely to end these attacks on her than anything else she could think of. It would be silly to refuse his help just because what he offered filled her with happiness.

Damaris was pulled from her reverie by Alec's return. She saw as soon as she opened the door that he had been successful in his quest, for his light blue eyes were sparkling with excitement.

"I found a ship going to Newcastle, and the captain was willing to take us for a fee. They're weighing anchor in two hours; we will need to leave soon. There was money left over from my transaction with the moneylender, so I picked up a couple of things. First . . ." He had been holding one hand behind his back, and now he brought it out, holding out to her a simple white dimity round gown.

"Alec!" Damaris clasped her hands together in awe. "You didn't! How—" Emotions swelled in her throat, and she was not sure whether she was about to laugh or cry.

"I picked up a few notions at the haberdashery, and it so happened they had a gown hung there to advertise their materials for sale. I was able to talk the shopkeeper into selling it to me. It may not perfectly fit you, but—"

"It's wonderful!" Impulsively Damaris hugged him. "Thank you!"

His arms closed around her, squeezing her to him for a

moment, before he released her and stepped back. "Careful. Don't want to break this." He reached inside his jacket and withdrew a simple wood comb. With his other hand, he pulled out a blue ribbon and a little box of hairpins.

"Oh, Alec!" Tears sprang into Damaris's eyes, and she pressed her fingertips to her mouth, unable to speak.

"There, now, I didn't mean to make you cry."

"I'm just—oh, you cannot imagine! I so wanted a comb! You are the best, kindest, most wonderful man!"

He chuckled. "If only I had known how much women valued a comb! To think that I have wasted my money all these years on rubies and diamonds."

Damaris made a face at him. "Do not think you can fool me into believing you did not do me a kindness. You knew very well how sorely I missed a comb. I do value it. And I thank you very, very much."

She took his hands between hers and gazed up into his face. She was afraid that she was perilously close to doing the very worst thing possible for her own well-being—falling in love with the Earl of Rawdon.

Fifteen

The ship Alec had found was a rather unprepossessing-looking vessel, a medium-size ketch with a faded and battered figurehead of a woman in a dress that must once have been blue, as the name *Blue Betty* was written on the side of the hull. Damaris clutched Alec's arm tightly as he led her across the gangplank onto the small ship. She had been on edge during the entire trip from the inn, and now that they were so close to the safety the ketch represented, her stomach was jumping with nerves.

All around them the crew was busy with their tasks preparatory to casting off, and only one or two men even glanced their way as Alec whisked Damaris across the deck and down the narrow steps into the narrow hallway below. He knocked upon a door at the forward end of the corridor, and when there was no answer, he opened the door and ushered Damaris inside.

"Good," he said, casting an eye around the snug cabin. "He has already moved his things."

"What things? Who are you talking about?"

"The captain. When I told him that I needed a cabin, since my wife was accompanying me, he offered to give up his own, as it was the only place suitable for a lady."

"Oh." Damaris gazed around the small space somewhat doubtfully. "It seems quite pleasant."

Alec chuckled. "Cozy, one might say."

"It is a trifle small, but then, that is the way it is with ships, isn't it?"

Damaris could not help but think about the fact that she and Alec were apparently going to be spending the night in this room, which made their chamber at the inn last night look positively spacious. There was not even a chair here for Alec to sleep in. Indeed, there was almost nothing besides the bed. This piece of furniture seemed to dominate the cabin, and she could not look anywhere without seeing it.

"So we are still a married couple?" she went on carefully.

"It seemed wisest, given the circumstances. You need not worry," he went on a bit stiffly. "I have no intention of taking advantage of the situation."

"I know you would not."

Damaris turned away, taking off her bonnet and setting it down on the bed. She had been unable to resist putting on the new frock Alec had bought her. It was entirely too short, showing much more of her ankles than was seemly, and the bosom was also a trifle tight; but all in all, it was heavenly to have on a clean dress again, particularly one that was at least a bit stylish.

However, she had not taken the time to use the comb Alec

had brought her; that, she knew, would take more than just a few minutes. Instead, she had merely stuffed the tangled mass of her hair under her bonnet so that it did not show. Now, however, it tumbled free again, and she took the comb out of her reticule and began the slow process of combing out the snarls.

There was a sound behind her, and she turned to glance at Alec. He was leaning against the closed door of the cabin, his arms crossed over his chest, watching her. There was something in the set of his mouth, the heavy-lidded look in his eyes, that stirred the now-familiar ache deep within her. Her hands stilled on the comb and dropped away. She could not look away from him, could not think of anything except the touch of his lips on hers, the curve of his hand over her breast. She could feel her body responding to that remembered touch, tingling and throbbing at the thought of its happening again.

He straightened, pushing away from the door. "I—ah, I should see how things are going. Um, on deck. Let you"—he made a vague gesture around the room—"get settled." He cleared his throat, then gave her a quick nod, turned, and left.

Damaris sank down on the bed, her knees suddenly giving way beneath her. She had the uneasy feeling that this night was going to be very long.

Sometime later Damaris felt the ship begin to move beneath her. She had finished combing out her hair and had pinned it up, then sat staring around her and wondering how to occupy her time. She knew that Alec wanted her to stay belowdecks until the ship left. It was, she suspected, not at all necessary: her would-be abductors were probably nowhere near Gravesend, and even if they were there, there was little chance of their happening upon this ship and recognizing her from the docks. However, she knew that if she went on deck, Alec would rush her right back down here, and anyway, there was no reason for her to be there, where she would only get in the way of the men doing their jobs.

But when she felt the movement of the ship, she got up, reasoning that it would no longer matter if she could be seen, and made her way up the narrow steps to the deck. The sails were fully open as *Blue Betty* nosed into the middle of the river. Behind them, Gravesend was receding in the distance. The wind tugged at the wide brim of her bonnet, and she put her hand up to hold it in place as she walked toward the rail.

The Thames was broader here than she had seen it in London, and it widened even more as they moved away from Gravesend. Ahead the river made a deep curve to the left. Relief washed through Damaris, and she could not help but smile. The men who had chased them could not catch them now; here on the water, she no longer needed to worry about the possibility of running into them again or being tracked down. It was a wonderfully freeing feeling, one she would not even have guessed at a few days ago.

"Have you ever seen the Thames from here?" Alec moved up beside her at the railing.

"No." Damaris turned to smile at him. "But I have to say, it looks wonderful."

He nodded. He was still hatless, and the afternoon sun danced along the pale gold strands of his hair. It was a beautiful summer day, and Alec was so handsome that it caught at her heart to look at him. From the moment she first saw him, she had found him arresting and intriguing, if somewhat cold. But now, she realized, when she looked at him she saw so much more—the strength, the subtle humor, the hidden kindness that lay beneath that arrogant high slash of cheekbones and square jaw. She knew how that firm mouth could soften and turn seductive, how his eyes could warm with admiration or passion or flash with anger. Now she found him immeasurably more attractive, the stark angles and lines of his face imbued with character.

He raised his brows at her inquisitively. "What? Have I sprung a third eye? A horn in the center of my forehead?"

"No." Damaris shook her head, smiling. "Far from it. I was just thinking how handsome you are."

His eyes widened and he drew in a sharp breath. "Dear lady...just when I think I have steeled myself to your charms, you sneak in beneath my guard and lay me low again."

Damaris looked away. "'Tis a wickedly forward thing for me to say, I know."

"I am particularly fond of 'wickedly forward' women." He reached out and brushed his hand over hers on the railing. "But you do not make it easy to hold on to my gentlemanly intentions."

"I beg your pardon."

"No. Don't apologize. I savor the temptation. Believe me."

He slid his finger down the length of her hand, light as a feather. "I know that looking at you will only make me want you more, and yet I cannot keep my eyes from you."

Damaris felt the warmth creeping up her neck and into her face, matching the one that spread deep in her belly. "We should speak of something else."

"No doubt. The weather, perhaps?" His finger continued that slow, tantalizing exploration of her hand, gliding up and down each finger. "It occurs to me that perhaps a man could be stirred so by the sight of you that he would hire someone to bring you to him."

"It seems an unlikely way to woo a woman."

"Perhaps he has been driven too mad by your beauty to care about 'wooing,' only desperate for the satisfaction of having you in his bed, however he gets you there."

Damaris sent him a sardonic look. "You think some man has been driven mad by the sight of me?"

"Each day I realize more how likely that might be." The faintest of smiles played at his lips, creasing the corners of his eyes.

"Of course. And who do you think that man might be? It obviously is not you, as you are standing here with me."

"Ah, but perhaps I am so clever that I created the danger so I could save you. Have you thought of that?"

"No. Anyway, you are much more direct than that, not to mention more principled. So if you are right, it must be someone else. Let's see ... what man in Chesley do you think is the likeliest candidate for your villain? The apothecary, perhaps?"

His smile broadened, his eyes on his hand as it strayed over hers and laced their fingers together. "I think not. He would merely have had to slip some sleeping draught into your tea one day, and he could have carried you off himself."

"Then it must be Squire Cliffe," Damaris said firmly, and Alec let out a laugh. "No doubt he has a whole harem of women back in Chesley, and he wishes to add me to them. Or the Reverend Daniel Bainbridge." Damaris giggled. "No, that is too much to imagine, even in jest."

"I fear that Daniel would be much more likely to be interested in you if you were a thousand years old and Roman," Alec agreed. "Very well, I accede to your wisdom. Perhaps it is not an ardent admirer."

"I don't want to think about it anymore." Damaris crossed her arms on the railing and leaned forward, looking down the river, which, after the sharp bend, was curving back to the right and opening out.

A gust of wind caught the scoop of her bonnet and pulled, knocking it back from her head. Damaris reached up to adjust it, but as she did so, the wind jerked it away completely, sending it spinning out over the water, where it dropped and floated on the current.

"Botheration." Damaris reached up to push back the tendrils of hair that were already coming loose from their pins.

"Don't." Alec reached out to still her hands. "I like to look at you this way."

"A complete mess?" Damaris asked skeptically.

"With the sun on your hair. Strands breaking free to drift on the breeze."

Damaris sent him a look, but she lowered her hands to the railing and let her hair do as it would. "It is too much trouble, anyway." She peered into the distance. "I wonder when we shall be able to see the ocean."

"Soon, I would think. I have never gone this way. We always come by road."

"I would guess that it is a grand procession."

"Indeed." Again his grin flashed. "Especially when Grandmother is with us. Fortunately she winters in Bath these days. But in years past, my grandmother required a caravan. Genevieve and I took our favorite mounts. There was at least one wagon—and usually two—to carry the servants who must accompany us—Grandmother's and Genevieve's abigails, the grooms, whatever valet she was currently trying to foist off on me—as well as the trunks of clothes and hats and the various household items that my grandmother cannot live without. Then there was our coach, of course, and it had to be the one her husband bought, not one of the newer ones. They were not 'grand' enough—which means that I have left the family crest off the ones I purchased. She believes the world should know that the Staffords are on the march."

"Your grandmother sounds faintly terrifying."

"More than faintly. She believes one is not a true Stafford unless ice water runs in your veins, and it is her duty to put it there."

"But surely she is a Stafford only by marriage, isn't she?"

Alec cast her a shocked glance. "Don't let her hear you say that. She may have become a Stafford by marrying one, but that was only a formality. She has been a true Stafford in her heart from the moment she was born."

Something she would never be, of course, Damaris thought, then wondered why she had let such an idea even enter her mind. "What is it like?" she asked, to break from the path of her thoughts. "This castle of yours that is so impregnable?"

His face changed subtly, and she could see both pride and affection in his eyes as he said, "It is a fortress. You shall see when we get there. It was built in a bend of the river, where the water is narrow, and it stands on a knoll, so that you can see it from afar—and from inside, you can see anyone approaching."

"And your tenants? You sounded fond of them."

"They are good and bad, I suppose, like anyone else. I like some, and others I'd as soon never see again. But they are all . . ." He paused, frowning, as if searching for the right words. "They are *connected* to me. The people of Cleyre are more than tenants. They are family. You may not like them very much, but they are still yours." He looked at her.

Damaris shrugged. "I fear family is something I know little about. There was only my mother and me. You can imagine that I never met any of my cousins."

"What about your mother's family? Were you not close to them, either?"

"I never met them. Mother didn't like to talk about them. I

gather that it caused a rift between her and her parents when she went on the stage."

"Ah." He took her hand in his again. "Not having a family may not be a terrible thing. You probably grew up happier for it."

Damaris raised an eyebrow. "I thought family was all to you Staffords."

"Oh, it is what has made us who we are," he replied, his voice dry. "That does not necessarily mean it is a good thing. I think I could have spent all my days quite happily without my father."

"He was a strict man?"

"He was a tyrant," Alec replied flatly. "The lord of the castle, and none of us ever forgot that. It was, I think, generally the way of the Staffords. He believed in absolute rule and in toughening up his son. There are those who found Eton harsh. I thought it was much more pleasant than home."

"I'm sorry," Damaris said softly.

He tightened his hand around hers for an instant, then released it. "'Tis somewhat absurd to whine about the rigors of one's life when one is an earl. Don't you think?"

"I think it is possible to have both arrogance and misfortune."

He looked at her and grinned. "At least you do not mince your words with me."

She smiled back. "Would you rather I did?"

"No. It is one of the things I like most about you. You are neither scared of me nor plying your wiles."

"Plying my wiles?" Damaris laughed. "Is that what women usually do with you?"

"The prospect of a title will have that effect on some ladies."

Damaris turned to look up at him, her expressive eyes brimming with laughter. "And, pray tell, exactly how do they ply their wiles on you?"

"Careful, you will make me blush."

"That is something I should like to see." She tilted her head and crossed her arms in the manner of a tutor awaiting an answer. "Go on. Tell me about these devious ladies. What do they do?"

"You should know that better than I," he retorted. "They flutter their eyelashes, just so." He held an imaginary fan to face and batted his eyelashes at her above it.

Damaris broke into giggles. "You are terrible at it!"

"And they carelessly drop a kerchief." He mimed tossing a handkerchief onto the deck beside him, then cast her a meaningful glance over his shoulder. "They put a hand on your arm, thus"—he reached over and took her hand, placing it on his arm—"so that they can lean in a bit and whisper to you." He leaned closer to her, his face only inches from hers.

Suddenly the playfulness dropped from his face, and she saw the desire spark in his eyes. A breathless excitement swelled in her in response, and for a moment the very air between them seemed to shimmer with possibility. Then he broke from her, stepping back, and turned to gaze out across the water.

"There it is," he said. "The sea."

Damaris followed his gaze. The river had been growing ever wider as they sailed, and now it spread out in front of them, emptying into the limitless blue sea. The sun was sinking, and the sky in front of them was growing darker, dipping down to mingle with the deep-blue water stretching in front of them. A shiver ran through Damaris, in part from the cool breeze of the approaching evening at sea and in part from anticipation. Alec put his arm around her, pulling her close to his side, and they stood together, watching, as the ship carried them forward.

Dinner was plain sailor's fare, a distinct decline from their supper the evening before at the inn. But they ate it as they had then, alone together in their cabin, the tray on the bed between them, and that made up for any lack in quantity or taste. After supper, Alec was restless, as if he could not find comfort whether he stood or sat. The cabin seemed to shrink around them, and the bed loomed larger as the minutes passed. Damaris ran out of topics of conversation; every time she thought of something to say, she realized that it contained some innuendo that rendered it unsuitable or would lead inevitably to a subject that was better left unsaid.

Being alone like this in a tiny cabin with a virile male like Alec made any situation fraught with a seductive undertone.

"Perhaps we should take a turn around the deck," she said finally as she watched Alec prowl the room.

He practically leapt to open the door, and they went up onto the deck. It was dark, with only a half-moon and the stars for light, and there was a hush over the ship, broken only by an occasional flap of a sail. They might have been alone in the world. They walked along the boards, talking in the hushed tones that the setting seemed to call for, and stopped at the prow of the ship to look out over the sea. Moonlight revealed the ripples of the waves before them, and the boat rocked soothingly as it sliced through the calm waters. The rush of air was cool against Damaris's face and sent the strands of her hair flying once again. Alec stood so close that she could feel the brush of his arm against hers, and the touch sent a shiver through her.

"Cold?" he asked, and shrugged out of his jacket to hang it about her shoulders.

The warmth of the jacket enveloped her. It smelled like him, a scent that was somehow both reassuring and exciting. She liked the feel of it around her so much that she felt obliged to protest, "No, you must not give it to me. Now you will be cold."

"Don't worry about that." His voice was smooth and deep, with an undercurrent of amusement and something else, something darker and dangerously alluring.

He wrapped his arms around her from behind, settling her back against his chest, his chin resting lightly on her head. She felt cocooned by him, warm and safe and yet vulnerable in a way that made her knees weak and her nerves dance with anticipation. They stood that way for a long time, lost in the beauty of the night, unwilling to break the moment of unspoken connection.

"I was married," Damaris said and stopped, surprised at herself. Her marriage was a story she never told anyone. Not even her best friend in Chesley, Thea, knew the particulars of that part of her life. Indeed, it was a time that Damaris herself would just as soon forget. Yet for some reason, here in the dark, surrounded by Alec's strength, the words had just popped out.

Alec made no movement. She could feel his solidity against her back, the steady rhythm of his heart. His lips brushed her hair. He did not speak or urge her on, but she could feel him waiting, his silence, his presence somehow encouraging her. The need to tell him swelled in her, and she began to talk, the story flowing out of her.

Sixteen

"*I was young—seventeen—and barely out of* school," Damaris began. "I was thrilled to be attending parties and plays and the opera. My mother and I were in Italy then, in Venice. My friends were Italian, but there were other Englishmen around. One of them was Barrett Howard. He was . . . oh, the sort of man young girls dream about: handsome and sensitive, with a very poetical lock of hair that fell engagingly across his forehead when he grew emotional."

Alec let out a derisive snort, and Damaris sighed. "Yes, I was very young and terribly foolish. He loved me, he said, and I was certain I loved him, too. My mother was charmed by him, but she said we must wait. I was too young. When I pressed her, she wrote to my guardian. My father was dead by then, but he had left us well provided for. There was a trust for us, and one of the trustees was a friend of my father whom he had named as my guardian. This guardian wrote back that he would not allow it. He would travel to Italy the next summer, when I was eighteen, and if we were still of a mind to marry, he would meet Barrett then."

She hesitated, and Alec's arms hugged her a little closer. "I take it this chap did not want to wait."

"No. No doubt you have already guessed the rest of the story. Barrett could not bear to be without me so long. We were too much in love; my guardian was a dry, cold, aged man who did not understand the strength of young love. I was flattered by the thought that Barrett could not live without me, and I, too, thought my guardian, who was not even a man who knew me well, was stuffy and unreasonable. I did not like being thwarted, especially by one of those aristocrats who belonged to the world that had taken my father from me. Even though he was my father's friend, I felt certain he hated me and wanted only to hurt me. So when Barrett suggested that we elope and marry without their permission, I was happy to agree. When my gaurdian saw how much we loved each other and how we could not be kept apart, then of course he would give his permission."

"Which he did."

"Yes. After I had run off with Barrett, my reputation would have been in tatters if I had not married him. As it was, of course, it was a scandal. And it brought one of the other trustees to Italy—not my father's friend, but his solicitor."

"Ah …" Alec said in a knowing voice.

"Yes. Ah …" Damaris kept a firm rein on her voice as she went on, "Mr. Carstairs proceeded to explain the terms of the trust to Barrett. Neither my mother nor I had any control over the trust. Even after I turned twenty-one, the money would not yet be mine. It would continue for my mother's benefit and then for mine, and would not come to me until I was thirty."

"In other words, Mr. Howard would not get his hands on the full amount."

"Precisely. He could not have the principle or, indeed, any money that the trustees did not want to give us."

"I see."

"So did he. He was infuriated. He railed at Carstairs, to no avail, and then he came home and railed at me. He told me that he did not love me; indeed, he had no interest in me except for my money." Damaris's voice caught and she waited a moment, swallowing as though to force down the old emotion that threatened to rise in her.

"He was a fortune hunter," she went on in a dispassionate voice. "He came to Venice looking for some wealthy woman to swindle or some heiress to marry. I am not even certain if Barrett Howard was his actual name. When he saw me, he thought he had found the perfect victim. Local society was not aware of my exact origins; there were various colorful rumors about me. I believe he thought I was the granddaughter of some wealthy merchant or banker who had been sent abroad to acquire polish and an aristocratic husband. He had no desire to shackle himself to a wife, but I was a more appealing prospect, apparently, than some raddled old widow. He had thought that once he was married to me, my money would all be in his hands as my husband. And then, he said, he had planned to take my money and leave."

Alec turned her in his arms, pulling her in and bending to

lay his head against hers. "The man was a scoundrel," he said fiercely. "And a fool."

Damaris breathed out a little humorless laugh. "*I* was the fool. I didn't see him for what he was."

"How could you? You were seventeen, and he took great care not to show you what he was. You can scarcely be blamed for believing his lies."

"I found out soon enough. Barrett told me he refused to live with me for the next thirteen years until my trust came to me, begging for scraps from my trustees. The morning after Carstairs visited us, I found that Barrett had disappeared during the night. He had taken my jewels and all the money Carstairs had given us to set up household. I suppose he thought that would somewhat make up for not getting all my money."

Alec let out a ripe curse. "He should have been horse-whipped. I'd like to get my hands on him for a few minutes." His hands knotted into fists at his side.

"Thank you for the sentiment. But I am afraid that has been taken out of your hands. He was caught in a fire in an inn a few days later and burned to death."

"Good," Alec responded unsympathetically. "It is the sort of death he deserved. Though I am sorry he is not still around so I could show him what I think of him."

Damaris smiled, leaning back a little to look up into Alec's face. "You are a fierce man."

"No doubt that's true." His face softened and he raised his hand to brush her cheek. "But not to you. Never to you." He took her chin between his thumb and forefinger and leaned down to kiss her.

His mouth was gentle on hers and tender. Yet it caused heat to rise in her, filling her belly and spilling out all over her body. Damaris wrapped her arms around him, rising up on her toes to kiss him back. In an instant, the kiss changed, turning hot and needy. Alec slid his hands around her beneath his jacket, pulling her up and into him as his mouth moved against hers greedily. His skin flared with heat, and his body grew taut as he pressed her to him, his hands roaming her back.

Damaris's body responded to him reflexively, her breasts heavy and aching, and a fiercer, hotter need sprang to life deep inside her. She dug her fingers into Alec's back, pressing her body into his as if she could melt into him. The fire he had started in her the other morning, banked since then, roared to life. She knew how it had felt to have his hands caressing her, and she wanted it. She remembered the pleasure rippling through her, the breathless burst of delight. She wondered what it would be like to lie under him, to have him inside her, to hear his labored breath, to feel his damp, hot skin sliding over hers.

Perhaps it was wrong to want him this way; maybe her nature was truly wanton, and she was a wicked widow. Right now Damaris did not care. All she cared about was him—the taste and sound and feel of him.

Alec broke their kiss. He raised his head, gazing down at her, his eyes glittering fiercely in the dim light, his breath rasping in his throat. "We should not. Anyone could see us."

"I don't care."

He let out a little groan, tipping his head down to rest his forehead against hers. "You make it very hard to act the gentleman."

"I don't want a gentleman," Damaris replied boldly. "I want you."

Alec let out a breathy chuckle and pressed his lips against her head. "You should go below."

Despite his words, his arms did not loosen around her, and Damaris smiled to herself, leaning her head against his chest. "All right."

He released her, his arms falling away from her reluctantly. Damaris took his hand and started toward the steps.

"No." Alec remained where he was, their arms stretching between them. "I should stay here for a while. It's, um, better that way. Safer."

Damaris looked at him. Her heart was hammering wildly in her chest. "I don't want 'safer.'"

She started once more for the stairs, and Alec followed.

Inside their cabin, Alec closed the door and turned to face Damaris. His face was taut, his eyes bright and intent on her face, his whole body fairly radiating tension. He picked up her hand and brought it to his mouth, laying a kiss in her palm. His skin seared hers; his lips were soft as velvet. "Are you sure?" he asked.

She nodded, not trusting herself to speak. He pressed his lips against her palm again, then cradled her hand to his cheek. He moved even closer, cupping her face in his hands, and bent to kiss her, touching his lips softly to her forehead, her cheeks, her eyes, before settling finally on her mouth. The kiss was leisurely, exploring, signaling that they had all the night before them and he intended to savor each moment of it.

Damaris relaxed against him, and his arms slid around her. Damaris had never been so aware of her body. Every inch of her was alive and tingling, and where his hands moved over her, her skin blazed. A pleasurable ache started deep in her abdomen and grew with each kiss, each caress. He let his hands drift down over her back and up again, moving with a feather-light touch. They curved over her buttocks, and his fingers flexed, digging into the fleshy mounds and lifting her up against him. She could feel the rigid line of his manhood pressing into her, pulsing and eager.

He guided her back to the bed and tugged her down to sit on the edge, then went down on one knee before her. He lifted one of her feet, placing the sole of her half boot upon his bended knee, and began to unbutton her shoe. Damaris realized with surprise that something stirred deep inside her at the sight of him tending to her. She wasn't sure what it was— the nimble movement of his long, agile fingers on the leather or the care he took with her or perhaps it was simply the thought of him serving her—but heat blossomed between her legs and sent teasing tendrils up through her.

When he had removed her shoes, Alec stood, taking Damaris's hand to pull her up with him. He found the few remaining hairpins that had not been dislodged by the wind and plucked them from her hair, sending it tumbling down around her face and shoulders in a heavy curtain. Then he pulled her to him, burying his face in her tresses.

His searching lips found her ear, and he took the fleshy lobe between his teeth, worrying it gently, then tracing the shell of her ear with his tongue. Hot shivers of longing shot through her, bursting into a liquid ache low in her abdomen. He kissed his way down her throat, and Damaris let her head fall back, exposing the tender flesh to him more fully. He nibbled at the taut cords, his tongue trailing designs over her skin, working his way ever lower.

She drew in a sharp breath when he reached the soft top of her breast, and he pulled his head up. Damaris feared for a moment that her reaction had stopped him, but Alec took the top button of her dress in his fingers, slipping it through the material. He looked down into her eyes as he unfastened the neat little row, his gaze holding her as surely as his hands had. She felt each movement of his fingers, so close to her skin, and her breath hitched in her throat.

As each button fell to his advance, the dress sagged open more, revealing the creamy tops of her breasts above her shift. His fingertips brushed the valley between her breasts, and her insides quivered, a dark ache starting low inside her. Slowly he eased the dress from her shoulders and pulled it down, letting it drop to the floor. He ran a forefinger along the neckline of her chemise, the touch sending a trail of fire across her skin. He watched the path of his teasing finger, his eyes turning dark and heavy-lidded, then slipped his finger inside the soft cotton, gliding his nail over her nipple.

The bud tightened in response, and Damaris felt the movement all through her. Alec untied the center bow, loosening the garment, and rolled it slowly downward, revealing her breasts to his gaze. The cotton rubbed over her nipples, and he watched, with a sultry satisfaction, as the buttons of flesh prickled under the caress of the cloth.

Damaris was filled with a curious combination of embarrassment and pride as Alec drank in the sight of her bare breasts. No man had ever looked at her so. During her brief marriage, she had never undressed before her husband, and he had never removed her nightgown when they lay together. Certainly he had never gazed at her like this, as if he could consume her whole, as if his life lay in watching her.

The chemise soon joined her gown on the floor. Alec cupped her breasts in his hands, taking in the weight of them, and he brushed his thumbs over her, teasing her nipples into hardness. Then he bent and ran his tongue over one nipple, and Damaris let out another soft noise of surprise and pleasure. Nothing had ever felt like this, so hot and damp and compelling, and when his mouth closed around her breast, sucking softly on her sensitive flesh, she quivered with delight.

He took his time with each breast, stroking and kissing, rubbing her nipples between his lips, until Damaris was whimpering with desire. She moved her hips involuntarily, and his hand came down to slip between her legs, moving through the cloth of her underthings over the hot, damp center of her passion. A low sound, somewhere between a groan and a growl, issued from his throat.

"So sweet," he murmured against her breast. "So warm." He raised his head and looked down into her face. He was flushed, his mouth slack with desire and darkened by their kisses, his eyes piercing. "Just like yesterday morning," he went on thickly, his fingers working their magic on her flesh.

Damaris drew in her breath at the intense pleasure his agile fingers created, then gasped again as the implications of his words hit home. "You mean—you were awake then! When you—" Her cheeks flushed bright red with embarrassment.

He smiled slowly. "Did you really think I could sleep through that?"

She was indignant—or, at least, she wanted to be indignant. He had knowingly touched her. He had—he had—but, oh, sweet goodness, he was touching her like that now, and all she could think of was the hot, itchy, wonderful way it felt to have his hand on her. She could only shudder out a sigh and move unconsciously against his hand, her eyelids fluttering closed in pleasure.

This time she was certain the noise Alec made was a growl. He stepped back from her and bent down to yank off his boots and socks. He straightened, reaching up to the front of his shirt, but Damaris nudged his hands aside and began to unfasten the ties herself. He watched her, his eyes burning, as she took the end of each narrow strip of cloth and dragged it slowly apart, revealing inch by inch the bare skin of his chest. Sliding her hands up under his shirt, her fingers spread wide over his skin, she slowly made her way up his sides. At last she hooked her fingers into the hem of his shirt and tugged it upward, and he bent over to let her pull it off over his head.

Marveling a little at her nerve, Damaris moved to the top button of his breeches. Alec's stomach muscles twitched at her touch, but he did not move away. Damaris's eyes roved over his bare chest as she unfastened his breeches, watching his chest rise and fall more rapidly with each of her movements. The garment drifted dangerously lower and lower on his hips as she freed him, until at last, with an impatient movement, Alec reached down and skinned the breeches down his legs and stepped out of them, revealing his naked body.

He was lean and powerful, his legs long and his hips narrow. She understood now why he had enjoyed looking at her naked body. It did wicked things to her insides to see his bare flesh, to watch his muscles bunch and lengthen, to think of how they would feel beneath her hands, hard and strong under his smooth skin. Her fingers itched to explore his body, and she laid her palms flat on his stomach, drifting slowly up over the outlines of his ribs and around to his back, then returning to smooth her thumbs across the hard outcropping of his pelvic bones. She stopped there, not bold enough to let her fingers follow the path of her gaze onto the flat plain of his abdomen . . . to curl around the hard, thrusting proof of his virility.

Damaris blushed and jerked her eyes away from the fascinating view of his naked body and back up to his face. He was watching her, but the look in his eyes sent any thought of embarrassment flying out of Damaris's head. There was nothing in his expression but hunger, a deep, primitive need that left no room for thought or shame or anything but an answering yearning within her.

She untied her petticoat, letting it slide off onto the floor, then followed it with her pantalets. Alec watched her, his chest rising and falling in deep, uneven breaths. He came to her, his hands settling on her waist.

"You are the most beautiful woman I have ever seen," he said in a low voice, his thumbs moving along her skin, stroking her. He bent and swooped her up in his arms and laid her down upon the bed.

He stretched out beside her, propping himself up on one elbow. Slowly, softly, he began to run his fingers over her body, beginning at her chin and working his way slowly down her torso. Damaris watched his face as he caressed her, loving the way desire etched itself on his features, each stroke of his fingertips showing in his eyes even as it reverberated throughout her own body.

Damaris shifted beneath his hand, reveling in the slow building of passion within her, even as the ache inside her grew. He handled her as if she were priceless and delicate, and with every stroke, she longed for more. Her hands moved restlessly, itching to touch him as he was touching her, and yet she held back, afraid he would find her too brazen. His hand slipped between her legs, gliding up the inside of her thigh, and he bent to take her breast in his mouth again.

Damaris trembled under the force of her passion, her skin quivering as his mouth roamed over her, following the trail of his hand. He kissed her breasts, her stomach, even her thighs, teasing her with teeth and tongue and lips as his fingers explored her most intimate places, until she moaned and twisted beneath his touch, aching for release.

Then he turned her over and paid the same depth of attention to her back, kissing and caressing, moving with infinite slowness down the long curve. His fingers slipped into the crevice between her legs, startling her, but she forgot all modesty or hesitation and opened her legs to him, reveling in his touch.

She rolled over onto her back, reaching out to him, and at last he moved between her legs. He slid into her, opening her and filling her so slowly and powerfully that she had to clench her teeth to keep from crying out. She wrapped her arms and legs around him, shifting to accommodate him, and his breath rasped out in a groan.

He murmured her name as he began to move within her. Damaris dug her fingers into his shoulders, clinging to him as the world tilted and shook around her. He moved in long, hard, rhythmic strokes, his thrusts carrying her deeper and deeper into the hot swirl of pleasure. Instinctively Damaris ground her hips against him, matching his movements, delighting in each shock of pleasure.

The rushing sweep of passion he had created in her the

other morning swelled in her again, but this time it was even stronger, taking her over, mind and body, until she felt nothing, knew nothing, except Alec and the powerful force within her—the turmoil, the hum, the need that clenched ever tighter, until she hung, poised on the brink.

The moment exploded into ecstasy, and she heard Alec's hoarse cry against her neck, felt him jerk and shudder against her. She clung to him as the intense pleasure washed over her, leaving her limp and exhausted. He held her just as closely, his arms tight as iron around her, breathing out her name like a prayer.

Seventeen

$\mathcal{D}$amaris lay in the circle of Alec's arms, her head nestled on his shoulder. Her hand rested on his chest over the steady thump of his heart. She felt almost boneless and a little dazed after the cataclysm she had just experienced. Alec's arm was heavy across her back and arm, and she wondered if he was asleep. Damaris raised her head a little to peek at Alec's face. He slanted a look down at her through slitted eyes, and a lazy smile spread across his lips. He ran his thumb down her bare arm as though to emphasize that he was awake, then bent to press his lips against her head.

"Dear wife," he said in the teasing tone he reserved for those words. "Did you think to catch me napping?"

Damaris spread her hand wider over his chest, indulging her urge to touch him. "You seemed . . . quite relaxed."

His low laugh rumbled beneath her head. "Indeed, I am quite relaxed. But this feels too nice to sleep."

She snuggled closer, drawing lazy designs upon his chest, following the hard centerline of his chest, the flow of his muscles, circling the flat bud of his nipple. His skin quivered a little beneath her hand and she cast a quick questioning glance up at him, thinking that perhaps she had done something wrong. But the look in his eyes was far too warm for reproach, and he pulled his arms up above his head, stretching lazily, in a way that seemed to open himself to her touch.

Damaris was happy to oblige. She loved the feel of his skin beneath her fingertips—smooth and firm, with the soft crinkle of hair down the center of his chest. She wondered how it would taste if she touched her lips to him, her tongue, as he had done to her. That, too, seemed a very bold thing to do, but it made the now-familiar warmth coil low in her abdomen.

Alec tangled his fingers in her hair and combed them through, letting the soft strands slide over his skin. "You have hair like midnight," he told her, his voice gravelly and still heavy with passion.

"Then yours is like sunlight," she replied, resting her fist on his chest and propping her chin on it. She reached up and pushed a strand of his hair back from his forehead. "Or perhaps it's more like moonlight."

He grinned, more relaxed and boyish than she had ever seen him. "My hair is not so poetical as either one. 'Tis pale as a ghost is all."

"'Tis far too shiny for that," Damaris disputed. "You obviously have not seen it in the sun."

"I confess, I rarely look at my hair when I'm indoors, let alone take a mirror outside."

"You have seen your sister's, and 'tis the same color. Men have told *her* she has hair like spun silver, I'll warrant."

"Not in my hearing, they don't."

Damaris giggled at the scowl that formed on his face. "It would take a brave suitor indeed to face a brother like you. Poor Genevieve."

"Poor Genevieve?" His eyebrows soared. "Poor me, more like. I am the one who has to chase them away when they grow too tiresome." He grinned a little. "Though, I must say, Genny is able to scare a good many away on her own."

Damaris shivered and realized that she was growing cold now that the heat of desire was fading from her body, leaving her skin bare to the evening air.

"Cold?" Alec asked, rubbing his hand up and down her arm.

"A little." Damaris nodded and sat up. "Perhaps we should get under the covers instead of lying atop them."

Alec seemed distracted by the sight of her naked breasts as she moved, but he let out a sigh and swung off the bed to pull the covers down. He crawled in beside her again and turned away, leaning out to lift the lantern onto the small chest behind them.

Damaris studied his back, enjoying the stretch and pull of the muscles as he moved. She reached out and ran a finger down the knobbed ridge of his backbone. Her fingertip touched a thin raised line, tiny and almost silver in the glow of the lantern light. Her brows drew together and she edged closer, spreading her fingers across his back.

There were more of them across his back, little lines of differing lengths, almost too pale to see, narrow but slightly ridged. "Alec?" She slid her fingertips across his back, moving from one ridge to another. "What are these?"

He went perfectly still beneath her hand, then shrugged. "Nothing." He remained turned away from her as he reached down to pull the covers up over his back.

Damaris grabbed the covers and held them in place. "They aren't 'nothing,' Alec, they look like . . . scars." She felt faintly ill and suddenly she wished she had not brought up the matter.

"I told you, my father was a disciplinarian." His voice was cool, even dispassionate.

"But what made—" Damaris stopped and shook her head. "I'm sorry. I shouldn't pry."

"It doesn't matter." He rolled over onto his back, concealing the marks, and linked his hands behind his head in a pose that would have looked casual had it not been for the muscles bunched in his arms and the flat, remote expression on his face. He did not look at her as he talked. "There is little enough to tell. My father believed that the appropriate punishment for a boy of my willful nature was birching."

"Birching!" Damaris sat up, appalled. "He beat you with a birch rod?"

"Well, to his credit, he used an Eton rod, not one of the larger prison rods. When I was still in the nursery, it was on the backs of my legs, of course, but as I grew older, he took to my back and shoulders as well. Nor was I a stranger to the rod at school." The corners of his mouth crooked up in a smile that was more a grimace. "A stiff neck is rarely appreciated by schoolmasters or prefects, though I believe that my father, oddly, valued my refusal to knuckle under at school, rather than deeming it the sin it was to defy him."

"Oh, Alec . . ." Tears welled in Damaris's eyes. "I am so sorry."

"'Tis all in the past," he said in the same careless, flat way. "Not worth talking about, really." He rolled up onto his elbow again, stretching his hand out to turn down the wick in the lantern.

Damaris reached out and smoothed her fingertips along one of the scars. He went still, not looking at her, not speaking, and she bent to press her lips softly against the slender ridge. Alec made a low, inarticulate noise in his throat, and his fingers curled into the sheets beneath him. She kissed the tiny line above it, then another. The tears swimming in her eyes welled out and plopped onto his skin.

He turned onto his stomach, his back fully exposed to her, his arm crooked up over his head as if to cover his face. Damaris wanted to cry, but she swallowed the tears and continued to kiss his scars. Her mouth was soft and tremulous, brushing over each thread. Alec lay rigid beneath her lips, his muscles taut as a bowstring. When she had kissed each scar she could find, Damaris slid her body over his, her arms going around him and slipping beneath his chest, so that she was pressed against him all the way up and down.

Alec moved at last, his hand coming up and finding her arm, then gliding down it until he covered her hand beneath him. His fingers slipped between hers.

"When I was little, I could not escape him, though ofttimes the servants would help me elude him a bit," he said in a quiet voice, the flat quality gone, but with a weary tone, as if he were exhausted. "I grew more cunning as I got older, and I found better places to hide. When he caught me, I would kick and scream, fighting him. That only made it worse, for then I embarrassed him because I did not take it like a Stafford. I acted like some common boy from the fields, he would say, and he'd whip me until the blood ran. I didn't care; I enjoyed infuriating him. But once when I fled, he hauled Genny out of the schoolroom and started to use the flat of a ruler on her legs."

"No! Oh, Alec!"

"He knew me well. After that, I stayed and took it, and he never touched Genny again. It was our unspoken agreement. Until I was fifteen, and I came home on holiday from school. I was always large for my age, and that year I spurted up. I was taller than he, and I had become accustomed to giving as good as I got if the prefects decided I needed to learn a lesson. My father thought to start on me—he claimed I had grown soft in the south, you see—and this time I took that bloody rod and broke it over my knee. He laughed and called me a proper lion's cub. I considered pinning his throat to the wall with one of the pieces, but I didn't. But he saw it in my eyes, and I think he believed me when I told him that if he ever tried that again, or if he raised a hand to Genevieve, I would kill him. He left me alone after that."

Damaris was so filled with turbulent emotions that she didn't know what to say or do. She wanted, fiercely, to remove the pain that lingered in Alec. She wished she knew how. But since she did not, she did the only thing she knew. She kissed him. First his shoulder, then his neck, and when she felt his body relax beneath her, she worked her way down his spine, laying soft kisses along the way. She rested her hands on his sides to steady her as she moved, gliding down his ribs.

He stirred, a low noise of satisfaction rising from his throat, and this emboldened Damaris to slide her hands lower, tracing the hollow of muscle in the sides of his hips and curving back up over the rounded form of his buttocks. That brought another soft noise from him, and Alec whipped over onto his back, putting his hands on her hips and lifting her up over him so that she straddled him.

Damaris glanced at him, a little surprised and unsure, but he settled her firmly against him. His eyes gleamed as he studied her. She could feel the engorged length of his manhood prodding at her soft, vulnerable flesh, and the movement stirred the embers of her own desire. Hunger grew and twisted in her as Alec covered her breasts with his hands, then swept his hands down her body and back up again, searing her skin with his heat.

It was absurd, she thought, that he could have such power over her, that the mere touch of his long, supple fingers on her skin could turn her hot and yielding, like molten wax. They had made love less than an hour ago, and she was already churning with desire for him again.

Alec dug his fingers into her hips, lifting her and sliding into her. Damaris gasped with surprised pleasure as she sank down on him, taking the full measure of him deep within her. She wriggled a little at the sheer pleasure of it, and she saw in his slumbrous eyes how much her movement aroused him. Delighted at his reaction, she rose up almost to the tip of his shaft, then eased back down.

Alec let out a low groan, his breath ragged, his fingers twisting into the sheet below. Damaris smiled, unaware of how seductively her lips curved, and began to ride him in slow, smooth strokes, pausing now and then to circle her hips. Every motion she made seemed to drive him deeper into desire, his skin flushing, his eyes feverishly bright.

Damaris reveled in his pleasure even as her own desire expanded and pulsed, begging for release. It was a slow, delectable torture of the senses, holding the aching need at bay while she pushed it ever higher. Alec slipped his hand in between them, his thumb finding the small, aching center of her coiling hunger. He stroked the slick bud, knotting the need within her tighter and tighter until at last she could hold back no more. The wave took Damaris and she trembled, a sob of pleasure escaping her lips. His hands went to her hips, holding her as he slammed into her, driving up into her as if he could reach the center of her very soul, until at last he, too, cried out as he reached his own peak.

She collapsed against him and started to roll aside, but Alec wrapped her arms around her, holding her in place.

"Stay," he murmured, his lips against her hair. "Stay with me."

And so she did, lying atop him as she slid into sleep.

Damaris awakened the next morning, squeezed into a narrow space where the small bed met the wall. It was a bed meant for one person, and when someone the size of Rawdon was in it, there was little room left for anyone else. As they slept, he had spread out, so that Damaris had been nudged farther and farther to the edge. It was a good thing that the bed was built into the wall or she would have fallen off entirely.

She rolled onto her side, back against the wall, and propped herself on one elbow. Dawn had crept through the grimy portholes on the opposite side of the small cabin, washing the room in pale light. Damaris was well content to just lie there for a while, gazing at Alec.

He was lying on his back, one long arm crooked over his head, his other hand resting on his stomach. Since he created enough heat for a banked fire, the covers had gotten pushed farther and farther down so that they now covered only enough of him for the bare minimum of modesty. His far leg had kicked free of the covers and was bent back over them, exposing the long line of his leg, lightly covered in pale gold hairs. The sheet slanted up across that hipbone, and above it was the wide plain of his chest.

Damaris was able to look her fill, as she had not been in the darkness of night and the heat of passion. He was a powerful specimen of a man, his body hard and padded with muscle. Her eyes moved slowly over his face, slack and peaceful in sleep, without his usual tight control, then down onto the wide hard points of his shoulders, taking in the lines and hollows of his collarbone, the sprinkling of light-colored hair that formed an inverted V. She thought of following that beckoning V with her finger, dipping down to where it disappeared under the sheet. It would be terribly unladylike, of course. It had been one thing to caress his body last night in the midst of passion, but quite another to express such curiosity in the full light of day, with her mind unclouded by desire.

She cast a quick glance up at his face, still blissfully asleep, then reached out a careful finger, hooking it under the sheet and sliding it ever so slowly downward, revealing the flat table of his stomach, the shallow dent of his navel, the satiny skin stretched tightly over his pelvic bones, the line of hair widening now to burst out in full force all around the staff of his maleness. She stared for a moment in fascination at the member, thickening even in his sleep.

She stretched her hand out, then drew it back.

"Go ahead."

Damaris glanced up, surprised, at the deep rumble of Alec's voice, and found him watching her through heavy-lidded eyes. She blushed at being caught in such immodest behavior, but the rich timbre of his voice and the heated look in his eyes stirred her almost as much as his nakedness. She hesitated briefly, then placed her hand on his chest and slid it across him, her fingertips finding and circling the dark flesh of his nipples. Her belly warmed to feel them prickle and stiffen beneath her touch.

Alec linked his arms behind his head, offering himself to her touch without defense, and the gesture stoked the growing warmth in her abdomen. Damaris answered his invitation by letting her hand roam over him, delving down onto his stomach, edging ever close to the throbbing center of his desire, until finally her fingers touched the quivering flesh. She curled her fingers around him, fascinated by the silken feel of his skin, stretched over the swelling hardness.

He swallowed hard, his whole body tightening, and when she bent to take his nipple in her mouth, he let out a sharp exhalation of breath. She trailed her lips over him, tasting the faint salt of his skin, her tongue circling and teasing his nipples. Alec was taut, ruthlessly restraining his hunger, allowing her to explore his body with infinite care. But, at last, he fisted his hands in her hair, and with a low growl, he dragged her head up to take her mouth in a long, deep kiss.

Desire stormed through them. Alec pulled Damaris beneath him and plunged into her. Damaris accepted him eagerly, wrapping her arms and legs around him, clinging to him as he moved in long, smooth strokes. With every movement, passion built and spiraled. Damaris dug her nails into his shoulders, unable to hold back a thin, high cry as he shuddered within her, sending them both over the edge into a trembling explosion of pleasure.

It was much later that they pulled together the strength to arise. Alec brought them back a plain breakfast that differed little from their supper the night before, but they wolfed it down with appetites sharpened by the night's activities.

Afterward, they spent a long, lazy day together, talking and laughing, occasionally going up on deck to stroll around and look out over the limitless blue of the ocean. Though the sailors were around them, going about their jobs, Damaris and Alec were separated, in a sense as alone together as they were in the intimate cabin belowdecks. Cocooned together, freed from the usual constraints of society, without even the constant presence of servants, they came to know each other in a warm intimacy.

Alec talked to her of his home and family, his pride and love for Castle Cleyre shining through his mundane descriptions of the place and people. He told her about his closeness with his sister, the two of them growing up united against the world, and, smiling, he spoke of their aunt, Willa, who now resided at Castle Cleyre.

"You will like her, I am certain. She is my mother's sister, not a Stafford at all."

"Ah, so then she is not your grandmother's child?" Damaris asked, leaning her head against his shoulder. They were sitting curled up together on the bed, having just taken their third perambulation around the deck.

"Good heavens, no." Alec chuckled. "Aunt Willa is terrified of the countess. She would not even come live at the castle until Grandmother began spending most of the year in Bath instead. Willa is a trifle vague—you will see—but she is the kindest of people. She feared my father as well, but for our sakes, she would brave him and Grandmother in order to visit us each year, and she managed to convince them to let us visit her in Cumbria in the summers."

"Was she close to your mother?"

"I don't know. I scarcely remember my mother. She died when Genevieve was only two and I was seven. She died in childbirth, the baby as well. She was a beauty, I can tell that from the portraits of her. Aunt Willa was a paler version of her—eyes not so blue, hair not so blond, face not drawn so finely. Nor did she marry as well, though it was by all accounts a love match. Her husband was a jolly sort, though I fear that when I was young I viewed him with the scornful eyes of a Stafford. He wasn't, I thought, what a man should be."

"And what is that?" Damaris rested her head in the hollow of his shoulder, turning to press her lips briefly to his neck.

"Oh . . . all ferocity and pride, I suppose, as my father was. Grand in stature and feared by all."

"And yet you did not follow your father in that way."

"No. I refused to be him. But I am still a Stafford."

"You are far more than that," Damaris protested, turning to sit in his lap and twine her arms around his neck, planting soft kisses over his face, punctuating each of her words with another kiss. "You are strong and brave. A good friend."

"Ahem. I believe it was you who designated me Lord Frost at your Twelfth Night gala, was it not?"

Damaris laughed, her breath touching his cheek in soft little gusts. "You will hold that against me always, won't you? Perhaps I did find you a trifle cold—you did not, after all, pay me the slightest attention."

"Ah, there you are wrong; I was quite aware of you." He stroked his hand down her leg and slid it back up beneath her skirts. "I still am."

"Indeed?" Damaris cocked an eyebrow at him. Her skin was already beginning to tingle in anticipation, her insides threatening to turn soft and waxen. "I think you will have to prove that to me."

"Will I?" He grinned, hooking his hand in the waistband of her underthings and tugging them downward. "I think that I can do that." His fingers slipped between her legs to find the hot secret center of her.

Damaris choked back a gasp, closing her eyes at the hot, sweet pleasure, and she sagged back against his supporting arm. Alec never took his eyes from her face as his fingers played with her, stroking and teasing until her face was flushed with passion and her hips moved urgently against his touch. He watched, desire stamped on his features, as pleasure took her, sending her moaning and trembling into the maelstrom.

Only then did he shift her and sink deep within her to ride out his own fierce passion.

Afterward, sated and warm and lazy, they lay together, naked and unembarrassed, as Damaris told him of her childhood, loose and free and bound around with love in a way that was foreign to Rawdon. She talked of the cities in which she had lived, of the sophisticated, glittering continental society in which she had moved.

"And yet you chose to live in Chesley," he said, leaning on his elbow and looking down at her quizzically.

"Do not discount Chesley," Damaris warned. "It has a very particular charm."

He smiled, twining a strand of her hair around his finger. "I think its most particular charm is you."

Damaris stretched up to kiss him lightly on the lips. "I wish—"

"Wish what?" Alec prompted when Damaris stopped.

"I wish that we could stay like this forever, that it did not have to end," she went on in a soft voice. She lifted her chin, looking at him almost defiantly. "Despite everything—those men and not having enough money, all of it—this time has been ... magical."

Alec curved his hand over her cheek, his eyes warm. "It does not have to end. We will still be together." He bent and brushed his lips over her cheek. "We will still have the nights." His lips touched hers. "In a much more comfortable bed." His mouth strayed to her other cheek. "And I intend to make full use of it."

Damaris smiled faintly. "I am sure you will." She ran her fingers slowly back through his hair. "But it won't be the same. I like having you in my bed."

His mouth widened sensually, his eyes suddenly brighter. "As do I." He touched his thumb to her lower lip, dragging it softly over the tender flesh. "I have no intention of losing you. We are both fully grown and independent. There is no impediment, no one to gainsay us. I shall make certain no servants talk, and there will be no stain to your name. Whether you are at Castle Cleyre or Chesley or London, believe me, I will find my way to your bed."

Damaris's heart twisted within her. Much as his words stirred her, she could not help but notice that in Alec's future, there was no talk of marriage. He might want her, but she would never be anything but his mistress. Of course, she had always known that. And if she had had any doubts, that fact had been driven home to her when he spoke about the effect the scandal with Jocelyn had had on his family. He would marry the sort of woman a Stafford should—and a woman born in scandal and wedded in scandal would not qualify.

She told herself it made no difference. When she had turned to him on this ship and invited him into her bed, she had realized how it would be. She had accepted it. And she would not cry about it now. She would take what she could have and leave the rest to worry about later.

So she smiled and wrapped her arms around Alec's neck, pulling him down to her. "I will hold you to that," she whispered, and kissed him.

Eighteen

The next morning, their ship sailed into Newcastle, and with some regret, Damaris and Alec left behind their cabin and their pretense of marriage. Here, so close to his home, it took little time for Alec to secure them an excellent breakfast in an inn, as well as a room where Damaris could bathe and wash the salt spray from her hair. When the maids had filled the tub with deliciously warm water and left the room, Damaris turned to Alec, beaming.

"Thank you! You cannot know how much I look forward to it."

"Oh, but I do. I am looking forward to it, too," he told her, a grin spreading across his face as he began to undo his shirt.

Damaris's eyes widened. "Alec, what are you doing?"

"I am equally in need of a bath. Why waste the water?" He stripped his shirt off over his head and tossed it aside. "I can wash your back, so it will be quite practical."

"Alec! We cannot," she scolded in a tone of mock indignation, though in fact the thought of his wet soapy hands on her body set up a distinct twinge in her nether regions. "We must be on our way; there is no time for what you're thinking."

"There is always time for what I'm thinking," he retorted. And, indeed, it turned out that there was.

It was a great while later (and with a good deal of water splashed on the floor) when they emerged, clean and smiling, from the tub. Damaris was by now no longer surprised to find that Alec had also managed to procure clean clothes. She deemed it prudent not to ask where he had obtained the dress he handed her, but its low neckline led her to suspect that among the people Alec knew well in Newcastle were some women of less than good repute. Still, it was, at least, not gaudy in either color or material, and a lace fichu from a notions shop soon made the bodice respectable. He finished off his catch with gloves and a rather fetching little hat, and Damaris breathed a sigh of relief that she would not arrive at his home looking like a ragamuffin.

"You really are the most perceptive of men," she told Alec as he handed her up into their post chaise.

"Am I?" Alec widened his eyes in surprise and sat down beside her. "I believe you are the first woman to espouse that notion."

Damaris wrinkled her nose at him. "I know you like to pretend that you are cold and uncaring, but no woman who has been around you for any length of time would believe that. You obviously knew how uncomfortable it would be for me to wash up on your doorstep, ragtag and travel-stained, and you went to a lot of trouble to ensure I would have something suitable to wear."

Alec took her hand in his. "Perhaps I am merely gratifying myself. I like looking at you in that frock—though I do think you could have left off the scrap of lace." He reached out and drew a finger across the top of the neckline.

Damaris slapped his hand away playfully, but she could not disguise the shiver his touch sent through her, nor did she object when he leaned over and kissed the soft slope of her breasts hidden beneath the lace.

"You are insatiable," she murmured, running her hand over his soft, shaggy hair.

"I know." He raised his head and smiled at her with unapologetic desire. "'Tis the effect you have on me. Every time I look at you, I am filled with lust." He sighed and shifted over to the seat across from her. "However, I feel sure you have no desire to arrive at Cleyre looking as if you have been making love in a post chaise, so I shall have to rein in my base nature."

They rode along with the curtains pushed back, gazing out at the countryside. Damaris could see the pride and affection in Alec's face, and it grew stronger as they drew nearer to his own lands. The sun was in the west when they clattered across a stone bridge that obviously meant something to Alec. His eyes brightened, and he sat down beside Damaris so that he could more easily see ahead.

As they rounded the next curve in the road, he said, "There it is. That's Castle Cleyre."

Damaris leaned over to look out the window, and she drew in her breath sharply. "Alec!"

She had thought she knew what to expect, but it was clear that her imagination had fallen far short. Alec's home was a fortress. It stood on a commanding hill above a curve in the river, almost as if the gray ribbon of water had been forced to wind around the castle's solidity. High gray battlemented walls faced the land, anchored at either end by a square Norman tower. Behind them rose the towers, both square and round, and the walls of the castle itself. Huge wooden gates stood open, and above the smaller gatehouse towers waved blue flags bearing the arms of the Earl of Rawdon. Damaris felt almost as if they had been transported back five hundred years.

"You grew up here?" she asked, looking at him.

He nodded. "'Twas a wonderful place for a boy, full of forbidden rooms to explore and all kinds of nooks and crannies to escape one's governess."

Damaris could not help but think of Alec's tale of hiding from his father and his birch rod, but she did not mention it, only slipped her hand into his, offering comfort as much as seeking reassurance at the overwhelming sight of his birthplace. He squeezed her hand lightly.

"Don't worry. You won't get lost. 'Tisn't as confusing as it looks, and most of it is never used, anyway."

The road they were on curved around the bottom of the castle hill toward the distant spire of a church, but their vehicle took the narrow driveway up to the castle. It was a slow climb for the horses up the long, low hill, but finally they clattered over a wooden bridge built across the long-dried-up moat and into the inner ward of the castle.

Damaris could see off to the right that most of that portion of the outer wall had fallen or been removed, replaced with staggered terraces of gardens leading gently down the hill. In front of them, the drive continued through a wide green lawn to curl past the front steps of the castle and on to the stable yard beside it.

By the time the chaise had pulled to a stop in front of the house, both of the imposing doors had been flung open, and a flurry of servants poured out. Footmen and maids dressed in neat black and white formed a line leading from the carriage to the front door. A majestic figure sailed out of the front door, his wide girth encased in a black jacket, a snowy white shirt showing between the lapels.

"Oh, my." Damaris's stomach felt suddenly cold as she gazed at the display. "How very . . . regal."

Alec chuckled. "It used to be even more so. Grandmother still had the footmen in livery before I countermanded that. Parsons—he's the fellow in front—finds me a poor sort of employer, I fear; he preferred my grandmother's sense of what is due the lord of Rawdon."

Alec stepped out, turning back to hand Damaris down from the carriage. She could feel the weight of a host of curious eyes turned on her. She was, she thought, beginning to understand much better the hint of arrogance that clung to Alec like a perfume.

"My lord." The butler stepped forward, bowing. "Allow me to welcome you home, sir. I fear you will find us sadly disorganized. Had we but known you were coming …"

"Yes, Parsons, I apologize for not letting you know," Alec told him, acknowledging the faint note of reprimand in the butler's statement. "In truth, I did not know myself until a few days ago, and it hardly seemed worth the bother, since I would have arrived with the notice, if not before."

"Your room, of course, sir, is always ready for you." Parsons glanced discreetly toward Damaris before adding, "Which other room should we prepare?"

"The blue chamber should do for Mrs. Howard," Alec told him.

They started down the line, the butler giving the plump woman at the head of the line the honor of introducing her by name, Mrs. Cuthbert, which Damaris took to mean she was the housekeeper, second in importance in the household only to Parsons himself. After that followed an array of servants who, Damaris was amazed to notice, were each greeted by name by Alec, often with a comment or question thrown in. They had reached the last maid and were approaching the broad stone steps when a charcoal gray and white animal came running around the corner of the house toward them.

Damaris pulled up, barely stifling a shriek as he charged, long hair flying, ears flapping, lips pulled back to expose long, curved teeth obviously meant for tearing apart his prey. But Alec laughed and spread his arms, bracing himself as the huge dog reared up to set his front paws on Alec's shoulders.

His head reached Alec's chin; he would have been taller than a man of more ordinary height. His tail wagged furiously and he whined with delight as he wriggled and tried to lick Alec's face.

"Shadow! Down!" Alec laughed, shoving the dog back down to all fours. "Mrs. Howard will think you are tragically ill-behaved. Damaris, I would like to you to meet Shadow."

"Your wolf?" Damaris asked drily.

"My wolfhound," Alec corrected, scratching a spot behind the dog's ears that seemed to send him into ecstasy. "He is descended from a line of wolfhounds given to my great-grandfather by Lord Kerry. Aptly named, since he is, sad to say, a mere shadow of those warlike animals."

Shadow, in his delight at being reunited with Alec, began to jump and whirl and fling himself at Alec's feet, where he promptly rolled over and waited expectantly for his stomach to be rubbed. Alec complied, but after a few minutes, he gave the dog a final pat, and they set forth again for the front door. Shadow fell in happily beside them, darting forward now and then to whip around and look at Alec, tail wagging, as if waiting to see what wonderful thing Alec would do next.

They stepped into a cavernous entryway. A long gallery ran off to one side, hung with gloomy-looking portraits, and two other corridors stretched away in other directions. A collection of swords hung in a circular design on one stone wall beside a suit of armor. On the wall opposite the front door hung a huge, ancient-looking tapestry filled with medieval figures doing something, though Damaris could not immediately discern what that activity was.

"Alec! Dear boy!" A short, plump woman hurried down the wide central staircase of the house, beaming and holding out her hands to Alec. "What a wonderful surprise!"

"Aunt Willa." Alec grinned and swept her a bow before he kissed her on the cheek.

"I could scarcely believe my ears when the maid told me you had arrived. You only just left, didn't you?" She gazed up at him through round spectacles, her gray eyes puzzled. "One does so lose track of time."

"Yes, I know, but you needn't worry," Alec assured her. "You are right. I have been gone only a few weeks. I had to return, you see; I fear I missed you terribly."

His aunt giggled and gave his arm a playful push. "Such nonsense as you do say!" She glanced curiously toward Damaris.

"Aunt, allow me to introduce you to Mrs. Howard. Damaris, this is my aunt, Mrs. Hawthorne."

Aunt Willa took Damaris's hand in hers, smiling sweetly up into her face. "Oh, my, what a lovely girl you are. I should very much like to paint you."

"Oh." Damaris blinked. "Of course."

"Aunt Willa is an accomplished artist," Alec told Damaris, with a proud smile for his aunt.

"Silly child, I am nothing but a putterer, I'm afraid. But I do love it. Not watercolor, I think; that's much too pale for you. No, that coloring is meant for oils."

"Careful," Alec warned. "She will have you posing for hours if you let her."

They continued bantering as they strolled to the drawing room, where the butler himself soon carried in a tray of reviving tea for the travelers, along with an assortment of scones, cream cakes, and other delicacies. The interval apparently allowed the servants time to whip Damaris's room into proper readiness, and after teatime, Alec's aunt led Damaris up the stairs and along the hallway to her room.

"Here you are, dear," the woman said, smiling at Damaris in her sweet, vague way, and patted her on the arm. "Mrs. Cuthbert will send one of the maids to help you. I am sure you should like a bit of time alone to freshen up."

Willa left, closing the heavy door behind her, and Damaris turned to face the room. There was a marble-manteled fireplace on one end, with a comfortable-looking chair set cozily before it. Two long windows overlooked the side gardens, and centered on the wall between them was a large bed with a tester covered in blue damask above it. Blue draperies at the window and corners of the bed obviously gave the room its name. The room was so large that it also held a dresser, vanity table and chair, and massive armoire, without seeming in the least crowded. A high ceiling added to the general sense of enormous space.

Damaris went to the window and looked out. Her room lay in the wing facing the gardens that spilled down the hillside, and her view was open all the way to the sheen of the river curving in the distance. She shivered, feeling suddenly quite lonely.

She had known that everything would be different when she and Alec reached the safety of his home, but she had not expected this degree of grandeur and formality. She thought of the long stretch of corridor separating her bedchamber from the one Aunt Willa had pointed out as the earl's. She thought, too, of his aunt and the myriad servants that would be around them. The cozy intimacy of their days pretending to be husband and wife were clearly at an end.

The castle had also brought home to her just how far apart she and Alec were in their backgrounds and manner of living and, well, almost every other way she could think of. This was his life, not only great wealth but also great position. He had been raised as the heir to an old, powerful family, the sort of people who likely regarded the royal family as mere German upstarts. This was Alec's life, and clearly there was no room in it for the bastard daughter of Lord Sedbury and his actress mistress.

Tears prickled at Damaris's eyes, and she hastily wiped them away as the door opened to admit a neatly dressed upstairs maid, loaded down with an armful of dresses. "His lordship sent me to bring you these, mum. 'Tis some of Lady Genevieve's frocks that might suit you."

Damaris was reluctant to borrow Alec's sister's clothes without her even knowing, but she knew Alec was right. She had nothing to wear besides what she had on and the simple dress Alec had gotten for her in Gravesend. Neither was anything she could appear in at a formal dinner in this house. She would have to wear borrowed clothes while she was at Castle Cleyre. So, with a little sigh, she helped the maid to sort through the gowns, picking out those that best suited her coloring. Though Genevieve was a little taller and slimmer than she, the clothes would fit well enough with some hemming, though her breasts might strain at the bodice a bit more than was entirely modest. That aspect of the gowns, she thought wryly, would probably suit Alec quite well.

She accepted the maid's suggestion that she lie down and rest after her journey. It was wonderful, she thought as she popped between the covers, to have a whole bed to stretch out in. But the truth was, she would have given all this up gladly to have spent another night squeezed into the captain's bunk with Alec.

Several hours later, Damaris made her way downstairs, clad in a light lavender gown that suited her best among the icy colors of Genevieve's wardrobe. The maid, Gilly, had helped her dress, then had pinned her hair up into an appropriately formal style of knots and curls. Damaris made a few wrong turns before she found the dining room, where Alec and his aunt waited for her in formal splendor.

The long room was centered by an almost equally lengthy mahogany table. A chandelier of glittering prisms hung in the center of the room, supplemented by candelabras on the table and the sideboard. Marching down the center of the table, between the two sets of candelabras, were a large silver epergne filled with fruit and two smaller ones. Vases of roses adorned the sideboard, casting their perfume upon the air.

Alec, Damaris, and his aunt took their places at one end of the vast table, and no less than four footmen stood at the ready to serve them under the watchful eye of Parsons. Damaris glanced at Alec, elegant in his snow-white shirt and black jacket. He looked so formal and distant that she hardly knew what to say to him. He asked if she found her room adequate, and she complimented its space and comfort. Aunt Willa commented on the weather and later asked Damaris where her home was.

The conversation limped along in the same manner throughout the long meal. Damaris wondered if it always took so long to eat here or if this was a special effort of the kitchen in honor of the earl's return. When it was finally over, she and Aunt Willa left Alec to his Port and retreated to the music room, where Damaris occupied herself by playing the piano and Aunt Willa soon drifted off to sleep. She awakened with a start when Alec came in, though, and they continued their polite conversation until Damaris could not stand it anymore and excused herself to retire to her room.

Gilly helped her undress and get into one of Genevieve's nightgowns of finest lawn. Damaris sent the girl on her way and sat down to brush out her hair. It was a relief to do so after the string of nights with only a cheap comb with which to try to manage her hair, so she brushed it until it floated around her shoulders like a jet-black cloud. Smoothing her hands down its length, she contemplated plaiting her hair to keep it from tangling as she slept. It was what she often did at home, but Alec liked it loose and free.

She thought of his fingers drifting through her hair and the way he'd wrap it like a silk cord around his wrist. Had their nights of pleasure ended, she wondered, gone with their journey? Here, with all the servants and his aunt nearby, he might not risk coming to her room. She had just taken off her dressing gown and was about to blow out the candle before climbing into bed when the softest of taps sounded at her door.

Her heart began to pound as she went to open it, telling herself that perhaps she had only imagined the faint sound. She found Alec leaning against the doorjamb. The hallway was dark behind him, lit by only a single sconce halfway down the hall. He smiled at her, and she stepped back quickly to let him in.

"God, it's been forever," he said, grasping her shoulders and pulling her to him to kiss her. "I thought supper would never end."

Damaris giggled. "I didn't know if you would come to me tonight."

"Always." He wrapped his arms around her and rocked a little from side to side. "I thought about telling Parsons to put you in the chamber next to mine, the one for the earl's lady, or even the one above mine, where one of the former earls' mistresses was wont to stay and which has a clever staircase leading to it from my chamber."

"Alec!" She looked up at him in amazement. "There is a secret stairway in your room?"

He nodded and grinned boyishly. "I'll show you one night, if you'd like."

"I would indeed. That is just like one of Mrs. Radcliffe's stories."

"Mm." He bent and kissed her ear, tracing the shell-like whorl with his tongue. "Except with a happier result."

Damaris giggled again, his tongue sending shivers through her. Suddenly her stay at Castle Cleyre seemed much brighter.

"But it would have been obvious to everyone that we were lovers if I had put you in one of those rooms, so I could not. Though, Lord knows, the servants no doubt guessed it anyway, the way I could not keep my eyes off you all evening." He kissed his way down her neck. "I am looking forward tonight to a full, soft bed in which to love you."

Alec bent and swept her up in his arms to carry her to bed. Damaris laid her head against his shoulder and smiled dreamily. It appeared her happiness had not ended after all.

Nineteen

Her time at Castle Cleyre turned out to be nothing like Damaris had feared. She soon learned that the servants' devotion to the Earl of Rawdon meant that they turned a blind eye to any hints that the relationship between Alec and Damaris was not platonic. Aunt Willa seemed not even to notice if now and then Alec took Damaris's hand and kissed it or sometimes swept her up in a hug. And no one said a word about the fact that they were together nearly all the time.

Their days were spent rambling about the estate—walking through the gardens or exploring the labyrinth of rooms and corridors that lay in and around and beneath the castle complex or riding out to a secluded meadow to share a picnic beneath the trees. And if their journeys together often wound up in an embrace or a kiss, there was no one to disapprove.

The nights they spent in Damaris's bedchamber, locked in passion or murmuring in the dark, dozing in the warm glow of their satisfaction. The only thing that spoiled Damaris's complete happiness was that each night before dawn, Alec slipped out of her bed and down the hall to his own room. She understood—and was even grateful—that he sought to keep her reputation untarnished. But still, she could not help but think of the days during their journey when she would awaken each morning with Alec's warm body next to hers.

Sometimes her mind drifted to the men who had tried to capture her and she wondered anew who lay behind the attempt. They should, she knew, do something about finding those men. But, in the face of her happiness, it was easy to let such thoughts slide by. The Bow Street Runner Alec had hired back in London would be bound to find something soon, just as Alec had told her, and then it would be time enough to take some action. Right now it was far too sweet to spend her days with Alec.

After supper, they usually visited with Aunt Willa in the music room or engaged in a spirited round of three-handed whist. And when his aunt retired, Alec and Damaris often lingered on the terrace, gazing at the moon and murmuring softly to each other.

One evening as they stood there, their fingers entwined, Alec gave her hand a squeeze and said, "Come. I want to show you something."

Intrigued, Damaris followed him inside. He picked up a candlestick and climbed the wide central stairs to the next floor. There, taking her hand again, he pulled her up the next flight to the floor above.

"Where are we? Is this the servants' floor?"

He shook his head. "They're in the wing down there." He

pointed toward the end of the dark hall, where another corridor shot off at a right angle. "This contains the nursery. Down there is where Genevieve and I lived with our governess."

He did not go in that direction, however, but stopped in front of the nearest door and opened it. The room was obviously unused, its furniture draped with dust covers that cast eerie shadows in the dim candlelight.

"I trust you did not bring me up here to meet a mad Stafford you have locked away," Damaris said lightly.

"No, all the mad Staffords are on the loose, I assure you." He led her to the fireplace, where he pushed at one of the carved panels on the mantel.

To her astonishment, it slid aside, revealing a lever, which Alec pulled, and a portion of the wall next to the fireplace swung open. Damaris gasped. "The secret staircase!"

Deviltry lit his eyes. "Yes. Care to explore?"

"As long as you promise we will not get locked away in the walls and wither to skeletons."

"I think it's safe to say we won't. I've used it a few times when I wanted to leave the house without my grandmother knowing. Follow me." Holding up the candle, he started down the steep, narrow stairs. They curved down in a circular way, ending at a small doorway. Alec turned the handle and pushed open the door, and they stepped into a large, elegant bedroom.

"This is your room?" Damaris glanced around. It had to be.

The fact that Alec had always come to her room at night

made being in his bedchamber seem somehow more illicit. It was a grand setting, as befitted the lord of the castle, furnished with dark massive pieces and heavy burgundy draperies. In front of the fireplace stood a high wingback chair with an ottoman and, facing it, a sturdy old rocker. A small table piled with books lay between them. The bed itself was equally impressive, high and wide, with tall columns at each corner and a wooden tester across the top, matching burgundy velvet drapes tied back with gold cords at the posts.

"I wanted you in my room," Alec told her, setting the candlestick aside and sliding his arms around her from behind. His voice was thick with desire. "In my bed."

His hands came up to cup her breasts, and he bent to nuzzle the crook of her neck. Damaris closed her eyes, her insides immediately turning hot and liquid. She leaned back against his chest, arching up a little as if to offer him her body. He was quick to take her up on the gesture, moving his hands without haste over her breasts and down her front, then back up, awakening every nerve in her body.

Releasing her and stepping back, Alec began to strip off his clothes, yanking off his boots and tossing them aside, followed quickly by his coat and neckcloth. When Damaris reached behind her for the hooks and eyes that closed her dress, he stepped forward, saying, "No, let me."

Slowly he undid the line of fasteners, and as the sides of the dress fell apart, he kissed his way down her spine. She shivered, the molten heat in her belly growing with each velvety touch of his lips. When her dress fell at her feet, he started on her delicate undergarments, pulling loose the ribbons that tied them and lifting them from her. Finally he knelt and slid off her slippers, then peeled down each silk stocking, following the path of his fingers with his lips, until Damaris's knees were so weak she feared they might give way.

He stood, looking at her, his heavy-lidded eyes roaming over her creamy body, taking in each swell and dip of her soft flesh, the proud thrust of her dark rosy nipples. "You are so beautiful."

He bent to kiss each breast tenderly, almost worshipfully, then raised his head to look into her face again. "What have I done to deserve you?" he murmured.

Alec scooped her up and carried her to the high bed, laying her down on it with care. He unfastened his shirt and pulled it off, his eyes still drinking in her body. Suddenly a spark lit in his eyes, and he turned away, saying, "Wait here. Don't move."

Damaris watched, puzzled, as he disappeared into the dressing room. She heard the sound of a key in a lock, then a door opening, and a moment later he returned, carrying a small chest. Damaris sat up curiously as he set the chest down on the bed beside her.

"I owe you jewels, you know, to replace the ones you gave up in Gravesend."

Damaris made a face at him. "A pair of earrings."

He turned the key in the chest and lifted the lid. Inside lay a glittering array of jewelry.

She drew in her breath sharply. "Alec! How beautiful!"

"The Stafford jewels," he said, a smile tugging at the corner of his mouth. "No doubt all ill-gotten."

"They're lovely."

"Not as lovely as you." He bent and picked out a magnificent diamond tiara and settled it on her head. "Ah, now it looks much better."

Damaris chuckled, taking off the tiara and setting it aside. "You are indeed foolish."

"Which ones do you like best?"

Damaris peered into the box, her fingers trailing over a bloodred ruby necklace and another of equally brilliant emeralds and diamonds, then settled on a chunky old-fashioned gold necklace set with cabochon sapphires. It was not as elegant or as glittering as some of the jewels, but there was a sense of age and pride in the stones that touched a chord in her.

"These," she said.

There was a certain satisfaction in Alec's smile as he picked up the heavy necklace. "The Bride's sapphires. You must be a Stafford at heart, my girl." He laid it around her neck and fastened it. The chain hung heavy and cold against her skin, the large, unfaceted stones a deep blue that reflected her eyes. Reaching into the chest, he took out a matching bracelet and clasped it around her arm, ending by settling a circlet of gold, centered by a large oval sapphire, onto her head.

"They are the heart of the Stafford family. One Lord Rawdon before we were ever elevated to the earldom, so long ago no one knows for sure which ancestor it was, gave them to his Scots bride. Some say he stole her from her father, some from her husband. Others vow he won her in battle. I have always preferred the story that they fell in love, and she stole out of her tower at night and fled down the hillside to where he waited, bringing the sapphires with her."

Damaris gazed up at him, entranced by the story and his voice, by the passion that imbued both.

"I think he did just what I've done," Alec went on. "He draped them over her bare flesh." He bore her backward on the bed. "And he looked at her, thinking she outshone all the jewels."

He bent and kissed one pert nipple peeking out just below the chain, and the touch of his mouth sent a spear of lust straight down through her. Damaris dug her fingers into his hair. The strands of his hair were like silk against her skin, and the feel of it aroused her just as his mouth did on her breast.

Alec made his way down her body, worshipping her with his mouth and hands, opening her to him in the most intimate way. His tongue teased her into desire as bright and hard as the most glittering jewel, bringing her to the peak again and again, until she was almost sobbing with need, and only then did he send her over the edge.

And even as she relaxed, the ripples of passion fading away, he thrust deep and hard inside her. Damaris gasped, her fingers digging into his shoulders as he cast her once more into that delicious swell of pure need. They moved together, their bodies joined in a timeless ritual, and as he shuddered against her, his seed spilling into her, Damaris clutched him to her, lost in hot, dark pleasure.

Damaris awoke the next morning, reaching instinctively across the bed for Alec. When her hand found only empty space, she opened her eyes and looked around, blinking. She was back in her own bed. Alec must have carried her here sometime during the night to ensure that the maid would not enter Damaris's room to find her bed empty.

She sat up, memories of the night before rushing in—the thrill of sneaking down the narrow hidden staircase, Alec's hands and mouth on her, loving her, the exquisite pleasure so intense it had pierced her like pain.

The vague suspicion she had held for days hardened into certainty: she loved Alec.

It was impossible, of course. He would never marry her. A Stafford could not be allied to a woman like her. Her father's lineage, even her wealth, could not make the tint of scandal she carried acceptable. A bastard child—one, moreover, who had eloped, forcing a marriage to a fortune hunter? No, those were not the makings of a Countess of Rawdon.

Her heart, though, had made the decision she had sworn she never would. She loved Alec, and she could not live without him. The only solution, she knew, was to be his mistress. Little as she had wanted that life, it was one she would accept in order to be with Alec.

And, oddly enough, now that she had come to that decision, she felt no regret. There was no room for anything but happiness in her heart.

That happiness lasted only until the following evening, when she and Alec were leaving the dining room with Aunt Willa. Alec, heedless of his aunt's presence, took Damaris's hand as they strolled down the hall. They stopped abruptly at the sound of the heavy front door closing, followed by the raised voices of a man and woman bickering as they walked across the marble floor.

"Well, it wouldn't have happened if you hadn't insisted on coming along," the woman said tartly.

Alec let out a soft curse and exclaimed under his breath, "Genevieve!"

Twenty

Alec barely refrained from cursing. Of all the ill-timed moments for his sister to come back to the castle! He looked over at Damaris. She was gazing back at him with an expression of alarm.

The man in the entryway answered sharply, "I could hardly let you travel all this way alone, now, could I? A fine sort of gentleman I should be then."

And Myles was with Genevieve. It only grew worse. Alec sighed as Damaris untangled her fingers from his and took a step apart. Only Aunt Willa was smiling with pleasure. Alec was truly fond of both his sister and his friend, but at this moment he wished them at the devil—or, at least, in London.

Myles and Genevieve had stepped into their view now in the center of the hallway. Myles had removed his hat, and he ran a hand back through his hair, causing it to stand up comically. He was as neatly and fashionably dressed as always, but he looked in some disarray, his cravat rumpled, his coat wrinkled, and his watch hanging on its chain from his waistcoat, fobs dangling. His expression was that of a man pushed to the brink.

Genevieve, on the other hand, trim in a russet-colored traveling gown, a matching hat on her head, had not a hair out of place. It did not surprise Alec; his sister often seemed to be refreshed, rather than wearied, by a sharp exchange of words. Genevieve held her cat in her arms, and the fluffy white animal was watching Sir Myles with an expression that could only be termed smug.

"You would not have even known I was coming here if you hadn't happened to visit that afternoon," Genevieve reminded Myles. "I told you there was no need to put yourself out."

"As if I could allow Rawdon's sister go all this way without any protection," Myles retorted.

"Allow me?" Genevieve asked in a dangerously smooth tone, one eyebrow arching.

Myles, obviously realizing his misstep, quickly changed tack, saying, "Some ladies would be grateful to have an escort on the road, you know. Especially when she learned her brother had been attacked on the toll road."

"I don't know what Rawdon's attack has to do with me. It was an entirely different time and place, not to mention a different person. In any case, I had the driver and his under coachman to protect me. They always carry pistols and a blunderbuss. And the groom was riding Alec's horse as well."

"Yes, I know, the Staffords travel armed to the teeth. It's enough to make one wonder what you lot expect to encounter. But your servants aren't in the inns with you along the way. Not every lout hanging about knows that you are a Stafford and it's more than his life's worth to accost you."

"Alec taught me to shoot, and I am an excellent markswoman. I always carry the little pistol he gave me when we travel. And Xerxes keeps an excellent watch."

"Of course he does," Myles agreed sourly, eyeing the cat with disfavor. "Only you would have a watch cat."

"Yes," Genevieve agreed pleasantly, "and he's an excellent mouser. I never have to worry about vermin in my chamber."

"I had better step in before Myles explodes," Alec murmured to Damaris, and he strode forward. "Genevieve. Myles. What an unexpected pleasure to see you."

"Alec!" Myles swung toward his friend, looking relieved. "The pleasure is mine. Believe me."

Alec chuckled. "It sounds as though you two must have had, um, quite a trip."

"Myles is just fussing because Xerxes had a little accident as we came up the hill." Genevieve gave a dismissive wave of her hand.

"I don't see why the animal had to choose to cast up his accounts right on my new boots." Myles peered down at one foot. "Just got them the other day."

"Hoby?" Alec inquired mildly.

Myles nodded. "Of course. Leather's soft as butter, has a perfect sheen. Or at least it did." Myles cast a baleful glance at the cat in Genevieve's arms.

"Xerxes cannot help it. I told you that the motion of the carriage sometimes makes him ill."

"Perhaps if he had not insisted on springing at my watch fobs all the way, the ride would not have been so turbulent."

Genevieve struggled to suppress a smile. "Cats are attracted to shiny objects."

Myles lifted his watch chain and examined it with a sigh. "Lost one of the fobs. No doubt it's in his stomach."

"Then 'tis no wonder he was ill."

Myles rolled his eyes at Genevieve, but his lips twitched, and he had to chuckle. "Damme, Genny, but you are a brat."

"Hardly a surprise to you," she tossed back, "as you have known me since I was ten."

"Perhaps Myles thinks that one day you will grow up," Alec offered. He took the cat from Genevieve's arm and set him on the floor. "I am sure Xerxes would like to reacquaint himself with the castle while the rest of us visit."

The white cat gave them all a disdainful look and pranced off, tail raised like a flag. At his departure, their aunt, who had borne a healthy fear of Xerxes since the time he sprang from a cabinet top onto her back, came forward to hug Genevieve.

"Genny, darling. I am so glad you have come home. Is the Season over already?"

"'Tis winding down. Perhaps it's a bit early."

"Isn't that wonderful?" Aunt Willa beamed and turned toward Myles. "And you've brought Sir Myles with you. How lovely."

Myles, never one to ignore the social niceties, swept Aunt Willa an elegant bow. "Mrs. Hawthorne, you are looking splendid, as always. I hope you have not given your heart to another while I've been gone."

"Oh, you." Willa patted his arm, a pleased flush rising in her cheeks. "You are an utter flatterer."

"You know Mrs. Howard, of course," Alec said, bringing Damaris into the greetings.

"Indeed." Lady Genevieve turned her coolly assessing gaze on Damaris. "I trust that you have had a pleasant stay here, Mrs. Howard."

"Yes, thank you. Pray forgive me for making free with some of your frocks." Damaris touched the ice-blue gown she wore. "I hated to be so bold, but Lord Rawdon was certain you would not care."

"No, of course not. 'Tis far better suited to you. But no doubt you have sorely missed your own clothes. When I received my brother's letter, I realized at once that you were up here in the wilds without any of your things. Just like a man not to notice such mundane details, isn't it? I went straight to your house. Luckily, I caught your abigail before she left the city, and she gave me a trunk of your clothes."

"Oh, my lady!" Damaris smiled with real pleasure. Whatever trepidation she felt about Alec's aristocratic sister joining them, it was momentarily smothered by happiness at once again having her own gowns, her own brushes. "Thank you. Indeed. You are most kind."

Alec studied his sister as the others exchanged polite chit-chat about Genevieve and Myles's journey and the state of London and the *ton*. It was unlike Genevieve to leave London early. Though she could never be considered a convivial person, she did not love Castle Cleyre as Alec did, finding it boring to spend long, cold winters in what she termed "that great old pile of stones." He had assumed that she would stay in London until he returned to escort her home, or perhaps that she would have gone with their grandmother to Bath. He could not help but wonder what had prompted her to come dashing all the way up to Northumberland. He did not for a moment believe it was from some altruistic impulse to bring Damaris her clothes or to see that his horse was returned to him forthwith.

Genevieve glanced over and met Alec's eyes. There was something in her face that told him he was right; Genevieve had come here for some particular purpose and, unsurprisingly, it had to do with him.

"Have you eaten?" he asked casually. "I'll ring for some supper for you. I am sure Cook will be able to have something ready quickly. We've only just finished."

"But no doubt you'd like to freshen up a bit first," Aunt Willa added, and linked her arm through her niece's. "Come, I'll walk you upstairs to your room and you can tell me all the gossip from London."

"Of course." Genevieve smiled fondly at the short woman.

As they strolled off together for the stairs, Aunt Willa's voice floated back to them as she said, in tones of dread, "Your grandmother is not coming also, is she?"

Damaris turned to the men. "I am sure the two of you are eager to talk to each other. And I am growing a trifle tired. If you will excuse me, I believe I will retire now."

Alec hated to see the touch of constraint in Damaris's polite smile, and normally he would have tried to cajole her into staying with them, just to prove to her that she had no need to feel uneasy around his sister. However, he suspected that whatever reason lay behind Genevieve's visit, his sister would be unlikely to reveal it in front of someone she scarcely knew. So he did not press Damaris, just bowed over her hand, giving her fingers the slightest squeeze, and watched as she walked away.

He turned to find Myles regarding him. Alec smiled. "Care for a restorative brandy?"

"Lord, yes," Myles replied with heartfelt relief. "London to Northumberland with that maniacal cat is enough to send one straight to Bedlam."

Alec chuckled. "I have often felt the same myself."

The two men strolled back into the dining room, where Alec sent one of the footmen for food and brandy. Alec studied his friend as they seated themselves at one end of the massive table. "What brings Genevieve up here in such haste?"

"I haven't the least idea," Myles confessed. "I went to call on her and the countess the other day, and she had everyone dashing about, making ready for an immediate trip home. When I found out she was planning to set out alone, of course I offered to escort her. She refused, but fortunately the countess was present and she overruled Genevieve. As a result, Genevieve scarcely talked to me the whole way up."

"My sister dislikes being crossed." The servant brought in

the brandy and Alec poured it himself, sending the footman on his way.

"I assumed her reason for the trip had something to do with your disappearance," Myles went on. "She told me she had sent a groom down to recover your horse and pay some debts."

"Good. Did she get back the jewelry?"

"Is that what she was talking about? She was going on to the countess about paying moneylenders, and at first I thought it was Genevieve who had had to cover her debts; but then I realized she would never have mentioned that to your grandmother."

"Well, she needn't have mentioned my doing it, either," Alec grumbled.

Myles took a drink and settled back in his chair, eyeing Rawdon. "I have done my best to be polite, but blast it, man, what the devil brought you and Mrs. Howard to Northumberland?"

Alec chuckled and began to recount the tale of their journey, beginning with his learning that Damaris had fled London. He carefully expurgated such details as their masquerading as husband and wife, but even so, Myles's eyebrows soared higher with each new adventure.

"Is it the same men who abducted her in London?" Myles asked when Alec's story finally brought them to Castle Cleyre.

"I believe so."

"But why are they following her?"

"I'm not certain." Alec shook his head.

"Perhaps I can clear that up for you." Both men turned to see Lady Genevieve standing in the open doorway.

"Genevieve." The two men rose to their feet, Myles moving to pull out a chair for her. Alec regarded his sister warily as they sat down. "What do you mean? What have you been up to?"

"Watching out for your interests," Genevieve retorted. "Clearly someone had to, as you seem to have taken leave of your senses."

"I beg your pardon?"

"Pray do not give me that look. I have known you far too long to be intimidated."

"Have you?" Myles asked with apparent interest. "I have known him since school days and that look still makes me quake in my boots."

"Oh, don't be buffoonish, Myles." Genevieve shot him a withering glance before returning her attention to Alec. "You have clearly lost your head over Mrs. Howard. When you sent me that bizarre missive about highwaymen and leaving Erebos in some farmer's barn—not to mention popping off to Northumberland on money secured by your tie pin, leaving me to retrieve all your things—well, it was obvious that I needed to do something."

"Besides the matters to which I actually *asked* you to attend?"

"Yes, Alec, besides those peculiar tasks. Given your behavior, I thought it was wisest to do a little checking into Mrs. Howard's background."

"Genevieve!" Alec clenched his jaw, his eyes flashing with

temper. "You went about asking questions about Damaris?"

"Yes, and you know what I discovered? Nothing. No one knew her. No one had ever heard of her or met her before that night when you invited her to our party. She appears to have sprung up from nowhere."

"I told you, she is from Chesley. She was merely visiting London. Good Gad, Genevieve, she is a friend of the More-combes."

"Pardon me if I do not find that the highest recommendation," Genevieve replied drily. "Finally, someone recalled seeing Mrs. Howard talking to Lady Sedbury at our party. Apparently they had a rather charged conversation. So I went to call on Lady Sedbury."

"Bloody hell!" Alec jumped to his feet. "What the devil did you think you were doing?"

"Looking after you!" Genevieve shot back, rising to face him. "Since you were clearly thinking with parts other than your head! Mrs. Howard is the by-blow of Lord Sedbury. Her mother was an actress. When Lord Sedbury died, he left her practically all of his fortune that was not entailed; it was a grievous insult to his family. She and her mother took off for the Continent, and when she was just barely out, she got married in a havey-cavey fashion. Lady Sedbury did not know the details, but there was some sort of scandal involved."

A cold rage rushed through Alec. He could not remember ever having felt such anger toward his sister. "Damn it, Genevieve! How dare you go sticking your nose into my business? Gossiping with that old crow about Damaris's life!"

"I was trying to protect you!" Genevieve's face was ashen except for the two bright spots of color on her cheekbones, and her light blue eyes shone with a silvery fire very like her brother's. "I could not stand idly by while some conniving woman sank her claws into you."

"You will not speak ill of Damaris in my presence," Alec warned her, his face as cold as if she were a stranger to him. "Do you understand me? Nor will I stand for your gossiping about her with anyone, let alone Lady Sedbury, who has been in no way kind to Damaris. It is none of Lady Sedbury's business, and certainly none of yours, what Lord Sedbury chose to do with his own money. There is no shame in his having loved his daughter. As for 'protecting' me, I am a fully grown man, and I don't need you trying to order my life as you please."

"Oh, no, you have done such a stellar job of keeping it in order in the past!"

Alec stiffened, and Myles murmured, "Genevieve."

"Damaris is not Jocelyn," Alec told his sister in a glacial voice. "And I am not naïve enough to mistake a pretense for love again."

"I am sorry." Genevieve looked abashed. "I should not have brought up the past. I did not mean to hurt you."

"Then what *did* you mean to do by carrying tales to me about Damaris? What happiness could you have thought you would bring me?"

"I did not want you taken in by—" She stopped as he raised a brow in warning.

"Then you should be pleased to know that I have not been

taken in by Mrs. Howard. She has already told me all of this. I know who her father was and what he did. I know that her husband was a scoundrel who maneuvered her into marriage in the hopes of getting his hands on her fortune. I know that her grandmother treats her with disdain. Did your new friend Lady Sedbury also happen to mention that she had set four ruffians with guns upon Mrs. Howard and me?"

"Lady Sedbury hired your attackers?" Myles asked in astonishment.

"I don't know," Alec admitted. "But I have no other candidates for the villainy." He swung his fierce gaze back to Genevieve. "And I must say that I find it rather disconcerting to learn that my own sister is in league with the people who hired men to hunt us down."

"Really, Alec, I am not 'in league' with anyone!" Genevieve retorted hotly. "You just said that you did not know whether or not Lady Sedbury hired your attackers; it seems most unlikely to me."

"Oh, well, that no doubt makes it perfectly all right for you to go about spreading rumors about Damaris and me."

"I did not spread any rumors!"

"Genevieve. Alec." Myles stepped between them and turned in appeal to Rawdon. "Genevieve does not know Mrs. Howard as well as you and I do, Alec. I am sure that once she gets to know her better, she will realize her mistake. She was trying to protect you, which—"

Myles was rewarded by receiving furious glares from both the combatants.

"I don't need you to defend me, Myles," Genevieve said pointedly.

"I don't need protecting," Alec declared at the same time.

Myles turned up his hands. "I should know better than to try to reason with either one of you. Heads like iron."

Genevieve turned to her brother, saying stiffly, "Pray accept my apologies, Alec. Perhaps it was wrong of me to pry, even though I did so only out of concern for you. I assure you that I said nothing concerning you or your interest in Mrs. Howard to Lady Sedbury or anyone else."

Alec nodded. "I know that is your only interest in the matter. I am not angry, really." That, of course, was a blatant lie. A cold, hard fury still coursed through him, seeking outlet. But he knew that it was not reasonable; he could trust Genevieve to find out information without revealing anything about him or his situation.

His sister offered him a faint smile in reconciliation. "And now, of course, that I know you are aware of Mrs. Howard's past, I shall not worry about your doing something foolish. One expects men to take mistresses, after all." She blinked, somewhat taken aback by the sudden flare of fire in her brother's eyes. "Alec? What is the matter?"

"Damaris is not my mistress," he said tightly. But, of course, that, too, was a lie. What else would one call her, when he slept every night in her bed? It was just that it jabbed him like a hot poker to hear someone label her so. His fingers curled into fists at his side. He found that he wanted very much to hit something. "I will not allow you to treat her with contempt."

Genevieve's eyes widened a little. "I have no intention of being *rude*, Alec. Do you think I am unable to play the game? That I cannot pretend that nothing is going on even though everyone kno—"

"There *is* nothing going on!" Alec jammed his hands into his pockets and took a step back. He felt strangely cornered. "Mrs. Howard is—she is a lady who is eminently worthy of your respect."

The butler appeared, tray in hand, followed by two footmen similarly burdened. Alec seized on the opportunity to escape. "Excuse me. Clearly I am in no humor to be among friends. I will leave the two of you to your supper." Ignoring Myles's and Genevieve's astonished expressions, Alec turned on his heel and left the room.

Well, he thought as he strode rapidly away, he had certainly handled that like a novice. His clumsy protestations had no doubt thoroughly convinced his friend and sister that he and Damaris were lovers. One would think that he had never engaged in an affair before.

Like Genevieve, he knew how these games were played. It was simple: if one kept a lower-class mistress, she did not mix with polite society, and if one was engaged in an affair with a woman of one's class—a married woman or widow, say— one pretended to all and sundry that nothing was transpiring between the two of you, then slipped secretly down the hallway or knocked quietly on her back door. Everyone knew exactly what was going on and pretended not to notice—as long as one did not flaunt the affair.

Damaris was a lady, of course. He scowled at the thought that anyone might label her otherwise. She was not the sort to whom one would offer a carte blanche. She was a woman of breeding and refinement, no matter her parents' lack of wedding lines. He would not dream of setting her up as his mistress. But, he wondered suddenly, what did he plan to do with Damaris?

He stopped and glanced around, finding somewhat to his surprise that he had wandered onto the back terrace. He walked over to the stone balustrade and stared out at the moon-washed garden. The truth was, he *had* no plans concerning Damaris, nothing but a tumult of desires and joys and aching needs, a desperate wish to be with her every moment, to look at her, talk to her, hold her close, to go to sleep with her in his arms each night and wake up the same way every morning.

That was madness, of course. No matter how sweet it had been on the trip to wake up with Damaris warm and willing in his bed, that sort of thing was impossible outside of marriage. And he could not marry Damaris. Not that she was beneath him—Damaris was a finer lady than most noblewomen he had met. But Alec was done with romantic notions. Any marriage he made would be for duty only, the sort of alliance a Stafford should make. He had done enough harm to his family by following his heart with Jocelyn; he would not do so again. Damaris herself would be better off not married to him; she, like his sister and grandmother, would bear the brunt of the scandal much more than he. The men at his club would not turn away, but Damaris would be ostracized by most of the women of the *ton*. She would feel every snub, every cut. No, marriage would be a misstep all around.

But his sister's words had stung. Her easy assumption that Damaris was his mistress was like acid to his soul. And, perversely, the fact that making Damaris his mistress was what he was doing only made him resent Genevieve's words all the more. He hated the thought that his sister would look down on Damaris, that she assumed Damaris was a woman of easy virtue.

Alec set his jaw and turned around, leaning back against the half wall and crossing his arms, his head sunk in thought. If Genevieve saw him clandestinely going to Damaris's room or leaving it in the morning, that was exactly what she would think. He had to be careful not to dishonor Damaris, not to damage her reputation. However little he liked it, it was clear that now he must be more circumspect in his behavior. He thought of Damaris's room, which lay on the opposite side of his sister's. He would have to be bloody careful if he wanted to keep Genevieve from knowing he was staying there at night.

Indeed, he had to be more than careful, particularly tonight, with Genevieve having just arrived. He would think of some way for him and Damaris to be together soon, but he could not go to her tonight. Tonight he would have to play the gentleman. With a sigh, he resigned himself to a long and lonely night.

Twenty-one

$\mathcal{D}$amaris awakened late the next morning. She lay for a long time gazing up at the ornate tester above her bed. It was no wonder she had slept so late, she thought. For long hours last night, she had lain awake, her ears alert for the gentle tap of Alec's hand on her door. Even after it had sunk in on her that he was not coming to her bed, she had waited, hoping against all logic that she was wrong. Miserably, she had buried her head in her pillow, fighting her tears.

She feared that Alec had not come to her because his sister and friend were here. He was ashamed of her, she decided, afraid that they would discover his affair. She told herself that it was not so dire, that he was only being a gentleman now that others were here; he did not want to harm her reputation. But she was well aware that he could walk down the empty hall in the middle of the night and enter her room unseen by anyone. Even if Myles or Genevieve did happen to see him, they would not remark on it. Such things took place all the time; she had often heard of assignations at country houses where gentlemen tiptoed from their own beds to those of willing ladies.

Her heart squeezed within her chest. She could not bear to think of the possibility that Alec was embarrassed by her. That he might be done with her.

She got up and washed and rang for the maid, who brought her tea and toast, then bustled cheerfully about the room, opening the drapes and bringing Damaris's dressing gown and slippers to her. "Isn't it grand, having your own things to wear now?"

"Yes." Damaris made herself smile as she put on the robe and sat down at the vanity for Gilly to brush her hair.

The girl picked up Damaris's silver-backed brush and began to run it through her hair, carefully easing out the tangles sleep had put in it. "'Tis a lovely morning today, miss. The gentlemen went out early."

"Oh, really? Where did they go?" Damaris struggled to keep any hint of disappointment out of her voice.

"Hunting, they said, miss. They took that great lummox Shadow with them, though, so they may not come back with anything. That dog's more likely to frighten the birds away than find them."

Damaris had to smile at the thought of the happy, foolish dog bounding about in the fields, barking at birds, though her heart sank, knowing that she would not see Alec this morning. She could not help but wonder how it had come about that he and Myles had decided to go out hunting. Had it been

Myles's suggestion? Or was Alec avoiding her yet again, as he had last night?

On such dismal thoughts, Damaris dressed and went downstairs, unable to force down more than a piece of toast. She found Aunt Willa and Genevieve in the sitting room and passed the next hour with them in stilted conversation. Pleasant as Damaris found Aunt Willa, Genevieve's cool, aloof manner left her feeling awkward and vaguely out of place. They passed the time exchanging pleasantries about the loveliness of the day and the history of the castle and the area.

It was a great relief when Willa departed for her usual long tramp through the countryside. Damaris was quick to excuse herself as well, declaring that she wished to read a bit in the garden. In the library, she pulled out a book at random and went outside. It was easier to breathe out here, she thought, strolling along the neatly ordered path, bordered on each side by roses. She walked through the leafy green arbor and down the steps into the lower garden.

A man suddenly stepped into the path a few yards in front of Damaris, startling her, and she jumped, her heart pounding. He stood in the shadow of the hedge, his face unclear, and Damaris's thoughts went immediately to the men who had tried to abduct her. She thought of how far it was back to the house and whether she could reach the door before this man caught up with her. She began to back up, saying, "Who are you? What are you—"

She stopped as the man stepped out of the shadows into the sunlight. The color drained from her face.

"Why, Damaris, do you mean to tell me that you don't recognize your husband?" he asked as he sauntered toward her. "How careless of you."

Damaris stared at him, unable to move. "Barrett!"

He looked much the same despite the eleven years that had passed since the last time she saw him. It was the same thin, sensitively handsome face, the same dark hair, a lock falling in poetic disarray onto his forehead, the same melting brown eyes.

"But you—you are dead!"

"As you can see, I am very much alive." He spread his hands out to his sides. "And I am also very much your husband."

"Oh, my God." Damaris's knees went weak beneath her, and it was all she could do not to crumple to the ground. She sat down heavily on the nearest stone bench. Her brain was a jumble of thoughts and emotions, and overriding them all was one name: Alec! What would he do? What would he think?

"What happened?" Damaris asked. "Why did you not tell anyone you weren't killed in that fire?" Suspicion crossed her features. "Did you plan it? Did you set fire to it yourself? You did it to hide from your creditors, didn't you!"

He chuckled. "What dreadful things you accuse me of! I did not set the fire. I simply slipped away from the inn before dawn in order to avoid settling my accounts. But when I heard that I was believed dead, well, it suited me perfectly well. So much easier to start a new life when no one knows you're still alive."

Damaris's lip curled in disgust. "Why are you here? Why

do you—" Her eyes widened, and she jumped to her feet. "It's you! You are the one who sent those men after me! You tried to abduct me!"

He grimaced. "I could hardly allow you to start running about London, now, could I? It caused me no end of trouble, having to leave Lady Rawdon's party early for fear you would see me. Obviously I couldn't risk running into you somewhere else. One of us had to go, and I was not about to leave London myself." His face darkened. "You always were the devil of a nuisance! Whatever possessed you to enter London society after all these years? I knew it would be the end of Dennis Stanley if you recognized me."

"Dennis Stanley—oh! So that is your identity now? Very clever—taking on a last name of a highborn family, just as you did last time. Never actually claiming to be one of them, just passing it off modestly if someone asked outright, saying you were not an *important* member of the family."

"Yes." He ignored the bite in her tone, preening a little, as if she had complimented him. "It was inspired, I always thought."

"You tried to kidnap me to keep me from recognizing you and revealing who you really were?"

"I could hardly let you ruin everything when I had the shy little bird right in my hand." He held out his hand, cupped palm up, and snapped it closed. "The Engleton heiress was all but mine."

"What did you plan to do? Kill me to keep me from talking? Hold me prisoner the rest of our lives?"

"I wasn't sure. I couldn't decide whether to take you out of the country and threaten you so you wouldn't return or just keep you locked away somewhere for a few months until I could secure the silly chit. I thought of selling you to white slavers so you would disappear entirely but, alas, I did not know any."

"You are a vile creature." Damaris looked at him with contempt. "Is that why you are here? Do you mean to snatch me out of Rawdon's garden? Knock me over the head and lock me up somewhere? You are a fool if you think you can go against the Earl of Rawdon. Alec will crack you like a nut."

"His mistress's husband? I think not." Barrett's smile was not reassuring. "You see, I thought about the matter more closely after those fools managed to lose you time and again. It was excessively annoying, but then I realized that perhaps it was all for the best. I wasn't looking at it the right way. Why bother with that bacon-brained Eleanor Engleton when I already possessed an heiress? One, moreover, who is not plump as a pigeon and possessed of a fatuous giggle. It has been eleven years, after all, and I realized that you will soon come into your fortune. You'll get it at age thirty, isn't that right?"

"And, being my husband, you could get your hands on it." Damaris narrowed her eyes.

He smiled. "I think a trip abroad would appeal, don't you? We could go back to Italy, revisit the places where our romance blossomed."

"You are mad if you think I would go anywhere with you."

Damaris whipped around and started toward the house, but Barrett caught up with her, grabbing her by the wrist and pulling her to a stop. "What are you doing?" Damaris tried to jerk her arm from his grasp. "Let go of me, or I shall scream. If you have any sense, you must know that Alec will tear you apart."

"You forget, I have made a study of the wealthy and titled for some years now. I know very well who the Staffords are. I know that while they are a—how shall I put it—a vengeful lot, they are also unbearably proud. Arrogant, some say. And the Earl of Rawdon will not subject his family to scandal just for the sake of his bastard mistress."

Damaris paled, and Barrett let out a chuckle.

"Ah, that hit home, did it not? We both know you are enticing enough for Rawdon to dally with, but not enough to ruin his good name for."

"He will not let you take me," Damaris said through gritted teeth. However little Alec might want a scandal, she was positive of that. "He may not want a scandal, but if you know the Staffords, you know that no one takes what is theirs. Castle Cleyre has fearsome dungeons, I have heard."

She had the satisfaction of seeing her no-longer-dead husband flinch at hearing those words, but he recovered quickly, digging his fingers into her arm and giving her a shake.

"Then I guess I shall have to make sure you leave now before he comes back." Barrett grinned at her expression. "Ah, you underestimated me. Not surprising, since you are accustomed to dealing with clunch-headed nobleman like Rawdon.

I know the earl is not here; he went out hunting with his friend and won't be back for hours. Which gives you ample time to go back to your room, gather a few of your things, and come away with me. I have our horses waiting in the copse below."

"I told you—I am not leaving with you!" Damaris jerked her arm back, and this time he released it, so that she stumbled back and came up hard against a tree, scraping her arm.

"Oh, I think you will. You see, if you do not come with me, I shall reveal to the world that you are my wife. It is uncommon, true, for a husband to apply to Parliament for an act of divorce, but I shall do it. On the grounds of adultery. I have a clear case against you and, of course, the earl. As the guilty party, Rawdon shall have to pay a tidy sum, but that will hardly compare to the scandal it will bring upon him and his family. No doubt his sister will find it a trifle difficult to make a suitable match with that stain on the family name. It won't be as much money as I would get when you turn thirty, but then I would be quite free to marry again, with none of these worries about being found a bigamist. And it might just be worth it to see the Earl of Rawdon brought low."

Rage rushed through Damaris, filling her until she thought she might explode. "You snake! You absolute, utter blackguard. Go away and leave Alec alone. I shall pay you to do so. I shall arrange with my trustees to fund you; they accede to my wishes now that I am older. And when I turn thirty I shall pay you more to stay out of our lives!"

"And allow my wife to continue to cuckold me with the fair-haired earl? I think not. Besides, I shall have full right to all your money in two years. Why should I settle for only a part? No, the only way for you to make sure your precious lover survives his mistake of sleeping with you, without drowning in public humiliation, is for you to come away with me now, quickly and quietly. Go upstairs and pack. Oh, and leave him a short note explaining that you are ending your affair. We don't want him following us, after all."

"I cannot keep him from doing that."

"He won't stoop to chasing you if he thinks you are tired of him. Don't beg him for help or imply that I am forcing you."

"You *are* forcing me!"

"I am merely offering you a chance to let your lover escape the scandal. It will be all for naught if he chases us down and we have a very public brawl. And since I have no doubt that he would come out the victor in any such struggle, well, I would simply have to forestall that by shooting him as soon as he appears. No court would find me guilty of murder for shooting the man who was diddling my wife. On the other hand, if you tell him you are ending it, pride will not let him crawl after you."

Damaris stared at him, numb with shock. "You would *murder* him? I would not have thought that even you were that low."

"My dear girl, I have no desire to lose several of my teeth or have my jaw broken by that lovesick giant. I would shoot him in an instant."

It was all Damaris could do not to fling herself at him, clawing and kicking. If she had had a gun in her hand, she would have fired it at him—indeed, she thought she would have attacked him with a knife or stick or anything that was at hand. But she held not even her trusty hatpin, and the fury just burned through her, leaving her empty and shaking.

"I—I will be only a few minutes," she said dully. "Wait for me here."

Damaris turned and started back to the house. She felt numb, as if she were stuffed full of cotton batting. Her mind worked frantically, searching for some way, any way, out of this nightmare, but her thoughts skittered all around like leaves in the wind. She could not pin them down, could not think, for any thought was swept away by the cold, hard image of Alec lying dead on the floor.

She had no doubt that Barrett—or whoever he was now—would follow through on his threat to shoot Alec if Alec attacked him. Nor did she have any doubt that Alec would attack him if he believed the man had seized her or hurt her. The only way to keep that from happening was to do as Barrett had suggested. She must write Alec a simple note ending their affair in a cold, clear fashion. The only way to save him was to cut him to the quick.

Tears filled her eyes at the thought of Alec discovering that another woman had run away from him, and her resolve almost melted away. She did not have to go with Barrett. She could stay inside the castle and be safe until Alec returned home. She would tell him what had happened. But no, she knew if she did that, Alec would charge out into the night to find Barrett. As soon as he drew close enough for Barrett to see him, Barrett would kill him.

Barrett clearly had no moral qualms, and he was right in thinking that any court would rule shooting his wife's lover justifiable. Barrett would not hesitate to hide somewhere and shoot Alec in cold blood as he approached.

If she could by some miracle keep Alec from pursuing him, Barrett would do as he had threatened and put Alec squarely in the center of a scandal. His reputation would be in tatters, especially after the beating it had taken when Jocelyn jilted him a year and a half ago. Damaris might tease him for his arrogance, but she could not bear to see that proud tilt of his head change. She refused to be the cause of his humiliation before his peers. And he would not be the only one who suffered; his family would be hurt as well. It would damage both the countess and Lady Genevieve, and while Damaris had no great fondness for either of them, she could not let innocent persons be harmed. More than that, she knew how Alec would suffer at the thought that his actions had hurt his sister and grandmother.

No, she could not allow that to happen. She had to go with Barrett. Later ... well, later she would find a way to take care of Barrett. Once they were far away from here, where whatever happened could not damage Alec, then she would do whatever it took. That resolution was a cold, hard lump in her chest. But right now, the most important thing was to keep Alec from following her.

When she reached her room, she stuffed a few of her things in a satchel. Her hand lingered over the comb Alec had bought her, then she dropped it into the bag, too. She could easily leave most of her things, but that gift from Alec she would keep and treasure forever. She wavered over her gun as well. She was not sure how she would deal with Barrett, but it would be of great help to have a weapon. However, the gun was empty, and she carried no powder or shot for it. Nor did she know where Alec kept such things.

Slipping out of the room, she tiptoed down the hall to Alec's bedchamber. If she was lucky, Alec would not have bothered to take the small knife that he often carried in his boot, since he and Myles had gone out with a full complement of guns for their hunt, not to mention the gamekeeper and his assistants and all the dogs. The knife was not lying handily about on top of the dresser or table, so she eased open a drawer and checked inside it. She felt rather guilty, sneaking about, looking through Alec's things, and she hoped a servant would not chance to come in and find her.

Finally, in the narrow drawer devoted to socks, she found the lethal weapon, as well as the scabbard Alec typically strapped on his calf to carry it. She had to buckle the scabbard around her thigh to make it fit, but it stayed, and she slid the knife into place and shook her skirts back down. Feeling well satisfied, she scurried back to her room, where she sat down at the delicate mahogany secretary and took out a piece of paper to write Alec a note.

But she found that the words would not come. She wrote two sentences, then scratched them out, certain that they revealed too much. Finally, she ended up scribbling down a terse declaration that she was leaving. "The affair is over. It was enjoyable, but I have grown tired of it." Was that enough to stop him? she wondered.

Barrett was right in saying that Alec was a proud man. Surely his pride would not let him chase after a woman who no longer wanted him. Thea had told Damaris that Alec had not pursued Jocelyn when she ran away, at least not at first, because of his pride. Following on the heels of that betrayal by his fiancée, surely he would be yet less likely to run after Damaris. She was not even engaged to him. If he made no fuss about it, no one need know that she had run from him.

But, she knew, nothing could take the sting away. She was fleeing from him exactly as the woman he had loved before had run from him. Damaris's heart clenched at the thought of hurting Alec. She did not flatter herself that he loved her the way he had loved Gabriel's sister. Certainly he was not planning to marry her. But even so, her leaving would be a slap in the face to him—salt in the emotional wound that Jocelyn had left.

Everything in her rebelled at the thought of hurting him this way. But she knew, too, that the hurt would serve to keep him from following her, perhaps even more than his pride would. He would not let her or anyone see his pain. For that reason, she could not take away any of the sting, as she longed to do. She could not write that she loved him or that she regretted her actions. She could not beg him not to think badly of her.

And so, tears spilling out her eyes and splashing onto the

notepaper, she signed her name in a hand as small and tight as she felt inside, then folded and sealed it. She wrote his name on one side, and dashing the tears away from her cheeks, picked up her satchel and trotted down the stairs. She went first to the silver tray on the narrow table near the front door, on which calling cards and the mail were placed. Slipping the note onto the tray, she turned and started quietly down the hallway to the garden door.

"Mrs. Howard?"

Damaris stopped, inwardly cursing, and turned toward the stairs. Alec's sister stood on the bottom step, her hand resting lightly on the newel post. Her pearly white cat sat a few steps above her, tail curled around him, staring down at Damaris with an imperious stare identical to his mistress's.

"Oh. Lady Genevieve. Good afternoon. I mean, good morning, I guess." Damaris offered a nervous smile.

Genevieve's eyes flickered to the satchel in Damaris's hand. She stepped down to the entryway floor and started toward Damaris. "Are you going somewhere, Mrs. Howard?"

"Yes. I—I am leaving. I have left a note for Lord Rawdon." She glanced toward the folded paper on the tray.

"Indeed? Then you have not spoken with him?" Genevieve's tone was glacial.

"No. I—I cannot. I mean, my nerve may fail me." Damaris swallowed against the tears that threatened to rise in her throat, and she took a step closer to the fair-haired woman. "Please . . . you know that it is better if I leave. I don't want to live as any man's mistress. Even Alec's." She saw no need to add that, little as she wanted to, she had already decided to accept that half-life in order to be with Alec.

A faint ripple of emotion touched Genevieve's perfect face, but she said nothing.

"Alec may be angry, I know, but in the end . . ." Damaris swallowed again. She could feel the tears swimming in her eyes, but she blinked them away. "It will be better for him. I know you think so too."

Genevieve's eyes flashed. "I will not have him hurt." There was a fierce tone in her voice that echoed Alec's.

"I'm sorry. I do not want that either. I never wanted . . ." She stopped, certain that she would break into sobs if she continued. Whirling, she ran down the long hallway toward the far door. No footsteps followed her.

Twenty-two

Alec strolled across the yard, casually chatting with Myles. Shadow loped along in front of them, his tongue lolling out, wet and muddy and looking as smugly pleased with himself as if he had actually behaved like a hunting dog instead of charging around, barking madly at the birds and generally getting in everyone's way. Alec knew how he felt. They had bagged only a few grouse, but it didn't matter. It had been a nice tramp with a good friend and his dog, and now he had the rest of the day with Damaris to look forward to.

A footman opened the door for them, then recoiled in horror as Shadow lumbered in. Alec jumped forward, hooking his hand around the dog's collar, catching him just before he launched into a thorough shaking to remove the water and mud from his coat.

"No you don't, my fine friend," he told the happy dog. "The housekeeper will have my head if I let you dirty her nice clean floor. Here." He handed the dog over to the footman. "Take him down to the kennels and tell one of the men to clean him up before he comes back in."

Shadow, seeming aware of the bath that lay in his future, stiffened his legs and leaned back, doing his best to sit down as the footman dragged him away, but his paws slid easily over the polished marble, and in a moment he was out the door, tossing back a final pleading look toward Alec.

Myles chuckled. "Poor Shadow. You'll be in his black books now."

"Not him. He won't remember by the time he returns to the house. He'll simply be happy to see us again. Unlike Genevieve's cat, who remembers the slightest transgression and holds it against you for days."

The cat in question was seated on the flat top of the newel post at the bottom of the stairs, studying them with a cool, unswerving gaze. Both men cast a wary eye at the animal.

"I think he rather holds it against me that I exist," Myles confessed.

Alec glanced down and saw a folded piece of paper lying in the silver salver on the entry table. His name was written across it, and though he had not seen her write more than once or twice, Alec was certain that the flowing script was Damaris's hand. His heart stuttered in his chest, and he was touched by a sudden, inexplicable dread. He stopped and looked at the table, curiously reluctant to pick up the note.

"Alec?" Myles, a few feet past him, realized that his companion had stopped, and he turned back toward him. "What is it? You look—" He frowned.

Alec made no answer, just picked up the note, turning it over to carefully break the seal. He unfolded it and looked at the paper, where words and whole sentences had been scratched out. It was blotched here and there, the letters streaking, but it was short and simple, and the import was clear: Damaris was gone.

"Alec!" Myles's voice was alarmed, and he crossed back to his friend in two quick strides. "What the devil—"

Alec merely held out the paper to him. His face was as white as the marble floor on which they stood, his eyes distant, as if the man inside were far away. Myles grabbed the note and read it quickly, his eyebrows soaring upward. "'The affair is over. I have grown tired—'" He raised his head, staring at Alec in astonishment. "What does this mean?"

"I think it is clear enough. She has left me. She is running away."

"No! Bloody hell, Rawdon, Damaris is not Jocelyn."

"I would have sworn not." Bitterness laced Alec's voice. "And yet, she is gone. I seem to have a peculiar effect on women."

He had not felt the pain yet. Not really. That would come later, Alec knew, alone in the dark in his room, as the full measure of what he had lost swept through him. Right now he was numb.

"Don't be absurd! I have seen Damaris with you. If she isn't madly in love with you, then I know nothing about women. And I must remind you that I have a whole brood of sisters."

Alec swung his ice-cold gaze to his friend. "You have the letter in your hands. I do not know how you could doubt it."

Footsteps sounded on the marble behind them, and they turned to see Genevieve hurrying along the long side gallery toward them. "Alec!" Her eyes went to the paper in Myles's hand and back to her brother's face. "You have seen it."

"Yes. I have seen it. When did she leave?"

"A little less than an hour ago." She came closer, her light eyes intent on Alec's face.

"You knew?" Alec's eyes flashed, and color sprang up along the sharp edge of his cheekbones. "And you did not stop her!"

"What was I supposed to do?" Genevieve shot back. "Hold her here against her will? She is a grown woman."

Anger and frustration flared bright in his eyes. "Why? Did she deign to tell *you*, at least, why she felt impelled to run?" He snatched the letter from Myles's fingers and crumpled it in his fist. "Heaven help me, why am I such a fool about women?"

"She said she did not want to live her life as your mistress," Genevieve replied. "It—it is hard for a woman. She could never be accepted by the *ton* if everyone knew. Even if you were discreet—which, I must point out, you have not been— for someone like her, born on the wrong side of the blanket, to be dallying with a gentleman . . . well, she will be snubbed. You must see that."

"I would have their hide if some old cat dared to cut her!" Alec snapped.

"If you were there," Genevieve replied, putting her hands on her hips and not backing down. "But you would not always be with her."

"Damaris does not care about the *ton*," Alec said almost sulkily, turning aside.

"No woman wants to be a pariah." Genevieve hesitated,

studying her brother's face. "Alec . . . it is probably better this way. I know you are upset right now, but . . ."

"Upset?" He let out a hollow laugh, not looking at her or Myles. "No. Never. I am a Stafford, am I not? We do not indulge in emotions."

Genevieve cast a worried glance at Myles and turned back to her brother. "I—perhaps you should sit down and rest. I'll ring for some tea."

Alec let out a wordless roar and swung around sharply, raking his arm down the hall table and sending a vase of flowers, the silver tray, and two ornate candelabras flying. "I don't want any bloody tea!"

His companions jumped back as the vase crashed spectacularly, scattering water and long-stemmed flowers and shards of ceramic everywhere.

"I will not have it!" Alec swung toward them, and Myles stepped quickly between Alec and Genevieve. "I will find her."

"Alec, think," Myles began reasonably. "You cannot carry Mrs. Howard back here by force."

"The hell I cannot!" Alec glared at him. "I am going to bring her home, and she is going to tell me, face-to-face, why in the hell she doesn't lo—" He broke off and strode away.

"Alec! Wait!"

He took the stairs two at a time, ignoring his sister's voice behind him. Rage and pain boiled within him, flooding over the dam he had built with painstaking care for so many years. He charged down the hall to his room and flung himself down on the ottoman to pull off his walking boots. He jerked at the bellpull;

then, too impatient to wait, he stuck his head out into the hall, shouting to the startled housemaid to have his horse saddled.

How the devil had Damaris left? he wondered as he took the riding boots from his wardrobe. Had the grooms saddled a horse for her? He'd have their hide if they had. Surely she hadn't set out on foot. Was it possible that she had arranged for a post chaise from the village? Had she been planning this for days? The thought that she might have deceived him, pretending to be happy while all the time plotting to run away, sent pain lancing through his chest.

He curled one hand around the bedpost to steady himself, and at that moment his sister hurried into the room. She let out a small cry of distress and reached out toward him with both hands, as if she could catch him even though she stood several feet away. It was no wonder, he thought; he, too, felt as if he were falling, no matter how upright he was standing.

"Alec, please . . ." Genevieve walked toward him, her forehead knotted with worry. Myles came up behind her, hovering uncertainly in the doorway. "What are you doing? You cannot mean to chase after Mrs. Howard."

"I mean to *catch* Mrs. Howard," he replied flatly, and sat down to pull on his boot.

"For what purpose?" Genevieve's voice squeaked in a way it never did. "You cannot force her to remain."

"I refuse to allow Damaris to slip through my fingers." He looked up, his eyes so bright and fierce that Genevieve took an unconscious step backward. "I will talk to her, make her see . . . I will convince her to stay."

"Alec, she left with a man!" Sympathy and sorrow mingled in his sister's face as she visibly braced herself for his response.

The boot slid from Alec's fingers and he stared at her for a long moment. "What? What do you mean?"

"She ran out the back into the garden, which I thought very odd. So I went up in the tower and looked out. There was a man in the garden waiting, and she joined him. They left together."

His face looked frozen in ice, only his light eyes shining with fury. Alec stood up and went to the dresser, opening a drawer and pulling out a case. He opened the case to reveal a set of pistols, which he methodically, silently, began to load.

"Alec! What are you going to do? You cannot just *shoot* Mrs. Howard!"

"I have no intention of shooting Mrs. Howard," he replied in a deceptively mild voice. "I intend to shoot *him*."

"Alec! No! Myles, stop him." Genevieve swung toward Sir Myles.

Myles raised his eyebrows. "You expect me to stop Rawdon with a gun in his hands?"

Genevieve let out an exasperated breath. "I expect you to be of some use!"

"I *am* of use," Myles protested and turned to Alec. "I'm going with you."

"Myles! I meant stop him from killing someone, not help him to do so!"

Alec shook his head. "No. I shall manage it alone."

"But what good will it do? Why must you go after her?" Genevieve cried.

Alec looked at her, his eyes dark and empty. "I cannot breathe without her."

Genevieve let out another cry of distress, and tears sprang into her eyes. "Oh, Alec . . ." She twisted her hands together, watching him as he finished loading the pistols. She swallowed hard and lifted her chin, saying, "Very well. If that is what you want . . . I watched them leave. I took the spyglass and went up onto the battlements and watched them. There was a post chaise waiting on the road, all bay horses. They drove west."

"Then I know they aren't going to Newcastle. I imagine they're headed to London. Or perhaps to Chesley." He gave her a tight smile. "Thank you."

Genevieve sighed and stepped back, still frowning. She hesitated for a moment, then added, "She was crying."

Alec looked at her sharply. He turned away and went to the dresser, opening the narrow drawer on the left. A puzzled frown formed between his eyes, and he thrust his hand into the drawer, pawing through the neatly arranged socks.

"My knife is gone." He turned toward Genevieve.

She stared at him blankly. "Well, I haven't got it. Perhaps one of the maids moved it."

"They opened my drawer and moved the knife and scabbard I'd put in there?"

"You mean the sticker you wear in your boot sometimes?" Myles asked. "Are you sure that is where it was?"

"Of course I am sure." He frowned, the bright blaze of anger in his gaze muting and turning thoughtful. "Could she have taken it?"

"Mrs. Howard?" Myles asked in astonishment. "Why would she take your knife?"

"I'm not sure . . ." Alec sat down and thrust his feet into his boots, his movements quick and purposeful. The red-hot rage inside him had changed, turning into something cooler, sharper, and more determined, threaded through with a new, faint note of hope—and, with it, fear.

He picked up the pistols and thrust them into the large pockets of his hunting jacket as he strode from the room past his sister and Myles. He marched down the hall to Damaris's chamber, ignoring the others as they trailed after him. He cast a comprehensive glance around. A couple of drawers in the dresser stood open, empty. A single stocking lay crumpled on the floor.

"What did she take with her?" he asked.

"Just a small bag. One of the ones I brought from London."

He looked at the dresser. The top of it lay empty. There was no sign of the plain comb that he had purchased for Damaris in Gravesend. "Genevieve, did you bring Mrs. Howard's brushes?"

"What? Yes, of course. I saw the maid pack them myself. It was a lovely silver-backed set of brush, comb, and mirror."

Alec slid his fingertips across the smooth surface of the dresser. It was no surprise that Damaris had packed her elegant silver vanity set. But why, then, he wondered, would she, as she eloped with another man, pause to take along the cheap, ordinary comb Alec had given her?

Why, indeed?

He whirled and left the room. By the time he went through the front door, he was running.

Damaris ate her supper in stony silence. The truth was, she had no desire to eat anything, but she knew she should keep her strength up and her wits sharp. She needed to be ready, though she was not sure what she was going to do. She had no intention of staying with Barrett, she was certain of that. She had spent all her time in the post chaise going over her options. She had no intention of allowing this scoundrel to acquire her inheritance in two more years, but she had to do something about him before then. She could not bear the thought of living with him, and there was no possibility of divorcing him. She would have gladly borne the time and expense of pursuing the act of Parliament necessary for a divorce, but if she did, Barrett would pull Rawdon into it, as he had threatened, and she could not allow that.

The solution, she knew, was to make sure Barrett did not leave this trip alive. It was why she had taken Alec's knife and hidden it in the scabbard on her leg. Now and then, as the chaise jolted along, she had laid her hand on her leg, reassuring herself that the instrument of her delivery was still there. The question, unfortunately, was whether she would be able to wield the weapon. She hated Barrett Howard with everything in her, and she was certain that the world would be a better place for not having him in it.

But did she have it within her to kill him in cold blood?

In that moment when she had picked up the knife, resolved to give up her happiness with Alec, she had thought she could. But as her blood cooled, she had grown less certain. She tried to imagine slipping into Barrett's room while he slept and plunging the knife down into his chest, and the idea sickened her. Damaris believed that she was capable of killing someone to defend herself or someone else, but the idea of plotting out a murder and following it through with icy purpose was another matter entirely. She wondered if that meant she was a good person . . . or merely a coward.

"Decent roast pork," Barrett said now, taking a bite from his fork. "Though the duck was dreadful, and that soup was thin as water. What one would expect, I suppose, in an out-of-the way place such as this."

Damaris took a sip of her drink, not answering him or even glancing in his direction. Barrett had kept tossing out similar conversational bits all through their drive, as if he thought she would simply fall in happily with him and act like a normal married couple. She could not decide if he was that much of a fool or if he was doing it to aggravate her. Either, she supposed, was possible. She did not know the man, had never known him, really, even during those exciting weeks when he had pursued her so ardently. Everything about him had been a lie.

"I wonder what they have in the way of rooms here," he went on lightly. "Though I suppose we really should get farther along. Just in case, of course, your jilted lover takes it into his head to pursue you."

A quick, yearning hope sprang up in Damaris at the thought of Alec riding to her rescue, but she sternly quashed it. He would not have any interest in finding her after the note she had written him. Doubtless he would toss her letter in the fire and label her the same sort of fickle female his fiancée had been. Besides, she could not want Alec to follow her. Not with Barrett armed and ready to shoot him.

When Damaris again made no response, Barrett heaved an exaggerated sigh and tossed his napkin on the table. "Really, Damaris, do you intend to keep up this silence for the remainder of our married life?"

She turned her glare on him, finally goaded into speaking. "It is my devout hope that our married life will last a very short while."

His lips thinned. "I should not wish for that if I were you, since it would mean that you would be resting cold in the ground."

"What I wish for is *your* demise."

Barrett stood up swiftly, the heavy chair scraping over the stone floor. "Not bloody likely. I think it is time that you were reminded of your situation, wife."

His heavy emphasis on the word Alec had teased her with time and again sent a spear of pain and anger through Damaris. She fought it down, rising from her seat with unhurried dignity.

"I am going to get a room here and go to sleep," she said with icy calm. "I have no interest in traveling any further tonight."

"You'll go to bed when I say you will!" Barrett stepped forward and wrapped his hand tightly around her wrist. He jerked her to him, his other arm curling around her waist. "But since you are so eager to climb into bed, I shall agree." He brought her up hard against him and bent her backward over his arm, looming over her. "Though there's no need for a room; here should do well enough."

Damaris threw her arms up between them, pushing against him with all her strength. "Are you mad! Do you think that I would sleep with you?"

"I think that you will if I want you to. It is your marital duty, after all."

Damaris squirmed and twisted, trying to free herself and avoid his suddenly questing lips. "Let go of me! What is wrong with you? You don't want me; you told me so yourself!"

"Of course I don't want you, you shrew! But you clearly need to be taught your place. And it occurs to me that a babe might be just the thing to keep you docile."

The thought that he would take her, intending to impregnate her, with the motive of making her easier to control, that he would use something as sweet and longed for as a baby, sent red-hot rage pouring through Damaris. She let out a shriek and swung at him, raking her nails down the side of his face as she struggled to break from him. Barrett cursed viciously and slammed her back against the table, setting the crockery to rattling. He bore her back over the table, planting one arm across her chest and pressing her down with all the force of his weight and strength.

"Bitch," he spat out, panting. "You'd best think: once I've gotten a babe on you, I'll have no more need of you alive. Your money goes to your child, does it not? And who but the father would be her guardian? It would behoove you not to displease me."

"You'll never get your hands on any child of mine!" Damaris began to kick and fight, but her struggles only seemed to excite him. She could feel his manhood swelling against her, and her gorge rose in her throat at the thought of him touching her, forcing himself into her.

He grinned, his eyes lighting up nastily. "Go ahead. Scream all you want. The door is locked. And who is to gainsay a husband teaching his impudent wife a lesson?"

He reached down with his free hand and shoved her skirts up, then began to unbutton his trousers. Damaris contorted, reaching down until her hand touched the hilt of Alec's knife. She pulled it free and swung as hard as she could, stabbing it into Barrett.

Unfortunately the knife did not plunge in deeply but slid along a rib. It was enough, however, to slice a long furrow through his flesh, and he let out a howl of pain and staggered back, clutching at his side. The knife caught in his jacket and tore from her hands, clattering to the ground. Damaris did not waste time trying to find it but jumped to her feet and ran for the door. She reached it and was fumbling at the key, when Barrett slammed into her from behind, knocking her to the floor.

She scrambled backward, trying to pull herself away, but

he sat astride her, pinning her to the floor, and dragged her arms above her head, holding them immobile. She struggled, but he just grinned down at her.

"Go ahead," he said, wriggling a little against her hips. "Squirm. I rather like it." He secured both her wrists in one hand and hooked his other hand in the neckline of her dress. "Now, I think payment is in order for what you did to me."

He ripped downward, tearing the dress, and Damaris screamed.

Twenty-three

*A*lec rode as if the hounds of hell were after him, driven by an inchoate mix of rage, hope, and fear. Questions bombarded him. Why had Damaris taken his knife? What did it mean? Why would she take that cheap comb with her when she had a far better set of her own?

Because he had given it to her.

He told himself he was being a fool. Taking the silly comb meant nothing. Nor was the fact that she had been crying any proof that she did not want to leave him; her tears could have just as likely meant she was unhappy at Castle Cleyre. And perhaps she took his knife simply because she wanted a little protection with her. But if she was meeting a lover, why would she need protection? On the other hand, who was to say that the man was her lover?

That had been his first assumption, when jealousy had ripped through him. He had been certain that, like Jocelyn, Damaris had run away with another man. But now, with cooler blood, he had to wonder whether the scene Genevieve had witnessed actually meant what she had assumed it did. Was Damaris eloping on a romantic tryst?

However foolish Alec had been about Jocelyn, even a large dose of jealousy could not make him believe that Damaris would act as Jocelyn had. She was several years older than Jocelyn, for one thing, a grown woman who had loved before, who had known sorrow and bitterness. She was not the sort to get herself into the type of situation Jocelyn had, and if she had, she would have been much cleverer in getting herself out of it.

Damaris would not have carried on an affair with Alec if she were in love with another man. On that, he realized, he would stake his life.

Besides, where and when would Damaris have come up with a lover? There had been no sign of a man in Chesley, and Rawdon was convinced that not only would someone have known if Damaris was being wooed, but also that if one person in Chesley had known it, everyone in the town would know it. Thea would have told him if Damaris had been seeing a man.

So this man would have to be someone Damaris had met during her brief stay in London, which seemed unlikely. Or he was someone from her past. Someone she had loved from long ago? She had not mentioned anyone but her husband, and it could not be him, since he was not only dead, but also someone Damaris would have been more likely to spit on than leave with.

Of course, she had not necessarily told Alec everything. There could have been a man with whom she had fallen in love but who was married or could not for some other reason be with her. Perhaps he had shown up after all this time, and she had been overcome with joy at seeing him. Perhaps whatever she felt for Alec could not compare to her love for this man, and so she had left with him, after shedding a few tears for the hurt she must inflict on Alec.

Painful as it was, the notion made sense. Until, of course, one considered how this man could have known to find her at Castle Cleyre. And why had Damaris, if she regretted hurting Alec, not taken the time and trouble to write a more thorough explanation?

What seemed much more likely was that that this sudden and inexplicable departure was tied to the danger they had spent the past weeks eluding. What if the man was one of her abductors and he had somehow forced her to leave?

Well, admittedly, that did not make sense, either, for she had clearly packed and left the house on her own, as well as written him a farewell note. A note so final, so terse, so likely to wound, that he would not pursue her.

Perhaps he was merely fooling himself again, but something about that idea struck a chord in him. Could Damaris have written the harsh missive simply to ensure that he would not follow her? No, that had to be wishful thinking. And yet . . . such a blatant lack of concern was in no way like the woman he knew . . . the woman who had gently kissed the threadlike scars on his back, her tears falling on his skin.

Or perhaps it was not one of the ruffians who had attacked her, but the man who had been behind it. Perhaps it really had been her family who had orchestrated the attacks, and the man with whom she left was an uncle or cousin.

And so his thoughts ran on, one moment filled with hope and the next crashing into a despairing certainty that he was playing the fool over a beautiful woman once again. But, whichever the case was, he was not about to give up. Not this time. However much it hurt, however foolish and duped and lovestruck he would appear, he had to find Damaris. He would not, could not, let her go until he had heard from her own lips that she did not love him.

He paused now and then to question someone he passed about seeing a post chaise headed this direction. Not everyone had seen it, but enough assured him that one had passed on the same route earlier that he believed he was continuing on the right path. As dusk fell, he began to worry that he might ride past them, that they would stop for the night and he would continue blindly on. So, despite the time it took, he began to stop at each inn along the way to see if Damaris was there. Fortunately, he thought, Damaris was a woman whom any man would have noticed and remembered.

At each stop he met with blank stares or head shakes until at last he slid down from his horse and asked the ostler his usual query and the lad's eyes lit up in a telltale fashion.

"A swell mort?" the fellow asked. "A prime article?"

"The most prime," Alec agreed, his spirits lifting a little. "Black hair and blue eyes. She likely was with a man."

"That's 'er," the lad agreed. "They're inside, gettin' fed."

"Are they, now?" Alec tossed him a coin and started toward

the inn. His blood was up now, and even though his stomach turned to ice, thinking of what might lie before him, he strode forward rapidly, drawn toward Damaris like a magnet to true north.

He stepped inside to find the public room curiously empty. A few further steps took him into a hallway where a clot of people were gathered outside a closed door. On the other side of the door, there was a crash and a woman's cry. Alec's heart leapt into his throat.

"Damaris!" He shoved his way through the crowd. "What the devil's going on here?"

They parted, and the man closest to the door turned toward him, his face relaxing as he recognized authority. "We don't know, sir. It's been going on like that for a bit. Shouting and screeching and banging about. But the door's locked. We can't get in."

Alec shoved the man aside and crashed the heel of his boot against the door. The other man, presumably the innkeeper, let out a cry of protest, but Alec paid him no mind, just kicked the door again. There was another cry from within, and Alec threw every bit of strength he had against the door.

It crashed open. Alec saw Damaris on the floor, a man straddling her, pinning her to ground, his hand reaching obscenely for his crotch.

With a roar of rage, Alec charged into the room.

Damaris had closed her eyes, turning her face away from the sight of Barrett's red face, stamped with lust, but at the sound of the door crashing open, her eyes flew open and she swung her head toward the door. She stared in shock and disbelief as Alec threw himself at Barrett. He slammed into the other man, tearing him off Damaris and onto the floor beside her, landing heavily on top of him.

Rearing up, Alec rained blows down upon the man's face. Barrett's nose broke with a sickening crunch, and blood spurted from it, soon joined by a stream of blood from a cut above his eyes and another from his split lip.

Damaris staggered to her feet and glanced over at the doorway, which was filled with a crowd of strangers, all staring in fascination at the sight of Alec pounding his fists into Barrett's face. She turned back to Alec and could not deny a certain vicious satisfaction in seeing him destroy the man who had just capped off his crimes against her by trying to rape her.

But, a more rational part of her brain reminded her, she could not let Alec put himself in the position of killing a man. "Alec, no! Stop!" She went to him, grabbing his arm as he pulled it back. "Stop. You will kill him."

He turned and looked up at her, his face stamped with such primitive bloodlust that it would have made most men quail. "That's exactly what I mean to do," Alec assured her, but when she stood firm, continuing to gaze at him calmly, his blazing eyes lost their wild look, and he rose to his feet. Casually stepping over Barrett's inert body, he pulled her into his arms. "Are you all right?"

Damaris let out a choked cry and flung her arms around him, burying her face in his chest and giving way to a storm of tears.

He cradled her against him as she cried, stroking her hair and back soothingly . "Shh, love, shh," he murmured, kissing the top of her head. "It's all right. You're safe. He shan't hurt you again."

"I know. I know," she managed to gasp out. "I was so scared."

There was a collective gasp from the people still clustered at the doorway, and suddenly Barrett's voice rang out. "You doxy!"

Damaris and Alec whirled to see that while they were wrapped up in each other, Barrett had rolled away and pulled himself to his feet. He was standing against the wall, leaning back against it for support. Blood covered his face grotesquely, and one eye was already swelling. And in his trembling hand, pointing straight at Damaris, was a gun.

"You have ruined yourself now," he went on, his words distorted by his swollen lips and battered jaw. "I have every right to shoot you and your fine—"

"Barrett, don't!" Damaris cried. "Think! This will not help you."

"Barrett!" Alec stiffened, his eyes narrowing.

"I disagree," Barrett told her. "It will give me a great deal of pleasure."

"It is I you want to shoot, not her," Alec said calmly, sticking his hands into his pockets in a casual way and stepping in front of Damaris.

"Don't worry. I intend to shoot both of you," Barrett replied.

"Ah, then you have two pistols?" Alec asked. "Because, you see"—his hands swept up, still in his pockets, and two shots rang out simultaneously—"I do."

Bright red blossomed on Barrett's hand and chest. The gun went flying from his hand, firing harmlessly into the china cabinet, and Barrett stood for a moment, staring at Alec with a look of astonishment, before collapsing on the floor.

For an instant, everyone remained frozen. Then one of the women watching let out a high-pitched shriek and collapsed in hysterics into the nearest man's arms. Alec pulled his hands out of his pockets, the emptied pistols still in them. He glanced from the man lying on the floor to the innkeeper.

"Is he—is he dead?" the innkeeper asked in hushed tones.

Alec strode over and dropped to one knee beside Barrett, reaching two fingers to his throat to check his pulse. "Yes, it would seem so."

"Who is he?" The innkeeper came closer, staring at the body with a sort of frightened fascination.

"I've never seen him before," Alec answered, and a flicker of his gaze to Damaris told her to keep silent.

The innkeeper turned toward Damaris. "What did you say to him, missus? Did you say his name?"

Alec answered before Damaris could open her mouth. "I believe what she said was, 'You daren't! Don't!'"

"Ah . . ." The innkeeper nodded, his eyes going back to the dead body.

Damaris sat down hard in the nearest chair and watched as Alec opened the dead man's jacket and reached into an inner pocket. He pulled out a silver card case and flicked it open, and his eyebrows rose slightly.

"Well, it seems as if his name was Dennis Stanley." Alec

snapped the case closed and dropped it onto Barrett's still chest. He rose to his feet and turned his most lordly expression on the innkeeper. "I have no idea why, but this man abducted my guest out of the garden at Castle Cleyre a few hours ago." He glanced at Damaris. "'Tis easy to guess what his purpose was." He cast an expression of disdain at the body. "Obviously he was a man of low morals and no honor, but other than that, I know nothing about him. No doubt you should call for the coroner. I am not sure who your local magistrate is."

"Judge Rickard, sir."

"Ah, yes, I believe I have met him. Good fellow. Tell him to feel free to call on me at the castle if he has any questions. I shall be happy to attend the inquest, of course." He patted the pocket of his jacket, then said, "Pardon me. I was out hunting when I received word of the crime, and I haven't any cards on me. Just tell the judge it is Lord Rawdon at Castle Cleyre, should he need me."

"Yes, my lord." The innkeeper bobbed a nod of respect, clearly overawed by Alec's title and manner.

"But now I must take my guest back to the castle to recover from this harrowing event. I fear it has been a dreadful shock to her nerves."

"Of course, my lord."

Alec had the post chaise brought around, with fresh horses harnessed to it, and he whisked Damaris out to the vehicle and handed her up into it. For a moment Damaris feared that he was going to ride his stallion outside the carriage, but as she watched, Alec spoke to one of the ostlers, handed him a gold coin, and climbed up into the post chaise with her. With a flick of his wrist, he closed the curtains on either side, then pulled Damaris into his lap, cradling her to his chest.

He bent his head to hers, pressing his lips against her forehead. "Sweet Lord, Damaris, I thought I had lost you."

"Oh, Alec . . ." Tears began to flow from her eyes again, and she nestled deeper against him, clutching the lapels of his jacket with both her hands. "I was so scared. I could not believe it when you broke into the room!"

"That man was your—he was really Barrett Howard? I thought he was dead."

"He was! I mean, I thought he was." Damaris straightened up so that she could look into his face. "They told me he had died in a fire in an inn. I have believed him dead for the past eleven years. I nearly fainted when he walked up to me in the garden."

"At the castle? He came to you at Cleyre?"

"Yes. At first I was stunned, but then it all made sense. It was he who sent those men after me."

Alec's eyes narrowed. "I should have known it was simply a man who desired you."

Damaris let out a humorless laugh. "It wasn't from desire, believe me. He apparently saw me at that ball at your house. He thought I was about to try to enter the *ton*, I think, and he was afraid I would recognize him and reveal who and what he really was. He was apparently engaged in the same sort of scheme he used when I met him, trying to deceive some heiress into marrying him. It would have been a disaster for him if I told everyone he was already married to me. The silly part was that I never even saw him. His secret would have been safe if he had just left me alone."

"But why did you go off with him? Why did you not stay in the house when you came back inside? Why did you write me that letter?"

Damaris saw the flash of pain in his eyes, quickly shuttered, and she let out a low cry. "Oh, Alec!" She put her hands on either side of his face and leaned in to kiss him. "I did not want to hurt you, I swear it!"

She kissed his lips again, and he reached up to hold her head in place, sinking his mouth into hers possessively. It was a long time before they broke apart, and when they did so, their color was up and their breathing uneven. Alec closed his eyes and leaned his forehead against hers.

"Don't ever leave me that way again," he murmured. "I was nearly wild."

"I'm sorry." Tears choked her throat. "I did not want to. He threatened you."

He raised his head, the old familiar look of arrogance, now so dear to her, settling on his features. "You thought I could not handle him? That he would get the best of me?"

"I thought he would shoot you," Damaris retorted bluntly. "He said that if I did not go with him right then and there, he would seek a bill of divorce, and he would accuse you as the man with whom I had committed adultery. He would drag your name through the mud. And it would not be just you who suffered, you know that. Your entire family would be caught up in the scandal. All because of me! Because I was so foolish as to have married that blackguard! The only way I could stave him off was to go with him. I had to get him away from there, from you. I was afraid of what your temper might lead you to do."

"I would have done exactly what I did. He was a dead man either way."

"I didn't want you to kill a man for me. I did not want to be the cause of your having his blood on your hands."

"My dear girl." Alec's voice was tinged with faint amusement, and he picked up her hand and brought her fingers to his lips. "Did you really think it would cause me any regret to have ended that snake's existence?"

Damaris glanced at him. "I don't know. It seems it should."

"He hurt you," he said simply. "He deceived you; he took you from me; he was about to rape you. There is no way I would let him live."

"I suppose I should not feel happy about that, but I do. I did not doubt that you could overcome him in a fair fight. But he was carrying a loaded pistol, and he said that if you came after us, he would shoot you. Any man can fall if taken by surprise and at a distance. I could not take that chance."

"And so you wrote me that note."

"Yes." Tears sprang into her eyes again. "I am so sorry to have hurt you. I did not think, after that, that you would come for me."

"I will always come for you."

Damaris snuggled into him, feeling, finally, safe and warm. The rocking of the carriage lulled her, and she closed her eyes, drifting into sleep, secure in his arms.

Twenty-four

$\mathcal{D}$amaris awakened when the carriage rolled to a stop in front of Castle Cleyre. Damaris sat up drowsily as Alec set her aside and climbed down from the carriage. Damaris followed him, looking up at the great stone edifice of the castle, its windows glowing warm and bright against the darkness. To her surprise, instead of giving her his hand to step down from the carriage, Alec reached in and swooped her up in his arms, carrying her up the steps to the door.

"Alec!" she protested, smiling. "Whatever are you doing? I am not an invalid."

"Humor me." He carried her inside, and she thought he would surely set her down there, but instead he started up the wide sweep of staircase.

She caught a glimpse of Lady Genevieve and Sir Myles popping out of the drawing room door and staring up the stairs after them, eyes wide with curiosity. Damaris closed her eyes again and put her head on his shoulder, grateful not to have to face any questions from Alec's sister. Genevieve had never been friendly toward her, and Damaris suspected that the woman thoroughly disliked her now.

When he reached her room, Alec set Damaris down carefully on the bed, ringing for a maid to bring a tray of food and brandy as well.

"Alec . . ." Damaris laughed, sitting up and leaning back against the massive headboard. "I am fine. Truly. 'Tis very nice of you to cosset me, but not necessary."

"You have been through an ordeal that would send a large number of ladies into hysterics."

"Ah, but I am not a lady."

"Don't talk nonsense." He turned bright, fierce eyes on her. "You are the finest lady I know." He ran his knuckles down her cheek. "Now, you eat up and drink your tot of brandy like a good patient."

The butler himself carried in the small silver tray containing brandy and two glasses. He was followed a moment later by Alec's aunt, who hugged Damaris and exclaimed over her, though she seemed rather vague as to what had actually happened to her. She also insisted on laying one of her own crocheted throws over Damaris's legs, positive that whatever ailed her could be combated by heat. It was all Damaris could do to persuade her not to have more logs added to the fire. They were soon joined by Myles, offering jests and pleasantries, as well as by Lady Genevieve, who was, unsurprisingly, more reserved in her greetings.

Finally, Alec herded everyone out of the room, then came back to stand by the bed. "Would you like to be by yourself?"

"No." Damaris reached out to take his hand. "I would rather you stay, if you don't mind."

"Hardly." He sat down on the side of the bed. "Though my grandmother would have hysterics about my being alone with you in your chamber. The fact that I am sitting on your bed would probably render her speechless."

"'Tis not the first time you have been with me here," Damaris said softly, rubbing her thumb over the back of his hand.

A light sparked in his eyes. "Vixen," he said affectionately. "You tempt me, knowing I cannot stay."

"You need not stay. You could return."

She felt his skin flare with heat under her fingers, and he lifted her hand to press a kiss to her palm. "You have no idea how much I want to. But I dare not. It was different when it was only Aunt Willa; she sleeps like the dead and would never whisper a word of sanction even if she saw me entering your room. But it's a different matter now that Genevieve and Myles are here."

"You worry they will gossip?"

"Lord, no. But …" He looked down at her hand, interlocking their fingers. "I want no hint of stain on your name."

Alec cleared his throat and looked away. He was clearly reluctant to discuss the matter, so Damaris changed the subject.

"How did you find us so quickly?" she asked. "I mean, how did you know which way he had taken?"

"Genevieve told me." When Damaris glanced at him, surprised, he went on. "She thought there was something odd about it all, so she watched you leave. She saw the two of you get into the post chaise and saw which direction it turned on the road. After that, it was easy enough to follow."

His words surprised Damaris. She would have guessed that Alec's icy sister would have been happy to have seen the last of her, not help him find Damaris. However, it hardly seemed polite to say that she thought Genevieve thoroughly disapproved of her. She was silent for a moment, picking at the covers, then asked another question that had been tugging at the back of her mind.

"Do you mean to pretend that Barrett is unknown to us?"

Alec shrugged. "I saw no reason to admit any connection, especially since it turned out so fortunately that he was passing himself off as someone else."

"It seems wrong to let him be buried under a false name. His mother ... someone ... may wonder the rest of their days what happened to him."

"Are you certain that Barrett Howard was his name?" Alec asked.

"No. It probably was not. Like Stanley, it is the name of an aristocratic family, and I imagine that he assumed it, too, to aid in passing himself off as some outlying member of that clan. You are right: I have no idea who he really was."

"You thought he died years ago. I presume that everyone else who knew him by that name thought the same."

Damaris nodded. "The trustees of my inheritance certainly believed him dead. They were as relieved as I." Her lips curled in contempt. "That is the reason he wanted me to come with him."

"What was?"

"The terms of the inheritance my father left me. At first, his aim was to smuggle me out of the country long enough for him to marry the heiress he had been dangling after. But he remembered that I would come into my inheritance in another couple of years, and he decided it would be better to be my husband again so that he could get his hands on my money. He said . . . he said if I was difficult, he would get a child on me and then do away with me and be the guardian of the money my baby would inherit."

Alec's eyelids drooped a little, covering the fierceness that leapt into them, and he said in that deceptively mild tone she had become familiar with, "I am sorry that I killed him so quickly."

She squeezed his hand. "I did not want you to have to kill him, but I am grateful that you did. That is why I took your knife, you know. I thought I would get him far from you, and then I would slip the knife between his ribs."

"Ah, my bloodthirsty girl. I am so proud of you."

"Well, I could not. I mean, not in cold blood. I stabbed him when he attacked me, but it didn't do much damage."

"I know. I saw the blood on it when I picked it up off the floor." He raised her hand to his lips again. "I was proud of you."

There was a noise at the door as the maid came in with the tray of food, and Alec popped to his feet. He stayed with

Damaris while she ate, but after she finished, her eyes began to droop, and Alec rose, bowing over her hand.

"You need to sleep. I shall go." He bent and kissed her lightly on the lips, but Damaris curled her arm around his neck, and his kiss deepened. It was with some effort that at last he pulled away. His voice was hoarse as he said, "Sleep well."

Perversely, once the maid had returned and solicitously helped her dress for bed, Damaris found that she was no longer sleepy. She lay down and spent a long time staring at the pattern of the tester above her head. Then she slipped out of bed and sat down in the chair by the window, watching the moonlight on the outer walls of the castle.

She missed Alec. How, she wondered, had she managed to get into such a state after only two weeks of being with him? She wanted to lie beside him. Well, the truth was that she wanted much more than that, but aside from the sweet, deep ache that yearned for the temptation and surcease that only he could bring, she missed lying in bed with Alec at night, feeling his warm body curled against her back. She missed the kiss he pressed upon her shoulder before he would slide into sleep, and she missed waking up in the dark hours before dawn, feeling the hard urgency of his desire as he, too, awakened.

Damaris sighed and got up, strolling restlessly around the room. She had heard the others' footsteps as they came upstairs. She had heard the quiet movements of their valet and maid as they slipped away later. Everyone was in bed. She suspected that they were all asleep but her.

She went to the door and eased it open, peering out into the hall. It was quiet and dark, lit only by the moonlight filtering in through the tall, narrow windows at the end of the hall. Impulsively, Damaris slipped out of her room, closing the door silently behind her, and crept down the hall to the staircase. Lightly she went up the stairs and into the room above Alec's, where she copied his actions at the mantel and the secret door opened for her. At the bottom of the narrow stairs, she turned the handle and slipped into his room.

Alec was lying in his bed, the sheet up to his waist. His head was turned away, toward the open window, but she saw the flash of his open eyes, and she knew that he was lying there as awake as she had been. He turned his head toward her, his eyes sweeping down her form. She knew that he took in the dark circles of her nipples beneath the thin cloth of her gown, that as she walked toward the bed, he followed the movement of her legs under the cotton, the soft swaying of her breasts.

She came to stand beside him, and he looked up at her. "You should not be here." His voice was low and hoarse.

"Do you want me to leave?"

"You know I do not." He reached up and laid his hand flat over her stomach, watching as he glided it over her body, caressing her hips and thighs and breasts through the material. He bunched the gown in his fist, tugging her onto the bed.

She crawled up onto the high bed and slid over his body, the faint groan he made as she did so turning her hot and soft inside. She stopped when her mouth reached his, and she kissed his upper lip, then the lower one, then settled in to taste him thoroughly.

Damaris seduced him slowly, using her hands and mouth all over him, and when he reached up under her gown, she pulled away and stripped it off over her head. Then she returned, taking his hands and pulling them up over his head as she returned to kissing him, and he let her pin him there just as though he could not easily break her hold. She teased at his flat masculine nipples with her teeth and tongue and lips, then moved down over the ridges of his rib cage. Her hair trailed behind her like a dark cloud as she moved, gliding over his skin in its own gossamer caress. He jerked, his flesh quivering, as her mouth reached the soft flat plane of his belly.

She took him in her hands, stroking and cupping, gliding the edges of her nails along the satin-smooth shaft. He made an inarticulate noise and his hands clutched at the columns of the headboard above him. His fingers dug into the wood as she teased him into exquisite tension, pulsing and hard. His fingers dug into the wood behind his head, and his head was arched back, the veins in his neck throbbing, his breath ragged in his throat.

Damaris straddled him, easing down onto him, taking him fully within her until her heart clutched within her chest at the delicious joy of it. With long, slow strokes she moved upon him as he had taught her to, and with every deep glide, she was pierced by the ecstasy of it until at last she shuddered into the dark, mindless pleasure she sought.

Alec whipped over, pulling her beneath him, still hard and full within her. Straining to hold back his own fulfillment, he moved his hips in slow, deep thrusts, arousing the need in Damaris once again until she was trembling all over, aching to reach that elusive peak. He teased and tormented them both, holding back, until finally he slammed into her as he crested, muffling his cry against her neck, and as he did, Damaris reached her own shattering explosion.

He collapsed against her, and she clung to him, both of them spent and incapable of movement.

Twenty-five

$\mathcal{D}$amaris awoke and lay for a moment feeling strangely disoriented, for she was no longer in the bed where she had gone to sleep. Then she remembered awakening before dawn and creeping back through the hidden staircase and down to her room. She let out a soft sigh of regret at not awakening beside Alec, but she pushed the thought from her mind. The world was as it was, and she must get used to it.

She rolled lazily out of bed and stretched, aware of all her aches and bruises after yesterday's adventure. It was already past breakfast, she was sure, so she settled for having tea and toast on a tray in her room. After that, she rang for a bath and spent a long time soaking in the warm water. All through the bath and afterward, as she sat in front of the low fire, brushing out her wet hair and drying it, she thought about Alec.

It was impossible to deny anymore that she loved him. But she was not foolish or naïve enough to think that their future lay together. He could not marry someone like her; she was well aware of that. The only question was whether she was willing to grab for the joy of being with him now, bartering for that happiness with the life she knew and enjoyed.

Clearly the danger that had sent her and Alec to Northumberland was now over. There was no reason for her to remain with him here at his home, and it would be awkward to continue living at the castle now that Genevieve was in residence. Sneaking about, creeping down the hall to his room at night and returning before the sun came up, rarely alone with him during the day and interacting with him in the formal manner of a houseguest, was simply not enough to satisfy Damaris.

It was time for her leave, to pick up her life again. The only question now was what that life would be like. And how much of a part Alec would play in it.

Damaris had never been one to avoid harsh reality, so once she was dressed and her hair dry and swept up into a simple coil, she went downstairs to talk to Alec. However, when she stepped into the drawing room, she found only Lady Genevieve there.

"Mrs. Howard." Genevieve popped up from her chair. "I hope you have recovered from your ordeal."

"Yes, I feel quite well." Damaris resigned herself to delaying her search for Alec for a few minutes and came farther into the room. "I wanted to thank you. Lord Rawdon told me that it was you who told him which road to take yesterday to find me."

"Yes." Genevieve nodded a little stiffly. "I—Alec was ... very distressed. I cannot bear to see him hurt." She hesitated, then went on, "Sir Myles tells me I have been rude to you."

"Oh, no, he should not," Damaris replied quickly.

"Sir Myles no doubt does a number of things he should not," Genevieve said tartly. "However, I will bow to his knowledge in this regard. I am not—I know that I often seem aloof. I—I am not good at talking to people." Pink tinged the ridges of her cheekbones, reminding Damaris of her brother.

Because of that similarity, Damaris could not help but soften toward the young woman. "Pray, do not worry. I am often at a loss for conversation myself."

Genevieve smiled faintly. "Thank you for saying so— though I think that is probably a bouncer. You seem very much one of those women who put everyone at ease. But what I am trying to say, with so little success, is that if I have in any way offended you, I hope you will accept my apologies. I love my brother very much." She gave Damaris a searching look. "I do not want there to be enmity between us."

"Nor do I," Damaris assured her. "Alec is—" She hesitated; she could not simply blurt out to this reserved woman that she loved her brother. Finally, she finished, somewhat lamely, "He is dear to me as well."

"Good. Then . . . well, I should go tell Alec that you are up and about. He wanted to know when you came downstairs." Genevieve turned and started toward the door, but before she reached it, she turned back and fixed Damaris with a hawklike gaze. "But if you hurt Alec, I promise you, I will make you regret it."

On those words, she whipped around and walked out of the room. Damaris gazed after her for a moment, wondering exactly what to make of their conversation. Of course, she reminded herself, it did not really matter whether Genevieve warmed to her or not. She was unlikely to spend any time with the woman in the future, given the decision Damaris had made.

At the sound of hurried footsteps in the hall, Damaris turned and saw Alec step into the room, and her heart lifted inside her. Would there ever come a time, she wondered, when she would not melt looking at those high, fierce cheekbones and shocking blue eyes? She smiled and saw the same breathless burst of excitement and pleasure mirrored in Alec's face.

"How are you?" he asked, coming forward and reaching out to take both her hands in his. "Genevieve said you looked well. That doesn't begin to describe how lovely a sight you are."

He was standing so close to her now, she had to bend her head back to look at him. Damaris would have liked more than anything to put her arms around him and lean her head against his chest. It was almost frightening how much she wanted—needed—to be close to him. She wondered if she really must talk to him immediately, if it would not be better to put it off a little while longer. It did not matter, really, did it, if they had to share the next few days with others? They would find bits of time to be together.

Sternly she reined in her thoughts and said, "I wanted to speak with you."

He smiled. "Did you? Curious. I wanted to speak with you as well. Shall we take a turn about the garden?"

Damaris nodded. It would be better to have this conversation outside, where there would be no listening ears, no chance of someone popping into the room. She tucked her hand into his arm and they walked out, taking the rear door down into the garden.

"What did you want to say to me?" she asked, thinking to put the moment off.

"No, you first." He smiled down at her. "I may need to bolster my courage."

She gave him an odd glance, but she was too wrapped up in what she had to say to wonder about his choice of words. Drawing a breath, she began, "I should return to Chesley soon."

She felt his arm stiffen beneath her hand, and he came to a dead halt. "What? You are leaving?"

"It—it is awkward here, with Lady Genevieve and Sir Myles so close. We have to monitor our words, our movements."

"I will tell them to leave."

Damaris had to chuckle. "No, you cannot do that. 'Twould be rude. The thing is: if I stay here while Genevieve is here, there would be gossip about it later. People would criticize you, and it would be uncomfortable for Genevieve."

"Criticize me for what? What people? Damaris . . . what notion have you taken now? There will be no gossip about this—well, mayhap a small amount if word reaches the *ton* that I shot that man. But it will not touch upon you; I will make sure of that. We did not even give those people your name yesterday."

"No, it isn't that. Oh, I am going about this all wrong. I have been thinking and thinking about this, and now my tongue just seems to get twisted up." She drew a breath and started again. "Alec, it will cause gossip that you had your mistress in the house with your sister there. You know 'tis not at all the thing."

"Is that what you are worried about?" His brow cleared. "No one will know about that."

"Yes, they will. Oh, I am not saying that your sister or Myles will reveal anything, but word will get out. Later, in London, when we . . . I think that I should move to London. Buy a house where you can come to me."

He stared at her in astonishment. "Damaris, what are you talking about?"

"I am talking about our future." A frown started between her eyes. "Alec! Do you not—have I presumed too much? Do you intend to break it off between us?"

"No!" He scowled at her in frustration. "It is you who are talking about leaving."

"Only to go to Chesley and take care of matters there. I shall have to close the house. It would put Gabriel and Thea in an awkward position."

"Gabriel and Thea! What the devil! Damaris, tell me plainly." He took her chin in his hand and tilted her face up to gaze down intently into her eyes. "What plans are you so busily making for us?"

"Plans so that we can be together. If I take a house in London, you can come to me there. You will not have to worry about who might see us or hear us. You can leave my bed when you want, not when you have to, and if I want to sit on your lap in broad daylight in the middle of the drawing room, then I will do so, and no one will object."

He grinned, the corners of his mouth turning up. "That sounds a very pleasant prospect indeed. Perhaps we should start right here."

She made a face at him. "Alec, I am serious."

"I can see that you are." He stroked his thumb across her chin, then bent to press a light kiss upon her lips. "Damaris, are you talking about establishing yourself as my mistress?"

"Well, yes, I suppose I am . . ." Damaris said somewhat crossly. She had thought he would be happier about her decision. "Although I do not plan to make a pronouncement about it."

"Is that what you want? To live the life your mother did?"

Damaris looked away, pulling her chin from his grasp. "'Tis not that I wish to live that sort of life. But . . ." She looked up at him, bracing her shoulders. "I want you."

Alec sucked in a quick breath, his skin going taut over his face and his pale eyes lighting. "My sweet . . . beautiful girl."

He cupped her face in his hands and kissed her, hard and quick, then pulled away, taking her hand and leading her over to the nearest bench. He pulled her down to sit, both her hands in his, and went down on his knee before her, looking deep into her face.

"Damaris, my love, I don't want you for my mistress." She blanched, feeling as if she had been slapped; but before she could move, he tightened his hands on hers, holding her down, and went on, "I want to marry you."

Now she felt even more as if she could not breathe. Damaris stared at him. "Alec ... if you are jesting ..."

"No! What an odd notion you must have of me. I am asking you to be my wife."

She could feel herself trembling and she tried to stop, but she could not. Damaris gripped his hands hard to control their shaking, and he responded by bringing her hands to his lips and kissing each one. "Well," he asked, quirking a brow, "do you mean to keep me in suspense?"

"You cannot!"

"Ah, but I can." He smiled, the corner of his mouth quirking up. "Haven't you heard? Border lords are a law unto themselves."

"I am Lord Sedbury's by-blow! My mother was an actress. My own family abhors the scandal I represent. And that is not all of it, either! If one digs a little, they will find that I ran away with Barrett and had to marry to save my reputation. Your family would be touched with the stain of my name."

"Genevieve and my grandmother will manage," he replied shortly. "Do you believe that I give a tinker's damn what other people think when it comes to you? Good God, Damaris! When that man took you, when I thought that you were fleeing with another lover, I followed you. Even then. I could not let you go. I was going to find you and make you listen to me. I would have given anything to make you stay. I would have gone down on my knees and begged. Do you really think that whispers behind my back would keep from having you as my wife?"

Tears shone in Damaris's eyes. Everything in her wanted to throw herself into his arms, to cry out that she would marry him a hundred times over, but she retained a sliver of control, enough to say, "But you will have me anyway. Whenever you want. However long you want."

"I don't want you hidden in some house in London. I don't want to slip away to see you when I can or spend my nights here at home by myself. I want you with me, always. In my bed. In my drawing room. In London or Chesley or Cleyre or anywhere I am. I want to wake up with you and eat supper with you and hold your hand whenever I bloody well feel like it. I want you to be my countess. My temptress." He pulled her forward to kiss her lips, and his hands settled on her hips, pulling her down from the bench and into him. He murmured against her ear, "I want you to be the mother of my children."

"Alec!" Damaris let out a sobbing laugh, clutching his shoulders.

"The question is: what do you want?" He leaned back, looking at her. "Will you marry me?"

"Yes!" She grabbed his face and kissed his lips, his cheeks, his chin, punctuating her words with kisses. "Yes, yes, yes! I will marry you." She gazed into his eyes. "I love you. I want all those things, too; you have no idea how much. And I pray you will not regret it."

"Never. I will never regret loving you. And I will never stop."

Alec pulled Damaris to him and kissed her.

Can't get enough of Candace Camp?
Read on for a sneak peek of the first novel
from her new Secrets of the Loch series

TREASURED

Prologue

APRIL 1746

He walked swiftly, footsteps muffled on the dirt path, barely noticing the damp stone walls around him. He had taken care of the gold, putting it in safe hands—hands in which he would entrust his very life. Now he was free to find the prince and his fleeing Highlanders. Despite the crushing defeat, he was certain that they could recover, given time and fierce resolve . . . and the fortune he had brought back for them. He had no doubts that he could find them. This land was his, and he knew every cleft, every cave, every bramble that might offer shelter. If he could not evade the Redcoats and find the men they so zealously pursued, then he was not worthy of the name Laird of Baillannan.

But that search was for tomorrow. Right now, Malcolm Rose had a far different quarry. His mind was on only one person. One place. One night before they must part again.

His heart sped up as he neared the end of the tunnel, wanting, as it always did, to burst out of his chest at the thought of seeing her. Even after all these years, even though he had been with her only yesterday, he was still as eager as a lad.

He opened the low wooden door at the end of the tunnel and bent to step through it. As he raised his head, the sight that met him was so unexpected that for a moment he could not speak, could not think. "You!"

"Yes. Me." The smile that accompanied the words held a bitter triumph.

"What the devil are you doing here?" His secrets were shattered. He knew that. Yet there was a relief in having it known. Over and done with.

He took a step forward, and so intent was he on the confrontation before him that he did not hear the whisper of movement behind him until the thin blade of Toledo steel slipped between his ribs and into his heart.

I

APRIL 1807

I   t was raining. It had been doing so, Jack thought in dis-
     gust, ever since he set foot in this benighted land. Some-
     times the water fell in slanted sheets, lashing him like
bits of iron; other times, it subsided into a steady, miserable
drizzle. But even when the rain stopped briefly, mist still
hung over everything, as if the very air were so laden with
moisture it could not hold it.

A cold drop of water slid between cloth and skin, trick-
ling down his back, and Jack turned up the collar of his
greatcoat as he gazed out across the bleak landscape. The
road—if this rutted, narrow path could be termed that—
cut across thick mats of heather and disappeared into the
distance. There were few trees between him and the gray
curtain of mist, only the brown and green land and a few
scrubby bushes. Off to his right, a trench had been dug into
the ground, exposing a straight wall of black earth. Rocks of

all sizes dotted the lumpy, irregular ground, adding to the image of desolation.

What had possessed him to come to Scotland?

He had asked himself that question last night as he'd lain on the thin straw mattress in the grim little inn in Kinclannoch—indeed he'd asked it almost nightly for the past week, and had still not come up with a satisfactory answer. There was no reason to see the house that was now his or to talk to the people who worked on the estate. His only desire was to sell the place, which fortune had dropped in his lap like an overripe plum. Whatever little tickle of proprietary instinct had made him want to see it, whatever odd pull he'd felt at the thought of being a landed gentleman, the truth was his impulsive journey up here to claim the estate made him as big a fool as the bird-witted Scotsman who had wagered his home on the turn of a card.

Still, it made even less sense to turn back now, when he had drawn so close to his destination. If he had understood the innkeeper's thick brogue, the house could not be much farther.

His horse whickered and shifted as a gust of wind whipped through them, driving the rain into Jack's face and nearly taking his hat with it. He grabbed the once elegant, now sodden hat, jamming it more firmly down on his head, and leaned over to stroke a soothing hand down the horse's neck. "Steady on, Pharaoh."

Now, blown by the wind, the mist receded, and he could see the narrow loch and, at last, the house. It lay on a shelf of rock beside the water, a long, straight line of stone unbroken by curve or ornamentation. As gray and dreary as the loch and the sky above it, the house might have been formed out of this bleak landscape itself.

Baillannan.

If Jack had harbored some hope that the sight of his new home would lighten his mood, he knew now he was doomed to disappointment. Nothing could have looked less welcoming. Suppressing a sigh, he dug in his heels and started forward.

✳   ✳   ✳

Isobel was carefully pulling out the last few stitches in her embroidery when her aunt startled her by exclaiming, "We have a visitor! How nice! Barbara, did you know someone was coming?"

"Isobel," she corrected automatically, and her aunt nodded vaguely.

"Yes, dear, of course."

"Who is it?" Isobel set aside her needlework and stood up, suddenly hopeful. "Is it Andrew?"

Aunt Elizabeth squinted down at the courtyard below. "I don't think it's anyone I recognize."

"A stranger?" Isobel joined her aunt at the window, but their visitor had already disappeared, and she saw nothing but the groom leading off an unfamiliar bay horse.

"He looked soaked, poor man," Elizabeth went on sympathetically. "Perhaps he's a traveler seeking shelter from the rain."

"A traveler to where?" Isobel asked pragmatically. "It's my guess he's gone astray. No doubt Hamish will set him straight."

"It would have been nice to have a visitor," her aunt said wistfully. "So many people have left, one hardly sees anyone anymore."

"Yes, since the Clearances began, our closest neighbors are now sheep," Isobel agreed tartly.

"The MacKenzies would not have sold if Ronald was still alive. Poor Agnes; she will not enjoy living in Edinburgh, however much her son may have profited."

Agnes MacKenzie had been Elizabeth's closest friend, and Isobel's aunt had been lonely with her gone. Isobel could not help but feel that the loss had affected Aunt Elizabeth's mind as well as her spirits; she had grown more forgetful the last few months.

Isobel murmured a vague agreement, not wanting to set her aunt off on that unpleasant path. She returned to the sofa and picked up her embroidery hoop, saying, "I fear I've made a shambles of my stitches. What do you think I should do?"

Elizabeth was distracted by Isobel's plea for help, and she started toward her niece. But she had scarcely taken a step when the quiet was interrupted by the sound of a voice rising in agitation downstairs. Surprised, both women glanced toward the door. A moment later, there was the clatter of feet on the stairs, and one of the maids burst into the room.

"Miss Isobel!" The girl's face was flushed and her voice trembled with excitement. "Hamish says come quick. There's a man here, claiming Baillannan is his!"

"What?" Isobel stared at the girl. Her words were so absurd that Isobel thought she must not have heard the maid correctly.

"A man, miss, at the door. An Englishman. He says he owns Baillannan. Then Hamish says he maun be daft, but the man says, 'Nae, it's mine,' and shows him a paper, and Hamish sends me to fetch you."

"Isobel . . ." Aunt Elizabeth turned toward her, frowning.

"I don't understand. An Englishman, here? Who is he? What does he mean?"

"I have no idea. It's nonsense, of course." Isobel started toward the hall. "Don't worry, Auntie, I will straighten it out."

At the foot of the staircase Isobel was met by the sight of Hamish, the man who had been the Rose family butler all her life, standing, arms crossed, as if he would bar the man from the stairs physically. His weathered face, usually set in stoic, even grim, lines, was red as a beet, bushy brows drawn together, dark eyes glittering with dislike.

Opposite him stood a stranger, tall and dark-haired, his face creased in frustration. He would have been a handsome man, she thought, if he had not been soaked to the skin, his cravat a soggy lump around his neck, starched collar points utterly wilted, and his fine wool jacket stretched out of shape by the weight of the water it had absorbed. He held a waterlogged hat in one hand and a many-caped, gray greatcoat hung over the same arm, both of them puddling water on the stone floor beneath him. His boots were caked with mud, and between the sides of his open jacket, his wet shirt clung to his chest. It was made of fine lawn and the water had turned it almost transparent, so that she could see every line and curve of his chest and stomach. As she watched, he reached up and shoved the mop of hair back from his face, stripping water from it. His hair was thick, and slicked back as it now was, it left his face in sharp relief, emphasizing the square set of his jaw and the high slant of his cheekbones. An errant drop of water trickled from his temple, sliding down his cheek and curving over his jaw to disappear in the cloth of his cravat.

Isobel realized that she was staring, and she quickly

averted her eyes, a faint flush rising in her cheeks. "Hamish? Is there a problem?"

The stranger looked up at her, relief flooding his face, and burst out, "Ma'am! Thank heavens, you speak English."

Isobel raised her brows, her voice faintly amused. "I do indeed, sir. I believe you will find that most of us do."

"Not so I could tell," he responded with a dark look at the butler.

"I canna help it if you dinna understand clear speech." Hamish set his jaw mulishly.

The stranger ignored his retort, addressing his words to Isobel. "If I might be so bold as to introduce myself, I am Jack Kensington, ma'am, at your service." He swept her a polite bow, elegant in spite of his drenched condition.

He was clearly a gentleman, his speech and manners as refined as those of her brother or cousin—perhaps more so—and she suspected that his clothes were equally sophisticated when not soaked by the rain.

Isobel was as intrigued as she was puzzled, and she came down the last few steps and held out her hand to him. "I am Isobel Rose, sir. I'm pleased to make your acquaintance."

Mr. Kensington looked taken aback, but he recovered quickly and took her hand, bending over it politely. "Mrs. Rose. An apt name for such a lovely woman."

"Miss Rose," Isobel corrected him, pulling her hand back. His words were too forward and no doubt meaningless flattery, but she could not deny the lift of pleasure at his compliment.

"Dinna trust him, Miss Isobel," the butler warned, taking a step toward her protectively. "This Englishman is trying to swick you. Or he's daft. He says he owns Baillannan."

"I'm sure his intent is not to swindle us," Isobel replied. "Perhaps he has been misled." She turned to Kensington. "I am sorry, sir, but you are mistaken. Baillannan belongs to the Rose family."

"It did," Kensington responded tersely, his courteous manner giving way to irritation. "But it is mine now. I have it from Sir Andrew Rose."

"No!" Isobel stared at him in astonishment. "Andrew would never have sold Baillannan."

"He did not sell it, ma'am. He wagered it on a game of whist. And lost."

"No," she repeated, but the blood drained from her face, and for an instant she thought she might faint. "I don't believe you."

"Then believe this." He shoved a piece of paper into her hand. "It is Sir Andrew's chit."

Isobel stared at the familiar writing, the bold swoop of the *A*, and this time she did have to reach for the newel to stay upright.

"Miss Isobel?" Hamish stepped forward anxiously and took her arm to support her. "What is it? The young laird never—"

"Yes." Isobel kept her gaze on the words, now swimming before her eyes. "I fear he did. 'Tis Andrew's hand. He wagered Baillannan," she finished bitterly.

"I have the deed, as well," the Englishman added mildly.

"No doubt." Her stomach was roiling. She wanted to scream and shred the note, to toss it back in the stranger's face and tell her men to toss *him* back out into the rain. But she was a Rose, and so she must put iron into her spine. Isobel blinked back her tears—she refused to let him see her cry.

He was holding out the deed to her, and she took it, running her eyes down it as if she were reading it, when in truth she could not take in any of the words, her mind overwhelmed by something close to terror. She had no idea what to do, so she clung to the behavior that one expected from the lady of Baillannan, a stoicism that hid the turmoil inside.

"Welcome to Baillannan, Mr. Kensington," she said tightly as she handed him back the papers, though she could not manage to look him in the face. "Hamish, show Mr. Kensington to a room. I am sure he would like to get dry. And no doubt he would appreciate a cup of tea, as well."

"Miss Izzy!" Hamish went an even deeper shade of red, and his eyes bulged. "You canna mean to give him your home! Your father . . . your grandfather . . ."

"Hamish," Isobel said firmly. "I cannot undo what Andrew has done. Baillannan apparently belongs to Mr. Kensington now."

Hamish set his face mutinously, but finally he bobbed his head. "Aye, miss."

He seized Kensington's coat and hat, grabbed up the satchel at his feet, then went to speak to the servants, shooing them toward the kitchen.

Isobel turned back to their visitor in awkward silence, then rushed to speak. "I apologize that your room is not ready."

"No, no need to apologize. Indeed, I should do so for the shock I have given you. I thought Sir Andrew would have written, but no doubt his letter has not had time to reach you."

"No doubt. If you will excuse me . . ." She gave him as close to a smile as she could muster and turned away.

"No, wait." He followed her to the foot of the staircase. "Please."

Isobel stopped on the stairs and turned reluctantly to face him. He was a step below her, so that his head was level with hers, only inches away. His eyes, she realized, were not black or brown as she had thought, but a dark blue, shadowed by thick black lashes. The odd color, combined with the high slash of his cheekbones, gave his face a faintly exotic look. She found it unsettling.

"Are you—I'm not entirely sure I understood what that fellow said, but it seemed—are you related in some way to Sir Andrew?"

"I am his sister."

"His sister!" His eyes widened. "I'm sorry. Sir Andrew never mentioned . . . I didn't know . . ."

"There is no reason you should." This time she could not manage even an attempt at a smile. Whirling, she ran up the stairs.

"Isobel?" Her aunt stood outside the door of the sitting room, looking a trifle lost.

Isobel pulled up short, barely suppressing a groan. Aunt Elizabeth's memory had been growing hazier the last few months, and Isobel had found that any unexpected occurrence tended to make her condition worse. But Isobel was not sure she could explain the situation calmly when she felt as if she might shatter into a storm of tears herself.

"Isobel, who was that man? Was he talking about Andrew?" Her aunt's face brightened. "Is Andrew here?"

"No. Andrew is in London. Or at least I suppose he is, since he has not bothered to write."

"He is so careless that way." Aunt Elizabeth smiled indulgently. "Of course, young men have better things to do than write home."

"He might have thought of something besides himself for once."

"Isobel? Are you angry with Andrew?"

"Yes, I am." She added, softening her tone, "A bit." She couldn't give in to her feelings in front of Elizabeth.

"But why was Hamish upset? Who is that man?"

"He knows Andrew. I—he is staying here for a time."

"Oh. How nice—a visitor. He was quite a handsome young man, I thought." Elizabeth's eyes gleamed speculatively, and for a moment she seemed like her old self. "It will be good for you to have someone your own age here."

"Don't." Isobel felt as if she might choke. "Please, don't try to matchmake. It's impossible."

"Nonsense. Now come in and sit down and tell me all about him."

"I cannot." Isobel pulled away, ignoring the faint hurt in her aunt's eyes. "I will come back later and tell you everything I know. But right now I must go. I—I have to fetch something. From Meg."

Her aunt frowned. "Meg?"

"Meg Munro, Auntie; you know Meg. Coll's sister. Their mother Janet was Andy's wet nurse."

"Of course I know Meg."

The vagueness in Elizabeth's gray eyes made Isobel doubt her aunt's words. I cannot bear it, she thought.

"I must go," she repeated, and fled down the hall without looking back.

Inside her bedroom, Isobel closed the door and sagged against it. She wasn't sure how she had gotten through it without breaking down. Her knees were jelly, her hands trembling. She heard the sound of footsteps and voices in the hall outside her door as Hamish and the Englishman walked past, a bitter reminder that her home was gone.

Not just the house she had grown up in, but the loch, the earth, the rocks and caves, every inch of this land and its wild, harsh beauty. Her very life was tumbling down around her, ripped away by her young brother's folly. Even her beloved aunt was being taken from her bit by bit each day, her mind retreating.

She could not hold back a sob. Grabbing up her cloak, she ran from the room, tearing down the stairs and out into the yard as if pursued by devils.